"Maya Banks writes t...
—Lora Leigh, #1 *New York Times* bestselling author
of *Secret Sins*

Praise for the novels of Maya Banks

"Incredibly awesome . . . I love Maya Banks and I love her books."   —Jaci Burton, *New York Times* bestselling author

"Maya Banks . . . really dragged me through the gamut of emotions. From . . . 'Is it hot in here?' to 'Oh my GOD' . . . I'm ready for the next ride now!"   —*USA Today*

"[A] one-two punch of entertainment that will leave readers eager for the next book."   —*Publishers Weekly*

"For those who like it naughty, dirty, and do-me-on-the-desk HAWT!"   —*Examiner.com*

"A cross between the Bared to You or Fifty Shades series and the Wicked Lovers series by Shayla Black."
          —*Book Savvy Babe*

"Hot enough to make even the coolest reader sweat!"
          —*Fresh Fiction*

"You'll be on the edge of your seat with this one."
          —*Night Owl Reviews*

"Definitely a recommended read."   —*Fallen Angel Reviews*

"[For] fans of Sylvia Day's *Bared to You*."
          —*Under the Covers*

continued . . .

WHEN DAY BREAKS

MAYA BANKS

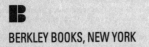
BERKLEY BOOKS, NEW YORK

THE BERKLEY PUBLISHING GROUP
Published by the Penguin Group
Penguin Group (USA) LLC
375 Hudson Street, New York, New York 10014

USA • Canada • UK • Ireland • Australia • New Zealand • India • South Africa • China

penguin.com

A Penguin Random House Company

WHEN DAY BREAKS

A Berkley Book / published by arrangement with the author

For information, address: The Berkley Publishing Group,
a division of Penguin Group (USA) LLC,
375 Hudson Street, New York, New York 10014.

ISBN: 978-0-425-26378-5

PUBLISHING HISTORY
Berkley mass-market edition / July 2014

PRINTED IN THE UNITED STATES OF AMERICA

10 9 8 7 6 5 4 3 2 1

Cover art by Craig White.
Cover design by Rita Frangie.
Interior text design by Laura K. Corless.

In loving memory of Pat Pattarozzi.
She was a true "Mama Kelly" and will be missed by many.
I hope you enjoy your angel's wings
as you lovingly look after your family from heaven.

CHAPTER 1

BIG Eddie Sinclair sat behind his aged wooden desk in his big empty house—a house that had once been filled with love and laughter—his gnarled, callused hands *shaking*.

Sweat beaded his forehead and ran in thin rivulets down his temples, tracing a line over grooved, aged, weather-beaten skin. His hands shook so badly that the papers he'd been holding fell, scattering on the desk, some sliding onto the floor.

He stared up, his gaze unconsciously seeking out the mantel over the fireplace his wife had insisted on having installed in his working space. She hadn't wanted him to ever get cold. The idea that Big Eddie Sinclair's gentle wife had been concerned that he'd get *cold* would have gotten him laughed out of the barracks. His badass buddies would never let him hear the end of it.

Eddie was a big man. A killer. Trained by the best. And in turn he had trained the best. But right now he felt as helpless as a newborn babe. Fear, an emotion that until the day his first child was born had been completely alien to him, gripped him by the balls, freezing his insides. He rubbed at his chest in an effort to alleviate the discomfort and closed his eyes, trying to rid himself of the images the threat had invoked.

He'd lived his life knowing that he was invincible. He wasn't egotistical. Men who served with the men he served with didn't think they were good. They knew they were good.

And none of that ability had been able to save his precious wife.

He closed his eyes more tightly against the betraying sting of tears. Even years later, thinking of the love of his life had the power to bring him to his knees. A lifetime of regret stored in the years since she'd died, leaving him with three young children to love, protect and raise on his own. And by God, he'd done just that. He'd made certain they were protected above all else.

And now his precious Eden, his only daughter, was a target. All because of him and the life he'd led, the choices he'd made. The mistakes he'd made in the past. All coming back to haunt him. Still fucking haunting him every goddamn night.

She was the image of her mother not only in looks but in all aspects. Gentle. Loving. A heart of gold. Sweet and innocent. Always willing to look for the good in people. Never seeing the bad.

It wasn't said in so many words, the threat. But he knew. His gaze fell on the blown-up glossy photos of his daughter. Taken in a moment of unguardedness, a rarity for Eden because he'd taught her to never let her guard down. She might have the face of an angel and pose for cameras for a living, but she had the mind of a soldier. Eddie had ensured that.

I'll take from you what you took from me. I won't stop until pain is all you see, all you feel, all you know. I'll take every single thing you love and then you'll die. Beautiful, isn't she?

The note, so simple and yet so life changing, stared back at him, ugly, black.

The photos of Eden glimmered in his vision. Taken of her when she thought she was out of the camera's eye. None of the glamorous clothing or makeup. If he weren't so terrified, he would have softened at the real Eden. More comfortable in sweats, hair in a ponytail, face devoid of cosmetics. So beautiful it hurt to look at her because she reminded him so much of her mother.

He reached for the phone, dialing her number before he thought better of it. As it rang, he nearly hung up, but Eden would only call back. What could he possibly say to her?

He had security around her. The best money could buy and yet he knew there was better out there. It wasn't her he needed to talk to. He needed to speak to others. People who would ensure her safety and put their lives before hers. That kind of blind loyalty was hard to find. Not many men, no matter what, were willing to sacrifice their lives for someone else.

Civilians couldn't possibly understand that kind of self-lessness. They lived in their little bubbles never thinking about the thousands of young American men and women who gave their lives so the rest of America could exist in willful, ignorant bliss.

He didn't need private security. What he needed was military.

Eden's voice came over the line just as he started to disconnect.

"Hi, Dad!"

Her cheerful voice hit a deep part of his heart that never failed to tighten whenever she was near.

"Hi, baby," he said gruffly. "How are you?"

"I'm good. What's up?"

"Nothing," he said hastily. "I just . . . I just wanted to hear your voice."

"Is everything all right? Are you okay, Dad?"

The worry in her voice shook him from his dark thoughts. The very last thing he wanted was her worried and distracted. If she was focused on something else—him—then she wouldn't be paying attention like she should. She'd make a mistake. Slip up. Allow someone the chance to get to her.

"I'm fine, baby girl," he said, making his voice stronger. "I just wanted to see how my girl was doing."

"I'm good. Just got done with the afternoon shoot. If I never see another froufrou yip-yap dog it'll be too soon," she grumbled.

Despite the gravity of the situation, Eddie smiled. No. His girl wasn't one for irritating furballs. She'd much rather be surrounded by bigger, stronger dogs. Her "baby" was an English mastiff well over two hundred pounds.

"King is going to be pissed when he smells these other dogs on me," she said in disgust. "I'll have to bribe him with treats for a week."

"Are you resting enough?" he asked. "Don't let your agent work you into the ground, Eden."

She laughed. "If anything I work him too hard. You know that, Dad. He's always after me to slow down. And well, maybe one day I will. But right now I have to hit it hard while I'm still in demand. In another year or two, no one will want me. There's always someone younger, prettier coming up the ranks. And you know that I'm getting old in model years."

He rolled his eyes and let out a grumble. Didn't make a damn bit of sense to him. Eden was only twenty-four years old and yet she talked like she was some middle-aged nag about to be put out to pasture. She constantly reminded him that for a model, she was old.

"Oh hey, let me go, Dad. That's Ryker calling now. We've been playing phone tag all day and I have to tell him happy birthday."

Eddie's chest tightened at the mention of his middle child. Eden's older brother. The two were as thick as thieves. Always had been. Eddie hadn't forgotten his son's birthday. But he'd put his call to him off because he knew what he'd say wouldn't be the best birthday message in the world.

"Talk to you later, then. Love you," Eddie said gruffly.

"Love you too, Dad," she sang out just before the line went silent.

Still gripping his phone, he hesitated only a brief moment before punching in a seemingly endless series of numbers and codes. He'd sworn he'd never involve Guy again. Not after what he'd done for Eddie in the name of revenge after his wife had died. No, she hadn't just fucking died. She'd been murdered.

Eddie closed his eyes in frustration when once again he

failed to connect to the one person he trusted with Eden's life. A man who'd never allow anyone to hurt her.

"Hancock," Eddie said raspingly, clearing his throat in order to leave yet another message. "It's me. Big Eddie Sinclair. I need your help. It's Eden. I'm afraid . . ." He broke off, refusing to allow his weaknesses to be aired over even a secure line. "I need your help. Call me as soon as you get this."

He ended the call and then leaned back in his chair, dreading what he had to do next. Weariness and dread assailed him. His sons wouldn't understand. How could they? Eddie had never confided in them that their mother's death was no accident and that her killer had been ruthlessly hunted down and taken out. Though he hadn't been present, he knew without asking that his wife's killer's death had been slow and painful. The mission had been deeply personal to Hancock as well, for Eddie's wife was in all ways a surrogate mother to Hancock himself.

Now Eddie had to call them. Because he had to ask for their help if they were going to close ranks around Eden.

He punched in Raid's number and waited, knowing that unless his son was out on a call, he'd answer. Two seconds later, his idea was confirmed when his son answered.

"Hey, Dad. Shouldn't you be calling the worm today? It's his birthday, not mine."

"Hold on while I conference him in," Eddie said in a short, grim voice.

Raid fell silent. It was a testament to his training and discipline that he didn't immediately demand to know what was wrong. A moment later, Ryker answered with a short hello.

"Son, Raid's on the phone as well," Eddie said by way of greeting.

"Ah great, a twofer," Ryker said cheerfully. "I just got off the phone with Eden. Now my day is complete."

"What's wrong, Dad?" Raid asked, cutting through Ryker's mood.

"I need you both to come," Eddie said. "I can't discuss it over the phone. I'll explain everything when you get here. I need you to hurry."

CHAPTER 2

"**SMILE!** Come on Eden, give me sultry. That's it. One more. Perfect!"

Eden arched her neck, flipped her hair over one shoulder and sent her most smoldering glance straight into the camera lens. Her neck ached and she wanted a break, but there was still the dogs to contend with.

"Okay, that's a wrap. Justin, where are the goddamn mutts?" the photographer bellowed.

On cue, two chihuahuas were carried onto the set while another assistant changed the backdrop. As Justin shoved one of the dogs into her arms, the tiny dog snarled at Eden and began to yap furiously.

"Yeah, yeah, the feeling's entirely mutual," Eden growled back. "Stupid hairball."

"Uh, Eden, they don't have much hair," Justin said in his tinny voice.

She rolled her eyes. The guy was so literal. "It was an expression," she said uselessly.

"Well, whatever, but be nice to them. We need to get these shots and you can't be scowling, nor can they be growling at you. You're supposed to be laughing. Flirty. Cute even."

Eden had to call back the growl that rumbled in her throat. King, her mastiff, wouldn't forgive this transgression. As soon as he smelled other dogs on her, he'd sulk for eternity. That is, until she broke out the treats as a peace offering.

Pasting on her brightest smile, she cuddled, or as much as she could when the dog was a wiggling mass of unhappiness, and turned her attention to the camera.

The photographer shot rapid-fire, capturing every angle. He barked commands at Eden as if she were the dog, and then she got on her knees and the two dogs gathered around her as she acted out playing with them, her smile bright, cheeks aching from the effort.

She had a huge, huge shoot the day after tomorrow and if they didn't get this wrapped up today, there went her one day off to get some much-needed downtime before the Aria cosmetics commercial shoot.

It had been a huge coup to land the lucrative contract. It would set Eden up enough that she could retire if she so chose, though she planned to work a few more years. She would only be in demand a few more years at best. There was always someone younger, more beautiful, more eager climbing the ranks. While Eden might be the big thing today, there was nothing to say that tomorrow she wouldn't be yesterday's star.

But she did plan to slow down some at least. She had already planned a vacation after the Aria account was finished. Already she was imagining being home with her father and brothers. Maybe she'd take them someplace nice. To the mountains. They all loved it there. It didn't really matter, though. She just wanted to be around her family again. It had been months since the last time she'd seen them for more than a day here and there. Though it had made her schedule tight and taken away from much-needed rest, she'd scheduled flights home occasionally when she had only a day between gigs.

"Are you with me, Eden?" the photographer snapped. "Believe me, sweetie, we all have things we'd rather be doing, but don't let me hold you up. By all means take all afternoon."

Eden shot him a glare before snapping back to the task at

hand. She was bone weary and she was just ready to be done
with it so she could sleep about twenty-four hours before flying to Paris for the Aria shoot. She had to look her absolute
best. Fresh. Rested. Sparkling with life.

For another half hour she suffered through endless smiles,
ignoring the dogs that seemed to hate her and getting them to
cooperate for the camera. At one point, Eden slid her hand
underneath the belly of one of the pooches, intending to scoop
him playfully so they were nose to nose. Only the dog wasn't
having it and sank his sharp teeth into Eden's hand.

"Ouch! Damn it!"

She dropped the dog and held her hand in her other palm,
glaring at the offending dog, who looked supremely pleased
with himself.

"Okay, that's a wrap," the photographer said in an irritated tone. "Get someone to look at her hand, damn it. Are
you up to date on your tetanus shots, Eden?"

She gritted her teeth, still glaring at the smug dog she was
positive was laughing at her.

"I'm fine. He didn't break the skin." Thank God. Her
hands would be predominantly on display in the upcoming
commercials, as would the rest of her body. She didn't need
any blemishes or cuts.

Still, one of the assistants rushed over with a first-aid kit
and clucked and fussed over Eden until he was satisfied that
the spot was only red and would likely fade within a few hours.

She listened as he rattled off a ton of instructions for how
to treat it, moisturize it and care for it so her skin was perfect
for the upcoming shoot. She tuned it all out and glanced to
where David and Micah waited in the wings.

They recognized it for the SOS it was and pushed forward, flanking her and herding her toward the exit.

"Thank God that's done," Eden muttered.

"Oh, I don't know," Micah drawled. "You looked kind of
cute with the little hairless rats."

She shot him a dirty look that guaranteed payback.

The two men her father had insisted oversee her personal
security and travel with her everywhere she went situated her

between them as they left the studio. They were nearly to the waiting car, the driver having been alerted by David that they were coming out, when the world seemed to explode around them.

Screams sounded shrilly in Eden's ears as she went down hard, a two-hundred-pound man on top of her. There were hoarse shouts, more screams and the sound of scrambling people on the sidewalk. More glass shattering, windows of the building being broken out.

A car roared up, a barrier between Eden and whatever the hell was doing the . . . shooting? She dimly registered that it sounded like bullets smacking into concrete and glass, and she was certainly acquainted with what bullets sounded like.

Then she found herself hauled up and thrown into the back-seat of the car and then Micah's hoarse shout of "Go, go, go!"

The car screeched, tires burning rubber on asphalt as they careened away from the scene.

"What the hell's going on?" Eden gasped.

Her body felt bruised and she dimly wondered if she would be scraped and bloody for the Aria shoot. They wouldn't be happy with any delays. They were on an extremely tight production schedule and were cramming two weeks' worth of filming into just a few days.

"Shooter," David said grimly.

"But why?" Eden asked in bafflement. "That's crazy! You mean some random sniper just started shooting at people on the sidewalk?"

"If it was random," Micah bit out.

She turned wide eyes on him. "This wasn't personal."

But it sounded more like a question than the statement she intended it to be.

"I'll make some calls when we get to the hotel," David said. "The cops are going to want to talk to you regardless. They'll make noises about you leaving the scene, but they can hardly blame you for staying safe. But they'll want to question you since we're all eyewitnesses to a crime."

"But I didn't witness anything," Eden said. "Oh God, I have to call my dad. If this hits the news he'll freak!"

"It doesn't matter what you saw. The police will still want to question you," Micah said, his tone soothing.

They rolled up to the hotel and Micah all but dragged Eden out, placing her firmly between him and David. He wrapped his heavy coat around her despite the warmth of the day, shielding her from view, though the sight they likely presented would be a huge tip-off to any lurking paparazzi.

At the front desk, Micah spoke in hushed tones with the clerk and then was presented with several key cards. Eden stared at him in confusion as he herded her onto the elevator and hit the button for a floor that wasn't the one she was currently staying on.

"We don't know what the hell is going on, but I'm not taking you back to your hotel room until it's cleared," Micah said. "For now, you'll stay in a different one on a different floor until this is all sorted out."

She allowed herself to be led into the large suite, identical to the one she had occupied the last several nights, and then plopped into one of the armchairs, her hands shaking so badly she couldn't control it.

Then, remembering she had to call her father, she picked up the phone. Across the room, David was already on the phone, explaining the situation to the police and that Eden was safely inside the hotel. She purposely waited for David to finish his call, wanting to be able to give her father as much reassurance as possible.

When he finally hung up, he turned, his expression tight. "They're sending two detectives here now. They were very certain to say you weren't to go anywhere in the meantime. And Eden, it's likely they'll detain you further while they sort out this whole thing. The press is going to be all over this."

She made an *ugh* sound and then stared down at the phone. With a sigh, she punched in her dad's number, knowing he was going to have a heart attack when she told him she'd been shot at, whether randomly or as the intended target. Either option wouldn't be acceptable to Eddie Sinclair.

CHAPTER 3

EDDIE stared at his two sons, unease gripping him by the balls. He was sweating. Even his hands were damp. His legendary cool under pressure had flat deserted him.

Ryker and Raid were staring at him expectantly, their expressions grim and worried. Raid had come from work, his shoulder harness still on, gun holstered. Ryker's hair was still damp from a shower and it was obvious he'd thrown on the first thing he'd come across in his haste to answer Eddie's summons.

"What's going on, Dad?" Raid asked in a low voice.

Eddie wiped his palm down over his face. "It's a long story. One I need to tell you from beginning to end so you understand what we're dealing with."

Ryker frowned and glanced over at his brother. No doubt they weren't used to seeing their father in such a state of agitation. Eddie had never been anything but assured and confident.

"Sit," Eddie commanded, gesturing toward the couch.

His two sons did as he directed and then looked expectantly at him, but he didn't take a seat. He was too jittery, too *gutted* by what he had to tell his boys. How could he ever look any of his children in the eyes again once they knew the truth?

"You're worrying me, Dad," Ryker said in a grim tone.

Eddie closed his eyes and then ran a hand raggedly through his hair.

"Your mother's death wasn't an accident," he said.

Shock registered on both his sons' faces.

"I don't understand," Raid said, his tone as grim as Ryker's had been moments earlier. "What the fuck are you saying, Dad? Did you just find this out? How the hell did you find this out anyway? And if her death wasn't an accident . . ."

"Who killed her?" Ryker asked hoarsely.

The knot in Eddie's stomach grew, clenching painfully. "It's a long story, one that begins before you were born."

"We're listening," Raid said tightly, his features drawn into a mask of pain and confusion. And worry.

Eddie finally slumped into one of the armchairs across from the couch where Raid and Ryker sat and bleakly stared at his sons.

"You both know I served in the military."

They nodded, impatience simmering in Ryker's eyes. He wanted his dad to get to the point.

"I served in a special ops group, one that didn't officially exist. Our missions weren't the usual run of the mill. We took on missions that were it discovered the U.S. had a hand in them, the fallout would have been messy. One particular mission took us three years to complete. Three long years of waiting and watching for the right opportunity. Raul Sanchez was our mission. Taking him down and dismantling his operation. Three years and two months into our operation, we caught a break. We got intel that he was going to be in a particular location for a family gathering. His daughter's birthday. This was a man who was as slippery as an eel. More than one country's military was after him. We just happened to get to him first.

"We set up surveillance on the compound where he was going to be. Everything went off without a hitch. But then the unthinkable happened. We believed his wife and daughter had already left in a car. We waited until they were clear of the compound and then we went in."

He broke off, regret and guilt surging and pumping through his veins as if it had happened just yesterday. For years he'd lived with his mistake. A mistake his wife had paid for, his entire family had paid for. And now it would appear Eden would pay for it if he and his sons didn't prevent it.

"A firefight broke out. Our entry wasn't clean. A guard got lucky and deviated in his patrol, saw one of my men and all hell broke loose. I was leading the group of men tasked with taking out Sanchez. We burst into the study he was holed up in. He had two men with him and they drew on us. We had no choice but to return fire and . . ."

He scrubbed his hands over his face, tears burning his eyelids.

"What happened?" Raid asked quietly.

"Sanchez's wife and daughter got caught in the cross fire. God, she was just a little girl. Holding the doll she'd been given as a birthday present. There was blood everywhere. God, I can still see them in my dreams, my nightmares."

"Jesus. I'm sorry, Dad. That's a big burden to carry around all these years," Ryker said.

"Sanchez and his son got away, in the chaos and my horror over the wife and daughter being caught in the cross fire. My priority was trying to get them help, and Sanchez and his son escaped.

"We cleaned up best we could. Collected the information needed to dismantle his operation and rounded up a lot of the key players in his business. He had a hand in a lot of different pots. Drugs. Arms trafficking. God, he even had a lucrative human trafficking operation going. Selling young girls into sexual slavery to the highest bidder."

Raid made a sound of disgust.

"I thought . . ." Eddie took a deep breath. "Years went by and I thought I'd put it behind me. I retired after that debacle. I just couldn't do it any longer. You children were born and your mother and I were happy. And then . . ."

He choked off, emotion knotting his throat as tears gathered in his vision.

"Sanchez waited, biding his time, planning his revenge. He was responsible for your mother's death and he wasted no time in letting me know he was taking an eye for an eye. A wife for a wife."

"What the fuck?" Ryker demanded. "And you never told us? You just let him get away with that? Killing our mother?"

"No," Eddie said quietly. "No, I didn't. I called Guy."

"Hancock?" Raid asked in a puzzled tone.

Eddie sighed. "There's a lot you don't know about Guy. He joined the military, followed in my footsteps in more than one way. He belonged to a group that was buried so deep that according to military records, they were all killed in action. They no longer existed. They weren't supposed to have any ties to the outside world. They lived, breathed and ate their missions. But he kept me in the loop. He wasn't supposed to, which is why I never let on to you or Eden. All you knew was that he was serving and off the grid. And it's why we never see him. I hear from him sporadically. He never tells me much, just that he's okay from time to time. He's made a lot of enemies over the years and now the government has cut ties and likely has orders to eliminate him if he ever surfaces."

"So you contacted him after Mom died. Why?" Ryker demanded.

"Because I wanted revenge," Eddie said in a low voice. "I wanted to go after the bastard and make him pay for what he took from me. For what he took from all of us."

"Jesus," Raid breathed. "And? Did you? Did you find him?"

Eddie was silent a long moment before finally nodding. "Guy went after him. He didn't want me involved. I gave him all the intel I had. I called in a lot of favors to get the information he needed."

"So he killed him," Ryker said bluntly.

Again Eddie nodded.

"Christ, Dad. And you didn't think we deserved to know

all of this sooner? And why tell us now? What's going on?" Raid demanded.

Eddie paled, suddenly feeling years older. The weight of a lifetime of regret settled like a ton of bricks on his shoulders and his heart.

He reached up to the mantel and picked up the photos and the note he'd received. With shaking hands, he shoved them toward his sons, simply waiting for them to look them over and draw their own conclusions.

"Holy fuck," Ryker exploded. "Eden is being threatened?"

"His son," Eddie said in a strained voice. "It has to be the son. We weren't able to find him. Just Raul. But his son would want revenge because not only did he lose his mother and sister but then Guy took out his father and now he's looking for revenge. By hitting me where he knows he'd hurt me the most. Through Eden."

"Son of a bitch," Raid swore. "What the hell are we going to do? Where is Eden now? What are we going to do? She's not safe even for a minute. What if he's already found her? What if he's going after her as we speak?"

"It's why I called you both to come. I spoke to Eden earlier today. She seemed fine. I don't want to scare her. I don't even want her to know all of this. It would upset her. But we have to close ranks around her. Tighten security. What we have now isn't going to cut it. These people are ruthless. They have resources beyond our imaginings. She isn't safe. We have to figure out a way to make sure she's safe at all times."

Ryker went silent a long moment, his expression thoughtful. "I know people who could help us. It's what they do. They're all ex-military. I served with two of the brothers. Nathan and Joe Kelly. They got out when I did. That last mission that went all to hell. Some of us didn't make it back. Joe was injured and Nathan and another teammate were held prisoner for months in the mountains of Afghanistan. But their brothers run a special ops group. Some of it's private sector, but they also do a lot of government contract work.

Jobs that no one else can or will do. Hostage recovery, rescue, protection. You name it, they do it. And they're damn good. Nathan and Joe work with them now as does Swanny, the other guy I served with. We could call them in. They owe me a favor."

"How good?" Raid asked bluntly. "Because good isn't good enough. Not when it comes to keeping Eden safe. We need the fucking best."

"I'll call them. Set up a meeting immediately. We may need to fly out there so we can get the ball rolling sooner," Ryker said grimly.

"You do that," Eddie said. "I'm not losing Eden. Or you. Those bastards have taken enough from this family."

The phone rang, interrupting the tense discussion. Eddie glanced down to see that it was Eden calling.

"Hey, baby girl," he greeted, holding his hand to his sons.

"Daddy?"

At the tremble he heard in her voice, his blood went cold.

"Eden? What's wrong? Are you all right? What's happened?"

Raid and Ryker immediately came to attention, rushing over to stand closer so they could hear what was transpiring.

"There was a shooting," she said, her voice wobbling precariously. "But I wanted you to know I was okay. I didn't want you to hear about it on the news and worry."

"What do you mean there was a shooting?" he roared.

"I don't know anything yet, Daddy. The cops are coming to question me. David and Micah got me into the car and to the hotel. We're staying in a different suite. Micah and David were concerned that this could be personal."

Hell, Eddie *knew* it was personal. Son of a bitch, but he hadn't expected it to start this soon. He'd only received the threat today. His blood chilled in his veins. But the timing was impeccable. Had the killer planned it this way? For Eddie to receive the threat just a short time before Eden was killed?

Helpless rage gripped his throat, squeezing until he could barely breathe. Raid wrenched the phone from his hand, ignoring his father's immediate protest.

"Eden, this is Raid. Tell me where you are and we'll catch the first flight out we can," he said calmly.

There was a pause and then Raid said, "Okay, honey. Stay where David and Micah put you. We'll be there as soon as we can."

He ended the call and handed his father back the phone, his eyes nearly black with rage.

"So it's begun, then."

Eddie could only nod, fear and fury waging war in his mind.

"Then let's get the fuck out of here," Ryker said tightly. "I'll call Nathan and Joe on the way and have them meet us there if they can make it."

CHAPTER 4

DARYL "Swanny" Swanson picked his head up when the phone rang in the cabin he shared with Joe Kelly.

"Hey, can you get that?" Joe called from the bathroom.

Swanny hauled himself up from the couch where he was watching the baseball game and ambled over to pick up the cordless house phone. It was probably a damn telemarketer because no one ever called the landline. Everyone used cell phones.

"Hello?"

"Can I speak to Nathan or Joe Kelly? It's urgent."

The male voice sounded vaguely familiar, but Swanny couldn't place it. But whoever it was obviously wasn't someone who knew the brothers well or he would have known that Nathan lived in his own place with his wife, Shea.

"Can I tell him who's calling?" Swanny asked as he started toward the bathroom.

"This is Ryker Sinclair. We served together. It's important I speak to one of them immediately."

"Sin?" Swanny exclaimed. "Hey, buddy, it's Swanny. How the hell are you?"

There was a pause and then Ryker replied. "Swanny? I heard you were working with the Kellys, but I didn't expect to get you on the phone. Man, am I glad to hear your voice. How are you doing? How is Nathan doing? I haven't heard from y'all since we all got out."

"We're all doing fine. Nathan is married now. But hey, what's going on? You said it was urgent. Anything I can do to help?"

Ryker breathed out heavily over the phone. "Yeah, I need your help. I need KGI's help."

"Hang on, let me get Joe and I'll put you on speaker-phone."

Swanny beat on the bathroom door, holding the phone to his side. "Hey, Joe, get out here. It's Sin. Ryker Sinclair. He needs to talk to us ASAP."

The door swung open and Joe appeared, a frown on his face. "Sin?"

"Yeah, get in the kitchen so I can put him on speaker-phone. He said it was urgent and he needed KGI's help."

"Fuck," Joe muttered.

They strode back to the kitchen and Swanny punched the speaker button before replacing the phone on the receiver.

"Hey, man, we're both here," Joe said. "What's up? How the hell are you?"

"Not good," Ryker said grimly. "I have a problem. I need your help. KGI's help."

"You know we'll do whatever we can. Give me the rundown."

"I don't have time to get into it on the phone and I don't have all the details myself. We're on our way to where Eden is. She's in trouble. It's a long goddamn story and I know I'm not giving you much to go on, but I need you for this. Can you come?"

Swanny's eyebrows went up. Eden? She was Ryker's sister. His very *hot* sister. Ryker used to share her letters—and photos—with the guys when they were freezing their asses off in the Afghani mountains. She'd fired more than one wet dream. She was fucking gorgeous. And not in a bought-and-paid-for way either. She was a natural beauty through and through and she just sparkled. She had a million-dollar smile and her letters were always filled with love and humor. Her letters had brightened many otherwise shitty days when they were hunkered down with only her pictures—and their fantasies—to keep them warm.

He frowned. She was a model, if he remembered right. And she was in trouble? Swanny's protective instincts roared to life. What kind of trouble was she in that her brother needed KGI's help? Whatever it was, it couldn't be good.

"Tell me where," Joe said simply.

Sin had saved Joe's ass by shoving him down when their team came under fire. Sin had taken a bullet that would have otherwise taken Joe out. Swanny knew that if Sin needed help, Joe wouldn't refuse. No matter what it involved.

"We're flying to Boston now," Ryker said grimly. "Some asshole took a shot at her and they're holding her for questioning, so Dad and Raid and I are going there so we can find out what the hell is going on."

He paused a second, letting out a sigh.

"And there's more. A lot more. But I can't get into it over the phone. That's why I need you there as quickly as you can make it. I'll explain everything when you get there."

Joe and Swanny exchanged quick looks.

"I'll call up my team and we'll head out as soon as I can get everyone to the jet. Sit tight, okay? Let me give you my cell number so you can reach me."

"Thanks, man. This means a lot to me. And to Dad. I'll text you the hotel."

Joe gave him his cell number and Swanny's, and then they quickly took down Ryker's as well.

"Okay, give me a few hours and we'll be on our way. I have to run this by my older brothers, but we'll come. You can count on it," Joe said.

They rang off and Joe turned his frown on Swanny. "I wonder what the fuck that was all about."

Swanny shrugged. "I'm more curious as to what he meant

when he said someone took a shot at Eden. Did he mean someone hit her or actually tried to shoot her?"

Joe scowled at that. "Isn't she some hotshot model?"

"Surely you remember the pictures Sin used to show us," Swanny said dryly.

Joe's brow furrowed. "No, not really."

Swanny rolled his eyes. "Dude, she is hot. Smoking hot."

Joe's eyebrows shot up. "Wow. She must have really made an impression on you. I never hear you talk about chicks, hot or not."

Swanny rubbed a hand over the jagged scar that ran the length of his face. "Not much to talk about," he murmured. "They aren't exactly lining up to get with me."

Joe grimaced. "Sorry, man. Poor choice of words."

Swanny shrugged. "You want me to call Skylar and Edge? Get them heading in this direction? I'll let you tackle your brothers. They're going to want a meet-up at HQ. They aren't just going to turn us loose on the basis of a phone call saying we need a jet, and oh, by the way, we're taking the team but we don't know why yet."

"Smart-ass," Joe muttered. "But yeah, you're right. You call Sky and Edge. I'll call Nathan and Sam and we'll meet at the compound."

Swanny pulled his phone out of his pocket and turned away to start making his calls. If he lucked out, both would be at home since they roomed together in a house close to the compound so he'd only have to make one call.

"Edge," Swanny greeted. "Hey, man, is Sky with you?"

"Yeah, she's here," Edge replied. "What's up?"

"We've been called up. Load-and-go situation. No idea on how long, so pack accordingly. Meet up at the war room as soon as y'all can get there."

"Later," Edge said, and hung up.

Swanny grinned. As verbose as ever. Edge didn't say a whole lot, but people tended to pay attention when he did. But then he was a big guy. Most people were wary around him. Swanny often wondered how he and Skylar ever decided to room together.

Skylar was bubbly, outgoing and talkative. Edge was quiet and never instigated conversation. Swanny could well imagine Skylar driving the big man insane inside of a week of living together. But they'd been in the same house for months now and all seemed to be going well.

Joe was still on the phone with one of his brothers, so Swanny took off to his bedroom to pack his gear. He did a weapons check, although he was always meticulous about his gear and kept it ready to go at all times. It wasn't unusual to get a callout that required them to load and go.

Just another day on the job.

Only this job involved a very beautiful woman, and it pissed him off that someone had taken a shot at her, figurative or not. From what he'd gleaned in her letters to her brother and Ryker's stories about her, she had a huge heart and was completely down to earth, despite her glamorous life as a model.

An image flashed in his mind. A magazine Ryker had proudly produced on that last tour, the one that had effectively ended Swanny's career in the army, had Eden's face on the cover. She'd been chosen as the world's most beautiful woman, and Swanny could see why. She was so beautiful she made his balls ache.

Long, flowing blond hair. Not the bottled kind either. Eyes an unusual shade of aquamarine that glowed brightly against sun-kissed skin. And her smile. Man. Not a fake smile, but a genuine, from-the-heart-looking smile. Her eyes had sparkled with laughter. She hadn't done one of those serious, sultry poses. There was a hint of mischief shining in those ocean eyes. The kind that told a man he was getting a handful with her.

And those lips. Full, luscious. Just the right amount of plumpness and forming a perfect bow. No lipstick, just a hint of shiny gloss. For that matter, as he gained a firmer image of that picture in his mind, he remembered that she hadn't worn makeup, or if she had, it was the kind that made it look as though she wore none. She had a natural, all-American-girl look going. The girl next door, only ten times hotter. Men could only dream of the girl next door looking that damn good.

He shook himself from his wayward thoughts and stashed clothing in a duffel bag, took a quick inventory of his knives and the flashbangs he always had on him and then made sure he had sufficient ammo for the two pistols he carried.

He was acting like a goddamn teenager with a crush on the cheerleader. Yeah, he'd had his share of fantasies on those long nights in the cold with only his daydreams to occupy his thoughts. Eden wouldn't give a man like him a second glance. Or maybe she would, but it would be because she was doing a double take at the hideous scar that marred his face. That thought effectively put a damper on his imaginings and he got back to the task at hand.

He secured the ankle holster before sliding the smaller Sig into place and then put on the shoulder harness and secured the larger Glock. He grabbed the duffel bag carrying his clothes and the case holding the ammo and then carefully shouldered the straps of the two high-powered rifles. One was a semiautomatic, the other his .308 with the high-powered scope he used for sharpshooting. Anything else they needed would be on the plane in the weapons locker.

He wasn't sure what kind of trouble Eden Sinclair was in, but Ryker had sounded worried, and not much worried the Sinclair family. Their father was a badass in his own right. Raid, the oldest, was a seasoned cop and Ryker worked in private security, a smaller, less military version of KGI. All his jobs were on the up-and-up. Mostly personal security, which made it odd that he was seeking KGI's help for the trouble his sister was in. Swanny would have thought that if she was in any kind of trouble, the family would close ranks around her and handle it on their own. They were private that way. Which only reaffirmed his belief that the situation was dire. Ryker's vagueness on the phone bothered Swanny. He had a bad feeling about the whole damn thing. But there was nothing to do until they got there and heard firsthand what was going on.

He hurried back into the living room to see Joe stuffing his bags with clothing and his own personal arsenal, which was similar to Swanny's own. They all had their personal

preferences when it came to guns, but they all adhered to the
motto that many was sufficient but more was even better.

If the zombie apocalypse ever occurred, they were definitely prepared. The KGI compound could withstand a fucking war. The sheer number of legal—and illegal—shit that
was housed behind the walls of the compound would shock
the average citizen. Swanny had his own stash of C-4 and
enough grenades to repel a small army.

During his captivity, he'd sworn never again to feel that
kind of helplessness and fear. He'd accepted the inevitability
of his own death. He'd even embraced it. In his darkest
hours, he'd prayed for it. It shamed him now, but at the time,
death was the ultimate freedom. Escape from his dismal
reality.

Thank God for Shea, Nathan's now-wife, who'd inexplica-
bly reached out to him across thousands of miles, speaking to
him in his mind. Helping him and Swanny escape their captors
and certain death. And Grace. Shea's sister. God, she'd *healed*
him. She'd fucking healed him from injuries that would have
slowed his and Nathan's escape. He'd begged Nathan to leave
him. To save himself. And instead Nathan, with Shea's and
Grace's help, had healed him. Made it possible for him to soldier on, and they'd made it out of those mountains alive. Not
unscathed. But alive nonetheless.

He absently fingered the scar on his face. A memento
from his time in captivity. Insurance that he'd never forget
those endless days of torture and starvation. They'd carved
him and Nathan both up. They both still wore the scars from
their captivity, but Swanny's were more visible. His face had
been slashed and by the time they'd been rescued and hospi-
talized, there was little a surgeon could do, and he wasn't
vain enough to ever have plastic surgery.

No, he wore that scar as a reminder of what he'd survived.

His sex life had certainly suffered as a result, but sex
wasn't one of his priorities. Not since coming home alive. He
threw himself into his job. His new family. He shook his
head. He had no family. Not until Nathan. The Kellys and
KGI had embraced him. Marlene Kelly, the matriarch of the

Kelly clan, had adopted him as one of her own, and she treated him just like he was one of her many children.

Frank and Marlene Kelly had six sons, but Marlene had adopted others into her fold. Rusty Kelly, the sullen teenager who'd broken into her home but was now about to graduate from college, a vibrant, beautiful young lady who had the world at her feet. Swanny had no doubt she'd one day rule the world.

And there was Sean Cameron, a sheriff's deputy in Stewart County. Also adopted into the Kelly fold and treated much like all Marlene and Frank's other children. It was mind-boggling, the extent of the Kellys' generosity.

The family had grown and expanded. Joe was the only unmarried Kelly, and he definitely heard about it from Marlene on a regular basis. There were grandchildren aplenty and more on the way.

And here in the middle of it all was Swanny. He'd gone from a solitary existence with only the men he served with as his brothers. And now he had the entire Kelly family plus the KGI team members. All at his back. Ready to go to the wall for him. It baffled him, this unconditional loyalty.

He'd crawled back to the little house he'd inherited from his parents after he and Nathan had been discharged from the hospital. But he'd been restless and . . . lonely. His brush with death, facing his mortality and then his miraculous healing had brought him to Tennessee, seeking answers from Nathan about what had happened in those mountains before they were rescued.

And he'd stayed, first adopted into the fold instantaneously by Marlene Kelly and then offered a position with KGI. He'd joined the new team headed by Nathan and Joe and joined soon after by Edge and Skylar. They were his family now. And having family, people who accepted him, felt . . . good.

When he'd served in the army he'd had a purpose. His life had been consumed with the need to protect and serve. After his injuries and discharge, he hadn't known what else to do. There was nothing for him on the outside. He'd never be

happy with a nine-to-five office job or joining the rat race as
a civilian. KGI had given him purpose again.

KGI helped people. They protected the innocent and the
weak. They helped bring down the assholes in the world,
those who preyed on the innocents. Now when he woke in the
morning, he felt alive. Like he had a future. KGI had given
him that, and he'd be forever grateful to them for that.

He'd resigned himself to never settling down, having a family, things most people took for granted even if they weren't in
a hurry. He was surrounded by just those things. Each of the
Kelly brothers, with the exception of Joe, had met their soul
mates. Even the team leaders, Rio and Steele, had settled into
domesticity with an ease that still amused and befuddled the
men and women who worked under their command. Hell, even
Cole and P.J., two of Steele's team members, had hooked up
and were living in marital bliss, though he imagined theirs was
an interesting arrangement since P.J. could kick ass with the
best of them. It was for certain she kept Cole on his toes.

But that wasn't for him, and he accepted that just like he'd
accepted everything else. With peace and understanding. He
didn't just have scars on the outside. He was irrevocably
scarred—changed—on the inside. He wasn't sure how Nathan
was handling the memories. He was sure Nathan still had his
fair share of sleepless nights, but he had Shea to help him, to
lean on when the past reared its ugly head. But Swanny still
suffered nightmares. Flashbacks to his captivity. He still woke
in a cold sweat, fearing for a moment that he was back in that
hell. Chained in a cave waiting for the time when they came
for him. To carve him up, beat him and interrogate him.

They hadn't been able to break him. He took pride in that.
He and Nathan both had withstood all that their captors had
dished out and had never broken. Because in the end, that
was all they'd had left. Their pride and determination not to
let those cocksuckers win.

He had a good life now. No, he wouldn't ever have a wife
or children, and he was okay with that on most days. Every
once in a while when all the Kellys got together and he was
surrounded by so much love, the Kelly wives and the children,

he was instilled with a fierce sense of longing, but he'd long discovered it did no good to dwell on what would never be.

Most women couldn't even look at him without fear, disgust or pity. Pity was the worst. He'd take fear and loathing over their pity. Although it pained him for a woman to fear him just because of his appearance. He'd cut off his right arm before ever hurting a woman. It made him sick just to think about it. He'd seen enough violence in his life to know it would never be part of his makeup. Except when it came to taking out assholes who deserved what was coming to them.

He was a killer and he suffered no qualms about meting out justice where it was merited. As long as he could look at himself in the mirror every morning with a clear conscience, he could continue to do the job required of him as a member of KGI.

"You ready?" Joe called out, shaking Swanny from his thoughts.

"Yeah. All packed up. You call Nathan and Sam?"

Joe nodded. "Nathan's on his way over and Sam is calling Garrett, Ethan and Van to meet us there. I told him there was no need to call in Steele or Rio. This is our mission. Sin is our friend and I'm not letting anyone else head this mission."

"Agreed," Swanny said. "I don't know what kind of trouble Eden's in, but if Sin is worried then it has to be serious."

Joe nodded. "Let's get on the road. Nathan can fly us so there's no need—and we don't have the time—to call up one of the other pilots."

Swanny grinned. "Kind of nice now that we have a landing strip on the compound. That drive to Henry County was a pain in the ass. Not to mention it makes for a hell of a quicker response time when we get called out on a mission."

Joe slung one of the bags over his shoulder and then bent to snag the straps of the two rifles he shouldered. They carried their gear to Joe's truck and carefully placed it in the back before sliding into the cab to head the few miles down the lake to the compound.

CHAPTER 5

WHEN Joe and Swanny got to the compound, Nathan, Sam, Garrett and Ethan were already there. Swanny walked inside the war room and laid his gear on the floor next to the door. When he looked up at the others, he had to stifle a grin of amusement that would likely get his ass kicked if noticed.

Sam and Garrett were both holding their new babies. Well, not so new. They were a few months old now, but according to Joe, they were both in teething hell and had been giving their parents a lot of sleepless nights. Swanny could only guess the dads were giving their wives a breather and had hauled the infants to the impromptu meeting.

"The tykes keeping y'all up at night?" Joe asked with a grin he *didn't* disguise.

Sam and Garrett shot him disgruntled looks and Garrett made a quick *shhhh* and waved his free hand to quiet the others.

"I just got her to sleep," Garrett whispered. "She hasn't slept the entire goddamn night!"

Ethan chuckled, which earned him another glare from Garrett.

"Welcome to parenthood," Ethan said in a loud whisper.

"I'm glad to say that we're past that stage with the twins. They're sleeping through the night completely now. Mason is even almost potty trained! Not bad for an almost-two-year-old."

The proud note didn't go unnoticed by the rest. Sam rolled his eyes and made a rude gesture with his free hand.

"If only your wives could see and hear all the profanity and gestures y'all are making," Nathan drawled. "Sarah wouldn't be happy to hear your cursing around Kelsey."

"Fuck you," Garrett said in a low voice.

Sam shifted his son in his grasp and then thrust him toward Ethan. "Here. Since you're so *adept* at this now, you can hold Grant while I conduct this meeting."

Ethan happily took the infant and immediately began cooing to the gurgling baby.

Joe, Nathan and Swanny all exchanged eye rolls since they were the only ones without kids. Nathan and Shea were in no hurry to add to the growing pile of kids the Kellys were accumulating, and Joe and Swanny showed no sign of settling down any time soon.

Still, Swanny couldn't help the surge of envy as he surveyed the room of burly warriors, all making twits of themselves over their progeny. It was hard to imagine these men as the ultimate badasses when they were talking teething, babies and potty training. And yet they ran a tight operation. They were the best. And they employed the best.

Swanny had no false modesty when it came to his skills and abilities. He'd been good before he'd come to KGI, but KGI had made him better. He was at the top of his game, or at least he was getting there. He'd been a mere shell of himself when he'd returned from Afghanistan after months of imprisonment, starvation and torture.

But with the help of good friends, the Kelly family, the KGI organization as a whole, he'd put the pieces together again. At least the physical aspects. He wasn't sure he'd ever be the same mentally. He still had nightmares. Or night terrors, since the dreams he had weren't likely considered normal nightmares.

Most people didn't have nightmares involving being

carved up with a knife, stripped of their clothing and being held—and treated—like an animal. Hell, most animals were afforded better treatment than he'd received at the hands of his captors.

One day he'd make peace with it all. He hoped. And in the end, that was all he could do. Hang on to hope that his past didn't forever rule or tarnish his future. Maybe he'd live with his demons forever. But at least he was becoming more adept at surviving them.

But he didn't want to survive life. He wanted to live it. He'd die before ever becoming a victim again. Never again would he be stripped of his humanity, his very *soul*. When he thought back on the many times during captivity when he'd wanted to give up—*had* given up—it shamed him. Nathan had been stronger than Swanny, a fact that still bothered him after so many months. But never again. Nothing and no one would ever bring him that low again. It was a vow he'd made the moment their rescue had become reality and not just a seemingly impossible dream.

The door to the war room opened and Donovan strolled in unhurriedly, a smile on his face. As the newest brother to get hitched, he was in a perpetual good mood. Though Eve, his wife, hadn't become pregnant, she had two younger siblings that lived with her and Van. Travis was sixteen and enrolled in the local high school while Cammie, Eve's precious little sister, was now five years old and would be starting kindergarten in the fall with Charlotte, Sam's oldest child.

Donovan lifted one eyebrow when he saw the babies Ethan and Garrett were holding.

"Teething still?"

"Your day is coming, little brother," Sam warned. "And don't think you'll get an ounce of sympathy from the rest of us when you and Eve have babies."

Donovan grinned. "I'm looking *forward* to it. The kind of shit y'all bitch and moan about, I can't wait for. But we *are* going to wait a while. Eve is still young and she's been taking care of her brother and sister for a long time. I don't want to saddle her with added responsibility for a while. We both want kids. Lots of them. But we have plenty of time and I want her, Cammie and Travis to myself for a while before we add to the family. I don't want Cammie or Travis to ever think they come second to any children Eve and I have together."

Joe made a sound of impatience. "Not that I don't love all the domesticity that oozes from the walls, but we have a mission to focus on. Can we get on with it?"

"Spoken like a free man," Ethan drawled.

Swanny too was growing impatient. The phone call from Sin was still weighing heavily on his mind, and like Joe, he was ready to get moving on this.

The door opened again and Edge and Skylar walked in, looking focused and ready.

"Okay, everyone's here," Joe said. "Let's get started."

"Going to tell us what's up, or are you just absconding with a jet and taking off?" Sam asked dryly, subtly reminding them that though this was a family-run organization, he was still in command. Or rather he shared dual command with Garrett and Donovan, but for the most part, Sam ran the show, though he did include his brothers in all the decision making. Ethan was steadily coming into his own, but he had a lot of ground to make up, having only joined KGI when his wife, Rachel, had been rescued a few years earlier.

Edge and Skylar moved to the planning table where the others were gathered, but not before Skylar stopped to coo at Grant, who was still in Ethan's arms.

"Here, hand the little guy back to Sam so we can start planning," Ethan said, handing the baby to Skylar. "I think it's time for a diaper change and I've paid my dues in that department."

There were simultaneous looks of amusement—from the men who had children—and something akin to horror from the men who didn't.

Skylar didn't seem at all bothered by the prospect of a soiled diaper. She reached to take him from Ethan and bounced him gently in her arms before finally passing him back to Sam.

"He's adorable, Sam. And he looks so much like you! It's weird looking at your children because Charlotte is an exact replica of Sophie, and Grant looks exactly like you," Skylar mused. "You've totally got a Mini-Me!"

"Poor kid," Nathan muttered.

"Hello? Mission time?" Joe said in exasperation.

Garrett shifted Kelsey carefully in his arms like she was a bomb about to go off. He tensed and stared down at her, strain evident on his brow. Swanny saw the evidence of many recent sleepless nights in the big man's face, saw him visibly sigh in relief when his daughter squirmed once and then settled back to sleep, nestled in her father's arms. But there was also so much love and adoration in the big man's eyes that Swanny would have to be blind or completely oblivious not to notice it.

That little girl had brought Garrett to his knees, and she'd continue to do so for the rest of her life. One thing was for certain, though, and it held true for all the Kelly children. There wasn't a child on earth who'd be more protected and watched over than those babies. Swanny pitied the poor fool who ever tried to date the Kelly daughters. Being met on the front porch by a surly, overprotective father? Swanny would pay money to see that.

"So what are we looking at here?" Garrett asked in a low voice. "You didn't give us much to go on."

Joe glanced at Nathan. "Ryker Sinclair called. Said his sister was in trouble. He wouldn't go into detail. Said someone took a shot at her, but I have no clue what that means exactly."

Nathan frowned. "Isn't his sister a supermodel, or something? He used to show us pictures of her. She was chosen as the world's most beautiful woman by that magazine a few years ago. He showed it to us when we were on our last tour."

"Yeah, that's her," Swanny supplied.

Just the mention of that magazine cover—glossy, silky blond hair flowing as though she were out in a gentle breeze, eyes glowing and a megawatt smile—brought back the first time he'd seen her photo. He felt like an idiot for having nearly an identical reaction just from the memory.

"So you know this Ryker Sinclair?" Donovan asked.

Joe nodded, as did Nathan and Swanny.

"We served with him," Nathan explained.

"He saved my ass," Joe interjected. "Shoved me down and took the bullet intended for me. I owe him."

"We all owe him, then," Sam said simply.

And that was Sam. In his eyes, what debt one of his brothers owed was a debt the entire family assumed. That extended to the rest of KGI as well.

"He didn't go into a lot of detail," Joe continued. "But he sounded worried, and if he's worried then we should be too. His father served and his older brother is a cop. They likely employ a security company to protect Eden because I can't imagine Big Eddie leaving his daughter's safety to chance. So the fact that they've called us up tells me this is something big. Sin told me Eden's holed up in a hotel and they're flying out immediately to get to her. He said he'd be in touch as soon as he knew where we needed to meet them, but he asked that we get going in that direction."

Sam pinned Joe with his stare. "You'll let me know the minute you have more intel, and if it's something your team can't handle on their own, don't be stubborn. Call me for backup, and I can have Steele's or Rio's team in the air within a few hours."

"You guys in?" Joe asked, turning to look at Edge and Skylar.

"Hell, yeah," Skylar said in a tone that suggested Joe's question irritated her. "We're part of this team. If you're going, we're going."

Edge grinned, the action erasing the hard lines of his face and lighting the brooding shadows in his eyes. "Couldn't have said it better than Sky."

"All right then, y'all get in the air and holler when you land and get a better handle on the situation," Donovan said.

"I'll alert Steele and have him on standby," Garrett said in hushed tones, though he was still staring at his daughter as if afraid any noise would awaken her. He winced, obviously seeing something he didn't like.

Then sure enough, a wail sounded and a panicked look entered Garrett's eyes. He blew out a weary sigh. Swanny could almost summon sympathy, but how did you feel sorry for a guy who had the world at his feet? A beautiful, loving wife. A new daughter. The promise of future children. A future he didn't face alone. No, Swanny didn't feel sorry for him. He realized the internal flinch was . . . *envy*. Was this how Donovan had felt before Eve had come into his life when his brothers were falling one by one? Forging their own, separate path. Still firmly ensconced in the fold of the Kelly family but striking out on their own as well. Branching off, though all forks led back to the same place. Home. Kentucky Lake.

"Shit. I should probably head back home. She's probably going to want to nurse. I was hoping to give Sarah a longer nap," Garrett said with a grimace.

Without waiting for a response, Garrett all but ran for the exit, laughter in his wake. He only paused to raise his right hand and extend his middle finger before disappearing from the war room.

"I meant what I said," Sam said in a serious tone, turning everyone's attention back to him. "If this is something you think you need backup on, you call me immediately. Garrett and I are out of commission for the short term, but Van and Ethan as well as the other two teams can bug out on short notice. I'll put them on alert just in case we need them."

"We got it, big brother," Nathan said dryly. "We're big boys now. It's time to wean us off the tit and let us out into the world."

"Dick," Sam muttered. "It's my job to worry about y'all. I'm the oldest, so that falls within my job description."

"As long as you don't claim to be the brains of this operation," Donovan drawled. "That's my title. Super geek, remember?"

The others rolled their eyes, but then Joe picked up his pack and motioned for the others.

"Let's hit the road. We're wasting time. Sam, is the jet fueled and ready?" Joe asked.

Sam nodded.

Joe slapped Nathan on the shoulder. "Okay, little brother. You're flying the jet."

"*With* permission this time," Sam said dryly.

"Y'all are never going to let me live down the time I stole the company jet, are you?" Nathan asked in exasperation.

"It was a righteous cause," Swanny said sagely.

Nathan had commandeered a KGI jet and left home like a bat out of hell, but he'd returned with Shea. With a new lease on life. Swanny could see the difference in Nathan. He'd come a long way from the man who'd been rescued from the same hell Swanny had endured. Swanny had no doubt Nathan still dealt with his past, but there was a peace about him that was evident. He was . . . happy. Content. Wasn't that what everyone wanted in the end?

Donovan smirked. "Truth, but that doesn't mean we aren't going to give him shit about it whenever we get the chance."

"Fuckers," Nathan grumbled.

Skylar and Edge hauled their packs up and headed for the door. Swanny stooped to retrieve his bag while Nathan and Joe raided the KGI arsenal in a room just off the main staging area.

They walked briskly in the direction of the hangar. It was a pretty good distance from the war room, but by the time they shoved all their gear into multiple SUVs and drove to the airfield, they'd already be there just lugging it themselves.

Though petite, Skylar kept stride with the much taller men and didn't even look winded. She kept herself in impeccable shape. One thing Swanny had noticed from day one of her joining the new team was that she hadn't come in with a chip on her shoulder, nor had she seemed to think she had anything to prove just because she was a woman in a predominantly male organization. She was sharp as a tack, smart and confident. And the few times Swanny had actually not looked at her as a teammate—as just a part of a whole—she was beautiful in an effervescent way. But confident. Yeah. That was an attractive quality in a woman. Maybe some men didn't agree, or perhaps they felt threatened by a woman fully capable of taking care of not only herself but others around her, but Swanny didn't think there was a more beautiful woman than one who knew her mind and dared the world to take her on.

Perhaps not being the only woman in KGI had helped in
that regard—though Swanny acknowledged that probably
had little to do with it. Sky was her own person. She wouldn't
have needed P.J. to break ground for her. She could do plenty
of groundbreaking and ass kicking all on her own. She and
P.J. both, for that matter.

P.J. Rutherford . . . damn it, *Coletrane* now. He had to correct himself every time. She and Cole were married now but it
was hard to start thinking of her as P.J. Coletrane. At any rate,
P.J. was a kick-ass female warrior who could easily take down
a man—or men—twice her size. Skylar wasn't any less of a
badass and none of the guys treated her like . . . well, a girl.

Like P.J., she was one of the guys. As he'd already mused,
both women were more than capable of taking care of themselves, and more importantly, perfectly capable of backing
up their male teammates. Swanny had no qualms about having Skylar—or P.J.—at his back. He trusted Sky with his life
just as she trusted him with hers.

It was the way it worked in KGI. The chemistry had to be
just right within each team in order for them to perform and
function as a well-oiled machine. Their lives—and those of
others—depended on that fact.

As they boarded, Swanny was contemplating Eden. Her
image swam in his mind. Impossibly beautiful and sweet
natured, and she had a heart of gold by all accounts. He used
his phone to study up on her recent activities, curious about
the woman her brother used to talk about so much. And
where she was now in her career. If she'd been one of the
world's most beautiful women a couple of years ago, what
about now? Had she changed?

But as he stared at recent photos, courtesy of Google, he
realized that if anything she'd grown impossibly lovelier than
ever. *Lovelier.* The word amused him. He couldn't remember a
time that word had ever been a part of his vocabulary, and he
damn sure hadn't ever used it in actual speech. And yet he
couldn't think of a more appropriate word. *Beautiful. Gorgeous.* Those were common. Tossed around with enthusiasm.
But *lovely*? Somehow it seemed more elegant and timeless.

Like her. Her kind of beauty never went out of style. She would have been beautiful in any time period.

He flipped through other shots of her: professional poses, advertisements and some that looked as though she'd been caught in an unguarded moment. Those were the ones he studied the closest, looking for clues, insight into her character. What was behind the makeup, glamour and glitz. Not that it made any difference if she was a chameleon, her smile forced and her good heart only visible in public. He'd do the job because that was what he was paid to do. Whether he liked or approved of a potential client didn't mean shit if his team took the mission.

He couldn't make up his mind about her. But then how could he, having not met her and formed an impression? He was huge on first impressions and gut instincts. They rarely failed him.

He skimmed through various articles, some legitimate news sites, others nothing more than online gossip rags. But they all had one thing in common. She read like she was utter perfection. Donating to charity, helping to raise funds for charitable organizations. She visited sick children in hospitals and donated her time to various good causes.

It was a rare thing indeed for there not to at least be speculation or even blatant made-up shit published for hype and to sell lies. His cursory read didn't bring up a single negative thing about her. No secret pregnancies, drug use, crazy exes and for that matter no love interests. He frowned at that. A woman that beautiful or, rather, lovely would have no shortage of men trying to get in her pants. He was starting to wonder if the woman was a damn saint. He nearly snorted at the thought. No one was *that* perfect. Everyone had their faults. He wondered what hers were.

He wondered if everything he was reading was an extremely well put together and rigid public persona and what she was really like behind it all. Ryker would have him believe that Eden was everything the news reported and more, but he wasn't exactly an unbiased party. But he'd never heard Ryker utter a single bad word about her. He grumbled about Raid, his older brother, and even his father, calling him a set-in-his-ways old fart who still liked to bark orders like a drill sergeant.

He knew that Ryker had lost his mother when he was young and that it had deeply affected them all but his father had taken it very hard. By all accounts, Eden was a replica of her mother. Ryker said that his father bragged when they were growing up that she too could have been a model but hadn't wanted the spotlight. Her favorite place in the world was being at home taking care of her children and spending time with the family.

She'd been a military wife, and military wives were a very special breed of woman. They were often the unsung heroes when it came to service to their country. But they made sacrifices above and beyond what most women experienced in their lifetime.

When their husbands were away on a tour, they were at home by themselves, raising children, keeping the family intact and supporting their husbands. It took a special woman to unselfishly give up her husband for the protection of others. People those wives would never meet. People who would never be able to express their gratitude to the soldiers, much less to their wives.

Swanny had infinite respect for military wives just as he held deep regard for the Kelly wives and the team leaders' wives. For all practical purposes, their husbands were still military even though they weren't still enlisted.

But KGI could be called up on a mission as quickly as they had been today, and they dropped everything to take on a mission to protect or rescue others and the wives remained behind, never knowing if their husbands would come back. Yet they took it in stride and stayed strong. Resilient.

He glanced again at his phone, where a particularly stunning photo of Eden was staring back at him. It wasn't a glam shot. She was laughing into the camera, down on one knee, her arms wrapped around a huge mastiff. Her eyes sparkled with happiness; her smile was wide and natural, displaying perfectly straight, ultrawhite teeth.

When Joe plopped down into the seat next to him, he quickly shut down the browser page where he'd been staring at the photo of Eden.

He was practically mooning over a woman he'd never even met, and she was so far out of his league it wasn't even funny. She wouldn't see him. Few people ever did. He was quiet and usually kept to himself. He let others on his team do the talking. Making sure the mission went off without a hitch was his job. As well as his teammates'. Doing his job didn't require him to be verbose, and he liked it just fine that way.

And if people did see him . . . Well, the reactions were typical. Horror. Revulsion. Fear. And pity. He shook his head, knowing Eden would be no different than everyone else even if she had a heart the size of Texas.

She was surrounded by beautiful people. Wealthy people. People who were polished and refined. She was abreast of the latest fashion and Hollywood gossip, in all likelihood. And yet . . . her family, her immediate family were ex-military and a cop. Did they keep her grounded in reality? The image of a delicate beauty among three men who'd experienced the worst of humanity, had blood on their hands and honor in their hearts, was incongruous. A rose among thorns. Jesus. Now he was getting poetic.

Her career took her to places that were miles above the places he'd been to. Having wine in Paris at a swank cocktail party was a world away from being hunkered down on watch waiting for a five-second window of time to make a kill shot after going three straight days with no sleep, because if he lost focus, even for a tenth of a second, he might miss his opportunity.

No, Eden wouldn't look at him. And if she did, she certainly wouldn't look twice. But that didn't mean he couldn't look his fill of her. Somehow he imagined that just being in her presence would be like standing under the warm rays of the sun. He'd find out soon enough.

He could dream. No law against that. But he was pragmatic enough to know that for guys like him, dreams were an exercise in futility and inevitably led to disappointment.

CHAPTER 6

EDEN dragged a hand wearily through her hair, wondering if she'd be bald before this was all over with. She patiently explained, for the third time, the events that had transpired when she, David and Micah had exited the building after her photo shoot.

Micah and David had given their own statements, identical to hers.

"I simply don't know anything more, Detective Gibbs," she said tiredly. "It all happened so fast. The glass shattered behind us and I was shoved to the ground. It was all a giant blur. I was scared. And then the car roared up and they shoved me inside and we drove here, to the hotel."

The detective exchanged a frustrated look with his partner, both with notepads in their hands taking down what they likely thought was perfectly useless information.

"I'm sorry I can't be of more help," Eden added, uncomfortable with the sudden silence. "Have you made an arrest?"

And then another thought occurred to her, shaming her because she hadn't considered it until now.

She caught her breath and glanced urgently at the two detectives. "Was anyone hurt? Was anyone shot?"

Gibbs shook his head. "There were a few minor injuries from the flying glass. A twisted ankle from tripping as someone ran from the scene. But no one was shot."

"Thank God," Eden breathed.

An urgent knock sounded at the door followed by a distinctive bellow. "Eden! It's Dad."

Relief surged through her veins and she bolted from the sofa only to be restrained by Micah.

"David will answer. You stay put."

Eden simmered with frustration as David went to the door. As soon as her father and brothers entered, she shoved Micah away and flew across the room and into her father's arms.

"Eden, thank God you're all right," her father whispered against her ear.

"Thank you for coming so quickly," she said fervently. "I'm so glad y'all are here."

She was passed then to Raid, who swallowed her up in a bear hug, and then to Ryker, who held her every bit as tightly.

"You scared us, honey," Raid said when Ryker finally let her go.

Eddie looked past Eden to the two detectives and scowled. "What's going on here?"

Eden took his hand and dragged him toward the waiting detectives.

"Daddy, this is Detective Gibbs and his partner, Detective Barnes. They're questioning me about the shooting."

"Have you made an arrest? What the hell happened today?" Eddie barked.

"We're still in the preliminary stage of the investigation, sir," Gibbs said in a steady voice. "We're interviewing eyewitnesses, trying to put the pieces together."

"Do you know anything at this point?" Raid asked.

"You the cop?" Barnes asked.

Raid nodded.

"All we know is that the shots were fired at a downward

trajectory, not street level. We dug one of the bullets out of
the concrete and the angle puts it in the eight- to nine-story
level, so we're checking the hotel across the street and doing
a sweep of floors five to eleven. So far nothing has turned up,
but we're reviewing the hotel records of all persons staying
on those floors," Barnes supplied.

"Sniper?" Ryker asked.

"Looks to be," Gibbs said grimly. "There's evidence that
only four shots were fired, but we can't be certain. We've
done a thorough search of all the rooms that faced the street
and found no casings, so it's likely the shooter cleaned up
after himself. We're dusting for fingerprints but unless we
get lucky, this will likely take some time."

"Are you through with my daughter?" Eddie demanded.
"She looks exhausted. Have you been questioning her all
damn afternoon?"

Color scoured Barnes's cheeks. "It's procedure, sir."

"I'm all right, Daddy," Eden said in a low voice.

"No, you're not," Raid denied.

"They've been here several hours," Micah said. "I'd say
they're done."

Gibbs sighed. "We've got all we can get for now."

"Is she free to go?" Eddie asked.

Barnes lifted an eyebrow. "You in a hurry?"

Eddie shot him a glare that would shrivel most men. It
was a look Eden didn't often see, but it would certainly
intimidate her. Gibbs and Barnes weren't unaffected. Barnes
shifted uneasily before dropping his gaze.

"I have another shoot," Eden said quietly. "Day after
tomorrow. I have to leave tomorrow. It's important. The biggest of my career."

Her father and brothers exchanged uneasy glances but
kept silent.

"Leave me your contact numbers in case we have further
questions," Gibbs said. "We'll notify you if we make an arrest,
of course."

Eden supplied her cell number, as did Micah and David.

Then the detectives took their leave with a promise to keep them updated on the progress.

When the door closed behind them, Eden sagged onto the couch and closed her eyes. Raid and her father immediately sat on either side of her, and her father pulled her into his arms again. He trembled against her and she realized just how terrified he'd been. That made two of them.

It hadn't really sunk in just how close she'd come to death until afterward, when the detectives arrived close on the heels of Micah's call to them. She'd shaken for the entire first hour of questioning.

"I'm so glad you came," Eden said. "I was so scared, but you're here now and I'm all right."

Her father pulled away and framed her shoulders in his big hands. "I have some people coming, baby."

Her brow furrowed. "What people and why?"

"They're the best, or so Ryker informs me. I'm bringing them in to see to your protection for this next shoot."

Her mouth dropped open. "But what about David and Micah? That's what they're here for. And they did. They got me out and to safety. Why do we need more?"

Her father's features were implacable. "You almost died today, Eden. There will be no arguments. I want them around you at all times. David and Micah can take a well-earned break."

"But, Daddy . . ."

"He's right, Eden," Raid chimed in.

Eden glanced up at Ryker, her eyes pleading, but he looked as resolved as Raid and her father.

"They're the best at what they do," Ryker said, his jaw tight. "There's no way in hell you're going to that shoot without them. I know it's important to you, otherwise we'd have you home and under constant guard and fuck your career."

Heat washed over her face and anger surged. They were ganging up on her. Making decisions for her. She was a grown woman and she certainly had a right to make her own choices.

"They're right, Eden," Micah said.

She groaned. "God, not you too."

"You almost died today," David said. "If these people your father is bringing in are the best, then that's what you need. No one wants you dead."

"You're all making a pretty huge leap here," she pointed out. "From all appearances this is some random shooting and I just happened to be in the wrong place at the wrong time. Any one of those pedestrians could have been killed. Not just me."

She saw a flicker in her father's eye but it was gone just as quickly, resolve tightening his features.

"I'm not willing to take chances with your safety," he said. "Placate me, Eden. Because I'm about this close to hauling you home and telling your agent to call off the whole damn thing."

In the end it wasn't the threats that swayed her. When she looked at her father and brothers she saw stark fear in their eyes. And worry. She knew they wouldn't be swayed and if she refused the additional security, she had no doubt her father would make good on his threat to take her home and keep her under lock and key for as long as it took.

She sighed, massaging her forehead with her fingers, fatigue settling into her bones.

"You're tired, baby," Raid said. "Will you try to lie down and get some rest until the Kellys show up? They're on their way now and we need to make plans since you're leaving tomorrow evening for Paris."

David held out the prescription bottle the hotel physician had prescribed when he'd come by to examine Eden hours earlier. "Take it. You need the rest," he said bluntly.

The room was swimming in testosterone already. She shuddered to think how bad it would be when whoever her father had hired showed up.

Micah shoved a water bottle into her hand and then Raid propelled her to her feet and toward the bedroom area of the suite.

"I hate it when the men in my life handle me," she grumbled once Raid shut the door behind them.

Raid pulled her into his arms and hugged her fiercely. "We're scared, baby. Humor us, please? You have no idea what that call did to Dad. It will make him feel better to know you have the best at your back."

"You totally did that on purpose," she accused.

Raid pulled back, an innocent look on his face. "Did what?"

"You know damn well what," she said in disgust. "You're using Dad against me."

"Is it working?"

"Yes. Damn it."

He grinned and kissed her forehead. "Take your medicine and get some sleep, okay?"

"Whatever, big brother. But payback's a bitch."

"It will make Ryker and me feel much better too," he said, his expression growing serious once more.

She sighed. "I agreed, so lay off the guilt trip."

"We worry about you, baby. We love you and never want anything to happen to you."

"I love y'all too," she returned. "Now shoo so I can tackle that bed. I'm about to drop."

"Not until I see you take the pill," he said pointedly.

To emphasize his point, he crossed his arms and stared expectantly at her.

"You're all a bunch of tyrants," she muttered. But she did as he ordered and swallowed the bitter-tasting pill with a grimace. "There. Happy?"

"Yes," he said, leaning forward to kiss her forehead.

"Wake me when whoever gets here, okay?"

He nodded.

"Promise me," she pressed. "I'd at least like to be present when my future is decided."

He rolled his eyes. "Promise. Now get your ass into bed."

She didn't need much encouragement. She didn't even pull back the covers. She did a face plant on the bed and burrowed her head into the sumptuous down pillow with a sigh.

In the distance she heard the door shut behind her and she closed her eyes, exhaustion taking over.

CHAPTER 7

JOE parked the SUV toward the back entrance of the hotel and called up for Ryker to come open the door so they didn't trek through the lobby with their arsenal of weapons. Seconds later, Ryker opened the door and motioned them out of the vehicle.

They hurried inside, Ryker quickly shaking Joe's, Nathan's and Swanny's hands.

"Thanks for coming so quickly," Ryker said as they climbed the stairs.

"No problem," Joe returned.

"Eden's resting, which is good," Ryker said as they walked out of the stairwell and into the hallway. "Dad is determined that she not know what's going on, or at least not everything. Not saying I agree, but we're doing this his way. He'll give you the info you need so we can act accordingly."

He stopped outside a hotel room door and inserted the key card. He pushed it open and motioned the others inside.

Swanny's gaze swept over the interior, noting an older man he assumed was Eddie Sinclair and a younger man who must be Ryker's older brother, Raid.

Eddie met them halfway, his hand extended to shake theirs as introductions were performed.

Once they were all seated, Eddie leaned forward in his chair and kept his voice low. He glanced toward a closed door where Swanny assumed Eden was sleeping.

"As far as Eden knows, the shooting was random," Eddie said in hushed tones. "But I know differently. Just before the shooting took place, I received a threat. It's a long, convoluted story. It's . . . revenge."

Swanny's eyebrow rose and Joe frowned. "Care to elaborate? Do you know the source of the threat?"

Eddie ran a hand through his hair, his eyes dark with worry. "Years ago when I was in a black ops group, we had a mission that was totally FUBAR. We were supposed to take out Raul Sanchez, a big player in drugs and arms trafficking, with human trafficking as a strong secondary contender. He had his hands in just about everything. We finally got our opportunity. His daughter's birthday."

He broke off and went silent a moment, emotion simmering in his eyes.

"His wife and daughter got caught in the cross fire. Sanchez and his son got away."

"Damn," Nathan murmured.

"It didn't end there," Eddie said tiredly. "Years later, Sanchez came after me where I was most vulnerable. My wife."

He choked and had to visibly compose himself before continuing.

"He killed my wife."

"Jesus," Swanny muttered.

"I went after him," Eddie said in a grim voice. "I couldn't just let him get away with it. Not when I knew. So I tracked him down, called in someone to help and we took him out. And now . . ."

He rubbed both hands over his face and when they came away, tears glistened in his eyes.

"The cycle of revenge continues. The son now wants to take from me what was taken from him. His mother, sister, and then his father. He sent me pictures of Eden. Told me he would take from me what I loved the most. And God, just hours later, someone tried to kill her."

He leveled a hard stare at the members of KGI.

"She has an important shoot that begins day after tomorrow. It's inside, which is the only reason I'm allowing her to go. No way in hell I'd have her in open air where protecting her would be a nightmare. But this is huge for her. I can't shut her down, not when she doesn't have the full story, and I don't want her to know."

Joe lifted an eyebrow and Swanny could see the disapproval on his face. Swanny was having similar thoughts.

Eden's family was treating her like a pampered, sheltered princess and it would get her killed.

"The story is that I've called you in because I'm worried after what happened today and I want her protected. And I do. She has to be safe at all times."

"Where is this next shoot?" Nathan asked.

"Paris," Eddie replied. "It hasn't been publicly announced that Eden is heading Aria's new cosmetics campaign. So if we keep her off an official airline and don't leave a paper trail, then hopefully by the time this guy catches up to her, the shoot will be over and she'll be back home."

"We can fly her on the KGI jet," Joe reassured.

"So you'll do it?" Eddie asked hopefully. "You'll take the job?"

Joe's gaze narrowed. "We wouldn't be here if we were merely entertaining the idea, sir."

"Thank you," Eddie said sincerely. "But I want your word. Eden is not to know what I've told you. I don't want her to be hurt by the knowledge that her mother's death wasn't an accident. It was bad enough my boys had to know."

Joe sighed. "She won't hear it from us."

"Daddy?"

Swanny turned in the direction of the hesitant, feminine voice to see Eden standing in the now-open doorway to the bedroom. She was wearing a large man's button-up shirt, and though she was taller than the average woman, the tails clipped the tops of her knees, baring a good portion of the expanse of her shapely legs.

She sent an accusing look in Raid's direction. "You promised to wake me when they got here."

"They just did get here, honey," Raid said in a placating tone. "I was just about to go wake you. We've only finished introductions."

He didn't even blink over the lie.

Swanny's gaze was riveted to Eden. Tousled hair, sleepy eyes and legs to die for. As if realizing she was only wearing a shirt, she pulled at the hem, attempting to cover more of her legs, but the action tightened the shirt over her breasts, outlining them with clarity, and just a hint of her nipple was discernible through the material.

"I'll, uh, just go get dressed," she said, discomfort evident in her voice.

She quickly shut the door.

"You look at her and give me one good reason to break her heart," Eddie said in a low voice. "She sees the good in everyone. She's too soft for her own good. I don't want to ruin that. Not if I can help it."

Swanny shook himself from his reverie, glancing at his teammates to make sure no one had seen him looking inappropriately at Eden. If they'd noticed, they didn't make it obvious, thank God.

Quiet descended and then a moment later, Eden reappeared, dressed in jeans and a T-shirt, and her hair was pulled into a ponytail. She hadn't bothered with makeup, but Swanny had seen the pictures of her all glammed up and he preferred the more natural Eden. She was beautiful no matter the trappings. Perhaps he was less intimidated with the person instead of the supermodel.

"I'm Eden Sinclair," she said unnecessarily. She offered a smile to each of the KGI members as introductions were performed by Ryker.

Swanny tensed when Ryker got to him, and as was his habit, he turned the scarred side of his face to the side so she wasn't staring at it.

But her smile was warm as she shook his hand, her fingers squeezing his tightly.

"Swanny, of course I remember Ryker talking about you. And Nathan and Joe as well. I'm so glad to finally meet some of the men he served with."

She took a seat next to her father, her expression one of unease. "So what's going on, Daddy?"

Eddie sighed and took Eden's hands in his. "I'd feel better if you had more protection for this next shoot. I know how important it is to you, so I won't ask you not to do it. But for my peace of mind, I'd like KGI to take over your personal protection, at least for this shoot."

She glanced around, her lips pursed, as if she'd only just realized that David and Micah were no longer present.

"I sent them home. They're long overdue for a break," Eddie said, correctly reading the question in her eyes. "KGI will take over from here."

She sighed. "Don't you think you're overreacting just a little?" she asked gently.

"No."

That immediate denial came from Raid, who up to now had remained silent. Eden sent her brother a startled look.

"I'd much rather us overreact than underreact when it comes to your safety," Raid said. "If a few is good, then more is better."

Her shoulders sagged and resignation reflected on her features. "All right. But I can't have the set overrun with five hulking bodyguards. The photographer will have a cow."

"He'll get over it," Joe said bluntly. "I'll have a talk with all the people associated with the shoot and explain the necessity of our presence. We'll come to an understanding. You won't have to worry about us being in the way. But we will be there. Your protection is our number one priority and we don't care whose feet we step on in the process."

She blinked in surprise. "Well, okay."

"Now, I've ordered room service so you can eat, and then I want you to get a good night's sleep," Eddie said in a firm voice. "Your flight leaves tomorrow, but you won't be taking a commercial flight. I don't want a paper trail that would make it easy for someone to track you."

Eden paled. "You honestly think this shooting was directed at me?"

"We aren't willing to take any chances with your safety," Ryker said bluntly. "Until we have evidence to the contrary, we're treating it as a direct threat to you."

She heaved in a deep breath and sagged against the back of the chair. Then to her dad, "Nothing more than a salad. I can't afford to gain even a pound for this shoot."

Swanny's eyebrows went up in surprise and Eden must have noticed.

She shot him a rueful smile. "The camera adds ten to fifteen pounds. So for all practical purposes I have to be those ten to fifteen pounds underweight because the camera puts them right back on. The camera is very unforgiving. If I have any extra weight, it will show and I could lose my contract over it."

"You're perfect just the way you are," Swanny said bluntly.

Her smile warmed and color suffused her cheeks. "Thank you. But my photographer would disagree."

"Then he's a fool," Swanny muttered.

"I ordered a variety of food so everyone can eat. There are a couple of side salads so you can have what you like," Eddie soothed. "But swear to God, Eden, when this shoot is over, you're taking a break for a while and you're going to eat like a normal human being. You're too thin as it is. I worry about you."

She rolled her eyes. "It's not like I have an eating disorder, Dad. I work out and I'm healthy as a horse."

The doorbell to the suite rang and Ryker got up to go let the room service attendant in. A few minutes later, the food was all set up on the table and everyone ate buffet style.

Eden was studying each of the members of Swanny's team and he tried to stay back, out of her direct line of sight. Still, he felt her scrutiny and it made him uncomfortable. He sat as far away from her as possible while they ate. But it seemed not to make a difference. Every time he stole a glance her way—with his scarred side averted—she was studying him. He could swear he felt her gaze. Was she gawking, trying to get a better look at his scars? But no, when he chanced another glance at her she was simply staring at him thoughtfully.

"Swanny? What's your real name?" Eden suddenly asked.

Swanny's gaze lifted in surprise that she'd singled him out when she hadn't said a word to any of the other members of his team during the meal.

Her cheeks colored as if she regretted the impulsive question. Damn, but he was being rude by simply staring at her like a moron.

"It's just that in all of Ryker's letters he always called you Swanny and he did say it was a nickname formed by your last name, Swanson, but he never told me what your first name was," she said in a rush, as if trying to assuage him as to why she'd asked the original question.

"Daryl," Swanny said gruffly. "But nobody calls me that. Ever. I just go by Swanny."

She gave him a breathtaking smile that was like a punch to the gut. Her eyes were warm, with a hint of a spark to them. Or maybe he was imagining that.

"I'll remember that . . . Swanny," she said, her smile never wavering. "I'm very glad you made it home from Afghanistan. Ryker agonized for months that you and your teammates were MIA. And I felt like I knew you all from Ryker's letters, so it was very upsetting to me as well."

She was actually acknowledging *him*. Talking to him when she could have said the exact same thing to Nathan. But she'd never even looked at anyone else but him. Every time he glanced her way, she was staring at *him*.

He had no idea how to respond. What to say. His tongue was in knots and the words stuck in his throat. He finally managed a short thank-you, knowing he was being rude for not saying more. It shamed him that he was relieved when the rest finished their meals and Raid prompted Eden to go to bed.

Eden put up a fuss, saying she'd already taken a nap, but Raid wouldn't be swayed. He dumped two pills in her hand and stood there until she took them. It was already nine in the evening and they still had a lot of planning to do. It would be a hell of a lot easier if Eden were sleeping so she wouldn't by chance overhear anything her father didn't want her knowing.

After waving a disgusted good night to everyone, Eden allowed Raid to hustle her off to bed, but still they waited until half an hour later when Raid quietly went in to check to see if Eden was sleeping yet.

He returned with a thumbs-up. "She's out like a light. Today exhausted her, though she'd never admit it."

"Okay, so we obviously have Eden's protection covered," Joe said, "but what about the source of the threat? What intel can you provide us? I can call Sam and get a team working on that angle because until that's eliminated we're spinning our wheels."

"I hadn't thought past Eden's protection," Eddie admitted. "But of course the threat to her has to be eliminated. I've put in another call as well regarding the situation but didn't hook up so I'm grateful that you all can get on this now."

"I'll put a call into Sam," Nathan interjected. "I'll give him the rundown, but we need to know everything. Don't hold back anything that could help or hinder us. We can't be flying blind. Sam won't send a team in if it's going to get them killed."

Eddie nodded. "I'll give you everything I know. I appreciate this. More than you'll ever know."

"While we're in Paris with Eden, you, Ryker and Raid need to lie low. If this guy can't get to Eden, he may just go after one of you instead," Joe warned.

"I'm not hiding from this fucker," Raid said, his eyes glittering dangerously. "I have a job to do. I hope that asshole *does* come after me."

"Just watch your sixes," Nathan said. "We're going to make damn sure he doesn't get to Eden."

"That's all I ask," Eddie said. "Keep my baby safe."

"Edge, you call one of our pilots and tell him to bring the bigger jet. Tell him what's going on and to be ready tomorrow at three. For that matter call in the other pilot to hitch a ride so he can fly the small jet back to the compound." Joe said. "Nathan, you call Sam. Give him the rundown. The rest of you stand down. We need to get some rest while we can grab it."

"We can crash in Eden's room," Ryker said, gesturing to himself and his father and brother. "It'll leave more room for your crew to sleep out here."

"I need to call Nigel, her agent, and let him know what's going on," Eddie said. "He can also smooth the way with everyone on site. He's planning to arrive earlier than Eden so that will help, hopefully."

As soon as the Sinclairs retreated into Eden's room, Swanny began preparing a makeshift bed on the floor, using one of the cushions from the couch as a pillow. After Edge and Nathan made their calls, they joined the others in bunking down.

It was just another day on the job. Nothing they hadn't done a hundred times before. This was one they could do in their sleep. And yet Swanny found himself wide awake, replaying those brief moments when Eden had been in the same room.

He'd been right. Just being in her presence was like being washed in sunshine.

CHAPTER 8

EDEN came awake with a grogginess she normally didn't feel in the mornings. She wiped at her eyes attempting to rub some of the bleariness away and remembered the two pills Raid had forced down her throat.

She glanced at the clock and saw that it was just after eight. At least she hadn't slept the entire morning away. She had a lot to do before leaving for Paris.

After a quick shower, she went through her skin care regimen but left off makeup. Her skin needed to breathe so she'd look her best for the upcoming shoot.

She dressed casually in a pair of comfortable jeans and an oversize shirt. After slipping her feet into a pair of flip-flops, she went in search of the others, who were no doubt making plans without her.

She rolled her eyes as she walked from the bedroom. She had no doubt her father and brothers were overreacting, but they were genuinely worried, especially her dad. After her mother's death, he'd been extremely overprotective of her to the point of absurdity, but she didn't want to add to his worry, so she just went with it when he got in one of his moods.

Everyone was drinking coffee and the television was on a local station. She waved, not really knowing what to say to the group of people her father had hired to protect her. They seemed a quiet bunch anyway. Except Joe. He seemed to be the leader and so far had done most of the talking. And yet it wasn't Joe she'd noticed. It had been Swanny. There was something about the quiet man. In a group with that much testosterone it was odd that she'd hone in on Swanny but there was no explanation for it.

As she accepted a cup of coffee from Raid, she stood back, quietly observing the people she'd be spending the next week with.

Skylar was petite and cute with sparkling eyes and long blond hair, but in her case appearances had to be deceiving or how else would she land a job with a company like KGI?

Edge was a huge man with strong features. His ears had the beginnings of the cauliflower ears associated with boxers or mixed martial artists. His nose had a slight bump that told her he'd likely broken it at least once. He had dark eyes and hair that hung to the tops of his shoulders.

Her gaze drifted to Swanny. Quiet and observant. He had a scar down one side of his face that ended right at the corner of his mouth. It was as if someone had taken a knife and slashed open the side of his face. The scar was puckered, the ridges uneven as if he'd simply been sewn back together with little care for his appearance.

She wondered what had happened and how he'd gotten such a terrible injury.

As if sensing her scrutiny, his gaze found hers and he turned the scarred side of his face away from her. He did that often. She'd noticed when he caught her looking he always turned the scarred side of his face away. As if he were self-conscious about his appearance.

He fascinated her and she couldn't pinpoint why exactly. He wasn't handsome in a classic sense. But he had strong features and a rugged quality that appealed to her feminine instincts. He was a man who had complete honor. She was positive of it. Of all the team members of KGI, it was Swanny she put her trust in most, and damn if she knew why. As she studied him harder, it hit her like a ton of bricks. She was attracted to him. Sexually and emotionally, which was pretty stupid considering that (A) she was a job to him and (B) they'd only just met. He likely thought she was crazy staring at him all the time. She'd be mortified if he took her interest as merely gawking at his scars, like a train wreck she couldn't turn away from.

In her job she was surrounded by men most women would consider gorgeous and yet she found them too pretty. Too . . . perfect.

Swanny's gaze swung to her as if sensing her prolonged perusal and for a moment he held her gaze, returning it in equal measure. Faint heat flooded her cheeks but she couldn't make herself look away. His eyes mesmerized her, his gaze seeking as if he could see into the heart of her. She hoped she wasn't obvious in her attraction.

He averted his gaze first, turning away. Disappointment seeped into her chest because she'd seen no sign that he returned her attraction. Just a steady gaze, returning her study in kind. He probably thought she was some brazen hussy on the make.

She turned when she heard the local news break in with a special report. The entire group stopped what they were doing and listened intently as the reporter spoke in rapid tones.

There'd been another shooting, and a suspect was in custody. She caught her father's look of surprise and frowned. Before she could remark, her cell phone rang and she glanced down to see an unknown number on the screen.

Remembering that she'd given the detective her number, she hit the button to accept the call and brought the phone to her ear.

"Hello?"

"Miss Sinclair?"

"Yes, this is she."

"This is Detective Barnes. I wanted to let you know that another shooting occurred this morning."

"Yes, I just saw it on the news," she said. "They reported that a suspect is in custody."

The detective muttered a curse that sounded suspiciously like "fucking reporters" and then, "Yes, we do have a suspect in custody, but this is a slam dunk. I wanted to let you know so you didn't worry further. We apprehended the shooter and he confessed to yesterday's shooting as well. I can't go into further detail, but I thought you should know so you can rest easy now."

"Thank you for calling," she said. "I really appreciate it."

"No problem. Take care."

She ended the call and looked up to see every single person staring at her expectantly.

"That was Detective Barnes," she said. "He confirmed they have a suspect in custody and a confession for yesterday's shooting."

The result was complete silence as everyone exchanged glances, as if they didn't know what to say.

"So, um, I guess all of this is unnecessary," she said, gesturing toward the members of KGI.

"I disagree," Raid said firmly.

Her eyes widened. "But they've arrested the shooter and it obviously wasn't personal."

"I'd feel better if KGI accompanied you to Paris," her father said, a stubborn set to his face.

Her eyes narrowed. "What aren't you telling me?"

Ryker slid his arm around her shoulders. "Cut us some slack, Eden. You were almost killed. It would make us all feel better if you had tighter security for your Paris shoot. Besides, they're already here and plans are in place."

"Lay off the emotional blackmail," she muttered. "Raid has already poured it on thick enough."

Her father walked over to her and framed her shoulders in his hands, his expression serious. "Do this for me, Eden. Please. I'd sleep better if I knew you had the best protecting you."

She heaved a heavy sigh. "Okay, okay, whatever. But I'm going on record that this is totally unnecessary."

"Miss Sinclair."

Startled, she swung her gaze up to look at Swanny, who'd spoken her name softly.

"I think it *is* necessary," he continued. "You're already all over the news as having been involved in yesterday's shooting. There are hundreds of crazy-ass people out there, and the likelihood of a copycat is possible. You should absolutely tighten your security for the next while at least. Wait for things to calm down. You can't take this too lightly."

The rest of the group looked as surprised as she was that he'd said so much. There was a firmness to his voice that told her he was absolutely serious.

"He's right," Raid said grimly.

She held up her hands in surrender. "I already said I would go along with it."

"But you have to take it seriously," Swanny said. "Which means you do what we tell you and don't resist. Our job is to keep you safe, and we can't do that without your full cooperation."

She blinked but held his gaze, warmth invading her veins as he stared intently at her. This time he didn't avert the side of his face. He looked at her almost challengingly, daring her to look away first.

"You'll find I'm not a difficult person," she said softly.

Swanny grimaced. "I didn't mean to imply that you were. If I did, then I apologize."

She shook her head. "No, no offense taken. I just want you to know that I'm not some spoiled diva who throws a tantrum if I don't get my way. I'll cooperate fully. I don't want to make your jobs harder."

"We appreciate that, Miss Sinclair," Joe interjected.

"Please, call me Eden," she said, sweeping the entire group with her gaze, including them all in her request.

"All right, Eden," Swanny said.

It did funny things to her stomach to hear her name on his lips. She broke his gaze and looked to her father, sure that

her cheeks were flush with color. The last thing she wanted
was to be obvious. Or come across as desperate.

"When do we leave?" she asked, to cover the awkward-
ness.

Joe took over then, briskly telling her of the arrangements
that had been made. It awed her that they could pull something together this quickly. They were, in fact, taking this
very seriously, and for the first time, she felt a kernel of
unease. What if they were right? What if some idiot decided
to take a shot at her now that she was splashed all over the
news?

"We'll see you off and then catch a flight back home,"
Raid said. "I have to be back to work, but we expect you to
check in with us often and if anything happens, we want to
know about it immediately."

Eden nodded, swallowing the knot in her throat. Everyone was acting as if it were a foregone conclusion that something *would* happen.

CHAPTER 9

EDEN relaxed in the back of the jet, curling her feet underneath her as she leaned against the arm of the couch. The others were still up front in their seats, but she'd retreated to the back as soon as they'd taken off.

She didn't like the fear that gripped her. That wasn't the way she lived her life. Always fearing the worst in others. Her fame hadn't changed her, at least she didn't think so. Underneath the glamour was still the same girl she'd always been.

Her father and brothers kept her grounded. Even if she'd tried to become someone she wasn't or let her fame go to her head, they would have reined her in quickly.

A noise alerted her that she was no longer alone, and she swung her gaze upward to see Swanny standing in the entryway to the lounging area. He had an inquiring look on his face as he stared at her.

"Everything okay?" he asked in a quiet voice.

She stared back, drinking in his appearance. Then she nodded and gestured to the space next to her on the couch. "Sit, please. I'd like the company."

He hesitated and then to her disappointment, he sank into one of the armchairs catty-corner to the sofa.

"I figured you didn't want company since you came back here right after takeoff," he said.

She lifted one shoulder into a shrug. "It's not that. I just don't know any of y'all and this all came out of the blue for me. I actually don't like being alone and in fact I rarely am. When I'm not working, I go home and stay with Dad and spend time with him and my brothers."

"You keep pretty busy, it seems," Swanny said. "This Aria thing is a big deal for you, isn't it?"

She nodded. "Yeah. It's a career high for me. It's a huge account and I had some stiff competition. No way I'd miss it because some jerk went off his meds and started shooting at people."

A smile quirked the corner of his mouth. She noticed that on the scarred side, his upper lip didn't really move, resulting in sort of a half smile. It was a crooked grin she found endearing. She wondered if there had been nerve damage, resulting in the inability to move that corner of his mouth.

And then she wondered how it would feel to kiss him. To have that mouth on her skin. Betraying heat crept up her neck and she forced her thoughts back to the mundane. The curse of having fair skin was that she blushed vividly.

"I don't want you to worry, Eden," Swanny said, his expression growing serious once more. "We'll make sure nothing hurts you. It's what we do. And not to discount the importance of this mission, but we've faced a hell of a lot worse."

She cocked her head to the side. "Is that what I am? A mission?"

He looked surprised by her question, and as if only just realizing that he was completely facing her, he turned his scarred cheek away from her, presenting his profile.

"Why do you do that?" she asked softly.

His brow furrowed and he turned slightly in her direction once more. "Do what?"

"Turn away from me so I won't see your scar."

He looked surprised at her bluntness, and he went silent for a long moment.

"It's habit," he admitted.

"It doesn't bother me," she said, eager to ease his self-consciousness around her. "And if it bothers other people, that's their problem, not yours. If they judge you because of your scars, then they're assholes who don't deserve your respect or your regard."

He laughed, startling her with the rumbling sound that welled from his chest. The lines around his eyes eased and his gaze lightened to one of amusement.

He fingered the scar absently and then dropped his hand.

"Does it still hurt you?" she asked quietly.

He shook his head. "Only the memories."

He looked immediately chagrined, as if he regretted sharing something so personal with her. But she was delighted that he was actually talking to her. A real conversation that didn't revolve around the job he was hired for.

"How did it happen?"

He paused a long moment, shadows chasing away the lightness in his eyes. Then he expelled a long breath and sat forward in his chair, seemingly ill at ease.

"If I'm prying too much, just tell me to mind my own business," she said quickly. "It's not morbid curiosity. I'd like to know more about you . . ."

She trailed off before she said something really stupid, like that she was fantasizing about his mouth on hers and tracing the lines of that scar with her own fingers. She wanted to soothe away any lingering pain, though it sounded ridiculous that she could offer him anything at all.

"On our last tour, Nathan and I and a few more from our team were captured. We had split off from Joe and his team. They got out. We didn't. We spent months being tortured and starved before we were rescued."

He put his fingers back to the scar. "They carved me and Nate both up, and they did this. By the time we got out and to a hospital, there was little they could do except patch it up the best they could. They said I could see a plastic surgeon, but I opted not to. It's a reminder."

He went silent again, a faraway look in his eyes as if he were back there in hell and not here.

She slid to the end of the couch so not much space separated them. Tentatively, she reached out and put her hand on his knee, squeezing gently.

He flinched, sucking in his breath, his eyes suddenly glittering with fire. Her pulse ratcheted up several beats because she realized he wasn't unaware of the chemistry between them.

"How is it a reminder?" she prompted gently.

"That I was a victim and I'll never be a victim again," he said simply.

"It's not ugly," she said in a sincere voice. "It's a mark of courage. Of survival. I think you're beautiful."

He reared back his head, surprise flaring in his eyes. He stared at her like she'd lost her mind.

"Beautiful?" he said hoarsely. "*You're* beautiful. Not me."

She leaned in, knowing she was being bold—too bold— but she simply couldn't resist showing him with more than words that his scar didn't put her off in the least. She cupped his face and slid her fingers down the puckered ridges.

He flinched and tried to withdraw but she leaned farther, following him back as she continued her gentle exploration.

"I disagree," she murmured. "I think you're beautiful. Strong. A warrior. Your scar is a badge of honor. You forget, my father and brothers served in either the military or the police force. They have scars. They don't bother me in the least."

Swanny looked at a complete loss for words, but he remained frozen in place. Then he leaned slightly into the palm of her hand as if he enjoyed her touch.

"Can I kiss you?" she whispered.

Shock registered in his eyes. She knew she was being forward. Practically forcing herself on this man. But she knew he felt it too. This inexplicable pull between them. She wasn't imagining it.

"We shouldn't," he began. But she hushed him by fitting her mouth to his.

He let out a low groan and she licked over his lips, pushing gently so he'd open his mouth to her advance. And then, as she'd hoped, he took control of the kiss.

He pulled her into his lap, deepening the kiss, sliding his tongue across hers in a gentle exploration. Her body molded to his perfectly. She leaned into him, enjoying the hard wall of muscle against her much softer body.

She was tall, nearly five-ten, but he was still a head taller than her. If they were standing her head would tuck perfectly underneath his chin and she'd only have to angle her mouth up a bit to kiss him.

She was the first to break the kiss but she wasn't finished. Not yet. She started at the corner of his mouth where the scar began and she kissed a gentle line over the entire puckered slash that ended close to his eye.

"You are beautiful," she whispered. "To me, you are."

He framed her shoulders in his hands and pulled her away, regret simmering in his eyes. But there was also answering desire. He actually picked her up and deposited her back onto the sofa and then backed off, standing a distance away.

"That shouldn't have happened," he said hoarsely.

He dragged a hand raggedly through his hair and looked away.

"Besides the fact that my job is to protect you, you're so far out of my league it's not even funny. I don't even exist on the same plane as you."

Her eyes narrowed as she stared back at him, unwilling to give an inch.

"Don't you think it's me who gets to decide who's in my league?"

"A woman like you doesn't have to go slumming," he said bluntly. "You could have any man you want."

"Apparently not," she murmured, looking pointedly at him.

He stared back at her in clear confusion. "Why me?"

She smiled ruefully. "Attraction doesn't follow a set of rules, you know. But I know that I don't look at the others like I look at you. I don't feel any chemistry with them, or anyone else for that matter. Can you deny that you feel it too?"

His lips tightened and he cursed softly beneath his breath. "No, I don't deny it, but that's not the point. I have a job to do and I can't do that job if I'm distracted, and babe, you're definitely a distraction."

She smiled, pleased with the irritation in his voice. He didn't want to be attracted to her and he was fighting it, but he was. She'd just have to work a little harder to crack through all those barriers he was putting up.

Playing the temptress was definitely new to her. She wouldn't have thought she had it in her to be so bold. But then she'd never met a man who made her feel this way. She wasn't entirely sure what she was experiencing here, but she knew she wanted this man.

And yeah, she was a job, but people met and fell in love all the time. Who was to say it couldn't be that way for her and Swanny?

Whoa. Talk about getting way ahead of herself. She was already planning their future and he was pushing her away as quickly as she was pushing toward him.

"Don't push me away," she said in a quiet voice. "I'm attracted to you. I don't sleep around, though you might think so because I'm being so forward with you. I've just never met someone I've felt this kind of chemistry with. I'd be a fool not to see where it takes us."

He looked utterly shell-shocked. He swallowed visibly and then ran a hand through his hair again.

"Jesus," he muttered. "The world's most beautiful woman thinks I'm beautiful and I'm telling her we can't get involved. I either need my head examined or need to make sure my balls are still attached."

She laughed, her lips turning up into a broad smile. "Just something to think about. We'll be spending a lot of time together over the next while. I just want you to promise me you won't start avoiding me. I like you. I feel comfortable with you. Much more so than with the others."

"I don't particularly want to get my heart broken," he said dryly. "When you move on and the job is over, am I just supposed to forget about you and move on like nothing ever happened?"

Her brow furrowed. "Is that what you think I'll do? Break your heart? Here I was contemplating that you'd be the one to break my heart. But we're getting way ahead of ourselves here. I just want your promise that you won't try to avoid me over the next several days."

He sighed. "Okay, I promise. But I still think you're crazy and when you come to your senses, you're going to think you lost your mind."

She rolled her eyes. "You can't blame this on the situation or that I have some kind of savior complex about you. There are three other guys on your team and I feel nothing for any of them."

"Well, thank fuck for that," Swanny muttered.

"Will you at least come sit with me?" she asked. "We still have a long flight and I'd like your company."

He seemed to battle with himself over the simple request, and then he gave in and slid onto the couch beside her.

"You should get some rest," he said gruffly. "I looked over your itinerary and it's booked solid for the next several days. I don't know how you manage to work those kind of hours."

Without asking permission, she snuggled into his side and looped her arm across his midsection. He went still, his entire body vibrating with tension, but he didn't pull away.

Finally he carefully curled his arm around her waist, anchoring her to his side. She let out a blissful sigh and laid her cheek on his chest, tucking her head right below his chin.

"I'll rest better with you here," she said.

He toyed with a strand of her hair with his fingers before dropping them and resting his hand back on her hip.

His body heat soaked into her, making her feel warm and contented. She yawned broadly and closed her eyes, snuggling a little deeper into his embrace.

"You make me feel safe," she murmured.

"You are safe with me, Eden."

It was a vow, one spoken in solemn tones.

"I know," she whispered as her eyelids fluttered closed.

CHAPTER 10

WHEN they landed in Paris, Eden was hustled off the plane and into an armored Mercedes sedan. She barely had time to blink over the image before she was inside the backseat, flanked by Swanny and Skylar. Edge rode up front with the driver, and Nathan and Joe rode in another car that led the two-car procession to the hotel where Eden would stay.

She had only today to get her bearings and rest up because the following morning the shoot would kick off and her schedule was packed full, culminating in a formal launch party held by Aria at the end of the shoot.

They drove to the back entrance of the upscale hotel and Swanny issued a soft order for her to stay until he and the others were in position. When she finally ducked out, the five KGI members formed a tight boundary around her and hurried her inside.

Joe went up to the desk to handle the registration, and it occurred to Eden that she wasn't sure of the sleeping arrangements. She was used to having her own suite and her own space. She didn't even share quarters with Micah or David.

Having to share space with anyone would interfere in her plans to get Swanny into her bed. She mentally rolled her eyes and shook her head. She should be more concerned with her safety, but instead her thoughts were consumed with how to seduce Swanny and whether they would have the privacy she wanted.

When Joe returned, they began the trek up the stairs and when they reached her floor, she hesitated and turned to look at Joe, since he was holding the key cards.

"What are the arrangements?" she asked. "I mean, who's sleeping where?"

"Skylar will share a two-bedroom suite with you. The rest of us will take the other two bedrooms on either side of your suite."

Eden hesitated, unsure of how to put this without sounding either bitchy or just plain obvious.

"I'd rather not share a room with anyone," she said quietly. "It's just that I have so much stuff and I don't want to inconvenience anyone . . ."

She trailed off, knowing she sounded lame.

Joe's eyebrows furrowed and he exchanged quick glances with his teammates. Obviously they hadn't anticipated her resistance to someone sharing quarters with her.

"It's a two-bedroom suite, right?" she asked quickly, gathering her courage. Her face was flaming, she knew, but she just had to be more assertive and blunt.

Joe nodded.

"Then I want Swanny to stay in the other room with me," she blurted.

Skylar suppressed a quick smile, but she sent Eden a knowing look, and oddly enough Eden could swear she saw encouragement and camaraderie in Skylar's eyes.

"Edge and I can bunk together," Skylar spoke up. "Not like we aren't used to living together. That way you and Nathan can share the other room," she said to Joe.

Swanny looked a little poleaxed, and she supposed she couldn't blame him since no one had exactly consulted him in the decision making.

"I'd feel more comfortable with him," Eden said, refusing to give in to the embarrassment crowding her chest.

"Swanny?" Joe asked, looking in his teammate's direction.

Eden refused to look at the others, not wanting to see their expressions. She stared at Swanny, pleading with her eyes for him not to refuse her. She hadn't lied. She really did feel more comfortable with him.

"That's fine," Swanny finally said. "Her being alone isn't an option."

Eden sagged in relief.

Joe handed her a key card and then another to Swanny. "We'll be on either side of you, Eden, and it needs to be clear that you aren't to leave this room without one of us. For any reason. Where you go, we go. Period."

"Got it," she said, taking the key from him.

She pushed into her suite, Swanny following behind. Her luggage had been sent ahead and was waiting in the living room. Swanny's eyebrows went up.

"That's a hell of a lot of stuff for just a few days."

She grimaced. "Part and parcel of the business. One whole suitcase is nothing but hair and skin care stuff."

He glanced ruefully down at his large duffel bag. "Guess I pack lighter."

Her eyes widened as something occurred to her. "Oh my God. The Aria launch. If you all are going with me, and I assume you are since Joe said I wasn't going anywhere without you, then you're all going to need tuxes. Or at the very least a formal suit. It's a really big deal. Glitzy and glamorous. You'll need to blend in."

The deer-in-the-headlights look he gave her was hilarious.

"A tux?" he croaked.

She nodded solemnly, keeping a straight face. "I'll have to take you shopping and get you all outfitted. It'll be fun."

"Fun," he muttered as if it were the very last word he'd use to describe it.

"So, um, was I too obvious about you staying with me?" she asked hesitantly.

The corner of his mouth lifted into that half grin and his eyes gleamed with amusement. At least he didn't look pissed.

"Let's just say that Joe and Edge are probably jealous sons of bitches right now. Nathan is happily married, so he's out."

"So in other words, I *was* obvious," she muttered.

"I don't mind," he said mildly. "I like a straight shooter. It's nice to always know where I stand with someone."

"And do you know where you stand with me?" she whispered, staring into those mesmerizing eyes.

He cleared his throat. "I think so."

"So where do I stand with you, then?" she said quietly.

"Can't say I've ever had a conversation like this with a woman," he said ruefully. "You have to cut me some slack. You—this whole thing—is way out of my league."

"But you didn't answer the question," she said pointedly. "Look, Swanny, if you aren't interested in me, just tell me. I'm a big girl. I can take it. I'm not good at the coy meet-cute stuff in relationships. My father always said that I was a take-the-bull-by-the-horns kind of girl, and I guess he's right. I'd rather know now whether my attraction is reciprocated so I don't continue to make an ass of myself."

He crossed the short distance between them and hauled her roughly into his arms. He took her hand and guided it to his groin so she could feel his rigid erection.

"Does that feel like I'm not attracted to you?" he asked hoarsely.

She licked her lips nervously but she left her hand where it was, lightly caressing the denim of his fly.

"Jesus, Eden, you have to stop. This is starting to get painful."

"After we discuss where I stand with you," she murmured.

"What exactly are you after here?" he asked bluntly. "Am I a distraction to you? Something to keep you entertained for a few days before you move on to someone else?"

Hurt crowded her chest and she withdrew, her features carefully schooled. She was used to giving the camera whatever emotion or expression the photographer demanded. The last thing she wanted was for him to see that he'd hurt her with his frustrated statement. What must he think of her to have said that? But then she hadn't given him any reason to believe she wasn't exactly what he thought. Some bored spoiled woman looking for a good time and nothing else.

"Jesus, Eden. I'm sorry," Swanny said, regret swamping his face. "I didn't mean to hurt you."

So much for schooling her features.

"It's okay," she said lightly, proud of the way her voice didn't quiver betrayingly. "I understand perfectly and I get it. You don't have to beat me over the head with it. Now if you'll excuse me, I have to get unpacked. There's a lot to do between now and tomorrow morning. Perhaps we'll order in room service a little later."

Before he could respond, she turned and grabbed one of her suitcases and hauled it toward one of the bedrooms.

He cursed colorfully and called her name, but she ignored it and shut the door behind her. She'd venture out to get the rest of her luggage later. Right now she wanted a long soaking bath and to lick her wounds.

Swanny watched her go, helplessness seizing him. He'd royally fucked that up completely. But it baffled him that Eden was attracted to him. That she thought him *beautiful*, for fuck's sake.

He ran an agitated hand through his hair and stared at the suitcases still lined up in the middle of the living room. He should bring them into her room for her, but she'd likely locked the door behind her.

The hurt he'd seen in her eyes, just for a fleeting moment before her face had become expressionless, made him feel like he'd kicked a puppy. Most men would dream of having a woman like Eden throwing herself at him. But women didn't throw themselves at him, and he couldn't fathom the idea that Eden wanted him. She had to have an ulterior motive, but what?

She seemed genuine and sincere. She hadn't teased or flirted with any of the other guys. For whatever reason, she'd zeroed in on him and he'd solidly stuck his foot in his mouth and likely fucked up any chance he had with her.

He sighed and bent to pick up his duffel bag again before heading to the bedroom. He left his door open so he could stay apprised of Eden's comings and goings. The last thing he wanted was for her to take off from the hotel room because she no longer wanted to be around him.

To his surprise a knock sounded at the door and he hurried out, meeting Eden at her doorway.

"You stay put," he ordered, directing her back into her bedroom. "I'll see who it is. Don't come out unless I tell you."

She retreated, her features bland, but her eyes told a different story. Damn it, he'd hurt her feelings and that was the last thing he'd wanted. He wasn't an expert when it came to women, fuck it all. He had no idea what to do with Eden. Oh, he knew what he'd like to do, but just not how to get there . . . gracefully. Without appearing to be a bull in rut.

A woman like Eden deserved to be made love to. Not fucked without finesse and have it all be over in two seconds.

He looked through the peephole to see Skylar standing in the hallway gesturing for him to come out. Perplexed by what she could want, he followed her out and shut the door behind him.

A small smile flirted at the corners of Skylar's mouth. "Look, I'm here to save you from yourself. Because if I have to guess, you've probably already fucked this up royally. You can thank me later."

Swanny sighed. "I don't need you to tell me how badly I've fucked up."

"Yeah, you do," she said bluntly. "Look, Eden has a thing for you. I think it's wonderful. It's obvious she's not some obnoxious snob who thinks she's better than the rest of the human population. And she's very interested in you. While you're doing your best to fuck everything up. You couldn't have looked more displeased when she asked you to room with her. She looked crushed."

It irritated Swanny to be lectured by his own teammate,

but at least it wasn't one of the guys giving him shit. Skylar had a heart of gold and he knew he could count on her to keep her mouth shut.

"Look," she said quietly. "Eden appears to be a very special woman. I'd say even more special in my eyes because she recognizes the good man you are and isn't put off by the scars that would put off lesser, more superficial women. And she's beautiful. But more than the fact that she's beautiful on the outside, she seems to be genuinely beautiful on the inside. And that's what's more important. So don't fuck this up, Swanny. I know you. You'll spend all your time befuddled and asking yourself why instead of just going with it. I'm certainly not going to lecture you on not getting involved with a client because hell, the Kellys have made a regular practice of it. Not to mention our esteemed team leaders, Rio and Steele."

Swanny sucked in a deep breath, embarrassed at what he was going to ask Skylar. "What am I supposed to do?" he asked in a desperate voice. "I've already hurt her feelings by suggesting I was just a distraction for her, a quick lay to pass the time and that she'd move on when this was all over."

Skylar winced. "Ouch. Not cool, Swanny. No woman wants to hear that. That's more of a man's M.O. We women tend to be more emotional creatures. Having sex or making love, whatever you want to call it, *means* more to us than it does to men. I'd say you have some groveling to do with her now."

"You really think she wants me," he said bluntly. "Look at me, Skylar. I'm not a typical guy. Eden is surrounded by men a hell of a lot more polished and sophisticated than I am. Hell, she told me we all had to wear tuxes to her launch event, and I broke into a cold sweat."

Skylar grinned. "Now *that* I'm taking pictures of."

"Be serious a minute," he pleaded.

"Yes, I think she wants you, Swanny," Skylar said in a more serious tone. "She's certainly made herself obvious at great risk of embarrassment to herself. She doesn't strike me as the *ho* type who'll make it with any available dick. Most men would be on their knees because she chose them. Any particular reason you aren't?"

WHEN DAY BREAKS 75

He took a long moment to answer as he grappled with his thoughts. "No," he finally admitted. "Not a damn reason at all. I'm just not into the whole one-night-stand, casual-sex scene." He was a little embarrassed to admit that to Skylar, but her face softened in understanding.

"I know you aren't, Swanny. But if you think your scars make you any less desirable to a woman, you're an idiot. I see the looks women throw your way. You, on the other hand, are oblivious. You're so conditioned to see the worst in people that you never notice when you don't get just that."

He had no idea what to say to that. "You don't think I'm . . . ugly?"

Skylar's face softened even more and she briefly touched the scar that puckered his face. "I don't find you ugly at all, Swanny. In fact I find you very handsome."

The door opened and Eden stood there, a startled look on her face. Then crimson flooded her cheeks as she stared at Swanny and Skylar, Skylar's hand still cupped over Swanny's cheek.

"Uh, sorry to interrupt," she mumbled.

She hastily slammed the door back and Swanny swore viciously. "I can't do anything right with her, it would seem. Now she's going to think you and I are involved. Jesus, but when I fuck up, I fuck up big."

"Let me go in and talk to her," Skylar said. "It's a woman thing. I'll explain better than you. Men aren't so good when it comes to words. Give me half an hour. Go wait in the room with Edge. I'll be back in a bit."

CHAPTER 11

EDEN was mentally kicking herself in the head when a soft knock sounded at her door.

"Eden? It's me, Skylar. Can I come in?"

Eden let out a silent groan. The very last thing she wanted was a confrontation with the woman who was apparently involved with the man she'd just thrown herself at.

With a resigned sigh, she opened the door and gestured for Skylar to come in. Before Skylar could say anything, Eden took a deep breath.

"Look, I'm really sorry. I had no idea about you and Swanny. I know I way overstepped my boundaries. It won't happen again. I promise."

Skylar smiled, her eyes warming as she took in Eden's dismay. Then they softened in sympathy, which made Eden cringe all the more.

"Maybe we should go into the living room to talk," Skylar suggested. "I kicked Swanny out and he's hanging with Edge until we're done here."

Eden trudged into the living room on Skylar's heels, her embarrassment growing with every step. Of course Swanny

would be attracted to someone like Skylar. She was confident and capable of holding her own in a sea of testosterone.
She was kick-ass *and* beautiful. What man could resist that
combination?

"You completely misunderstood what you saw between
Swanny and me," Skylar said gently. "He was kicking himself
in the ass for hurting you, and I was attempting to offer encouragement. Swanny isn't the most confident when it comes to his
appearance. Now, in every other aspect, he's like *whoa*. He's
damn good at his job and he is not to be fucked with. But the
scars bother him more than he lets on. The memories of how
he got those scars are even harder for him to deal with."

"So you aren't involved?" Eden asked hopefully.

Skylar shook her head. "Nope. We're friends. Good friends
and teammates. We have a bond, but it isn't romantic."

"Does it make me a total slut that I'm relieved?" Eden
muttered.

Skylar's eyes sparkled. "I think you would be very good
for Swanny. But he's also worried about you breaking his
heart. Swanny isn't most guys. He doesn't fuck around for
the sake of fucking around. And you wouldn't be a notch on
his bedpost. I mean, it wouldn't go on his scorecard that he
made it with the world's most beautiful woman like it likely
would be for some guys."

"Ouch," Eden winced. "Talk about a shot to my ego."

Skylar smiled. "Just saying it like it is. I'm sure you have
your fill of guys who'd love to get into your pants for no
other reason than to say they've done it. But Swanny isn't
like that. I don't want him hurt, Eden."

Her expression became more serious as she studied Eden.

"But somehow I don't think I need to worry about you
breaking his heart. You don't seem like the type to fuck around."

"Thanks for that, at least," Eden muttered.

"Look, just cut him some slack. I think he's still in shock
that you're remotely attracted to him. And he's probably
arguing with himself because you're a job and our job is to
protect you, and if he gets emotionally involved, that will
fuck with the mission. But hey, most everyone in our outfit

met their significant other while on a mission, so it's not like it hasn't happened."

"Do I have a shot with him?" Eden asked in a low voice. "He told me a little about what happened. But I'm not at all sure what I'm dealing with here."

Skylar's expression softened. "If he told you anything at all, then that's a good sign because he doesn't talk about it to anyone. He still has nightmares. We've all witnessed them but we don't mention it because it makes him self-conscious. And yeah, I'd say you have a shot with him. You're just going to have to be patient as he wars with himself over whether he can juggle the job and a relationship with you too."

"I can be patient when it comes to something I want," Eden said softly.

Skylar's mouth quirked. "I like you, Eden. You're not at all what I was expecting."

"I'm not even going to ask," Eden said dryly. "But I'm glad that whatever you thought I was didn't turn out to be that way."

"I'm going to go kick Swanny back out of my room. He's stewed long enough. He's probably kicked himself in the ass enough that it's sore by now. Go easy on him. He's a man, after all, and they're incredibly thick when it comes to women. Believe me, I've seen it all," she added with a roll of her eyes.

"I like you too, Skylar," Eden said with a grin. "Anyone who can handle all that testosterone and hold their own certainly has earned respect."

"Swanny likes you," Skylar said bluntly. "Don't let him fuck it up, Eden. He's not used to contending with women wanting to be near him, and I'm guessing it freaks him out."

"Now that I know, you can be sure I'm not going to give up so easily," Eden said in a determined tone.

Skylar smiled again. "Awesome. Can't wait to see him fall hard. This will have to be documented for posterity."

Eden joined in her laughter, feeling at ease for the first time since this whole clusterfuck had begun. A few days in Paris, with Swanny basically her captive audience? It was plenty of time to work her magic, provided she had any.

CHAPTER 12

SWANNY let himself in the door as quietly as possible, though it was stupid of him to tiptoe around. But after making a total horse's ass of himself with Eden, and then Skylar having to smooth things over, he was feeling like a first-class moron.

Skylar hadn't said much, just that she'd explained "things" to Eden, whatever "things" was supposed to mean. Sky had worn a mischievous expression, though, and her eyes had sparkled with amusement when she'd told him to get his ass back over to his room and quit acting like an idiot.

Then her expression had gotten more serious as she'd told him not to fuck up his chance with Eden. What chance? And how had things progressed to this point so damn quickly? He'd only met the woman a little over twenty-four hours ago and it boggled his mind that he supposedly had a chance to mess up. *Or* get right.

He wasn't sure whether he was relieved or disappointed when he found the living room empty and the door to Eden's bedroom closed. He realized that he was a total chickenshit, which didn't sit well with him. When it came to his profession he had confidence in spades. But on a personal level? Relationships? *Confidence* wasn't a word that was exactly in his vocabulary. And definitely not with a woman like Eden.

What the hell did she see in him? It was a question that had haunted him for hours. Why was she even bothering with him, and why had she looked so hurt when he'd pushed her away?

He couldn't get that quick flash of hurt he'd seen in her eyes out of his mind. That he had that kind of power to hurt a woman of her caliber baffled him. Women like her likely left a trail of broken hearts in their wake. And yet she'd said rather bluntly that it was he who would likely break her heart.

He knew that shit like love at first sight wasn't some hokey crap only in fiction. He'd witnessed it firsthand. Well, maybe it wasn't at *first* sight, but pretty damn close. His teammates had certainly fallen hard for their wives, and it sure as hell hadn't taken very long to accomplish. But it wasn't something he ever envisioned happening to *him*.

How could he love someone he didn't know? How could she love or rather like or be attracted to someone *she* didn't know? They were, for all practical purposes, strangers thrown together by circumstance. Nothing more.

And yet she'd have him believe she felt something more for him. Would he be a fool to look the other way? To ignore what she was blatantly offering him? What was the worst that could happen? They'd have a fling and then go their separate ways? He could think of a lot worse things.

No one said they had to declare undying love or devotion to become involved physically.

Except that for him . . . sex wasn't casual. Or at least he didn't consider it a mindless act. Something to gain quick release and then go on his merry way. Perhaps that was why his sex life wasn't exactly lighting the world on fire. Well, that and the fact that one side of his face was a mangled mess.

The few women he had been with hadn't seemed to mind, but then he'd made damn sure he made up for his appearance by focusing on their pleasure. Keeping the lights off hadn't hurt either.

But who in their right mind would turn the lights off when making love to a woman as fucking gorgeous as Eden Sinclair? Hell, he'd want to memorize every part of her body. Every dip, every curve. He'd commit to memory the way her eyes glazed with passion, the way they flared when she orgasmed. Though he might be putting too much stock in his sexual prowess. Who was to say he'd even be able to satisfy her? A woman like her could certainly afford to be picky. And yet . . . she wanted *him*.

His groin reacted to the fantasy he was creating in his mind, and his dick swelled in his jeans, making it damn uncomfortable. He was going to wear the imprint of his zipper if he kept this up.

So what the hell was he supposed to do? March into Eden's bedroom, toss her on the bed and fuck her six ways to Sunday?

He shook his head in disgust. First he owed her an apology for acting like a dick. She deserved more than some crude fuck. She deserved to be seduced. And then made love to the entire night, everything devoted entirely to her pleasure. He wanted to make her forget any other man she'd ever had sex with. For her he'd pull out every single trick in his repertoire and learn a few more to boot. The idea of learning what pleased her appealed to him not only on a physical level but on an emotional one too.

"Swanny?"

It took him a minute to realize that Eden was standing in the doorway to her bedroom and that apparently she'd called his name more than once. He glanced up to see her wearing a worried frown as she stared at him, question in her eyes.

"Sorry," he muttered. "Was just thinking."

"Must not have been good thoughts," she murmured.

He almost laughed. If she only knew . . .

"I was asking if you were hungry. I was going to order room service. It's late and I need to call it an early night. Shooting starts early tomorrow morning and I need to look my best."

As if she could look anything else. This was not a woman

who had to work at looking good. If manufacturers could bottle her kind of beauty they'd be fucking gazillionaires. It was little wonder why she was so highly sought after. Having her back a product? Complete gold mine. She looked utterly approachable, not at all standoffish like he might expect someone of her celebrity to be. People likely flocked to her, drawn by her sweetness and genuine kindness.

"If you'll tell me what you want, I'll order for both of us," he offered.

She offered him a smile that took his breath. Bottled sunshine. That was her in a nutshell. He seemed to reference the sun a lot in her presence. But being in close proximity to her was like taking a bath in sunshine on a perfect spring day.

Jesus. Now he was some kind of damn poet? It was obvious she turned him into a blithering idiot, waxing poetic when she was around him. If he weren't careful, he'd start spouting the crap he was thinking and then she'd realize what he already knew. That he'd lost his damn mind.

"Just a fruit tray for me. I need to keep it light. Can't afford any extra pounds."

He snorted as he took in her flawless figure. "You look fucking perfect the way you are."

Her cheeks bloomed with color and she smiled again and that squeezing sensation in his chest grew, threatening to close off his throat. Jesus, but this woman was death on men. The entire male species, no doubt. She likely had them all throwing themselves at her feet, humbling themselves for just a crumb from her. A smile. Or just a few words. He should know because he was precariously close to being one of those men.

"But order whatever you want," she added quickly. "It's not going to bother me for you to eat something more hearty. You're a big guy. I'm sure you need the calories. Besides, I'll live vicariously through you and at least get to smell whatever you eat."

He frowned. "Do you ever get to eat like a normal person?"

She looked puzzled. "Of course. I mean it's normal for me. I just have to watch what I eat. The camera is unforgiving and adds pounds, so I have to compensate for that. I do splurge from time to time, but this shoot is too important to risk even one extra pound. When it's over I'll celebrate with a nice big steak."

"I'll take you out for one," he blurted out before realizing he was in essence asking her out on a date.

Her smile grew bigger, a dimple forming in her cheek and fascinating him. He wanted to run his tongue over it. And a whole lot of other places on her body.

"I'd like that."

"I'll, uh, just grab the room service menu," he mumbled.

"Why do I make you so nervous, Swanny?" she asked softly.

Their gazes connected and he forced himself not to look away, not to avert the scarred side of his face as he was so accustomed to doing.

Betraying heat crept up his neck and into his face. She'd been nothing but honest with him, so he could be no less with her. "You scare me to death," he admitted.

Her eyes widened. "I do?"

She sounded shocked, and he supposed it did sound absurd. He protected people for a living. Carried out missions that required courage and strength. He was tested on a daily basis and yet he'd just admitted that he was scared shitless by a woman half his weight. A woman whose bones he could break if he wasn't careful. His hands were big like the rest of his body. Not meant for a woman as delicate as Eden. They were a true study in Beauty and the Beast. And he wasn't a believer in fairy tales. He saw too much reality in his line of work. Knew there were too many unhappy endings to believe in too much goodness.

And yet he worked for an organization that prevailed in goodness and justice. For KGI—and him—failure simply wasn't an option. But here he was throwing in the towel before the very start. What a fucking pussy that made him.

"If I promise to behave, will you at least have dinner with me?" she asked, her eyes sparkling again.

He grinned crookedly. "Yeah, I'd like that."

She arched an eyebrow. "You'd like me to behave myself or you'd like to have dinner with me?"

He laughed this time. "Has anyone ever told you how incorrigible you are?"

"And how neatly you avoid the question. You're very good at that, you know."

"I'd like to have dinner with you. Whether you behave or not," he added.

"I wouldn't turn down a teeny bite of your steak, that is, if you're having one," she said, a look of longing in her eyes.

"A filet sounds really good," he admitted.

She pulled a face. "Now you're just being mean. That's my favorite steak."

"Then I'll make sure I order one and save you two bites. I can't think one extra will hurt."

She donned a thoughtful expression. "On second thought, order me a salad, no dressing. Then I can have those two bites."

"You got it."

He went to where the room service menu was laid on one of the tables and then called down their orders while Eden disappeared back into her room.

He felt her absence immediately. It was as though she took the sunshine with her, as corny as that sounded. But she just brightened any room she was in. He could honestly just stand in the same room with her and watch her. Could spend hours doing it. She was . . . genuine.

He felt guilty for the assumptions and accusations he'd levied at her. He'd acted like a first-rate dick and she hadn't deserved that from him. For whatever reason she seemed to genuinely like him—was attracted to him. And he was a dickless twit who didn't comprehend the magnitude of what this beautiful woman was offering him. Herself.

She'd asked for nothing in return. No hidden agenda. What could he offer her anyway? He couldn't think of a single ulterior motive she could possibly have for pursuing him, nor could he imagine why she wanted him. But as the saying went, he wouldn't look a gift horse in the mouth. Nor would he spend time questioning it.

If she wanted him, then he was damn well going to give her what she wanted. Just as soon as he figured out when and *how*.

CHAPTER 13

SWANNY felt horribly guilty for eating the succulent steak right in front of Eden. He didn't miss the longing in her eyes or the fact that her mouth was practically watering as he savored the perfectly cooked meat.

He'd never considered the sacrifices models had to make. He supposed he'd always assumed they were just naturally perfect and blessed with great genes and could eat whatever and never have to worry about weight gain.

But as they'd waited on dinner, Eden had explained her workout regimen, her diet restrictions and the arduous-sounding skin and hair care routine. It had to be exhausting. Add on to that the sometimes sixteen-hour days shooting and it sounded like hell to him. And yet she'd cheerfully listed her routine as if it were perfectly normal to work herself into the ground and carefully measure her caloric intake.

It was obvious that she made a lot of sacrifices for her career, and his respect for her grew the more they conversed. He was well aware of the stereotypes associated with super-models. But so far Eden didn't fit any of the negative assumptions so often assigned to women in her career.

He was as guilty of those assumptions as other people. He'd never considered the work involved in modeling and just assumed that it was a cakewalk and that all models were spoiled divas who were catered to and had their every whim granted. That beyond the practiced, polished exterior presented to the camera was a bitchy, completely fake personality.

Eden was quickly dissuading him of those notions, and he felt ashamed that he'd ever given any credence to those thoughts.

He cut off two large slices of the steak and laid them on Eden's plate next to the bowl that contained her salad. Her eyes widened but her mouth was watering as she stared down at them.

"That's too much," she said with a groan. "But man, I want them."

"Eat up," Swanny encouraged. "I'll get you up early and go down to the fitness center with you so you can work off those two bites before your shoot."

She smiled warmly at him, and his chest did that weird seize that seemed to occur with more frequency the longer he was around her. "I'd like that," she said, her eyes glowing softly. "Micah and David usually worked out with me, and believe me, they were grueling taskmasters! But I have to admit, they whipped me into better shape and they also taught me self-defense moves."

Swanny had to work to keep the scowl from forming on his face at the mention of the other two men. Hell, he'd take over any self-defense training. Him and only him, for that matter.

"You can show me your moves," he said, pushing away the jealousy that threatened to choke him. "I can always work with you when we have the time."

Her eyes twinkled mischievously. "Why, Swanny, if you keep this up I'm going to think you actually want to spend time with me."

"I think we've established the fact that I like spending time with you," he said in a quiet tone. "I worried about getting in way over my head, but if I'm going to be honest, I think I'm already there."

Pleasure spread over her pretty features, her cheeks dusty pink. "I'm glad I'm not the only one then," she said huskily. "I'm not some vamp on the make here, Swanny. I need you to know that. If you weren't . . . special . . . then I wouldn't be in this room with you. I wouldn't have gone to such lengths to put myself out there the way I did and risk rejection. It wasn't easy. I don't *want* to make a fool of myself."

Swanny's heart softened as he saw the honesty and sincerity shining in her eyes. The idea that he had the power to hurt this woman utterly baffled him. He was going to have to pull his head out of his ass and do everything in his power to assure her that her attraction was not one-sided and that he had no intention of rejecting her or rejecting anything she offered him.

"I've handled all of this badly," Swanny said, allowing his remorse to bleed over into his words. "And I'm sorry for that, Eden. You have to understand, this is new to me. And just as you said it wasn't easy for you, it's definitely not easy for me either. The idea that a woman like you has any interest in me . . ." He broke off and shook his head, still bewildered by it all.

She slid over on the couch so her left knee touched his right knee where he sat in the armchair diagonal to the sofa, their dinner spread out on the coffee table. She slid her hand up his leg, gently giving him a squeeze.

It wasn't a sexual move and yet his entire body went on alert the moment her heat seeped through his jeans. He felt every part of her touch. It burned a trail up his leg, ending where her hand came to rest and where she left it as she looked up at him.

"Any woman who doesn't see you as I do is a fool," she said in a determined voice. "I don't say things I don't mean, Swanny. Not even to make someone feel better. I think you're beautiful and I'm very attracted to you. I don't go around blurting out stuff like that to men I don't know. Or men I do know, for that matter," she amended. "So this is definitely new territory for me, and it's a little scary because you could so easily hurt me. And I'm not saying that to make you feel any obligation to give me something you don't want. I just need you to understand that to me you're something special. Maybe I don't know everything about you. Yet. But that doesn't mean that I don't want to learn. I'd like to think I at least have a chance with you."

This was a dream. An elaborate fantasy that he'd wake up from any moment now. He stared at Eden, knowing it was his turn to lay it out. That it had taken a lot of courage for her to be so forthright. He owed that back to her. But his tongue felt heavy and he couldn't form the words. His throat felt like it was closing in on itself.

Her eyes flickered, that same brief hurt he'd witnessed before, and she started to withdraw, pulling her hand away. Goddamn it, he wasn't going to do this to her again. He had to get with the program and start talking now.

He caught her hand, holding it tightly in his much larger one. It was a fascinating contrast, her tiny bone structure compared to his much larger frame. She had a delicateness to her that fired his protective instincts. Like if he didn't handle her with infinite care, he could break her—hurt her—and he'd die before ever causing her a moment's pain.

And yet that was precisely what he was doing by his boneheadedness. He was hurting her. Just not physically. A woman would only put herself out there so much before she gave up, and damn it, he didn't want her to give up on him. He had to get his shit together and man up and quit acting like a moron who'd never been with a woman.

"I don't pretend to understand what you could possibly see in me," he said hoarsely. "I can't even wrap my head around it. God only knows I have nothing to offer you."

"I only want one thing, Swanny," she said gently. "You. Just you."

"You make it sound so simple."

She shrugged. "It is. I mean, it can be as simple or as

difficult as we make it. I don't know how to make you understand that my feelings are sincere. I know you don't trust me
yet. But I *do* trust *you*."

"I've done nothing to deserve it or you," he said bluntly.
"I've been a complete asshole and I'm sorry, Eden. You have
no idea how sorry I am to have hurt you twice now. You
deserve so much more than me."

Her lips quivered into a faint smile. "You're repeating
yourself, Swanny. You keep saying the same things. Stop
analyzing why and figure out if you want me as much as I
want you. That's the only real issue here. Everything else
can be worked around."

"Hell yes, I want you," he bit out. "I can't think for wanting
you. You've consumed my thoughts since the very first time I
saw you walk into that hotel room where we met."

Her smile broadened and delight formed in her eyes.
"Okay, now we're getting somewhere. Finally!"

He sighed. "I'm not normally such an idiot. I'm not stupid.
Except when it comes to you, apparently. But you have this
effect on me that I can't even explain. I keep asking myself,
why me? What does a woman like you possibly see in me?"

She leaned forward and cupped a hand to his scarred
cheek, lightly caressing the ridges and the puckered skin.
"You keep saying 'a woman like me,' but turn that around
for a minute. Don't you think I'm asking myself what a man
like you could possibly see in *me*? You're a hero. You're a
survivor. You help people for a living. You put your life on
the line for others, and that takes a very special person to be
that selfless. What could you possibly want with a woman
who makes her living selling her looks and her body? You're
paid to save lives, and I'm paid to look pretty and sell a product. So who's the better person here?"

The way she very matter-of-factly levied her opinion of
him blew his mind. Whether he agreed with her assessment or
not, it was evident that she was absolutely sincere in her
thoughts and her analysis of him and his character. He felt like
a complete fraud. Because he felt that what she was seeing or
what she thought she saw was not the real Swanny.

Whatever lens she viewed him through was faulty. Was she merely temporarily infatuated with him? Perhaps intrigued by him? And what would happen when she realized that he wasn't all she seemed to think he was?

He'd prefer never to become involved with her rather than to become emotionally and physically involved with her only to see the way she viewed him change and to see the light dim in her gaze when she looked at him and really saw him for what he was. Flawed. Far from perfect. Still dealing with the demons of his past and the shame over his weakness during his captivity and how very close he came to giving up. The physical scars were certainly no cakewalk, but worse were the scars no one could see. The ones he could feel, ones that would always be there inside him, a stain on his soul.

And yet she sat there, mere inches away, looking earnestly at him as she asked what a man like him would see in her. *Her.* He couldn't even wrap his brain around that kind of question. She deserved so much more than what he could give her. She deserved a man who didn't come with the baggage he carried.

When he still hadn't answered her question—how could he?—she straightened slightly and gazed steadily at him, her lips firming with . . . resolve? And yet her voice was silky soft, as sweet as the rest of her and so fucking beautiful that it hurt to look at her, to listen to the musical tones of her voice.

"I'm not asking for anything you can't or don't want to give me, Swanny. And if you don't want this, if I'm completely off base here, then just tell me and I swear to you I'll never mention it again. I'll back off and all I'll be is a job to you and I'll room with Skylar from now on. All I want is for you to give me—us—a chance. To just go with the flow and see where this—whatever this is between us—takes us. But the ball is in your court now. I can't make you want me. I wouldn't want to make you feel anything you didn't on your own. That's not ever the reason I want a man to be with me, because I pressured him for something he didn't willingly give me on his own."

Left unsaid but perfectly understood by him was that this was his last and only chance. If he didn't make the next move, then she was done reaching out to him. It was a hell of a spot to be in. Scared to death to make a move and at the same time knowing that if he turned her away he'd regret it for the rest of his life. That he could very well be missing out on the best thing to ever happen to him. Even if his time with her was short lived and in the end they walked away and never saw each other again.

His courage had been tested countless times and he'd never felt as though he'd failed. But courage came in many variations and situations. He realized that to reach out and take what Eden was offering would be the toughest test of his courage he'd ever face. To allow someone inside him, where he allowed no one else. To let her see inside his heart and soul and trust that she wouldn't run as far away and as fast as possible once he did let her see what he hid so effectively from everyone else.

The easy way out would be to simply tell her no. That he didn't want to become involved and that they shouldn't. His job was to protect her, not to be fucking her, though he knew the minute he took her to bed, she would become his number one priority and that anyone trying to get to her would have to go through him in order to do so.

But nothing good was ever easy. Only a coward would take the path of least resistance and shut Eden out before he ever let her in. He wasn't a coward, had never been a coward, and he damn sure wasn't going to start being one now.

She was right in that he didn't trust her yet. Or perhaps he didn't trust what she said she wanted. But she trusted *him* and it seemed the height of disrespect not to give her his trust in return.

"I don't want you to go," Swanny said in a soft voice. He hated how vulnerable he sounded even to his own ears.

"Then what *do* you want?" she asked, just as softly.

He leveled his gaze at her, determined to be as sincere as she had been. And as honest. He sucked in a deep breath and put it out there. The same thing she'd done for him. Made himself vulnerable, as vulnerable as she'd made herself by putting it all on the line. Her pride. Her courage. Her heart. Because damn it, he'd sworn to her that she was safe with him. That he'd protect her at all costs. And now he realized that his protection had to extend further because he had to protect her heart and soul as well as protect her from any physical threat.

With his next words he'd be committing himself wholly to keeping her safe. Even from himself and any hurt he might open her up to.

"You," he said bluntly. "I want you."

CHAPTER 14

EDEN sucked in her breath, almost dizzy with relief. But the practical side of her insisted that she make sure that he did want her and wasn't just caving under pressure. She'd come on to him with all the finesse of a bull in rut, and he might have seen no other recourse than to wave a white flag of surrender.

And that wasn't what she wanted. Yes, she wanted Swanny. Was attracted to him in a way she'd never been attracted to another man. But she wanted him to want her in that same way without pressure.

"And why do you want me?" she asked softly, bracing herself for possible disappointment. "Because I don't want someone who feels pressured. I know I've put you on the spot and have been . . . brazen . . . for lack of a better word. I want you, yes. I've certainly made that clear. But I want you to want me for the right reasons. I hope I'm making sense."

His response was a low growl and then suddenly she found herself hauled from the couch and into his lap. She landed with a soft thud and he tilted her chin upward just before his mouth crashed down over hers.

He vibrated with want—need. It was impossible to fake. She could feel the erection straining at his jeans against her thigh.

He slid his tongue into her mouth, stroking and caressing, tasting her, allowing her to taste him. She let out a breathy sigh as she relaxed into his hold, his arms around her, anchoring her tightly to his body.

Such a muscled, strong body.

The kiss went on and on, their breaths mingling, until they were both panting between kisses as they sucked air into their starved lungs. She moaned from the exquisite sensations bombarding her. If she'd in any way imagined her attraction to Swanny, it was now confirmed. Her body leapt to life, every nerve ending painfully aware of the overwhelming desire singing through her veins.

Never had a man made her feel the way Swanny did. Never had she had the desire to go all the way. Something had always held her back. Now she knew why. Because she'd been waiting for Swanny. For a man to make her feel that she was safe, that he would take care of her completely.

Finally Swanny dragged his mouth away from hers. His eyes were half-lidded and heavy with desire.

"Now you tell me if it feels to you like I don't want you. Or that you're somehow forcing my attraction, because honey, it doesn't work that way. I can't fake my reaction to you. I can't even look at you without wanting you. The only thing I'm struggling with is my belief that a woman in your class could possibly want *me*."

She smiled, warmed by the sincerity she saw shining in his beautiful eyes. She lifted her hand to caress his scarred cheek, running her fingers lightly along the ridges. He didn't flinch or try to turn away, a huge victory because it meant he was becoming more comfortable with her.

She touched him often, wanting to tell him without words that she wasn't bothered by his appearance. She knew it would take time, but she wanted him to know without question that she wasn't put off by his scars. Not in the least.

"To turn your words back on you, I can't fake a reaction this strong. If you want an explanation I simply don't have

one. Some things just are, and for me that's you. I struggle
over the fact that we've known each other such a short time. I
mean, it never seemed possible to me to have an instant connection with another person like I do with you. But it's there.
It was there from the start. There was something about you
that just . . . drew me in. You'll find this hard to believe based
on the way I've come on to you, but this isn't normal for me.
I'm actually pretty reserved. I'm having my own share of
bewilderment over my boldness because it's not who I am, or
rather who I was," she said ruefully.

He nuzzled into her hand, pressing a kiss to her palm. "I
like your honesty. It's refreshing. There's no guessing with
you. I like that a lot. You don't play games. I don't find your
forthrightness to be bold or brazen at all. I like knowing
where I stand. And let's face it. If you'd waited for me to
make a move, you'd probably have waited forever because I
would have never imagined for a single moment that you'd
want someone like me. It would have felt to me like reaching
for the stars or wishing for the moon. I guess I needed a kick
in the ass and you provided that nicely."

She laughed, relaxing into his arms, resting her head on
his shoulder. There was nothing overtly sexual about their
position, but she felt comfortable and intimacy surrounded
them, pulling them into their own little cloud. The rest of the
world seemed miles away. There was only the two of them
with no intrusions or interruptions.

Knowing she was being bold—again—she turned her
head up just so she could see his face. "Will you sleep with
me tonight?"

His eyes instantly flared and she hurried to correct the likely
assumption that she was asking him to make love to her.

"I don't mean to have sex," she hastily amended. "I know
we're still feeling our way around each other and I don't want
to rush things. I'm liking where we are right now. But I'd love
to sleep in your arms tonight. To just . . . be with you."

He pressed a gentle kiss to her forehead. "I'd like that a
hell of a lot. And Eden, stop being self-conscious about saying what it is you want. I don't think you're some brazen

hussy. I hope you'll never hesitate to ask me for anything you want or need. Because I'll do pretty damn much anything to provide it for you."

She smiled ruefully. "I told you this isn't the normal me. It's actually really hard to lay it out like I have. I like you a lot and I don't want to ever put you off by being too demanding or pressuring you for something you aren't ready for."

"There's no pressure, honey. I think we've already established I want you pretty damn bad. You'll never come across as demanding or forceful by telling me what it is you want from me."

"I want you to do the same," she said softly. "I don't want you to worry about coming across too forcefully. I'd like us both to meet each other halfway. So if you make me promise to tell you what it is I want, then I want that same promise from you."

"Deal," he said gruffly.

He looked regretfully at his watch and then back to her.

"You said you have an early morning, and if we're going to get up and work out before your shoot, you should probably think about getting to bed now."

She nodded. Before she would have been reluctant to go to bed—alone—because she enjoyed his company and she would have lingered, giving up rest to spend time with him. But now that he was sleeping with her, she suffered no qualms about going to bed now.

He pushed her up with a gentle pat to her behind. "You go and get ready for bed. I'm going to grab a shower and then I'll meet you in your bedroom."

She leaned down and kissed his scarred cheek. "Don't be too long."

He grinned crookedly at her. "I'll likely set a speed record for this shower now that I know I'm sleeping with you tonight. I usually just wear boxers to bed. Will that bother you?"

She nearly laughed. Him in just his underwear and her getting to drink in the sight of his muscled physique? Her being able to sleep curled into that strong body and feel his skin against hers? Bother her? Ha!

"If you're okay with me wearing lingerie, then I'm certainly okay with you wearing just your boxers."

His expression was priceless. He looked as though he'd just swallowed his tongue. Then he groaned.

"You're torturing me. I hope you know that."

She gave him an innocent look. "I'll be more covered than you'll be."

He snorted. "I have a damn good imagination and believe me I'll be imagining what's underneath that sexy lingerie all night."

"Good," she murmured, a smile curving the corners of her mouth. "I like the idea that you'll be thinking about me."

On that note, she trotted off toward her bedroom, leaving Swanny sitting in his chair. She grinned and did a silly twirl as she gathered her nightclothes and headed for the bathroom.

Was this what falling in love felt like? She was certainly in lust with him. It was all so confusing. People didn't just fall in love at first sight. Love was something you had to work at. Something that was earned over time. But she could so easily see herself falling and falling *hard* for Swanny. Maybe she was already well on her way.

She let out a sigh. There was little sense in overanalyzing it all. She'd just have to wait and let the cards fall where they may. Already she was getting way ahead of herself. Though Swanny might be attracted to her, she was still a job to him. And they both had careers that took them to the opposite ends of the earth.

Maybe all she needed was an affair. Get him out of her system and when it was done and over with they'd go their separate ways and she'd have the memory of the time they'd spent together. But even as she thought it, she knew she was lying to herself. Because she highly doubted that having a hot fling with him would ever get him out of her system. If anything, becoming sexually and emotionally involved with him, even for a short time, would confirm what she already knew.

Swanny wasn't the type of man a woman ever forgot or ever willingly let go. The bigger question would be whether he wanted more than a temporary fling or if he would be the one to walk away when it was all over with.

CHAPTER 15

SWANNY found himself standing outside Eden's door, which was cracked a few inches. Though he'd said he wore only boxers to sleep, he hadn't considered the fact that there were more scars crisscrossing his torso, ones that weren't visible underneath his clothing, and he was seized by discomfort and self-consciousness at the idea of Eden seeing more of the imperfections of his body.

So he'd pulled on a T-shirt, noting that it made him a coward, but he couldn't face her yet. Maybe he'd turn the lights off when he entered if she was already in bed and then he could strip out of his shirt before getting into bed, although that didn't solve the problem of when they woke up because she's most assuredly get an eyeful then.

But she'd asked him to trust her. It was a lot to ask even though he knew she was utterly sincere. But still, it made him uncomfortable to bare himself when he hadn't ever let anyone else see the extent of the damage to his body from months of torture and degradation.

The psychological scars were every bit as bright in his mind as the daily reminder of his physical scars. In some ways the scars on his soul were more painful than the ones on his body, the ones that were visible. Those would take longer to heal. And maybe he'd never truly heal in heart and mind. But Eden gave him hope. Hope that he was afraid to allow himself to feel. She could so easily slip into his heart, and it would devastate him to see her expression change to one of pity or disgust, though he knew he was doing her a huge disservice by thinking she'd react that way. She'd shown him nothing but acceptance, had gone out of her way to convince him that his scars didn't matter to her. And still, he found himself holding back, not wanting to give her any reason to back away.

He finally pushed hesitantly into her bedroom to see her propped in bed, covers to her belly. She presented such a beautiful sight that it took his breath away and he found himself momentarily unable to draw air into his lungs.

"Care if I get the lights?" he asked gruffly, trying hard not to allow his self-consciousness to be too evident.

She stared thoughtfully at him a moment. "Why are you wearing a shirt, Swanny? What are you afraid of me seeing?"

The way she seemed to be able to read his thoughts, had instantly picked up on his mood, rendered him unable to form a response. What could he say to that anyway?

She pushed away the covers and slid from the bed wearing the sexy but modest sleepwear. She had a pair of silky shorts that rode high, displaying the long expanse of those gorgeous legs. And the top covered her but had little strings over her shoulders that would be so easy to slip down, baring her breasts. His need was a physical ache. Not want her? That she'd even questioned his wanting her? He'd have to be dead not to react to the sexy image directly in front of him and getting closer with every second as she walked toward him.

She placed her hands on his chest and looked up at him, such sweetness and understanding in her eyes that his throat swelled with emotion. She saw to the heart of him. What no one else ever saw. She saw past the front he displayed to others and he didn't know if that contented him or scared the holy hell out of him. Maybe some fucked-up combination of both.

Then she slid her hands underneath his shirt, pressing her palms to his bare skin. His breath quickened as did his pulse. His dick surged painfully and there was nothing to disguise it in the thin boxers he wore.

She pulled higher, gently removing his shirt, and he let her, standing there allowing her to do as she wanted.

With the shirt removed, she studied his torso, and then to his surprise, she pressed a kiss to one scar and then moved on to another and another until she'd covered every inch of his scarred flesh.

Now that he was down to his boxers, she took his hand, tugging him toward the bed, and he followed like a devoted puppy, eager to please his master.

She settled him into bed and then climbed in next to him, instantly curling her body into his, but she left enough space between them just so her hand would fit over his chest and the scars that dotted his torso.

"You don't have to hide anything from me, Swanny," she said softly. "Not from me. Never from me."

She caressed the lines of every scar, exploring them with her fingers and then as she'd done before, she kissed a line up each one, so sweet and gentle that it made his heart ache.

"You're beautiful," she whispered. "So very beautiful. I've never met a man as beautiful as you."

His heart damn near exploded and it took every ounce of his willpower not to turn her over and thrust into her as hard and as deep as he could go, making himself a part of her. Sealing the growing bond between them.

But she deserved more than that. And she wanted time. She didn't want to rush into anything and neither did he, but he knew that their making love was inevitable. It also wouldn't be long. Every other aspect of their relationship had moved at lightning speed and he knew that neither of them would hold out much longer.

Anticipation would make it all the sweeter when they did finally come together. He'd savor every single minute of their lovemaking, spend hours lavishing attention on her, learning everything that pleased her. He'd bring her to orgasm multiple times before he ever took his own pleasure. Her needs came first.

She placed one palm flat against his chest and then nestled her head on his shoulder so her hair tickled his nose. Then she slid her leg between his thighs as if seeking his warmth and touch. He was more than happy to accommodate her. He wrapped his arm around her waist, pulling her even closer as he wrapped his leg around hers, trapping hers between his.

She let out a contented sigh, the soft exhalation blowing over his skin.

Never had anything felt so . . . right. Contentment settled into his bones, relaxing him as pleasure seeped into every part of his body. She lay in his arms, a perfect fit, like she was made for him. Like she belonged there.

He might have initially fought his attraction to Eden and he might have doubted that she could possibly be attracted to him, but here and now he knew that what was between them was real. Their attraction was a living, breathing thing. Tangible. It danced in the air between them and when they were close, her in his arms, it smoldered like a slow-burning fire just waiting to ignite into an inferno.

He thought she'd drifted into sleep when she shifted and turned toward him, her eyes seeking.

"Do you like working for KGI?"

"Yeah," he said without hesitation. "They gave me purpose when I thought I no longer had one. I was at loose ends after coming back from that last tour. I suppose I was going through a self-pity stage and railing at the injustice of it all. It wasn't a pretty sight. But there were things that happened during our escape and rescue. Things I needed answers to, and so I went to see Nate. He wasn't faring much better than I was."

"What kind of things?" she asked curiously.

He hesitated, unsure of how much he should share. One, she'd think he was crazy, and two, he didn't want to betray

Shea or Grace. Not when they were the reason he was alive today.

But he also knew that if he and Eden became involved, she'd find out eventually. And he'd rather she heard it from him. So she'd know he trusted her and hadn't held out on her.

"You'll think I'm crazy," he said.

She pushed upward so she could look down at him, her hair spilling like a silken curtain over her shoulders and brushing over his chest. He could bury his hands and face in her hair and stay there for hours.

"I won't think you're crazy," she said solemnly. "You can trust me, Swanny. I won't judge you. I'll listen. And I'd never betray your confidence."

He knew that absolutely. Maybe it was crazy to trust this woman when he'd only known her such a short time. But he did trust her. She didn't have a mean or vengeful bone in her body.

He sighed. "When we were being held captive, Shea, Nathan's wife, though they didn't even know each other at the time, spoke to him, in his head from miles away. Telepathy."

Eden's eyes widened. "Really? That's so cool. I didn't think things like that truly existed."

"Yeah, she helped hold him together. She even took his torture for him. It sounds complicated, but she could draw away his pain and make it her own. She suffered for him so he could stay strong."

"That's pretty selfless," Eden murmured. "Especially for a man she didn't know."

Swanny nodded his agreement. "When Nathan and I escaped, I was busted up pretty bad. I knew I was fucked up internally and I knew I was dying. I was slowing Nathan down and I begged him to leave me so he could at least save himself. This is where it gets even more unbelievable. Shea's sister Grace has the ability to heal and as a conduit through Shea and Nathan, she was able to heal me or at least patch me up enough that I could continue on."

"It would seem I owe both those women my thanks when I meet them."

Swanny couldn't help the surge of pleasure at the matter-of-fact way she assumed she'd be meeting his extended family. Like she saw a future with him in it.

"We made it out. Nathan's brothers—KGI—got to us in time and they got us home. We were both busted up pretty bad, and afterward I went home and Nathan went back to his family. But I had no one. Just an empty house that used to belong to my parents. And it was driving me crazy. I had no idea what I was going to do with my life. And I still had all those burning questions about what had happened back there. So I looked up Nathan and while I was there, Shea contacted him, the first he'd heard from her since our escape. He went off the hinges and hauled ass to get to her. Two of his brothers and I went after him to help. I just sort of fell in with them and then they offered me a position on the new team they were forming."

"You're happy now, then."

He nodded. "Yeah. I feel like I have purpose again. Something to get up for in the mornings. I like making a difference. We help people and we take out those who prey on others."

She frowned. "It sounds dangerous."

"It is." He wouldn't sugarcoat his job. She needed to know what his job entailed. "There's always a chance of one of us not coming back from a mission. But we're good and we're careful. We've had a few close calls, but we haven't lost a man since one of Rio's men was killed before I ever came on board. He was taken out when the Kellys' mother was kidnapped from the hospital after her husband suffered a heart attack."

"Wow. It sounds like there's never a dull moment around you guys. I can see why this job would be a cakewalk for you and, honestly, far below your capabilities. I feel guilty for tying up an entire team. It seems like your talents are wasted on what amounts to a babysitting gig."

He pulled her back down into his arms, squeezing her against him. "We take your protection very seriously, Eden. You are our top priority. No job takes higher priority than another. Every mission we take gets our full attention. Besides, if we hadn't been hired to protect you, then you and I wouldn't be right here right now, and I'm liking exactly where we are."

He felt her smile against his chest. "You have a point there. I wouldn't have missed meeting you for the world."

"Me either," he said. "Now how about you get some rest. I have the alarm set for early so we can get in that workout. Don't expect me to go easy on you because I think you're cute. I'll work your ass off and then you're going to show me your self-defense moves so I'll know what else you need to be taught."

She chuckled but settled bonelessly into his arms, letting out a long breath that signaled her fatigue.

"Good night, Swanny. I'm glad you're here with me."

He squeezed her one last time. "I'm glad too."

CHAPTER 16

THOUGH Swanny had set the alarm on his watch, he had an internal clock that never failed him. If he knew what time he had to be up, he woke up five minutes before without fail.

He reached down to turn the alarm off, not wanting to jar Eden, who was sleeping soundly in his arms. He had five minutes before he needed to wake her up, and he intended to savor every one of those five minutes.

She was nestled in the curve of his arm, her hair spread out over his arm and the pillow. She was as beautiful in sleep as she was awake and alert. He studied her in the dim light from the bathroom, the door slightly ajar, using the opportunity to drink his fill when she was sleeping.

The straps to her top had slid down her shoulders, and it would take only the slightest movement to expose her nipple. As it was, the plump swells of her breasts were enticingly visible, the material just catching on her nipples so it didn't bare her further.

She shifted and he froze, but she simply snuggled deeper into his chest, let out a soft sigh and then settled back down again.

Damn, but he hated to wake her. He could lie this way for hours, simply watching and enjoying the sight of her in bed with him.

Their limbs were tangled, one of her legs between his, and his leg thrown over her possessively, anchoring her solidly against him. No, they hadn't made love, and he agreed that they shouldn't rush things, but the intimacy between them was as tangible as if they had made love.

And even though they'd both agreed not to rush, he was honest enough with himself to know that she would be in his bed and he would be inside her soon. They both wanted the same thing. Their consummating their growing relationship was inevitable.

All of his earlier wariness was gone, vanished. Now that he was certain of her and her feelings, he was eager to take that next step. Because sex with Eden wouldn't just be sex. He knew in his heart that it would be earth-shattering and that it would likely change the course of his life forever, no matter what happened between them later.

He refused to look too far down the road because their careers took them in completely separate directions. He was just focused on now and the time they would have together now. Looking beyond here and now would only bring him heartache.

They literally had to take it one day at a time and see where things took them. If they became serious, then they would simply have to find a way to be together. Love required sacrifice. He'd seen it time and time again. But where there was a will, there was a way. He had to believe that. Because if he thought too far ahead and imagined them saying good-bye and going their separate ways, it would devastate him.

He wanted nothing to interfere with what they had—and *would* have—now. All he could control was how they spent the time they had together. Anything beyond was out of his control, and so he had to concentrate on what *was* in his control: making damn certain that he gave Eden what she wanted—what he wanted—and enjoying every stolen moment together. If in the end they did go in different directions, then he'd savor every single memory of their time together and never regret a single moment. It was all either of them could do.

Knowing the quiet time he'd spent simply observing Eden unnoticed was over, he reluctantly brushed a hand over her cheek and murmured in a low voice, "Eden. Baby, it's time to get up. We need to hit the gym in twenty minutes if we're going to be on schedule for your shoot."

Her eyelids fluttered open and her unfocused stare found his, and then her entire face was transformed into a heart-stopping smile that took his breath away. The idea that she found so much pleasure from being in his arms, coming awake in his arms, made his chest constrict to the point of discomfort.

"Good morning," she said in a sleepy, husky voice.

He pressed a kiss to her forehead. "Good morning. Did you sleep well?"

"Like a rock," she admitted. "I've never slept better. I have you to thank for that. So thank you."

"For what, honey?"

"For sleeping with me. For holding me. Letting me sleep in your arms. I've never felt as safe and secure as I did last night."

Her frank admission twisted his stomach into knots. God, the woman was worming her way right into his very soul. She was already firmly entrenched, but every minute in her presence only strengthened the bond between them. Was this what love felt like? Was he already falling in love with her?

The practical side of him argued that it was much too soon to be making that kind of admission. But his heart and soul said very different things. That this was his woman. She belonged to him. Making love to her would simply cement what he already knew. That she was his.

He kissed her again, this time brushing his mouth over hers in a tender manner. "You're very welcome. But I have to tell you, I've never slept as well either, so you did as much for me as you say I did for you. I have . . ."

He struggled with the admission on the tip of his tongue.

It made him sound weak. And the last thing he wanted her to think was that he was weak.

"You have what?" she asked gently.

"Nightmares," he said in a low voice. "There doesn't seem to be a rhyme or reason to them. Some nights I don't dream at all. But others I dream about being back there, of the pain and despair I felt—still feel at times."

Her eyes shone with sympathy. With anyone else he would hate that sympathy. It was the last thing he wanted. But with Eden, he didn't feel the accompanying shame he so often felt over appearing weak.

"I can only imagine," she murmured. "It must have been such a horrible time for you, Swanny. I'm glad you had one night of peace. I'd hate to think that you were giving me so much and that I was giving you nothing in return. So it makes me feel good that you slept as well as I did. I think we make a good team," she said, a sparkle entering her eyes. "Maybe I'm good for you."

"I know you're good for me," he said with a growl. "There's no question of that. Now at the risk of sounding like an asshole, you've got to get up and get moving. I'll grab a shower in the other bathroom and then we'll go down and do your workout. If we have enough time, you can show me your moves and then I can analyze what you need further work on and we'll fit it in around your shoots. I don't want you to overdo it. I know this shoot is going to be exhausting enough."

"Oh, I'll be fine," she said as she climbed from the bed, taking her warmth and sweetness with her. "Besides, if it means getting to spend more time with you, then I'll *make* the time."

God, but she had him so twisted into knots that he didn't know up from down. How could someone so utterly perfect be interested in someone like him, who not only had physical scars but stains on his soul and emptiness in his heart that until meeting her he'd thought would never heal?

And yet within the short time they'd been together he could feel those missing parts starting to fill in. Like he was regaining all he'd lost during the horrific time he was held

captive and taken apart little by little, his very will to live
chipped away until he was ready to give up and end it all.

He hauled himself out of bed without the all-business
attitude that was his usual morning routine. After taking a
quick shower, he made a call to Joe to let him know he and
Eden would be down in the gym until it was time to take her
to the shoot. Joe had already made arrangements for the cars
that would take Eden and the rest of KGI wherever they
needed to go while they were in Paris.

"I'll send Skylar and Edge down to cover the entrance to
the gym," Joe said. "We can't be too careful and we definitely can't afford to let our guard down."

Swanny bristled at the notion that he wasn't adequate
protection for Eden, but he knew Joe was right. What
Swanny *couldn't* do was become involved with Eden to the
extent that he became distracted from their number one priority: keeping her safe at all times.

Her safety came first, above everything else. Even the
attraction between them. Nothing could compromise their
goal. This was a mission. A job. Their reputation, not to
mention Eden's life, was riding on this. He damn sure wasn't
going to be the reason they failed, and he definitely wouldn't
be the reason Eden got hurt or killed.

Yanked back by the reality of the situation, he went in
search of Eden, some of his earlier lethargy and the warm
haze that had surrounded him when he'd wakened in Eden's
arms replaced by a sense of purpose.

He stuck his head inside the bedroom door. "You ready?"

She came out of the bathroom finishing up the ponytail
she'd secured in her hair. She was wearing a tight-fitting halter
top and a pair of low-rise sweats that bared a few inches of her
abdomen. His body reacted instantly and he quickly reined
himself in, reminding himself of what was at stake here.

"I'm ready. You ready to get your ass kicked?" she asked
mischievously.

It was impossible to adopt a sterner, more businesslike
demeanor when she radiated warmth and sweetness.

"Pretty cocky for someone who hasn't sized up her opponent," he replied.

"Oh, I've sized him up," she said, letting her gaze wander over his body until he felt as though she'd stripped him of every piece of clothing with nothing more than her eyes.

"You're incorrigible," he said in mock exasperation. "Let's get moving. We're on a tight schedule."

She snapped to attention, giving him a soldier's salute. "Yes, sir. Lead the way."

Cheeky little wench. But he loved every bit of her sass. There wasn't a single thing about her he didn't like. She seemed impossibly perfect, and no one was *that* perfect. Everyone had flaws. So what were hers?

They took the stairs down to the second floor where the gym was located, and Edge and Skylar were already standing outside the door. Eden looked surprised to see them and maybe even a little chagrined. Swanny would have to have a talk with her later to remind her of everything he himself had discarded momentarily.

"It's clear," Edge said, his voice rumbling from his chest. "You and Eden will be the only ones inside unless someone else comes in after you. Sky and I will make sure that anyone who enters is on the level."

"Thanks," Swanny said. "We'll be an hour tops. Eden needs to eat before we head to her shoot."

"Just a vitamin shake for me," Eden interjected. "I'll need to shower again after my workout, so I can drink it on the way. But if y'all need to eat, go ahead and get room service ordered while I get all my stuff together. Hair and makeup will be done there, so I'll just wear sweats and a T-shirt to the studio. I won't take long to get ready at all. Just get my bag together and I'll be done."

Swanny shook his head but didn't comment. If it were up to him, Eden would be eating a hell of a lot more, but she knew what was best for her and it wasn't his place to interfere.

He used the room key to gain entry to the small fitness room and then grabbed towels for him and Eden.

She went straight to the stationary bike and immediately began a rigorous workout. He didn't join in because quite simply he enjoyed watching her work up a sweat. She was one of those women who didn't sweat. She glowed. A sheen of perspiration made her perfect skin glisten in the light and it made him want to do crazy things, like run his tongue over her flesh and suck up every drop of perspiration.

After fifteen minutes, she switched to a cardio stepping machine and put in another fifteen minutes there before moving to one of the benches to do abdominal crunches.

He was impressed by her stamina and the fact that she didn't look in the least winded. She was obviously in excellent shape. Her body certainly didn't tell a different story. She was toned. Hard in the places she needed to be hard and delectably soft in the places she should be.

Next, she went to the treadmill and threw a smile over her shoulder. "Give me fifteen minutes to cool down and then I'll throw you on your ass."

He grinned back and drawled out his response. "Keep dreaming, princess."

She rolled her eyes and refocused her attention on the treadmill, swinging her arms as she started out with a brisk pace only to back it down gradually until she finally turned it off and stepped down.

She made a show of cracking her knuckles and assuming the stance of a fighter as she circled him warily.

"I propose a wager," she said in a cocky voice. "I throw you and I get one request you have to fulfill."

"And if I throw you? Or you don't throw me?" he asked, lifting one eyebrow.

"Then you get one request of me that I have to fulfill."

His mind was immediately ablaze with all the possibilities. And judging by the calculating smug expression Eden was wearing, her thoughts likely mirrored his. Hell, in his way of thinking it didn't matter who won the bet because they very likely wanted the same things. But just in case, he wasn't about to let her win because it had suddenly become very important that he get what he wanted.

Her. In his bed. Him so deeply inside her that he felt swallowed up by her, heart and soul.

"Deal," he said in a challenging tone.

She was good. He had to hand it to her. Being up against a man twice her size would normally make it impossible for her to get the upper hand. But she was fast and she'd obviously been trained well.

He groaned when he saw that they had an audience outside the glass door leading into the fitness room. Joe and Nathan had joined Skylar and Edge, and they all were watching in obvious amusement.

His distraction almost cost him the bet. She went in for the kill and he stumbled but righted himself immediately and did a quick leg sweep while she was unbalanced and took her down, rolling himself underneath her so he took the brunt of the fall.

She stared down at him, panting softly, her hair in disarray. "I don't suppose since I'm on top and you're pinned down that I win?"

He laughed at the chagrin on her features. "Sorry, princess. I didn't want to hurt you so I took the brunt of the fall, but I definitely took you down. Victory is mine."

She pouted, which only made him laugh harder. She was so damn cute with that bottom lip stuck out and the puppy-dog look in her eyes.

"I hope your request will be at least as fun as mine was going to be," she grumbled.

"Oh, it'll be fun," he said softly. "I know I'll love every minute of it and I plan to make damn sure you enjoy it every bit as much."

Fire ignited in her eyes and for a moment he thought she was going to kiss him. But a quick glance in the direction of the doorway was enough to make her temper her reaction. She didn't want an audience any more than he did.

Instead she scrambled off him and then extended her hand down to help him up. He bounced upward and stood with his back to the door so Eden was shielded from view.

"You're good," he said sincerely. "But there's more I can

teach you. I can sharpen your skills for sure if you're interested."

She lifted both brows in an exaggerated expression of surprise. "Let's see. More one-on-one time with you and getting to wrestle you to the floor, no matter who causes the fall? Nah, I'm not interested at all."

"Incorrigible," he muttered, knowing he was using that word a lot when it came to describing her.

She flashed him a million-dollar smile. "So, um, when do I get to hear this request I'm supposed to fulfill?"

Making sure Eden was still hidden from view, he leaned in close so his lips brushed her temple and were close to one ear.

"Later," he murmured. "I'm thinking tonight, that is, if you aren't working too late and aren't exhausted afterward."

Her eyes gleamed and pink dusted her glossy cheeks, made so by the light perspiration of her workout.

"I can assure you I won't be so exhausted that I can't hold up my end of the bargain," she murmured.

CHAPTER 17

SWANNY'S respect for Eden's profession increased all the more as he stood back, watching the shoot for the commercials. It had to be exhausting for her but she worked steadily, took instructions from the director and responded perfectly, each and every time.

He didn't see what the problems were when the director yelled "Cut!" and then demanded a reshoot. She looked fucking perfect to him. But the director seemed like a real dick.

He'd thrown a fit when Eden had arrived accompanied by him and his team. He'd complained loudly about having so many people underfoot, and even though Eden's agent had arrived and pulled him to the side to explain the situation, it was obvious the director still wasn't happy.

He barked orders in a loud, obnoxious voice that made Swanny grit his teeth. The way the director talked to Eden made him want to plant his fist right in the fucker's face.

After several hours of shooting, the director called a halt and then barked for hair and makeup to go in and do touch-ups.

"She looks like shit," the director complained loudly. "I need perfect, goddamn it. Give me perfect."

"What a dick," Skylar muttered next to Swanny, perfectly echoing his own assessment of the asshole. "She looks amazing. The woman couldn't look like shit even on her worst day. What the hell does he want?"

Swanny growled his agreement, his stance rigid as he watched people rush in to touch up Eden's hair and makeup. How the hell did she work under these kinds of conditions? And further, how on earth could she keep that thousand-megawatt smile in place when some asshole was constantly criticizing her?

He knew this deal was important to Eden. She'd said it was the biggest break of her career. But hell, nothing seemed worth signing up for this kind of abuse.

Eden's agent came to stand beside Swanny and Skylar, watching the goings-on with a bored expression. As if nothing was out of the ordinary and this was just another day on the job.

"Is it always like this?" Swanny bit out.

Her agent looked surprised that Swanny was talking to him and then he blinked, clear confusion on his face.

"What do you mean?"

"Does she always have complete dickheads barking at her, telling her she looks like shit and complaining about every goddamn thing she does?"

Her agent actually took a step back, his expression wary, but then Swanny was sure he bristled with anger and his expression was probably *not* exactly pleasant.

"This director is one of the best in the business," her agent defended. "He may sound overly critical to you, but the end result certainly can't be argued with. He'll shoot until he's satisfied that it's not just good but perfect. This is too big an account to accept anything less than the best."

"He's still a dick," Skylar muttered.

Eden's agent laughed nervously. "I suppose it seems that way to someone not in the business, but Eden takes it with grace, just as she always does. She realizes the importance of having a flawless product and she'll work until she achieves that. It's what she does, and she's very good at what she does. It's why she landed this deal."

He glanced at Skylar and then Swanny before hesitantly extending his hand, first to Skylar. "I'm Nigel Blackstone, Eden's agent."

"I'm Skylar, part of Eden's security detail."

He was more reserved when he offered his hand to Swanny.

"I'm Swanny, also part of Eden's security detail," Swanny said shortly.

"Is she really in that much danger?" Nigel asked, concern flaring in his eyes. "I mean, I know the shooting turned into a random thing and they apprehended the man responsible. But is there something more I should know?"

"We're just taking extra precautions," Swanny said in a neutral tone. "With her name splashed all over the news, there's no guarantee some idiot won't get an idea in his head and take a shot at her. This shoot was important to her, and one she couldn't miss, so we've just tightened security around her for the time being."

He grudgingly gave Nigel credit. He did seem to be concerned for Eden and he hadn't uttered a single complaint about KGI's presence and had even intervened, explaining the situation to the director. Nigel had been firm and his tone had brooked no argument.

He might appear to be too slick and too polished, too damn pretty for a man, but he stood up for Eden and made it clear that the director could suck it if he didn't like the situation.

That, and his apparent concern for Eden's well-being, brought him up several notches in Swanny's esteem. He wouldn't say he *liked* the man. He was too smarmy for his tastes and he was a man Swanny could easily see being someone completely different under the facade. Unlike Eden, with whom what you saw was what you got. No fakeness. Just absolutely genuine to her bones.

"Of course Eden's safety has to take priority," Nigel rushed to say. "I hope I haven't given you any reason to doubt my commitment to her both professionally and personally. She's my biggest client, so whatever precautions need to be put into place, I'm on board completely."

"I'm sure Eden appreciates your support," Swanny murmured.

"She is my top priority," Nigel said, further pushing his point. "I'll handle any issues with the director. A lot of models would give their eyeteeth to land this account, but Aria isn't stupid. They want Eden because they want the best and if Lonnie—the director—causes any problems at all, I'll go over his head and either he'll be canned or he'll come around in short order.

"He's doing the shoot because like Eden, he's in the top of his field. But he *can* be replaced. Eden can't. That's not negotiable. I have an ironclad contract and if they did something stupid like try to get rid of Eden, they'd forfeit the payment already made to her. But between you and me, if anyone goes, it won't be Eden. Aria wants her too badly."

"If he keeps acting like a dick toward Eden, you'll have to find a replacement for him sooner rather than later," Swanny growled. "Because if he doesn't let up, I'll rearrange his face for him."

Nigel went pale, his nervous gaze flitting between Swanny and Skylar. "I'll have a talk with Lonnie as soon as we wrap up for the day. I also need to speak to Eden and, well, I suppose you as well since you're her security detail."

Swanny raised an eyebrow in silent question.

"As you likely know, there's a formal launch social at the end of the shoot. Everyone will be there," he said, emphasizing *everyone* though Swanny didn't have the first clue who *everyone* meant.

"Yes, she told me," Swanny replied. "She told me I'd need a tux so I'd blend in." He winced inwardly at sharing that particular piece of information.

Beside him Skylar snorted, and he shot her a glare to see her regarding him with a mischievous sparkle in her eyes.

"This I gotta see," she said, laughter in her voice.

"You have to dress for the occasion too," Swanny said dryly.

Skylar shrugged. "I'm perfectly capable of picking out a swanky dress with to-die-for shoes. Just because I spend most of my time in fatigues and face paint doesn't mean I don't know the art of socializing and 'fitting in.' "

Nigel cleared his throat, turning their attention back to him.

"In three nights' time, we'll be hosting a smaller soiree. Mostly just the Aria representatives and the crew working on the shoot. So I'd suggest buying that tux soon because you'll need it for both occasions."

Fuck me.

And goddamn Skylar was clearly enjoying his discomfort. He shot her another glare that would wither a normal person. But she only smiled more broadly and pressed her lips together in what looked like an effort not to laugh out loud. He was positive she was laughing her ass off on the inside.

"Guess I know what you'll be doing tomorrow," Skylar drawled.

"Yeah well, smart-ass. You have to come too. No way we're going to expose Eden any more than what is absolutely necessary."

"I'm looking forward to it," Skylar said, her expression sincere. "It's been a while since I got to dress up and actually use makeup that isn't camo paint. You'll have *two* hot chicks on your arms when we walk into the place."

He chuckled but didn't disagree with her statement. Skylar was indeed a very beautiful woman, in fatigues and combat gear or just regular street clothes. And she was a badass on top of that.

Something about kick-ass women like Skylar and Eden wearing spiked heels and cocktail dresses that conformed to their every curve just did it for him. Not that he looked at Skylar that way. Never had. She was his teammate, but more than that she was like a sister to him. They shared a strong bond, one he'd never compromise by making an impulsive pass at her.

Speaking of which, he now needed to go over the addition of the cocktail party with Nathan, Joe and Edge so they could prepare for it and ensure that Eden got there safely and that one of KGI would be in hearing distance of Eden at all times.

He'd speak to them after the shoot, but he planned to make

it brief because all he wanted to do was take Eden back to the hotel room, get her something to eat and then give her a full body massage, because she had to be uncomfortable as hell after so many hours of the same damn thing over and over.

The selfish part of him knew he just wanted her to himself. The previous night had been one of the best nights of his life and they'd never even taken their clothes off. But it hadn't kept him from imagining that perfect body scantily covered by that sexy silk negligee.

He had no doubt that despite their vow to take things slowly, she would be in his bed tonight. Even if they didn't make love, she would be sleeping with him. But he also knew that the combustible chemistry between them made having sex—soon— inevitable.

Action resumed and in this session, Eden had been transformed into a seductive siren wearing a bold red dress that would have men drooling at a hundred yards away.

They used props resembling iconic fixtures in Paris. She laughed, flirted and nearly drove him insane with the way she worked the camera. How could any red-blooded man possibly be within close proximity to her and not be out of his mind with lust? He knew he sure as hell wasn't immune.

A quick glance at the unattached males of his team told him they were doing their fair share of fantasizing as well.

He had to call back the growl that welled from his chest. He didn't want any man looking at her, seeing her as he saw her, even as he recognized the stupidity of such a thought. Eden was paid to look like every man's wet dream, and it was a look she'd certainly perfected.

It brought back all the insecurity he battled, and he questioned again why someone of Eden's caliber would even give him a second glance.

There were several outtakes of Eden standing with the Eiffel Tower behind her, looking sultry, her hair blowing from a fan that had been set up so it appeared she was outside on a perfect day, the silken mass lifted by the wind and scattering around her.

Even her lines drove Swanny to the brink of insanity. She

was in turns playful and full of mischief and then sultry and seductive, inviting her audience to try the product she was endorsing in a husky, throaty-sounding voice. Like she was speaking to a lover.

Like he wanted her to speak to *him*.

He checked his watch, impatient for today to be over with. He should be a gentleman and at least offer to take her out for dinner, but he couldn't imagine a more perfect evening than for the two of them to eat in the comfort of their suite. Spending time alone and allowing the evening to take them where it would. Or at least where he hoped.

But as far as he was concerned, Eden was in the driver's seat. He refused to put any pressure on her. Then again, he wasn't a flaming hypocrite either. He wanted her badly and from the signals she'd given him, it certainly seemed—however mind-boggling it was—that she wanted him just as badly.

His dick had grown another two inches just from the knowledge that this beautiful, fantastic woman wanted him. That kind of female attention would make any man's dick larger on principle. He hadn't considered he had an ego, but he actually found himself puffing out his chest, standing taller, and well, his dick was in perfect agreement with every other part of himself, so it certainly stood to reason that he'd add a few extra inches in his excitement and anticipation of having her laid out like a veritable feast on his bed.

"Earth to Swanny," Skylar said dryly. "They're wrapping up. We need to make sure the car is ready so we can hustle Eden out of the building with as little notice as possible."

Swanny shook himself from his thoughts and then nodded his agreement. "Have Joe and Nathan take the exit. Me, you and Edge will provide cover for Eden so we don't take any chances with her safety."

He'd run the soiree by his team when they returned to the hotel, but he planned to make it fast. It would give Eden long enough to shower and get into more comfortable clothing and then the evening would be theirs.

CHAPTER 18

SWANNY hustled Eden into her suite and gruffly told her to get dressed for bed, that he had to speak briefly with his team, but when he got back he'd order room service for the both of them. She gave him a look that told him with more than words she understood his plans for the evening and that even more, she was on board and had no objections. It was all he could do not to resort to a juvenile fist pump and make a first-class ass of himself.

He excused himself to go next door after making sure she locked and dead-bolted the door behind him so that even someone with a key card couldn't gain access to her room.

He knocked sharply on Edge and Skylar's door, knowing that Nathan and Joe would be inside waiting, as Swanny had instructed. He wasn't sure how he'd ended up being lead on this mission. Nathan and Joe were the actual team leaders, but Swanny had pretty much taken over anything to do with Eden's safety and to his team's credit, no one argued the point with him nor was there a pissing match over who was in charge.

Edge opened the door and gestured him in to where the others were gathered in the sitting area of the suite.

"So what's up, Swanny?" Joe queried. "Sky said there were some new developments but that you would explain when we all got back here."

Swanny shot Skylar a look of gratitude for allowing him to explain the situation even though she'd been party to the conversation between her, Swanny and Eden's agent.

"We all knew there was going to be a launch party when the shoot wrapped up and that we'd all need appropriate clothing to fit in, but Eden's agent said that in three nights' time there would be a soiree including everyone involved with the shoot. Eden will be expected to be there, so we will be too, which means that moves up our timeline to get appropriate evening wear so we don't embarrass Eden or stick out like sore thumbs."

The guys grimaced. Only Skylar smiled, seemingly happy with the opportunity to dress up for an evening.

"I thought we could break into teams so we get this done with as quickly as possible. Eden breaks for lunch tomorrow for an hour and a half. Skylar and I can accompany Eden to get us outfitted while the three of you remaining can go get fitted for a tux. I'm of the mind we can wear the same outfit for both nights. It's not about us anyway. It'll be Eden's night to shine and no one's going to give a fuck what we look like or who we are for that matter."

Nathan nodded his agreement, but Joe frowned. "Are you sure we should leave Eden with only two of us for protection?"

"Well, I'm thinking if we all go we'll draw a hell of a lot more attention than if just two of us go. Sky being a woman is helpful because for all anyone knows Eden is just shopping with a girlfriend. A girlfriend who happens to be able to kick the shit out of anyone who's a threat."

Skylar smiled warmly at Swanny, thanking him with her expression for his confidence in her.

"Okay, sounds like a plan, but we should at least go to the

same place," Nathan interjected. "Edge, Joe and I can hit the men's department while you go with Skylar and Eden to get what they need, but then you'll need to run by to get fitted yourself and all gussied up."

The amusement in Nathan's voice and the smirks on Edge's and Joe's faces just further irritated Swanny. As far as he was concerned, the conversation was over and he had a beautiful woman waiting for him in her room, and he'd promised her room service.

"I'll head back over. I'm supposed to order in room service for Eden. I don't think it's a good idea for her to be out and about. I'd rather keep her appearance here on the down low as much as possible."

There were several knowing grins that brought a growl to Swanny's throat, but he ignored them and headed for the doorway, anxious to get back to Eden.

He knocked on the door and waited, simmering with impatience. Then he heard the sound of the dead bolt being released and the door opened. He was greeted by the sight of Eden wearing sleepwear similar to the lingerie she'd worn the night before. All he could think about was sliding those thin strings down from her shoulders, just enough to bare her breasts.

She opened the door and he recovered enough to walk in and refasten the locks. She threw him a tempting, sultry look over her shoulder and headed for the sofa in the living area of the suite without waiting for him to follow. He quickly pulled himself together and hurried after her.

He disgusted himself. He'd never considered himself to be the caveman type, but Eden brought the primitive alpha male in him roaring to life. He wanted to haul her over his shoulder off to his cave and keep her tied to his bed until he fully sated himself, though he knew that would be impossible.

Because as soon as he'd had her once, had tasted her, touched her, kissed her, had been inside her luscious body, he'd never be fully sated. He'd want more and more until he ended up stifling her, and that was the last thing he wanted.

He didn't have a lot to offer a woman like her except to

spend every moment of making love to her an experience that would hopefully make up for his other faults. This was important. Too important to fuck up. He had to make sure that he took it nice and slow that first time, shower her with pleasure and show her that she was the only woman he even looked at.

She deserved to be on a pedestal, with him worshipping at her feet.

"You hungry?" he asked, finally finding his voice. He'd been standing there gawking at her like a moron. There was no telling what she was thinking. She was probably having doubts as to whether she truly wanted him as much as she'd stated. Not that he could blame her. But if she backed out now, he'd likely lose his mind.

"Yeah, I could eat," she said sweetly. "Want to split something? I put in a lot of hours today and didn't break for lunch, so I have some calories to spare."

"Tell me your pleasure and I'll make it happen."

Her cheeks pinkened and he found warmth chasing up his neck as well at the double entendre.

"They have a rotisserie chicken, a whole half, with vegetables and sides that sounds divine. If you don't mind sharing, I'll just eat part of the breast and the vegetables and let you have the baked potato and bread and the rest of the chicken, of course."

Since he was starving for her and food was the furthest thing from his mind, he simply nodded his agreement and then called in their order.

"While we wait, why don't you shower and get ready for bed too," she said softly. "That way when we're done, we can go to bed."

Her voice trailed off, but there was no doubt in his mind what she was saying between the lines. She wanted them to make love tonight. Thank God the hotel room came stocked with an intimate care package because he certainly hadn't packed condoms for a mission, for God's sake. Nor would he have ever dreamed that he and Eden would be making love. It still had the power to bring him to his knees.

He hurried through his shower, making certain he was clean and didn't smell like a goat. He winced as he dried off, seeing the scars that marked his body. The one on his face was bad enough, but the rest of him, mostly hidden by clothing, wasn't pretty in the least. He hoped to hell it didn't turn Eden off when it came down to actual intimacy.

He was already sporting an erection, so he pulled on jeans and a button-up shirt that he left open just to give her a chance to again view the sight of his scarred chest and midsection. She'd been sweetly accepting of them the night before, offering him reassurance, but he was just nervous enough to think she might change her tune once she got really up close and personal with him. After all, how would it feel against her skin when he was on top of her, the puckered ridges of the scars pressing into her flesh?

He was as nervous as a teenager taking his dream girl out on their first date. True, most of the pressure he felt was self-imposed, because Eden had been nothing but accepting of everything about him. But damn it, he wanted this to be perfect for her. For him, though he knew just being with her would be utter perfection in itself. It was her pleasure and happiness he had to focus on.

When he was done, he walked back into the suite just as a knock sounded at the door. Damn, but that was fast. Provided it was even the room service order. He damn sure didn't want it to be one of his teammates dropping in and infringing on his time with Eden.

Swanny motioned for Eden to stay right where she was, then went to the door, checking the peephole. It was indeed room service and he was paranoid enough not to just throw open the door without being prepared for the worst. Someone could easily pose as a hotel employee to gain access to Eden's room.

He reached for the Glock he'd set on the table just inside the door for occasions like this. For easy access if someone he didn't recognize or was wary of came knocking. He quickly stuck the gun into the waistband of his jeans and yanked out his button-up shirt so the tails hid the Glock from view. Wasn't the smartest thing in the world to shove a gun without a safety down his pants, aimed right at his dick, but improvisation was sometimes necessary.

He opened the door and motioned the attendant in with a gesture that clearly made the point to hurry. Swanny positioned himself between the young guy and Eden while the food was set up on the table. Eden was still lounging on the couch, wrapped in her throw as if she didn't want anyone but Swanny seeing her. That suited Swanny just fine.

Only when the attendant had left did she let the throw fall to the side, and Swanny nearly swallowed his tongue. If last night's lingerie outfit had him sporting a hard-on to beat all hard-ons, this one made it feel like he had a brick wedged between his legs. Thank God he'd worn jeans, though it was damn painful because if he'd donned boxers, his dick would be protruding out of the damn underwear in clear sight.

She stood, one of the strings sliding down her shoulder, giving him a tantalizing glimpse of one breast. Just a bit farther and her nipple would be exposed. As it was the material just barely hung over the tip, adding further to his already overactive imagination.

He pulled out one of the chairs for her and then took the seat catty-corner to her so he'd be closer to her and not across the table. He wanted to be as close to her as possible. The more time they spent in each other's company, the more the intimacy between them heightened, growing until it had taken on a life of its own.

Eden moaned when the dishes were uncovered. "This smells and looks divine. I have to admit, I'm starving."

Swanny frowned. "Do you often skip meals when you're doing a shoot?"

She shook her head. "Not always. Like tomorrow I'll have a lunch break, but sometimes, especially if we have to do a lot of retakes, we'll work through lunch and sometimes even dinner. As it gets closer to finish we usually work long hours to meet our deadline."

"Speaking of your lunch break tomorrow, Skylar and I plan to take you to buy whatever dress you want for the soiree planned in three nights, and the rest of the team is going to get outfitted as well so we blend in as much as possible. But I'll take you and Sky to get what y'all need and then I'll swing by the men's department to be fitted for a tux. I figured it wouldn't matter if we wore the same things to both events."

Eden smiled, her eyes sparkling. "That sounds like fun. I'll enjoy watching you be fitted for a tux. I bet you look absolutely irresistible all dressed up."

He grunted his reply. He still wasn't on board with all this, but he wouldn't ruin either night for Eden. For her, he'd do damn near anything.

She cut delicately into the roasted chicken and placed a tiny piece on her plate, leaving the rest for him. Then she selected some of the steamed vegetables, but as she'd promised, she left the baked potato and other sides for him.

He felt selfish, even knowing that she was extremely careful with her diet, but he hated eating so much in front of her, and her seeing it knowing she couldn't have it.

He wolfed down his portion, partly because he didn't want to be sitting there savoring a meal in front of her, but he was also impatient to get to the rest of the evening. He just hoped to hell he'd read the signals she was sending correctly and that he wasn't way off base by assuming tonight would be the night they took their relationship a step further. A huge step. Because for him, sex just wasn't casual unless he determined that going in and just wanted or needed a night to blow off some steam and have a one-night stand.

With Eden, it was a whole different ball game. She was a game changer of everything he'd experienced with women up to now. He wanted her desperately, but he wasn't willing to let his desire and impatience ruin something as beautiful as what was growing between them.

For all he knew she might only want a one-night stand and then she'd back off or move on. He was making a lot of assumptions, assumptions he had no right making. He was setting himself up for one hell of a fall if he allowed his emotions to overtake reason and read more into the situation than what it was in reality.

"Swanny?"

Eden's soft calling of his name jerked him from his thoughts, something that occurred with frequency when he was in her presence. In his job, absolute concentration was a must. Distractions could get him or one of his teammates killed, and so he was used to having absolute focus. But with Eden? He found himself drifting into internal conversations with himself. Pondering, wondering, self-conscious and a host of other things that crowded his mind when he was with her.

He glanced up to see that she'd set her fork aside and finished the small portion of food she'd allowed herself.

"Are you ready for bed or did you want to stay up a bit longer?" she asked.

Though the words were said steadily enough, he was now familiar enough with Eden to see behind the face she presented and the fact that her words were casual, measured even.

She was nervous and hesitant, almost as if she were worried that he wasn't on board for taking that huge step in their budding relationship.

"I vote bed," he said, his voice husky.

She smiled, but her lips quivered slightly. And then she rose from the table, once again giving him an eyeful of the sexy outfit she wore. He nearly cursed because his dick hardened even more and he'd already sported an uncomfortable-as-hell erection through the entire dinner. Seeing her right there in front of him, her nightwear leaving little to the imagination, turned his dick to stone, pressed uncomfortably against the confines of his jeans.

He got up and held out his hand to her, gauging her mood. She slipped her much smaller hand into his and he gave it a light squeeze as they headed toward the bedroom. It brought an instant smile to her face and lessened some of the tension he could feel radiating from her.

"I'll climb into bed if you want to get undressed," she said, heading toward the king-size bed in the center of the room.

It was telling that she hadn't told him to get changed but

rather *undressed*. The two had very different meanings. And suddenly he was nervous because he would be undressing in front of her, his faults and scars in plain sight once again.

He hesitated, uncertainty gripping him. Eden gave him a look of such caring and tenderness that he immediately felt shame for doubting her reaction even for a moment.

"I want to see you," she said. "All of you. There's nothing about you that will remotely turn me off, Swanny. I know words mean little, but I want to show you. I need to show you that I'm sincere."

Her words gave him the courage to undress, pulling his jeans over his straining erection, wincing at the discomfort. He gave an audible sigh of relief when his dick burst free from its restraints. But then he caught the look on Eden's face as she stared unabashedly at his cock.

Her cheeks had paled and she looked decidedly uncertain and . . . afraid.

She pulled aside the covers on his side of the bed, inviting him to crawl into bed with her.

"There's something I need to tell you," she said in a low voice. "I've argued with myself over whether to even tell you, and aside from that I didn't want it to change how you felt about me or your desire to make love to me. But you need to know. You deserve to know so that you can back out if I'm no longer someone you want. And I'll understand. I promise. I'm not going to throw some tantrum and make an ass of myself. I'd die before guilting you into something you didn't want."

Unease gripped him around his balls, squeezing to the point of pain. She made it sound as though she were a wanted criminal or had done something unforgivable, and Swanny couldn't imagine either scenario in the least.

He slid into bed next to her and automatically reached for her to try to soothe the unease he could see in her eyes. She didn't nestle into his side as he'd intended and instead moved closer but kept her head up so she could look him in the eyes.

"Eden, you can tell me anything," he said gently. "I can

guarantee whatever it is you're stressing about isn't going to change a damn thing about the way I feel about you, and it damn sure won't stop me from wanting you. I'm so hard right now that if you so much as touched me I think I'd come."

She smiled, some of the tension escaping her features.

"The other concern was whether you'd even believe me," she said in a quiet tone. "Because with the way I've been with you, so forward and bold, I can't imagine you would even believe what I'm about to tell you."

Now he was truly curious. Not worried because he couldn't imagine anything she could tell him that would put him off. Her past lovers didn't matter. What mattered was here and now and that she was going to be his.

"Just tell me, honey," he encouraged. "You're making yourself crazy over nothing I'm sure."

She sucked in a deep breath, seemingly gathering her courage, and then exhaled in a long sigh.

"I've never been with a man," she admitted in a faltering tone. "You'd be the first. I want *you* to be the first."

He stared at her, stunned, in complete disbelief. Of anything he thought she would tell him, this was the very last thing he would have considered. There were so many what-the-fuck thoughts barreling through his mind that he was utterly speechless.

Eden was a virgin? It boggled his mind. The world's most beautiful woman had *never* been with a man, and furthermore she wanted *him* to be her first? It humbled him and scared the shit out of him all at the same time.

What was he supposed to say to something like that? He didn't feel worthy. Her first time should be special, with a man who didn't look like he did. Someone more on her level. He suddenly felt clumsy and inept. He in no way underestimated the magnitude of the gift she was offering. But damn it, her first time should be perfect and he was suddenly seized by fear that he'd royally botch the entire thing up.

"Swanny?"

Her voice sounded fearful and she'd pulled the covers

farther up until they were tucked under her chin. She sounded as uncertain as he felt, and he cursed the fact that he was making a royal muck of everything.

"I don't know what to say," he finally managed to get out. "I had no idea, Eden. And the thought that you want me to be your first . . . I can't even fathom the magnitude of such a precious gift. Why me? You have to have had better opportunities—options. What could I possibly have to offer you? I feel like we're caught up in a modern Beauty and the Beast situation. I'm not handsome. Most would consider me ugly. I'm scarred not just on my face but on my entire body. How could you want someone like me?"

Her expression softened and her eyes gentled, and the look she gave him was so achingly sweet that it made his entire chest tighten with emotion.

She leaned down, brushing her lips over his, and then as she'd done once before, she slid her mouth over the length of his scar, pressing tender tiny kisses along every pucker and ridge.

"You're beautiful to *me*," she whispered. "I don't care what others think. They're idiots for not seeing beyond your scars to the heart of you. The person I know you are. As to how I could want someone like you, I can't give you a cut-and-dried explanation. It's just there. Something about you stirs me in a way no other man has ever been able to move me. I've waited because it never felt right before, and my virginity is something I considered precious, not to be given to just anyone. But it feels right with you. Perfect. I know without any doubts that I want you to be my first lover. But if it doesn't feel right to *you*, then I don't want it to happen. I don't want to pressure you into something you don't want."

"I want you more than I ever imagined wanting another woman," he admitted. "I'm blown away by the way you see me, that you still want me even seeing what I look like. I won't lie. I'm petrified because I want your first time to be something beautiful and precious, and I worry that I won't be able to give you what you deserve."

She smiled again, her hair falling like a curtain over her

shoulder and brushing over his chest. "And here I am worried that with my inexperience, I won't be able to satisfy you or that I'll fail miserably. I vote we do this together and to hell with expectations or fears. Let's just let it happen and we'll figure it out as we go."

He leaned up, cupping her cheek, and then pressed his lips to hers, sliding his tongue inside her mouth, tasting and savoring the sensation, the intimacy between them before they'd even taken that final step in their budding relationship.

"I think that's a perfect idea," he said gruffly.

CHAPTER 19

EDEN relaxed, letting go of her earlier bout of nerves. She had argued endlessly with herself whether to tell Swanny she was a virgin, but in the end he deserved to know. And, well, she wanted the experience to be wonderful, what she'd been dreaming of, and now that he knew, she knew he would take extra care with her and make it as special as she wanted it to be.

When she'd first told him and he'd looked astonished and baffled and speechless, for a while she thought she'd made a mistake and that he would back out. But then she realized that he was simply overwhelmed and humbled by the fact that she wanted him to be her first.

Her heart had simply melted at his reaction. He didn't feel as if he were good enough for her, and he was genuinely baffled by the idea that she wanted him when, in his words, she could have any man she wanted.

But therein was the issue. She hadn't wanted a man or felt right making love with another man. Not until Swanny. And as she'd tried to explain, she couldn't say why it was him. Just that for her, he was the one. Now, looking back, she was so glad she had waited. That she'd been discerning and holding out for just the right man, because she knew to her bones that Swanny was the right man to take this enormous leap with. He might have doubts as to why she wanted him, but she had none whatsoever, and if it was the last thing she did, she was going to make him see himself the way she saw him. Strong. Caring. Loyal. Tender. So very loving and humble. Her heart turned over just thinking of him being her first.

"Shall I undress or do you want to do it?" she asked him shyly.

He put his hand on her arm. "I'm going to undress you. I want to make this perfect for you, so I'm going to take this nice and slow and if there's ever a point where you want me to stop, just say the word and it stops then. I want you to relax and let me love you. We have all night and I plan to make the most of it."

She relaxed and then lay back on the pillow as he gently pulled the covers down to their feet, out of the way. She stared at his body, fascinated by the lean muscled contours of his body. Scars crisscrossed his chest and abdomen and even his thighs and upper arms. It broke her heart that this man had been subjected to unspeakable torture, but she also knew he was a survivor and that whatever hell he'd gone through hadn't broken him. Not many men could survive what he had and retain their sanity, and yet he continued to put himself on the line, where something just like what had happened before could happen again. Her admiration for him grew with every passing second.

He lifted his body over hers, his erection brushing against her belly where her top had risen to bare her abdomen. It was an electric shock and she looked down, wanting to see him intimately. Her eyes widened as they had the first time she'd seen his erection because it seemed enormous. She wondered if he'd even fit, especially since she was a virgin.

But she forced those fears out of her mind as he lowered his body carefully to hers until they were flush against each other. He kissed her lingeringly, so sweet and gentle her heart swelled and for some insane reason, tears burned her eyelids. The moment was just perfect. It seemed she'd been waiting for this—for Swanny—her entire life. And now it was here. She wanted him so very much that emotion overwhelmed her, consumed her until she was nearly bursting with it.

Breathing hard, he lifted his head and propped his weight on one forearm and reached to caress her face with his free hand.

"I'm going to be very gentle with you, Eden. I don't want you to be afraid. The very last thing I ever want to do is hurt you. I'll go as slow as you want. I want to know what pleases you, what feels good to you and what doesn't so I make sure I don't do it again. Your pleasure is my one and only priority."

"With every word you make me want you even more, and I do want you, Swanny. So very much. I ache," she whispered.

He groaned. "God, I want you too, Eden. So damn much I hurt with it."

"Then make us both feel good. I trust you."

He stopped, holding his head just above her, his eyes burning into hers with blazing intensity. She could see emotion glimmering in the fire, almost as if he couldn't quite get the words out he wanted to say.

When he finally did speak, his tone was husky and laced with awe.

"That you trust me with this—you—honey, I don't have words. You can't possibly understand what this means. That you waited. For me. And that it's me you want to make love to you. You undo me, Eden. There's never been anyone for me like you. No one who ever bothered to look beyond the scars and see the heart of me."

She stroked her palm over the scar-lined cheek, caressing and petting lightly. "They're part of you. Of who you are and where you've been. You're a hero. Willing to put your life on the line when so many others wouldn't. I'm so sorry you paid the ultimate price and for the pain the memories must still cause you. But I'm not sorry I met you. I'm not sorry you're here right now and that we're making love together."

He claimed her mouth again, moving his big body over hers. The silk nightwear was hardly a barrier to the hardness of his body. She could feel his muscles, the strength in this big man. Knew he could so easily hurt her but also that he never would and that she'd never be safer than she would with him. He'd never allow anyone to hurt her physically or emotionally.

The kiss deepened. She tasted him. Savored the intimacy of their kiss, her body coming to life underneath his. Her breasts swelled, her nipples hardening into tight points, and between her legs a pulse beat, making her restless and edgy.

Slowly and reverently, he slid the straps of her top down her arms, pausing just before her breasts were bared, almost as if he were savoring and anticipating the first glimpse of her unclothed.

She shifted restlessly, eager to be skin to skin with him, to feel his warmth and strength with no barriers between them. He kissed the hollow of her neck and then trailed his tongue downward to where he met with the barrier of her top and then slowly slid it downward, baring her breasts to his touch and gaze.

When his mouth tenderly closed around her nipple, she let out a low moan as pleasure cascaded through her body. Her muscles clenched and her clit tingled with anticipation. The pressure between her legs was making her edgy and needy.

She wanted to touch him and so she ran her hands over his shoulders and then thrust her fingers into his hair, telling him without words the pleasure he was giving her.

He pushed the top farther down and then lifted her hips so he could pull it the rest of the way down. He moved down her body, tossing aside the top, and then he hooked his fingers into her lacy shorts and slowly slid them down her legs until she was completely naked.

For a long moment he simply knelt there and stared, his heated gaze sweeping from head to toe, his obvious desire and appreciation for her body gleaming in his eyes.

"You're so beautiful," he whispered. "I never dreamed of having a woman like you, that you would want me. I'm overcome, Eden. I don't even know what to say. Can't possibly tell you in words what I feel right now."

"Then show me," she whispered back. "Love me, Swanny. Show me how beautiful it will be between us."

He began at her feet, kissing and tonguing every inch of flesh on his way up her body. He lavished attention over every part until she was mindless with desire. He gently parted her thighs, baring her vagina to his sight and touch.

He ran his fingers lightly through the wispy tuft of hair over her mound and then went lower, carefully parting her labia. He touched her clit, just a soft caress, but it was like a surge of lightning that electrified her entire body. She gasped and arched upward, seeking more, wanting more.

He pressed his thumb over her clit and stroked lightly until she was breathless and on edge. His fingers circled her opening, tenderly exploring the small piece of skin that signaled her virginity.

Then he lowered his head and nuzzled into her folds, replacing his fingers with his mouth and tongue. He licked and sucked lightly at her clit, seemingly knowing just the right amount of pressure to exert, expertly navigating the line between pleasure and pain.

He placed his open mouth over her opening and gently slid his tongue inside her, tasting her from the inside out.

"So sweet," he murmured. "So very sweet. Like honey dipped in sunshine."

His words and tongue were playing equal havoc with her emotions. She was so on edge that she knew she wouldn't last long and she didn't want to come without him inside her. She wanted this first time to be with him, inside her, together. Them coming together and experiencing it together.

She saw him reach for the box on the nightstand and for a moment didn't realize what it was until he tore it open and a condom fell out. She put a hand to his arm to stop him and he looked up, his gaze responding to her unspoken question.

"Do we have to use one?" she asked. "I mean, is it safe not to? Obviously I've never been with anyone, but I don't want my first time to be with a condom. I want to feel *you*. Not latex. Are you safe, and do you mind not using one?"

Swanny groaned. "God no, I don't want one. I was protecting

you, Eden. I'll always protect you. But to answer your question, yes, I'm safe. It's been a while for me and I've never not used a condom. And we have regular physicals and checkups on the job, so I know I'm clean. But what about pregnancy, honey? I'd never do anything to compromise your career."

Her cheeks heated. "I'm on birth control. I get a shot every three months. Which sounds silly given that I've never even had sex, but they regulate my periods and make them more bearable. After one shoot when I was on my period and was just miserable the whole time, my agent urged me to go to the doctor to see if there was something they could do so that my periods wouldn't interfere with my job. They suggested birth control and they gave me pain medicine for when it gets really bad. But the birth control has really helped on its own."

"If you're sure, then," Swanny said huskily. "There's nothing more I want than to have you skin to skin, to feel you surrounding me all soft and silky."

She smiled. "That's settled, then. Put them away and let's get back to the good part."

He laughed and tossed the box to the side and then lowered his head once more to her most intimate flesh and began working her up again, sucking, licking, kissing until she was writhing beneath him.

He slid up her body, fitting his to hers, but he made no effort to enter her yet. He caressed and sucked at her nipples, alternating between them until they were rigid peaks, straining upward. Then he kissed a path to her neck and nibbled just beneath her ear at the soft column of her neck.

When he reached her mouth he kissed her long and breathless, and then she felt him reach between them, positioning himself at the mouth of her opening. Her eyes widened at the feel of just the head stretching her opening.

"Relax, honey," Swanny said gently. "I'm going to take it nice and easy. If you need me to stop at any time, just tell me. I can't promise not to hurt you. I'm a big guy and this is your first time, but I'm damn sure going to try to make it as easy on you as possible."

Her heart softened and her body relaxed, going pliant

beneath his. "I know you will, Swanny. I trust you. I want this to be perfect for both of us. Not just me."

"There is no way my being with you can be anything but perfect," Swanny said in a fervent tone.

He slid his fingers over her clit, caressing and touching until she went wetter, and then he gently began to push forward, stretching her opening to his entry. He removed his hand and braced himself on his forearms on either side of her shoulders, staring down at her as he continued his slow entry.

She winced when she felt a slight tearing sensation and despite her best effort to hold them back, tears burned her eyelids. Swanny's eyes glowed with tenderness and he reached up to thumb away the tear that had escaped and slid down her cheek.

"I'm so sorry, honey," he said, regret reflected in his features. "Do you need me to stop?"

"No, it's okay," she said hastily, worried he'd call it all off. "I'll be okay. It's just a little uncomfortable. Please don't stop."

"I won't. I'm just going to go slow and give you time to adjust to having me inside you. The pain won't last long and then I'll make you feel nothing but pleasure. I swear it."

He moved forward just a bit and she flinched but held tightly to his shoulders. He stopped immediately and leaned down to kiss her.

"I'm going to stay right where I am for a bit. Let you adjust. You tell me when you're ready for me to go further, okay?"

She nodded and then focused on relaxing around him, savoring the sensation of having him inside her, albeit not deeply. Not yet. And she wanted that. Wanted him as deep as he could possibly be so they were one person. Connected in the most intimate way two people could be connected.

She shifted experimentally, testing the feel of him barely inside her. Some of the stinging pain had abated, leaving her with a restless, unfulfilled feeling.

Swanny groaned. "You're killing me, Eden. There's only so much restraint I can muster."

She smiled and slid her hands over his broad shoulders. "It's okay now. It doesn't hurt as much."

He propped himself up farther so he could see her face, gauging her reaction, and then he pressed forward, slowly and so very gently. She tensed, expecting more pain but other than the discomfort of stretching to accommodate him, the pain had diminished to a dull ache.

"Okay?" Swanny whispered.

God, but she loved how tender and caring he was being. She'd imagined her first time a lot over the years, but this far surpassed her wildest fantasies. It was beautiful. There was a poignancy that made her ache. Emotion swelled and knotted in her chest and throat. All she could muster was a reassuring smile and a nod to let him know she was fine.

He withdrew just a little and then pushed forward, a little more forcefully than he had before. She gasped, not in pain, but in wonder as pain and discomfort turned to intense pleasure.

"Just a little farther, honey. One more time and I'll be there. Tell me if this hurts you."

It shocked her that he wasn't already all the way in. It certainly felt like she had a lot of him inside her. But then she'd seen his size, had been nervous that he'd even fit especially since it was her first time, but her vagina was slick with her desire and gripped him tightly, inviting him deeper.

Again he withdrew, not all the way. He was still inside her and then he pushed harder and she felt his groin meet hers. Her eyes widened in wonder at the sensations bombarding her. She felt completely full, stretched tightly around him like a closed fist.

His face was taut, his features strained. He briefly closed his eyes and his breaths were short and raspy. She realized just what his restraint was costing him, and it endeared him to her all the more that he'd taken such care to make it as painless as possible for her.

When he reopened his eyes, they glittered with the same desperate need she felt. Her hips moved, unconsciously tilting upward to take him deeper, if such a thing were possible.

"I'm okay, Swanny," she said softly. "You feel so good inside me. I want this to be good for you."

He caressed her cheek with one hand and then fused their

mouths together as his hips rose and then he thrust back into her. His body covered her protectively and she wrapped her legs around his thighs, anchoring him to her, letting him know she was with him all the way.

She wrapped her arms more firmly around his shoulders, pulling him down even more to meet her mouth. Their tongues tangled and he mimicked the movements of his cock, thrusting his tongue in the same manner.

His breaths came quick and hot, mingling with her own. She inhaled deeply through her nose, trying to catch up as her body tightened and began the upward climb to the ultimate release.

"How close are you?" Swanny rasped out. "I want you with me, honey. I'm not leaving you behind. You come first. Always. Tell me what you need to get there and I'll make it happen."

She was so caught up in the overwhelming bombardment of sensation and feeling that it took a moment for his question to register.

"Close," she gasped out. "It feels close. I'm not sure what's happening, but it feels like I'm about to burst into a million pieces."

He smiled tenderly down at her, pushing inward with his hips again, and then slid out in a long, slow pull that had her vaginal walls clenching around him, resisting his withdrawal.

"That's what a good orgasm does," he said. "Just let go, honey. Let it happen. I'll be with you every step of the way."

He bent his neck so he could reach her breasts and sucked one nipple into his mouth as he surged forward again, burying himself to the hilt.

"You like that," he murmured.

Since she'd gone even wetter around his erection, he was stating the obvious.

She was nearly to the point of desperation. She was on edge, the tension growing until it was unbearable. He began to thrust harder, forgoing his earlier tenderness. He was careful to maintain control and he didn't thrust so hard that it hurt her at all, but he set a more rapid pace, plunging, retreating, then thrusting forward again until she was panting and writhing beneath him like a wild thing.

Her eyes flew open as the world seemed to shatter around her. The tension snapped, releasing the most intense pleasure she'd ever experienced in her life. She curled her fingers into his shoulders, holding on to him. Her anchor in the violent storm of her orgasm.

The room blurred around her. His features blurred but she focused on his eyes, drawing from the mirroring pleasure in his gaze. She bucked beneath him, arching, meeting his thrusts and using her legs to pull him into her over and over.

And then he let out a huge groan and his entire body tensed. He swelled within her, growing even more turgid, larger, and his thrusts became quicker, deeper.

To her utter amazement, as soon as she came down from the mind-blowing orgasm, his frenzied thrusts pushed her over the edge again. This time it was a quick buildup, no long leisurely climb to the top. It was explosive, not as lingering as the first, and her body quaked as a second orgasm flashed through her and he poured himself into her.

The heat of his semen flooded her, making the aftermath of her orgasm last even longer. He thrust with more ease as his seed eased his passage so he could easily slide to the hilt.

He let out a long groan and then finally collapsed over her, his warmth invading her whole body. She wrapped her arms around his back and shoulders and she caressed softly, enjoying having his weight covering her. She felt safe, like nothing in the world could hurt her at this moment.

She trailed her hands as low down his spine as she could reach and then traveled upward again, stroking and letting him know without words how she felt.

Finally he lifted himself off her and she immediately regretted the loss of his weight and heat. He propped himself up on his forearms, still buried inside her, and gazed down at her with such tenderness that she swallowed back the knot forming in her throat.

"Are you okay? Was I too rough?" he asked in concern.

She smiled and reached up to caress his face, paying special

attention to his scar. "It was wonderful, Swanny. I never imagined my first time would be this perfect. And maybe that's why
I held back. Something inside me told me that none of the other
men would give me what you've given me."

"It's you who have given me something more precious than
anything I've ever received," he said, sincerity shining in his
eyes. "You can't possibly know what it means to me that you
trusted me to be your first. I wanted it to be special for you. For
us both. In a lot of ways this feels like my first time as well. I've
never made love to a woman without a condom, and I've damn
sure never felt this way about any woman I've been with."

"I'm glad," she said, huskiness lacing her voice. "And it
was perfect, Swanny. You made it so special. I'll never forget
my first time for sure. You were so gentle and patient. *You*
were perfect."

Fire blazed in his eyes and he reached down to claim her
mouth. He kissed her lingeringly, sweetly and so very
reverently.

"I'm going to pull out now, honey," he said gently. "It may
hurt you a little but I'll go as slow and as easy as possible. I
need to clean us both up. I think I came a gallon."

She laughed and then braced her hands on his shoulders
as he began withdrawing inch by precious inch. As he'd pre-
dicted, she winced when he finally pulled free, but at the
same time she felt like she'd lost that connection with him
that she so savored.

He rolled to the side and got off the bed. He leaned down
to kiss her again. "I'll be right back. Don't move. I'm going
to try not to mess up the sheets any more if possible so we
aren't sleeping with a wet spot."

Then he disappeared into the bathroom and brought back a
warm cloth and carefully cleaned her sensitive areas before
wiping down his own groin and still semierect penis.

He checked the sheets, lifting her hips to feel beneath her,
and then frowned. "It's a little damp and I don't want you
sleeping on a sticky mess, nor do I want to have housekeep-
ing in at this time of night and put a damper on the mood, so

I can put a towel down over the spot and we can sleep like that."

"A towel is fine," she said, smiling at him. "I honestly just want to go to bed and have you hold me."

"That sounds wonderful to me too, but first I'm going to draw you a nice hot bath and let you soak for a bit. You're going to be sore and I don't want it to interfere with your shoot tomorrow. So give me a bit to draw your water and then I'll let you soak in the tub for a while and then we'll go to bed."

"That sounds heavenly," Eden replied, touched by the depth of his caring and the fact that he saw to her every need.

A little while later he came back into the bedroom and lifted her into his arms, cradling her against his chest. It was a novel experience to have a man pick her up and carry her anywhere. She was tall and though she didn't weigh much, she was still tall enough that a normal man wouldn't have been able to carry her.

But Swanny was hardly "normal." Could never be considered average. He was muscled, absolutely fit and so very strong. He made her feel cherished in a way she'd never dreamed of being cherished. She sighed as he lowered her into the bathtub and then sat on the closed toilet, watching as she relaxed into the water.

"There was a little blood on the sheets too," Swanny said quietly. "And I cleaned some off you and me. I hate the idea of having hurt you. I would have done anything to spare you that pain."

"You didn't hurt me," she denied. "It was a little uncomfortable at first, but as big as you are I think I would have felt that slight discomfort even if I hadn't been a virgin. You did everything right. Perfect. You were so slow and patient and so very gentle. I couldn't have possibly asked for a better first time. I mean that truly."

"I'm glad," he said gruffly. "I'm still just blown away by it all. It will take me a long time to come to terms with the gift you gave me, that you trusted and wanted me. It's hard to take it all in."

She slid deeper into the water, letting it lap to her neck, and sighed in pleasure at the hot water she soaked in. He was right. She was tender in her vaginal area, but the hot water was doing wonders to alleviate that discomfort.

"One day you'll see yourself the way I see you, Swanny. If it's the last thing I do, you'll see a loyal, fierce warrior, a survivor, not to mention a gentle man with a heart of gold and not an ounce of meanness in his body. At least not toward me. I know enough about your job to know you handle some sticky, hard situations, but with me? You're nothing like you present to the world. I see the real you, the man behind the scars, and I like what I see a lot."

"You have to stop," he said gruffly. "Because I'm an inch from hauling you back into the bedroom and making love to you all over again, and that's not what you need right now. You need time to heal and to feel better."

"But you can still take me to bed and hold me," she said wistfully. "I'm done soaking. What I really want are your arms around me and for me to sleep against your body."

"Now that I can do," he said as he moved forward to help her from the tub.

He took out one of the huge fluffy hotel towels and wrapped it around her body, wiping every inch of moisture from her skin until her flesh was pink and glowing. Then he dried the small amount of water that had gotten her hair wet and then guided her back into the bedroom, where he gestured for her to climb into bed.

As soon as she was settled, he slid in next to her and she immediately burrowed into his chest, seeking his warmth. She twined her legs with his and wrapped one arm around his waist, anchoring him to her.

He kissed her forehead and stroked away the strands of hair in her face.

"Good night, honey. Sleep well and dream of me."

CHAPTER 20

SWANNY awoke slowly, gradually climbing from the deep sleep he'd fallen into once Eden had tucked herself into his body. He was usually a morning person and never wasted time lying in bed once he awakened. At home or even on a mission there was always too much to do just to lie around and be lazy, but this morning?

He was sated and utterly content with Eden sleeping nestled in the crook of his arm, her head pillowed on his shoulder. He could spend all day just lying with her, holding her. He knew she needed time to heal before they made love again, but he was just as content to enjoy the intimacy that cloaked them.

He listened to her soft breathing and ran his fingers lightly through her blond hair, just wanting to touch her in some way. He checked the bedside clock and nearly groaned. He'd have to get her up in just a few minutes so she'd have plenty of time to get ready for her shoot. And all he wanted was to continue holding her in his arms, allowing the memory of their love-making to flash in his mind over and over.

Never had he experienced such a strong connection to

another woman. Or even another person. His team and KGI were his family now, but nothing compared to the way Eden made him feel. Like he mattered. That he wasn't just a man on a standard mission, in and out without any kind of emotional bond. He wasn't just a hired hand, he was a part of a team, but while he had a strong bond with his teammates, what was between him and Eden far surpassed what he felt for KGI—his family.

KGI—and his team—would always have his loyalty, and until now he would have said that nothing would ever be stronger than his commitment to his team. But Eden had changed all of that for him. He supposed this was what had happened to Rio and Steele, the leaders of the other two teams. They'd given KGI their absolute loyalty and the team came first, but after meeting their women, now their wives, he could understand why KGI now came second to their own families and to the women they loved.

It had happened to the Kelly brothers as well. Donovan had just met and married his wife and he was taking a more administrative role, as were Sam and Garrett since they had new babies. More and more the three brothers who'd founded KGI were giving more responsibility to the teams led by Rio, Steele, and then Nathan and Joe, the two men Swanny served under with Skylar and Edge.

And he did consider them family. They'd taken him in and offered him acceptance. He'd never forget that or take it for granted, just what all they'd done for him. They'd given him purpose again when he was at loose ends and had no direction after coming off that last tour that took him out of active duty.

But now he had Eden, and he wasn't at all sure where this would take them, but he knew without a doubt that she was a complete game changer for him. Already his priorities were shifting. He'd basically taken over her protection, although Nathan and Joe were technically in charge. But they seemed to realize that there was something between him and Eden, and they'd let him take the lead without argument—and thank God for that, because for the first time ever he would have openly defied their command when it came to Eden. He wanted this done his way. He wanted to be the one in charge of Eden's safety, and it wasn't that he didn't trust his team, but they didn't have the personal stake in this job that Swanny had. He wanted to be the one who shielded her, kept her safe. With him at all times. Such possessiveness was completely alien to him.

It wasn't that he was ever an asshole to the women he'd been with, but neither had he felt an overwhelming sense of possessiveness. The urge to keep her with him at all times. Not to let her go.

It hit him with startling clarity that in his mind she was his. She belonged to him. Not that a woman was some thing or chattel to "own," but his reaction to her was staggering. He also realized that this shoot was only a few days, and that might be all the time he had with her.

Panic surged because he hadn't given thought to the longevity of their relationship, and it occurred to him now that he wanted more. He didn't want to be a fling, her first lover, and then have her move on to someone else.

Their careers would take them to opposite corners of the world and he had no idea how they could possibly work that out. But damn it, there had to be a way. He didn't want to let her go.

If this was what being in love was all about, then he knew he'd already fallen hard for her. But the big question mark was how did she feel about *him*? He knew she cared for him. Hell, she'd gone out of her way to assure him that his scars and appearance didn't bother her. And she'd wanted him to be her first lover, so that had to mean *something*. But what?

All he knew was that he was already dreading the end of the shoot when she no longer needed KGI's services. Although the threat to her, according to her father, was still out there, so if that threat wasn't eliminated by the time the shoot was over, he might well want to keep them on.

He wanted any threat to her to be eliminated no matter how it was done. He wanted nothing to ever touch her or hurt her, but at the same time, as soon as the threat was eliminated she'd no longer need him or KGI, and he wasn't looking forward to the end of what they were sharing.

Eden stirred softly beside him, and he forwent his thoughts and turned to face her. She smiled sleepily up at him.

"Good morning," she said sweetly.

"Morning, honey. How do you feel this morning?"

Her cheeks pinkened as color rose up her neck and into her face.

"I'm fine, I think. I haven't really moved around much, but you took such good care of me last night I can't imagine that I'll suffer any discomfort today."

"As much as I'd love to stay in bed with you all morning, unfortunately we've got to get up and get moving if we're going to be on time for your shoot."

She grimaced, showing the same regret he felt.

"At least we have lunch together to go shopping," she said brightly.

Though it wasn't something he was looking forward to, being pushed into some posh, stuffy tux that he was *not* accustomed to wearing, the thought of getting to spend time—any time—with her quickly dissolved his misgivings over having to gussy himself up.

"It's a date," he said, kissing her lips. "Now why don't you hit the bathroom and do your thing. I'll use the other bathroom and take a quick shower and then we can hit the road. I'll call the others and make sure they're set and ready to go and have the cars ready and waiting in the back."

She sighed but pushed aside the bedcovers, baring her nude body to him. His dick hardened to the point of pain, but he kept a sheet over it until she disappeared into the bathroom. He was going to have to take care of the matter of his erection in the shower because there was no way in hell he could endure this kind of pain all damn morning. And for the most part, other than the very few women he'd had sex with, his hand had been the only regular release for his dick. Just imagining Eden and remembering their lovemaking the night before would finish him off in a minute flat as soon as he hit the shower.

Twenty minutes later and feeling only slight relief in his aching balls, he went in search of her to find her collecting up clothing and a host of other feminine stuff of whose uses he had no idea.

"Ready?" Eden asked, a broad smile curving her pretty features.

"Yep. No workout today, huh?"

She grimaced. "I try to do it every other day. I probably should do a daily regimen, and for a while I did when David and Micah took over my workouts. We worked out, ran and worked on self-defense. But after I got into better shape and more toned and lean, we cut back to three days a week. Sometimes more if I just need to work out my frustrations, but who wants to put themselves through that kind of torture every day?"

Swanny laughed. "Hate to say this, honey, but you're talking to a man who has a very strict training and workout schedule. When I'm not on a mission, that is."

"Of course," Eden grumbled. "People just aren't naturally blessed with the kind of body you have."

God, but he loved the way she didn't even seem to notice the extreme scarring and seemed to really like his body. The entire package. No one had ever made him feel this comfortable. Even with the Kellys and their family he was still reserved, and most of the time he averted the scarred side of his face even though he *knew* his scars didn't matter to them.

"I could say the same for you, the world's most beautiful woman," he said dryly. "And you're all natural. No enhancements. Your kind of beauty just doesn't happen to most women."

"No, I don't have enhancements, though I've had a few complaints that my breasts are too big," she said in a shy voice.

"What the fuck?"

Swanny stared at her in utter bewilderment. Too big? They were fucking perfect. Plump, perfectly rounded with nipples that were a delectable shade of pink. And they filled the palms of his hands perfectly, as if she were made especially for him.

She flushed again. "Most top models are tall, very slender

with not much cleavage. I have the tall and slender part down, but it's not like I could do a lot about my breast size and I refused to have a reduction."

Swanny looked at her in horror. "Breast reduction?" he croaked. "Who the hell suggested that to you? That's the dumbest-ass thing I've ever heard of. You're fucking perfect just the way you are."

Her eyes glowed in response to his heartfelt explosion. "Most of my gigs are cool with it. Occasionally when I'm doing a runway show they've sized a dress to fit the 'average' model and so they bitch about having to alter all the clothing I'm modeling. One guy was a raging asshole and told me that not only were my breasts obscenely large but my ass was also too big."

"Jesus," Swanny bit out. "I'd love five minutes with the bastard. You can be damn sure if I did, he'd never make the mistake of criticizing you again. I'd ask him how he felt about a *dick* reduction."

Eden burst into laughter, and she impulsively hugged Swanny to her. "I'm so happy around you. You just make me happy. I feel like I can be myself with you and not hide behind a facade or some fake pose for one of my photo sessions. I can't tell you how freeing that is. Till now, I've only been able to say that about my father and brothers. They certainly keep me grounded, and if I ever did get too big for my britches they wouldn't hesitate to have a come-to-Jesus session with me."

"You make me happy too, Eden," he said in a serious tone. "I know I sound like a broken record, but I have no idea why you chose me but I'm damn sure glad you did. What we had was *not* sex. We made love and until last night I really didn't know the difference between the two."

With anyone else he wouldn't feel comfortable baring his soul. He was the quiet, reserved one on his team. Edge was too, but perhaps not to the degree Swanny was. Except for now. When it came to Eden. He wasn't afraid to speak up and be vocal about how things needed to be. His teammates were probably thinking he'd gone off the deep end and, well, they wouldn't really be wrong.

But with Eden, he felt completely at ease with sharing his thoughts, his emotions, and he was not abashed to put it out there how he felt about her. He wanted her to know that last night was every bit as special to him as it had been for her. He'd never imagined making love could be so all-consuming. A melding of souls, hearts and minds.

He felt as though he were as much a newbie at the act of making love as Eden had been herself. Two people finding each other together. Figuring out what pleased the other. He found it immensely satisfying that though Eden had been a virgin, she hadn't shown any inhibitions, even before they'd consummated their relationship.

She'd been up front and honest with him from the start. She'd left no question as to what she wanted and that he was who she wanted. It was like Christmas, Valentine's Day and his birthday all wrapped up together. Hell, he felt like a kid at Christmas, full of wonder and excitement over something fresh and new and so intimate.

He knew he needed to be as blunt and as straightforward as she'd been with him, and he also realized that he needed to ask her some very direct questions about what was between them and what she saw in the future and if he was going to play any part of that future.

But now wasn't the time. He wanted no distractions for her shoot today, and he didn't want her pondering his questions when she needed absolute focus for the day ahead.

Tonight. Tonight when they went to bed, he'd lay it out to her, provided he didn't chicken out between now and then. But as he'd already reminded himself, she'd been nothing but straightforward with him and he owed her the same.

So when they were alone again, he would tell her what was on his mind and in his heart and just hope and pray that she was on the same wavelength.

CHAPTER 21

THE shoot was a lot more relaxed this morning. Either the director had taken his meds or perhaps he'd gotten laid the night before, but at any rate he wasn't the barking asshole he'd been the day before. He was even complimentary to Eden, praising her poses, the sultry looks she turned on like a switch being flipped, but as time wore on Swanny realized that she was focusing on him.

That he was the recipient of those sexy, seductive looks, and the director was eating them up with a spoon.

"Loving it, Eden!" the director called. "And Aria is going to love it too. You're the perfect face for their new product. They're going to make millions."

"She'll make millions as well," her agent muttered. "A model at Eden's level can afford to pick and choose her assignments. She's in such demand that her schedule is insane. I keep telling her she needs to slow down, but she's determined to work as long as her stock is on the rise and in a way she's right. Strike while the iron is hot. There's always new competition coming up the ranks, so it's smart of her to bank what she's making now so when she does retire she won't have to worry about money the rest of her life."

"You think she's too old to be modeling?" Swanny asked in bewilderment. In his opinion she was the most fucking beautiful woman he'd ever laid eyes on, and she didn't look a day older than a woman in her younger twenties. And that was considered old?

Her agent shrugged. "Models have short career spans. Not all, but most do. Some of the more popular supermodels continue to be famous and in demand well into their late twenties and even early thirties, but for the most part it's a younger woman's field, and Eden's breasts are larger than most, which is a strike against her. They like tall and lean. And, well, a year ago she gained a few pounds, so it became necessary for her to hire personal trainers to keep her fit. In her career, even one pound can make the difference in landing a contract or not."

Swanny growled low in his throat and her agent took a hasty step backward.

"There is not a fucking thing wrong with any part of her," he snapped. "She was forced to hire personal trainers because God forbid she gained a few pounds? And her breasts are definitely not too big, and I can't believe some jerk once told her she should consider a reduction. If I'd been there I'd have ripped his goddamn nuts off and shoved them down his throat."

"She told you about that?" her agent asked in surprise.

It didn't take much perception on Swanny's part to realize that Eden was apparently a very private person, especially given the fact that she was rarely in the news, so he'd likely just given away his relationship with Eden.

"Yeah, she did. I haven't gotten over that one yet, and then you hit me with forcing her into an exhausting workout regimen on top of an already grueling modeling schedule. Are you people even human? Because you sure as hell don't treat *her* like a human. More like some trained animal forced to obey your every whim. I've sure as hell been around her enough to know she's not some spoiled diva and doesn't expect everyone to obey her every desire. What gives you the right to do that to her? Do you forget that she's the boss and you work for her? That *she* signs your paycheck?"

Skylar, who'd walked to Swanny's side the moment it became obvious heated words were being exchanged, frowned, her lips tightening as her eyes narrowed. Then she scowled openly at Nigel.

"Seems to me that Eden does a hell of a lot of the work without reaping many of the benefits. She's directly and indirectly the source of income for a hell of a lot of people. You said yourself that she's your most important client. And if this Aria deal is so fucking important and they want Eden, then one would think they would have their noses up her ass on a regular basis. Not allow her to be treated like some fucking lapdog to be patted on the head, say 'good girl' and then toss a treat her way."

"I hardly think millions of dollars would be considered a mere dog treat," Nigel snapped.

"You're her agent," Swanny said in a pissed-off tone. "Isn't it your goddamn job to protect her from the kind of shit that went down yesterday?"

"I protect her best interests," Nigel said icily. "And this shoot definitely qualifies as being in her best interests even if it means dealing with a moody, temperamental director, who if you notice is a completely different person today."

"And they accuse women of having PMS. Let me tell you what PMS *really* stands for," she said with heavy sarcasm. "Putting up with Men's Shit. That's what PMS means. And while we women are afflicted once a month, guys have their own brand of PMS every fucking day. They're moody and difficult and act as though they're bipolar. One minute they're all smiles and the world is good. The next moment? They're pissed at the world and start snapping at everyone around them."

Swanny had to choke back his laughter, while Nigel didn't look at all pleased with Skylar's assessment. But he couldn't really argue with Skylar. He was honest enough and didn't have a big enough ego not to recognize the truth in her statement.

"I'd love to give him a permanent attitude adjustment," Skylar muttered.

"Who you threatening, Sky?" Edge rumbled out as he walked up to where Swanny and Skylar stood next to Nigel. Joe and Nathan were just behind him, bored expressions on their faces.

"Him," Skylar said, jerking her thumb over her shoulder in the direction of the director.

Edge shrugged. "Maybe he's back on his meds today."

The rest of the team chuckled, and Nigel, either disgusted or scared shitless by being surrounded by the entirety of Eden's security team, hurried away, quickly finding something to do that made him "look" busy. He pulled his phone to his ear, but Swanny could swear there was no active call taking place.

"This is boring," Joe mumbled. "I never thought I'd say that about my job, but right now I feel like a glorified baby-sitting service."

Skylar nudged Joe's ribs hard with her elbow, but Swanny caught her swift effort to make Joe shut it down. Swanny glared at Joe in clear reprimand.

"I don't consider the safety of a woman completely vulnerable to some asshole seeking revenge to be something as minor as a babysitting job," he said in an icy tone.

"I don't believe I said it wasn't important," Joe said mildly. "Just that it's definitely a change of pace and well, boring. I'm more used to being able to blow up shit."

Nathan chuckled.

Edge shrugged. "I've never been to Paris. Pretty cool to get to see the city, even as little as what we are seeing."

"Isn't Paris supposed to be the city of loooove?" Nathan asked innocently. "Because it appears to me that the bug has definitely bit one of us, and it ain't me."

Swanny shot Nathan a withering look.

"I think it would be amazing to fall in love in Paris," Skylar said wistfully. "So romantic. Think of the stories you could tell your children and grandchildren about how you met."

"Can someone explain to me why the fuck we're talking about falling in love when we're supposed to be focusing on a job here?" Swanny snapped.

"Chill man," Nathan said. "It's obvious there's some serious chemistry between you and Eden. I'm happy for you. We're just giving you shit. She's a beautiful woman, not to mention being genuinely nice and not fake in the least."

Swanny scowled. He didn't want his relationship bandied in conversation with his teammates, especially when he himself hadn't gotten to the heart of the matter with Eden. For all he knew there was nothing to talk about. They'd had sex. He was her first. Maybe that was all she wanted. His pessimism when it came to women reared its ugly head, and the insecurity that he loathed crowded into his chest.

"Okay, that's a wrap!" the director called. "I'm granting a two-hour lunch break since we got so much done this morning. Well done, everyone. I'll see you back here in two hours. Don't be late."

"That's our cue," Joe said. "Time to go shopping."

The others snickered, and even Swanny couldn't call back his groan. This was so not on his list of favorite things. But it got him two hours to spend with Eden, so he couldn't complain.

Eden hurried over, her face alight with happiness directed at Swanny. His stomach did a quirky flip-flop number, because how could he not react to the warmth she spread no matter where she went?

"Ready to hit the stores with me?" she asked with a grin.

"Yep," Skylar said with actual enthusiasm. "You know where we're going?"

"As a matter of fact, I do. It's not a long walk, but I don't know how you all will feel about that. It might be rather conspicuous for us to take armored vehicles and try to find street parking outside the boutique," Eden said with a chuckle.

The guys exchanged looks, questions in each of their eyes.

"I think as long as we flank Eden and make sure she's

covered and we have a very tight perimeter around her, walking would be okay," Swanny said. "Just how far is this, Eden?"

"Three blocks," she said cheerfully. "Not bad at all. And it's such a lovely day. It would be great to get a breath of fresh air after being trapped in the studio and hotel for two days."

Swanny lifted an eyebrow in Nathan's and Joe's direction. Joe just shook his head. "I don't know why you're looking to me now. It's not like you've listened to a damn word from me on this job anyway. You clearly took the lead on this, so you make the decision and we'll make sure she's covered on all angles."

Joe didn't sound pissy that his authority had basically been subverted, and for that Swanny was grateful because he knew he wouldn't back off even if he and Joe did get into a pissing match.

Swanny turned to Edge. "I think you and I should flank Eden. Since she's tall she needs someone taller than her on either side. A sniper isn't out of the question after what happened before. Nathan and Joe can position themselves in front of and behind Eden and Sky can place herself between Eden and whoever takes lead. That's a lot of people to go through to get to her."

Eden stood gawking at his team, her eyes wide as she took in everything they said. Maybe she wasn't taking this seriously since in her mind the first incident had been random. He'd have a talk with her later about taking her safety very seriously, right before he delved into the discussion about their relationship or if they even had one.

"You ready, then?" Swanny asked Eden. "You'll have to lead the way figuratively since Joe will be taking the lead, but you'll have to direct us to where we're going."

Eden hoisted her designer purse over her shoulder and said, "When we leave the building, take a right. Go three blocks and it's on the same side of the street as we're currently on. I'll tell you when we get there."

"All right then, let's saddle up and get the hell out of Dodge," Nathan quipped.

CHAPTER 22

EDEN grinned as she sat on a sumptuous couch just inside the section where the dressing rooms were and watched the men grumble and tug at their necklines as they walked out to let her view them in their posh evening wear.

Skylar seemed to be enjoying herself every bit as much. She smirked over the men's expressions, their groans when Eden would frown and shake her head and say, "No, not quite right."

So, she was having a bit of fun at their expense. Eden herself rarely went shopping for dresses for important events because there was no shortage of designers literally begging her to wear their apparel, and three gowns had already been delivered to her hotel for her to choose from for the soiree. Although the party would be mostly the Aria staff, production team, directors and staff, there would still be key important people and plenty of paparazzi to photograph their arrival, which was what the designers counted on.

And for the launch, Aria had already chosen the gown they wanted her to wear: the flashy red dress with the long slit up one side of her leg that she'd worn in the commercials.

This was their launch for their new ad campaign, so they wanted the woman from the television to come alive. She'd be playing the role of that woman the entire evening. Flirtatious. Sultry Mysterious. She wanted to roll her eyes at some of the things her job required, but overall it was a job she loved.

She loved traveling and meeting new people even though at heart she was a homebody, much more comfortable as the real Eden she could be when she was with her family. But her job gave her the best of both worlds. An opportunity to see the world and yet still be able to come home to her father and brothers. It was a career she wouldn't change a single thing about.

And, well, she knew realistically she likely had only a few more years, so there was still plenty of time for her to turn her thoughts to stuff like marriage and children.

"Eden?"

Guiltily, she swung her head up to see Swanny standing in the doorway of the dressing room. She hoped that her face hadn't given her away because he'd been very much on the fringes of her mind when she'd begun to think about the possibility of marriage and children. Which was pretty stupid considering they were still very much feeling their way around each other. But she'd always been impulsive and one to put the cart before the horse, so to speak.

She drank in the sight of him. He looked so damn delicious that she wanted to shove him back into the dressing room and have him against the wall while she devoured his mouth and a whole lot more.

He was dressed in a white silk dress shirt with a black coat and slacks. Usually a tie should accompany such an outfit, but there was something decidedly sexy about that top button being undone and getting a glimpse of that hard chest.

It was simple yet elegant and it made this beautiful man look even more powerful and dangerous than she already knew him to be.

"It's perfect," she finally announced.

"Thank fuck," Swanny grumbled. "We've already wasted

thirty minutes of your lunch break and we haven't even started shopping for you and Sky."

"Oh, I'm already taken care of," Eden said blithely. "And getting something for Skylar will be a snap. Her coloring is beautiful and with all that gorgeous blond hair, I already have a very good idea of what will look great on her."

Swanny stopped, his features scrunching into a scowl. "What do you mean, you're already taken care of? Wasn't that the whole purpose of this trip, to find you a dress for the party in two nights?"

Her lips curved in a grin. "Dahling," she said with exaggerated emphasis, "in my line of work, designers provide almost all my clothing for public appearances. They vie for my attention because they want the publicity. They provide a free dress in return for free publicity. Win-win. I have three gowns already delivered to the hotel for me to choose from, and I wouldn't be surprised if more showed up."

"You little heifer," Swanny said in a menacing tone. He shot her a glare that only made her laugh. "You totally set me up, didn't you?"

"Who me?" she asked, batting her eyelashes innocently. "I can't help it if you looked so cute grumbling your way through several outfits."

Swanny shook his head and then ducked back into the fitting room to take the suit off.

Skylar cracked up. "Well done, Eden. Well done, indeed. I quite enjoyed that. I have to say, you draw out a side to Swanny that most of us haven't seen."

Eden gave her a serene smile and picked an invisible piece of lint from her shirt. "He's too easy and it's so much fun to see him all riled up. He's too cute."

Skylar choked on her laughter. "Cute? I have to say I've heard Swanny described in many ways, but *cute* has never been one of them."

Skylar then cocked her head to the side. "You really dig him, don't you? I mean, it's not an act with you. You truly like him."

Eden flushed.

"I'm not saying that to make you uncomfortable or put you on the spot," Skylar hastened to say. "It's just that not many people look beyond his appearance to get to know the real man underneath. He has a huge heart, as I'm sure you know by now. I think it's really cool that you're so accepting of him. All of him. You look very good together."

"He's a very special man," Eden said quietly.

"On that we agree," Skylar responded.

They looked up to see Swanny come back out dressed in his jeans and shirt, and as good as he'd looked in his suit, Eden's mouth watered at those form-fitting jeans and the T-shirt that stretched over his broad shoulders and muscled chest.

He slung the suit on its hanger over his shoulder. Then he shot both women a glare. "Let's go see how the other guys fared since they didn't have you two tormenting them and making them go through half a dozen suits. I bet they chose the first one they picked out."

Skylar snickered and Eden lifted an eyebrow. "Oh, how little you know. I sicced the very nice saleslady on those three and told her my specifications. I can assure you that she made certain they didn't just grab and run. You were the lucky one, having me and Sky being the only witnesses to your pain."

"Poor bastards," Swanny muttered. "I think this qualifies for hazard pay. I'm definitely going to take this up with Sam."

"Quit being a baby," Eden scoffed. "Let's take your suit to the saleslady and then we'll outfit Skylar. I can't wait to get my hands on her. She's going to look amazing before I'm finished with her!"

With an exaggerated, indulgent sigh, Swanny meekly— or as meekly looking as a man his size could pull off— carried the suit to the beaming saleslady, who took it back to be wrapped with great care.

Eden clapped her hands, rubbing them together in antici- pation, just as the other team members joined them. "Now for Skylar."

Skylar's eyes sparkled with excitement. "I'm being dressed

by a supermodel. How many women can say that? I'm going to look *fabulous*! Man, I haven't looked forward to a swanky gig like this like *ever*. But I'm already fantasizing about a to-die-for dress, some kick-ass total fuck-me shoes and being made up by an honest-to-God professional makeup artist. And I get to hang out with Eden Sinclair! I can't believe I'm getting *paid* for this."

"Whoa, sweetcakes," Edge growled. "Remember the *job* you're being paid to do. Am I going to have to put you on a leash for the night? If we're having to watch out for you, our attention will be split between you and Eden, and that's *not* what we're being paid to do."

Skylar put her nose in the air and sniffed, sending him a glare. "Party pooper. Can't a girl have some fun?"

Eden threaded her arm through Skylar's and herded her toward the designer dress section, where the saleslady was already hanging up several selections for Skylar to try on.

"We girls will have fun," Eden said emphatically. "We'll just stick *together* and have fun. If we're in the same spot, then their attention will never be divided, right?"

Skylar sent her an admiring look. "I like the way you think. It's diabolical and pure genius. I love that you have an evil streak."

Eden grinned. "They need to be kept on their toes anyway, right? Since all this is to them is a glorified babysitting job."

Eden caught the wince on Joe's face as they caught up to her and Skylar and the color that rose into his cheeks and also the scowl that lit up Swanny's face as they both realized she'd obviously overheard Joe's assessment of their current "mission."

She and Skylar both bit into their lips to keep from reacting. Skylar's eyes sparkled with amusement and her expression was one of anticipation as well as a mischievous streak that for some reason her teammates weren't quite aware of. Or didn't seem to be, anyway. Eden wasn't familiar enough with the team dynamics to know what exactly they thought or knew about Skylar.

Figures, though, that they likely didn't know. Men were thick. They probably saw her as one of the guys. Safer that way. But Eden knew to her bones that Skylar wasn't just a kick-ass operative for a badass organization. She'd seen enough of her to know she enjoyed pushing the right buttons and yanking the chains of all her teammates without them even likely knowing they were being had.

That kind of wit was a trait Eden thoroughly enjoyed in other people but especially in Skylar, because it suited her to a T. If anything, she likely kept her guy teammates on their toes, which amused Eden all the more.

For a moment, Eden had a wistful thought of what it would be like if she and Skylar could be friends. *Real* friends. Without the job issue at stake. If she had anything to do with it, she planned to keep up with Skylar once the danger was over and KGI was off to its next mission. Her thoughts drifted to Swanny, her mood instantly diminishing. She slammed the door quickly on that train of thought. It did her no good to become upset over what was to come when she had beautiful days ahead of her. No matter how short the time span was. She fully intended to savor every moment she had with Swanny and suffer no regrets whatsoever when it came time to say good-bye. Well, *except* the regret of saying good-bye.

"How long will this take anyway?" Joe queried, glancing at his watch. "We're down to an hour twenty until lunch break is over, and I'm starving."

Eden stifled her laughter over the almost whiny tone reflected in Joe's question. As she'd guessed, the shopping trip had been a form of torture for them, but on the other hand, seeing four exceedingly handsome men decked out in fine evening wear? She might have to carry around a handkerchief all night to wipe the drool from her mouth.

She'd be the envy of every woman there, having the undivided attention of the KGI team. No one had to know they were her security team, after all. And then she almost laughed. Talk about fodder for the tabloids. She could see the headline now.

Supermodel Eden Sinclair on a night out with her male harem.

Hey, a girl could dream, right?

That was one tabloid she might actually read and frame any of the good photos that came of the flurry of picture taking.

"There's a café between here and the studio. They serve awesome croissants and to-die-for coffee," Eden offered. "We should have plenty of time to grab something. I'm going to wait for dinner and divine room service, but you guys can get what you like."

"Croissants?" Edge asked, his nose wrinkling skeptically. "Do they have anything a bit more substantial?"

She could see the same question in the other male members of the team and chuckled.

"Of course. You can get all sorts of baked goods. Sandwiches on fresh bread. A croissant with pretty much whatever you want on it. It really is good food. They have a pretty substantial menu, but you may want to send at least one of you ahead to order, because since it's lunchtime, and it's a favorite with the locals, it's likely going to be busy."

Swanny frowned at that, and Eden could see the battle he waged over leaving her even one man down from her protection squad, as she'd grown to think of them. Or rather protection army.

She felt like some kind of pampered, privileged, *important* member of royalty. Far more important than what she was in actuality. But she wouldn't lie, even to herself, and say she wasn't enjoying the extra attention and the fact that they were all so attentive—and determined to keep her safe at all costs.

"I think it's safe to say that I'll make it back with only four of you," Eden said dryly. "Joe could go place the order, since he and Skylar both were taking lead. That still gives you a tight perimeter around me. I doubt any of you want to starve because Skylar and I are dress shopping."

"Sounds like a plan to me," Edge said hopefully. His stomach rumbled, obviously voicing its agreement.

Joe looked chagrined that he'd somehow drawn the short straw on being the pack mule for the food.

"Hell, I don't even speak the language," Joe muttered.

"It's not that hard to point at what you want and hold up the number of fingers to indicate quantity," Eden said in amusement. "Besides, the citizens of non-English-speaking European countries speak better English than we do. I've never had a problem here."

"Okay, fine, I'll go," Joe grumbled. "But no bitching if you don't like what I pick out."

"Just none of that froufrou shit," Nathan said. "Try to make it edible, at least. At this point, I think I'd eat just about anything anyway."

"Is there a place you can just get a burger and fries?" Edge asked hopefully. "Or a good steak?"

"Save it for dinner tonight. I don't know if you've had the room service steak, but it's pretty darn good," Eden replied. "We shouldn't go overly long today. We got ahead by putting in a full day's work yesterday. That's the way this director works. He pushes hard the first day. Tests the waters, so to speak, so he can plan the rest of the filming time accordingly. Since everything went off without a hitch yesterday, he'll relax from here on out. Unless we hit a snag, and well, if that happens, all bets are off and we'll be in the studio until the wee hours of the morning if necessary."

Joe issued a short wave and all but ran from the clothing boutique as if the hounds of hell were on his heels. Eden and Skylar both giggled, which instantly gained them suspicious looks from the three remaining men.

Swanny turned to Eden as she held up the first dress for Skylar to try on. As soon as Skylar disappeared into the dressing room, Swanny got out what was obviously causing him irritation.

"So you've worked with this asshole in the past and willingly agreed to work with the dick again? I don't get it. Are you some kind of masochist? He's lucky I didn't beat his ass for talking to you the way he did yesterday."

Eden's features softened and she beckoned Swanny to sit on the small two-seat sofa in the waiting area of the dressing room.

"It's not always a cliché to say that directors are a moody, demanding and cranky breed of people. Most all of the ones I've worked with are perfectionists. *Anal* doesn't even begin to cover it. But it's what makes them so good at what they do. They have a talent for bringing out the best in their subjects. Of catching just the right look, setting the right tone, capturing the essence of what the advertiser wants. Lonnie can be difficult, yes. No doubt there. But you can be assured that when he calls it a wrap, it will be nothing short of perfect, which is what Aria wants, what Lonnie wants and what I want as well. A lot is riding on the success of this campaign. Not only for Aria and Lonnie and his reputation as a director—one of the best—but for me as well because I'm the spokesperson, the chosen face for Aria's new line of products. So it's a very symbiotic relationship between us all and we all want the same thing."

"So you're saying I'm overreacting and don't have an understanding of the business you're in," Swanny said, looking slightly chastened.

Eden smiled at him. "What I think is that it's very sweet of you to want to protect me from physical or emotional hurts. And in the beginning of my career, I admit I was young and not nearly as thick-skinned as I am now, and I didn't take criticism well. It hurt my feelings and I was often in tears because I felt like I was a failure. It was actually Lonnie, ironically enough, who sat me down and told me quite bluntly that I couldn't let what happens on the set affect me so deeply. That I wasn't a special snowflake and that all his models received the same treatment, the same demand for perfection he was asking from me, and if he didn't think I could deliver, he would have never signed on to do shoots with me.

"He acknowledged all the things you and I have just said about him. He was very direct about it. He told me he was a dick to work for and at times could seem unreasonable but only because he knew that his models, the few he exclusively dealt with, had the talent and the guts to make it in this business. But if I was going to let him make me cry every time he grew impatient or demanded more than what I was giving him, I needed to consider pursuing another career.

"But at the same time, he said he hoped I'd stick it out because he swore he'd never been wrong about a subject and he claimed to have known from the first time he looked over my portfolio and we worked that first gig together that I was going to be a star and he'd hate for me to allow my feelings to take that opportunity away."

"He doesn't sound like a *complete* asshole," Swanny said grudgingly.

Eden swallowed back her laughter. Swanny looked as though he'd swallowed nails having to make that particular admission.

"So I take it his talk with you worked, then?" Swanny said after a moment. "Because it's obvious you've definitely reached the top of your field and you're working with him on this shoot."

"Yes, it did actually," Eden said quietly, remembering those hard first few months when her confidence faltered and she felt as though she'd gotten in way over her head. "It was more his profession of faith in me, and my knowing he wasn't a touchy-feely kind of guy, and I was grateful for it. Because I was very close to walking away from it all. I was miserable and struggled with all the demands being placed on me. But once Lonnie spoke to me and laid it out so bluntly, I felt like a burden had been lifted and it suddenly didn't seem quite so impossible that I could really do this."

"I'm glad," Swanny said in a husky voice. "If you hadn't stuck it out I would have never met you. Never gotten the chance to have you in my arms."

Eden flushed just as Skylar came out of the door of the dressing room. The doors were thick and heavy but still, she hoped Skylar hadn't heard at least the tail end of their conversation.

Skylar did a little twirl as Edge and Nathan stuck their head into the small waiting area outside the dressing rooms.

"Suh-weet, Sky!" Nathan exclaimed. "Definitely your color."

Swanny looked at his team leader as if he'd grown two heads. "Since when have you gotten so in touch with what colors complement a woman's appearance?" It wasn't that he disagreed. Skylar did look dynamite, but then in his opinion she was just as beautiful in camo paint and fatigues.

"Since I got married and have gone through a myriad of questions from Shea about which color shirt looks best on her," Nathan said dryly.

"You look damn good," Edge said gruffly. "I think it's perfect."

"I feel like Cinderella," Skylar said, executing another twirl. "All shimmery and sparkly. This is to die for. All it lacks is a kick-ass pair of heels!"

Magically, or perhaps since the saleslady had all but glued herself to their asses the minute they walked into the door, she hurried in carrying a delicate pair of strappy sandals with an iridescent shimmer that were beaded and blingy at the toes and around the heel of the foot.

It gave the dress that much more pizzazz. Eden smiled as Skylar eagerly donned the shoes and then stood to her full height, which had grown by the two inches the heels sported.

"What do you think, Eden? I swear I don't even want to try on the others now. I think this is *the* dress."

"I agree," Eden replied, thrilled with Skylar's response over one of the dresses Eden had picked out herself.

The saleslady looked a little morose since one, it wasn't one of the dresses she had selected, and two, it wasn't nearly as expensive as those. But she recovered quickly, likely calculating the amount of money the four suits were bringing in, and chimed in with her own approval of the dress.

"Is that all, then?" the lady asked.

"Yes, we're finished, and thank you," Eden said warmly.

"Thank fuck," Edge muttered under his breath. Skylar rolled her eyes and shook her head in Eden's direction.

"Maybe I should try on those other dresses," Skylar said thoughtfully.

Eden almost laughed out loud. It was so obvious she was tormenting her teammates and enjoying every sadistic moment.

Her statement was immediately met with a chorus of denials, compliments and even begging. That one made Eden laugh the most. Three grown-ass men brought to their knees by an hour of shopping and being poked and prodded.

"The dress is perfect," Edge said, crossing his arms over his broad shoulders as he stared Skylar down. "Quit fucking with us. You forget. I know you far better than the others do and you're enjoying the hell out of torturing us."

"Well, there is that," Skylar said, not in the least abashed by Edge busting her.

The saleslady wore a confused look that suggested no matter how flawless her English was, she had no understanding of what was taking place. "Shall I have them wrapped and delivered to your hotel?"

"Yes, that will be perfect," Eden said graciously. "It will give us time to eat before we get back to the set."

"No, I'll come by and pick them up later," Swanny interjected before Eden could give out the name of the hotel.

Eden flushed. She'd never get the hang of all this covert nonsense. She knew they only had her best interests at heart, but she wasn't used to having to be this paranoid. Micah and David had always been cautious too. She was taking nothing away from them. But it was evident KGI was more highly trained and certainly more accustomed to matters of danger, threat and personal security.

"May I have the time you'll arrive so I can have them ready?" the saleslady asked, the hint of French in her impeccable English pleasant to Eden's ears.

Swanny checked his watch. "What exactly has to be done to them? Aren't they fine the way they are?"

The saleslady sniffed and put her nose in the air as she stared at Swanny through narrowed eyes, obviously insulted by his insinuation that her clothing wasn't of the finest quality and that they had to "fix" issues.

"Certainly they are, monsieur. I just thought perhaps you had more shopping to do and it would be inconvenient for you to have to carry them around. It was a courtesy, nothing more, something I offer all my customers. Courier service to the location of their choice."

Swanny frowned a moment, as if reconsidering his earlier

decision. Then he glanced Eden's way. "Give her the address of the studio. Have them leave them with the receptionist out front. That way we can grab them when we're done for the day. That is, if you can have them delivered that quickly?" he asked, directing his last statement to the saleslady.

"Of course," the woman responded.

"Then we'll do that," Swanny said, reversing his earlier dictate.

Dutifully Eden supplied the address and then gave the woman her credit card, which immediately made Swanny scowl.

"No fucking way you're paying for all this shit. Hell, you didn't even buy anything for yourself. I'll pay for it and collect from the others later."

Eden just laughed. "My father hired you, but technically you work for me, which means any expense you incur in doing the job you're required to do falls under business expenses."

"That makes no damn sense at all," Swanny grumbled as the saleslady hurried away to ring up the purchases.

A moment later, the lady returned with a receipt for Eden in an elegant receipt holder embossed with the boutique's name, along with the business card of the saleswoman.

"If you need anything else, please do not hesitate to come by or call. If I have an idea of what you want or need I can even take pictures in your sizes and send them so you can look, and if you want them I can take payment over the phone and have them couriered right over."

"*Merci*," Eden said, taking the envelope and tucking it in her purse.

As soon as they hit the pavement outside, the men all breathed a huge, collective sigh of relief. Eden and Skylar were smoothing their laughter and ended up with coughing fits instead, which earned them suspicious looks from some and outright glares from others.

"Such babies," Skylar mocked. "You can take on a group of terrorists only too happy to take themselves to the grave as long as you go down with them, and yet a shopping trip turns you all into giant pansies."

"Fuck you, Sky," Edge said rudely.

But Skylar just continued to grin, delighting in getting her digs in.

CHAPTER 23

DESPITE the misgivings over the food at the café Eden had recommended, not a single complaint had been registered when they met Joe who was waiting with their orders. Swanny had seen the look of disappointment on Eden's face when she'd asked if they could sit at one of the sidewalk tables and people-watch—one of her confessed addictions when she was in the city doing a shoot.

He hated seeing that look. It made him feel like he'd kicked a puppy. But damn it. As much as he'd move heaven and earth to make her happy, he damn sure wouldn't do so at the expense of her safety. And so they'd taken the food the short walk back to the studio and eaten in Eden's dressing room, which was large—worthy of the star she was—but stick six people in it and it suddenly seemed really damn small.

But then again, since he and Eden had claimed the small settee that caused them to sit thigh-to-thigh while the others either sat on the floor or leaned against walls, he wasn't complaining about *his* accommodations.

Just as they were starting to put away the takeout boxes, a knock sounded at Eden's dressing room door.

"On in fifteen, Miss Sinclair," one of the assistants called.

Eden scrambled to her feet. "Oh shit. Okay, everyone, shoo. Except you, Skylar. You can help me get into this crap so I'm not late. Lonnie has been in a good mood so far. If I ruin it now we may be here all damn night."

At that, the men all scrambled to their feet, but Swanny pinned Eden with a stare. "I'll be standing right outside the door. No one gets in here without clearance from me."

She waved her hand, motioning that she understood, but she was already hurriedly pulling together the outfit for the afternoon shoot.

A moment later the door closed and Eden grinned at the image of a big-ass surly bodyguard posted at her dressing room door. The assistants were probably drawing straws as to who had to come get her when it was time.

Although Lonnie was a stickler about time, one of his quirks was that he didn't want the models on his set until everything was in place and ready to go. It was a superstition of his, an inexplicable one, but Eden had always shrugged it off. Directors were a quirky breed, no doubt about it. And she had no problem with not hanging around an unfinished set wearing spiked heels that made her feet and thighs whine from standing so long.

"It must be awesome to wear something new and cool every day of the week," Skylar said as she helped Eden zip into the vibrant golden gown with the formfitting sequined top and flowing iridescent silk skirt that flared from her hips and fell elegantly down her legs. It gave just enough shimmer and sparkle to match the bolder sequins of the bodice.

Eden remembered in amusement Skylar's reaction to the dress she'd tried on and then purchased. A Cinderella dress. This one certainly came close to that same feel.

Eden gave her a rueful smile. "I suppose the grass is always greener on the other side. I'm honestly a lot more comfortable in a pair of worn jeans, a hoodie and a pair of flip-flops. But I won't lie and say I don't love my job. I do. I'm not one of these people who believe modeling objectifies or degrades women. Modeling is hard work. It's not just about selling our looks. It's complicated to explain. A director once told me that some women were just born for the camera and others weren't, and the ones who weren't destined for the camera weren't any less beautiful than the women who did model. They just had the talent to transform in front of a lens. Almost like a chameleon. Become whatever the photographer wanted. But believe me when I say, it's by far the most demanding job I've ever had. Not that I had many before I got into modeling, but I wasn't 'discovered' until four years ago, and I worked through high school and was in the process of putting myself through school waiting tables. Working at the register at a grocery store. Mowing lawns. You name it, I've done it," she added with a laugh.

"Wow," Skylar said. "I'm impressed. You obviously had ambition from the start. That's rare in someone so young."

"Stick your head out the door and holler for Bertrice," Eden asked Skylar. "She should be hovering close, waiting for me. She'll have to do a rush on the makeup, and hope Lonnie had a good lunch break or isn't PMSing. Again."

Skylar cracked up but immediately opened the door and reappeared a moment later with Eden's makeup artist.

"Swanny had the poor woman too afraid to knock to see if you were ready," Skylar said dryly. "He's standing outside your door like some avenging angel who will wreak havoc with the world if anyone crosses the threshold of your domain."

Eden burst into laughter. "You have such a flair for dramatics. You'd be a terrific actress."

Skylar looked befuddled and then she laughed, and laughed some more, holding her stomach in an effort to catch her breath.

"Oh God. Can you see me on a movie or television set? Unless it was something like *Rambo*. Now that would be killer. A woman version of *Rambo*. Me and P.J. could star. That would be a riot."

Bertrice looked baffled but said nothing as she hurried through the motions of redoing Eden's makeup. By Eden's count they had about twelve more minutes before Lonnie would either send someone to summon her like a subject to the king or bellow for her himself and ask her if she intended to hold up the entire production while she sat on her lazy fat ass.

She prayed for the former, because if he got all rampagy today, Swanny would likely kill him over the lazy fat-ass part. It was certainly something she'd heard before from Lonnie, but she knew how to take him, and after that first crying jag years back, she quickly figured out the best way to blow his bluster to smithereens was to blithely ignore him and kill him with kindness.

There was nothing Lonnie wanted more than to pick a fight and cause an emotional uproar when he was in one of his moods. But he'd only gotten that once from Eden and never again. She hadn't gained the reputation as being cool under fire for nothing!

"So who is P.J. exactly?" Eden asked, glancing at Skylar in the mirror. "I've heard her mentioned but was never sure exactly who she was or what connection she had to KGI."

Skylar grinned. "You'd like her, though she'd argue she doesn't want to be liked and doesn't really care if people like her or not. She's the original female member of KGI. I'm the second. I'm hearing down the grapevine that Sam has an eye on a female recruit for Rio's team but no idea where in the process they are with that. Rio . . . Well, he and Steele both kind of answer to themselves, as do their teams. To them, I mean. Technically you could say they work for KGI, meaning the founders—Sam, Garrett and Donovan. But Rio is two men down. He lost one during a clusterfuck of a situation when Frank Kelly had a heart attack and Marlene, his wife, was kidnapped from the bathroom of the hospital, killing one of Rio's men in the process. He lost the other when some bad shit went down on a mission Rio took a very personal interest in. Meaning, he had it bad for the woman he was protecting and one of his teammates risked her life for his own interests. He's lucky to be alive. I was shocked when I learned that Rio had let him live."

Eden's mouth dropped open, eliciting an instant frown from Bertrice, who was just finishing her lips.

"I'll be *finis*. Just few seconds more. Then I leave and you talk."

Skylar grimaced and clamped a hand over her mouth with a groan, but she waited until Bertrice finished up Eden's lip gloss and then stuffed her bag full of the stuff she'd taken out and left the room.

"Shit," Skylar muttered. "Shit, shit, *shit*!"

Concern wrapped around Eden's throat, squeezing her airway tight. "Skylar, what is it? Surely it can't be so bad."

"You shouldn't know anything about all the crap I just told you. Classified. All of it. That wouldn't earn me any brownie points for sure with the powers that be. But I swear, you're so down-to-earth and easy to talk to that I find myself just spouting out the least little thing. Like we're BFFs or something, for God's sake."

Eden smiled and then reached up to hug Skylar, squeezing her as lightly as possible so she didn't muss her hair or makeup.

"One, I'd never tell a soul what you just told me. And two, I'd very much like to consider us friends. Despite my profession being dominated by so many women, I'm not actually friends with any of them. This is a competitive, cutthroat business, and if the opportunity presents itself, they'd step all over me to climb higher in the ranks. So I have no illusions of true friendship or loyalty. I'm well aware of what's at stake in my career. If fucking me over will get them ahead of the game, they'd do it without a second thought."

Skylar pulled away frowning. "But, Eden, that's terrible. It's a terrible way to live and work. How do you handle knowing all of that? How can you even be nice to women you know would turn on you in an instant? In my job loyalty isn't just something. It's everything. We depend on one another for our very lives and I know without a doubt that any of my team would put themselves on the line for me in a heartbeat."

"I think that's awesome," Eden said wistfully. Then she laughed. "Listen to me. I sound like a poor little rich girl. I do have that. My father and brothers would lay waste to any threat to me. Hell, they hired you. But as far as outside my family, I don't have confidantes. People I know I can trust absolutely or who I don't feel have a motive for wanting to get close to me. Isn't that horrible?"

Skylar shook her head as Eden bent to pull on the pair of crystal heels with the hint of sparkle that matched the dress.

"I don't think it's horrible at all. It's called reality, Eden. I'm sure you've had your share of hanger-ons and a number of people who would take advantage of you in a heartbeat. I'm sure it's something all celebrities have to contend with. There's nothing wrong with being discerning about who you place your trust and faith in, and for reserving judgment and not wanting to be BFFs with the first woman who crosses your path."

Eden chuckled. "You are extremely astute. However do the men put up with you? I can't ever imagine them winning an argument with you. You have a solid, intelligent comeback for everything."

Skylar grinned. "Well, you mix intelligence with a streak of evil and that way they never know what they're going to get. Works best when you keep them off balance. Way easier to manage them that way."

"I seriously heart you," Eden said as they walked to the door where Swanny waited. "We are so keeping up after all this is over. No way I'm letting go of my first real potential girlfriend."

"Does that mean I get to accompany you on the red carpet at some swank Hollywood get-together sometime?" Skylar asked slyly.

"Yup. You and me both in killer dresses and fuck-me shoes? We'd have the room of men on their knees. Now carry that image with you while I work the rest of the afternoon."

Skylar laughed but Eden could see she was doing just that. Imagining her and Eden, partners in crime at some posh get-together where neither would give a rat's ass what anyone thought of them.

"Do I even want to know what the two of you are plotting?" Swanny asked warily.

"Nope," they said in unison. "Just girl stuff."

Most men couldn't back out of a conversation quick enough when the dreaded words *girl stuff* were mentioned, and Swanny was no exception. He cupped Eden's elbow and Skylar fell into step on Eden's other side as they hurried her down the hall to the studio.

There with two whole minutes to spare and Eden knew without false modesty that it didn't look as though she'd hurried through any of her preparation. She exuded calm and stood waiting patiently on Lonnie to bark his first instruction.

He glanced up at Eden, lifting one eyebrow as he checked his watch. Eden suppressed a smug grin. He'd so been itching to start bellowing insults and now she'd taken the wind from his sails.

And so the rest of the afternoon went. Lonnie—a completely different person than he'd been during the morning session—bellowed, bullied and was all-around difficult, and Eden only smiled wider, performed to his expectations and was completely unruffled by his bullshit.

Swanny, on the other hand, looked as though he was a breath away from choking the life right out of the director. Eden caught his eye once and gave a quick negative shake of her head and then mouthed "Later," hoping he'd catch her meaning that she'd explain everything afterward.

One had to know how to yank Lonnie's chains back. The minute Swanny got into his face and let Lonnie know how much he pissed Swanny off, it would become Lonnie's sole ambition in life to torment Swanny by tormenting Eden. It was far more satisfying to deny Lonnie what he wanted, which would only enrage him further and make him feel a fool when it was all over with.

Still, Swanny spent the rest of the afternoon glowering in the corner, looking as though he'd swallowed a lemon. The sad truth was that him all broody? Was sexy as hell. It made her want to go bite him. Where she wasn't even sure. Maybe on the thick column of his neck. Or even his chin. Or that rock hard abdomen. Either way she was salivating over the prospect.

His ass. Oh, now that was definitely a tempting prospect.

"Whatever the hell you're thinking about, keep thinking it," Lonnie barked. "Give me more of that. Love it. Sultry as hell, Eden. You'll have the world eating out of your hand."

She lifted her gaze to purposely meet Swanny's so he'd know exactly what she was thinking about. Or rather who.

His eyes became half-lidded and he returned her stare with a smoky, desire-laden one of his own that nearly had her squirming in her awkward pose. Hell, they were practically making love on the set of a commercial and they were half a room away from each other.

Lonnie was oblivious to the undercurrents, too deliriously happy with the results he was getting from Eden. But Skylar glanced between them with an almost wistful look in her eyes. But she also looked happy. She looked at Swanny with pride and at Eden with a warning in her eyes.

We may be becoming friends but if you hurt him you'll answer to me.

Eden acknowledged the silent message with a subtle dip of her head.

Eden listened to her instructions on autopilot, too absorbed in the moment with Swanny, imagining him undressing her. Her undressing him. Them making love. Her lips parted unconsciously and she licked them, ignoring the yelled encouragement from the director and photographer.

Her focus was solely on Swanny, watching his reaction to their mental lovemaking. His gaze promised her all she was imagining and so much more. His eyes bore into her until she could literally feel the heat between them, all consuming. And yet through it all she never faltered. She never moved. She was too much of a professional to allow herself total distraction. But still, she drifted further and further under Swanny's spell, counting the minutes until they could be alone again. Skin to skin. Mouth to mouth. Joined as intimately as a man and woman could be joined.

An ache began between her legs, spreading through her

body until her breasts were heavy and she was hyperaware. So sensitive that any touch would border on pain.

"Whoever he is, he's a lucky bastard," the photographer muttered as he snapped another series of photos.

That yanked Eden's attention away from Swanny and she glared down at the photographer, unsure of whether she'd heard what it was he said.

"What the hell are you talking about?" she demanded.

The photographer grinned. "Your lover, gorgeous. You must be thinking of him. Never seen you look quite so sexy as today and you've always been off the charts. But there's definitely something different about you now."

"Well since he isn't you, then I'd say it's none of your business," Eden said icily, staring him down until he had the grace to look way, color staining his cheeks.

"Get the hell off my set," Lonnie said in disgust. "And leave the memory card behind. You're fired."

The younger photographer paled. "What?"

"You ruined what was, up until now, one of the best shoots I've ever had the pleasure of directing with your big mouth. You think we're going to get that back now?"

He turned, acknowledging KGI for the first time, since he'd spent all his time trying to ignore their presence altogether.

"See that the gentleman is escorted from the building."

Swanny stepped forward before his teammates could, a scowl darkening his features. "With pleasure."

"I'll go with," Edge quickly said. Eden could see the slight concern in Edge's features that the photographer might have an accidental fall on the way out, courtesy of Swanny.

"The memory card goes with me," the photographer said firmly, his features changing from shocked surprise to ugly anger.

"That's where you're wrong," Lonnie said silkily. "Read your contract, boy. Those pictures belong to Aria. So take it out, and if you ruin it, I'll make sure you never work in this business again. Not to mention you'll be sued for millions of dollars that Aria will claim they lost because those photos wouldn't be able to be used in their campaign."

With a sullen look, the photographer carefully withdrew the memory card and thrust it toward Lonnie. But Lonnie still stood there expectantly, hand held out for the camera.

Swanny had gripped the man around his upper arm and now squeezed until the photographer winced.

"Give him the camera," Swanny said in a menacing voice.

Looking like a petulant child, the photographer handed over the camera and Lonnie proceeded to make sure every photo was saved to the card, and then went through deleting every single photo stored on the camera itself.

Lonnie nodded at Swanny. "He can go now."

Swanny turned him around and Edge fell into step on the photographer's other side and gripped his arm in the same fashion Swanny had as they propelled him from the studio.

When they got to the entrance they all but threw him out and he stumbled onto the sidewalk.

"I'll sue you for this," the photographer yelled. "I'll have bruises. I'll file assault charges."

Swanny gave him a bored look. Edge merely studied his fingernails, digging at invisible lint underneath one.

"Whatever makes you happy," Swanny drawled. "But understand me on this, boy. You fuck with Eden in any way, and I mean any way at all, and I'll come after you. There isn't a rock you can hide under where I can't find you. That's what I do for a living. I get rid of cockroaches just like you and crush them underneath my boot."

The young man went white as a sheet and then turned and fled down the busy street.

Edge laughed and clapped Swanny on the shoulder. "Let's go get your girl. I think Lonnie has pretty much called it quits for the day after that stunt."

CHAPTER 24

EDEN kept glancing in Swanny's direction on the way back to the hotel, and he could tell she was dying to say what was on her mind or had some burning question on her tongue. Several times she'd even parted her lips as if to speak, and then, as if changing her mind, she promptly shut them again.

This time Skylar was on Eden's other side so Eden was seated in the middle of the backseat between her and Swanny. Edge was riding shotgun, which left Nathan and Joe in the lead vehicle, along with their purchases made earlier in the day, as they traveled back to the hotel.

"Say what's on your mind, honey," Swanny murmured.

Then he wondered if he should have encouraged that since he had no idea what it was she wanted to ask and Skylar was right there, although Swanny knew damn well Skylar wasn't in the least fooled. She knew there were some serious sparks between Swanny and Eden and hell, the women had been thick as thieves today, whispering and likely stirring up mischief. He was just worried it was directed at him and wondered if he should be ducking and running for cover.

Eden hesitated and then turned slightly in her seat so he could see the silent plea in her eyes.

"Can we go *out* to eat tonight? I'd love to do one of those dinner cruises on the Seine. I've been to Paris multiple times but have never had anyone I would have wanted to share something like that with."

Swanny frowned, his heart sinking. God, but he hated saying no to this woman.

As if knowing he planned to do precisely that, she rushed on. "I know we can't go alone. I mean just the two of us. I understand the potential for danger. I'm not an idiot and I've actually given this a lot of thought."

He almost said *Uh-oh* out loud but wisely kept silent. Barely . . . Because a protest was already burning his lips.

"All of you wouldn't need to go. Just some of you," she persisted. "Edge and Skylar could go with us. To anyone looking we would just appear like two couples out for a romantic dinner. Surely the three of you can handle any possible threat, and you have to admit, there hasn't even been a hint of danger since that random shooting in Boston."

Goddamn it, but he wished her damn father had just been straight with her. Told her the truth from the start. He understood him not wanting his daughter to be ruled by fear, but fear kept people alive. It made them cautious and less trusting. Two things that could well save Eden's life if it came to that.

But at the same time, Swanny wasn't sure he could handle watching that sparkle disappear from her eyes and her constant smile and sunshiny disposition weighed down by sorrow and worry if she knew the truth.

What a fucking predicament to be in.

Swanny saw Edge immediately stiffen and go on alert. The damn man had the ears of an elephant, and Skylar was trying her damnedest to stifle her amusement but was failing miserably.

Swanny sighed. He knew he was a dead man, and should probably just save himself future misery by cutting his balls off, because there was no way in hell he could deny her anything. But the evening *did* pose a predicament.

"Uh, just how swanky is this sort of thing?" Swanny hedged.

"Oh it's totally casual, or at least in theory. Some people opt for total tourist clothing and others dress a little more formally, but nothing like what we'll have for the soiree and the launch party."

"There's a problem with that," Swanny said grimly. "I'm not going unless I'm packing."

"Ditto," Edge said, interrupting from the front.

Eden gave him a puzzled look.

Swanny's expression softened. "A gun, honey. We're pretty useless protecting you if we aren't packing heat."

She actually looked relieved, as if she had expected something far worse. He couldn't quite figure her out. Guns and potential danger didn't seem to bother her in the least. But the thought of being denied her wish obviously did.

"Oh that's not a problem," she said gaily. "We'll just outfit you in slacks and a dinner jacket. No tie. Just semicasual."

"*Another* shopping trip?" Swanny asked in horror. "We don't have time for that if you're wanting dinner, not to mention the planning involved in taking yet another trip to a clothing store. I'd have to clear it with Nathan and Joe and I can guaran-damn-tee they're not going to look at those doe eyes of yours and be swayed."

Eden laughed, making those doe eyes even rounder. On purpose, he was certain. The little heifer *knew* she had him wrapped around her finger, to his never-ending disgust. And she certainly wasn't above using that to her advantage. The hell of it was he didn't even mind despite his early disgruntled thoughts on the matter.

"No, silly. I have the very nice saleslady's card, remember? And she has all your sizes. I'll simply call her when we get to the hotel, tell her what we need, and Nathan or Joe can go pick it up, since they won't be going out with us. Besides, it'll take you guys half the time to get ready as it will us girls. By the time your clothing arrives and you get changed, Sky and I will be dressed and ready. I assume a jacket will conceal any weapons you carry?"

Edge grunted, which caused Swanny to grin. Edge's idea of packing was a little more detailed than most.

"And I'll just strap my thigh holster on," Skylar said, getting into the spirit. "Never know when a lady needs a gun when she's wearing a dress."

Swanny almost laughed. Despite the fact that Skylar was every bit as capable and kick-ass as P.J. on Steele's team, Skylar was unabashedly feminine and girly in her tastes, and no amount of teasing from her team seemed to faze her one iota. He liked that about her. That she could remain her own person and still operate within the confines of KGI and be such a valuable asset to their team.

"I'll totally have her send you over something as well," Eden volunteered. "Can't have you wearing the gorgeous confection we found for the parties. I'll ask for casual chic. She'll know exactly what will look perfect on you. Especially when I explain the occasion. Boutique salespeople have to have an expert eye. It's what sets them apart from all the other hundreds of independent boutiques. And they have impeccable memories, so you'll be in good hands letting her pick what you'll wear for tonight."

And so Swanny found himself, two hours later, standing in the middle of the suite dressed in khaki slacks and a button-up shirt that felt suspiciously like silk, with his shoulder holster and two guns, one on either side, concealed by the darker brown dinner jacket Eden had delivered from the boutique. He had a knife and one explosive strategically hidden, but there was no reason for Eden to know just how prepared he was. She'd just tease him mercilessly anyway.

A moment later, Eden came out of the bathroom and his mind went utterly blank. If he'd been pondering anything before, he sure as hell couldn't remember what it was now.

Eden was dressed in a long black sheath that clung to her every curve, with a scoop back that made it obvious she wasn't wearing a bra. The bodice was modest, covering her entire chest all the way up to her throat, where it looped around to secure at her nape. The only thing keeping the damn dress on her. He hoped to hell it was sturdy and there

were no wardrobe malfunctions because he'd be damned if
another man saw what he already considered his.

To further torture him, there were slits up both legs, coming together just at her hip bone so that every time she
moved, the long, smooth expanse of her legs was bared. And
the shoes? She was a tall woman but those shoes gave her at
least another three inches of height, which put the top of her
head right at his nose.

"You're trying to kill me," he muttered. "Is this punish-
ment for some infraction I'm unaware of?"

She laughed. "Not at all. I want to look good for you. And
even more, I want you to get a good look at what you'll be
taking off later when we get back to the hotel."

His entire body went rigid, his breath quickening. His
pulse was about to leap right out of his chest at the preview
she'd just innocently given him. The little vixen may have not
been sexually experienced in the physical sense, but he had to
remember that this was a woman well versed in seductive
looks and words.

And then the other thing she said registered with him and
he found himself frowning. She wanted to look good for
him? As if she could look anything else. But it stroked his
male ego that for whatever reason she'd singled him out in a
veritable sea of males who'd be on their knees for a chance
to get with her.

"Eden, honey. Unless you want to set a record for the
world's quickest dinner, you need to stop tantalizing me with
that kind of talk. If you keep it up, I guarantee we won't even
leave this hotel. Because I'll make love to you until we're both
exhausted and *then* I'll order room service."

A knock at the door prevented him from carrying out his
threat. Eden grinned and collected her handbag. Swanny
checked the peephole and saw Edge and Skylar standing outside. Edge was scowling and tugging uncomfortably at the
neckline of his shirt, and Skylar was grinning and looking
like a million dollars.

"All ready?" Skylar asked brightly as Swanny opened the
door.

Edge sighed and muttered something under his breath.

Skylar seemed as eager and as excited as Eden was over the evening. But then how often did a mission afford them the opportunity to play dress-up and actually relax a little? Not that he'd let his guard down even for a moment when it came to Eden.

He cast a glance in Skylar's direction, knowing that in order not to be a complete dickhead he needed to remark on her appearance. He was far more used to seeing her in fatigues and camo and with blood smears, but she was indeed a very beautiful woman.

"You look gorgeous, Sky," Swanny said sincerely.

Skylar actually gave him a shy look from underneath her lashes and flashed a smile through perfectly white, straight teeth. It amused him that the all-American cheerleader-looking woman was a kick-*ass* operative on a highly trained special ops team. Personal remarks had no place on the job, right in the middle of bullets flying and bombs going off, but here, though, it was not only appropriate but the right thing to do.

Skylar had been very nice to Eden. The women had acted as though they were well on their way to a friendship. And Swanny appreciated that because he wanted Eden to be accepted by his team. His family. He didn't dig too deeply into the reasons why, but they were there, hovering on the fringes, for him to ponder more deeply or perhaps admit to his own self that Eden was coming to mean a hell of a lot more to him than she should, given she was a job. A client.

Not that such a thing had ever ruffled any feathers within KGI, since most of the men had met their wives on missions. It had become a running joke in the ranks of KGI that if any of them had hopes of finding a woman, it would have to be on a mission since they were gone so much and a relationship with a hometown girl in Tennessee seemed impossible.

"You do look beautiful," Edge said gruffly, almost as if he'd been shamed by Swanny's compliment because he hadn't yet offered his own.

Skylar performed a cheerful curtsy and then to Swanny's shock pulled up one side of her dress. Then he realized why.

Holstered to the inside of her thigh was her smaller Sig
P250 sub-compact.

Then she unzipped the small clutch she held to show
them an identical pistol there with two extra clips.

"Never let it be said that vanity replaced readiness," she
said with a grin.

Swanny laughed. "I don't think anyone will ever accuse
you of not being prepared, Sky. You've earned your position
on this team and you've certainly earned your team's respect
and confidence. No need to prove anything to us. We're a
unit. Family," he said once more.

God, he was feeling actually mushy. Maybe it was the
effect Eden was having on him. She was definitely bringing
him out of his solitary existence, the wall of silence he usually stayed behind. He'd become practically *verbose* since
this mission had started, acting more like the team leader
than following the lead of the Kelly brothers.

Thank God they didn't have egos and act like he was trying
to subvert their authority. It had never been that way with their
team anyway. Rio and Steele? Absolutely in control of their
teams. Their authority unquestioned. Their teams did exactly
as they were ordered. Their team leaders commanded—
expected—immediate, unquestioning obedience. He admired
the two badass team leaders, but Swanny's team was different.

Their situation was different. They were led by not one
authority figure but two. The twins, Nathan and Joe. And the
two didn't handle their team as Steele and Rio did. He wasn't
critical of Rio or Steele in the least. They kicked ass and got
the job done no matter what. But Joe and Nathan included
their team in all the decision making. They worked as a true
unit. From the outside looking in, Swanny wasn't even sure
someone would even recognize who was considered the
"leader." They worked in perfect harmony, each stepping up
at different times when the need arose. Just like Swanny was
doing when it came to Eden. And well, he'd be lying if he
said he didn't have a very personal stake in this mission.

He was grateful that no one had tried to talk him down. Say
shit like he was letting his emotions get involved or warn him

that he was losing objectivity. They accepted it calmly just as they did everything else thrown their way. It was another thing he admired about his team. They never got worked up or sweated the small stuff. They were laid back except when it came to a job. Then they were all business and worked seamlessly, feeding off one another. That kind of loyalty and camaraderie was never just there from the start. It was something that had to be worked on. Earned. And for the first while after their team had been formed, they'd spent most of their time together, learning one another and bonding. It had made them stronger both individually and as a team.

They were a small team compared to the others. One fewer member than Steele's team. Two fewer than Rio's original team. Rio had lost one man several years earlier when the Kelly matriarch had been abducted from the hospital, and then he'd lost another more recently, though the man wasn't dead. Lucky, but not dead. Swanny understood now the control it must have taken for Rio not to kill his man after he betrayed Rio's woman, Grace. Because he'd damn sure lay to waste anyone who fucked with Eden. *Especially* if it was someone he trusted.

But Sam had made noises about adding another member to Rio's team, which would put them at six, which would then leave Swanny's team with five. They could probably use another man—or woman—but Swanny was reluctant to compromise what they already had. A tightly knit, loyal group that worked together like a well-oiled machine.

"Swanny?"

Eden's soft voice came from behind him, shaking him from his thoughts. Damn, but he was still standing in the open door, Skylar and Edge in the hallway while they talked stupid shit and Swanny was getting in touch with his inner self. He mentally rolled his eyes. Man, he had to pull it together. His mind was turning to mush and he needed to be on alert. Especially given that there would be only three people for Eden's protection tonight.

Eden pushed her way up beside Swanny and then smiled in delight at Edge and Skylar.

"Skylar, you look amazing!" Eden exclaimed. "Did I not tell you the saleslady would not steer you wrong? That dress looks absolutely stunning on you."

Skylar's eyes glowed with pleasure at the compliment from Eden. And it was said so sincerely that there was no doubt she wasn't speaking from the heart. No artifice or careful politeness from her. No, she was expressive and refreshingly honest and straightforward. Yet more things to add to the quickly growing list of things he loved about Eden.

"And Edge. Wow!" Eden said, casting an admiring gaze up and down his huge physique. "You clean up damn good. You look polished and yet you still have that air of danger that surrounds you, like someone would have to be the world's biggest dumbass to ever piss you off. I have to say, women totally dig that. Skylar will have to be careful or you'll have women crawling all over you tonight!"

Edge blushed. The big man actually *blushed*. Swanny blinked in astonishment because he'd never seen Edge remotely ruffled, and yet he stood there like a teenager being told by his dream woman that he was the total package.

Skylar caught it too and quickly lifted her clutch to cover her mouth, but her eyes sparkled with laughter as she watched Edge stare speechlessly at Eden.

But then Eden just had that effect on men and women alike. She was so freaking nice. And genuine. Not a fake bone in her body. Her smile was like being touched with sunshine, and Edge was no different than anyone else in that regard. He was as caught up in her spell as everyone else who came into contact with her.

"Glad I pass approval," Edge said, finally finding his tongue. "If you all are ready, I've arranged a ride. We'll go out the back. I've scoped the dropoff area. Eden said she'd have the tickets dropped off at the front desk, so I took the liberty of collecting those already. We don't want to spend any more time than we have to in line to board."

"They're VIP tickets," Eden said cheerfully. "We'll have a separate boarding area and separate dining area as well. Not as many people that way. I'll go ahead and admit that I bought out half the VIP tickets so we wouldn't have people on top of us. I figured that would put you all at ease more and perhaps you could enjoy dinner and the view better if you weren't constantly checking out our neighbors, worried they'd jump across the table or something."

Swanny sighed. The woman was smart. He and Edge exchanged disgruntled looks because it hadn't even occurred to them to set up such a thing. It gave him a measure of reassurance that Eden was taking the possibility of a threat very seriously and was acting accordingly. But then he should have known better because nothing she'd done suggested she was anything but a kick-ass, intelligent career woman with excellent business acumen, not to mention terrific instincts.

"I'm beginning to think you don't need us at all," Swanny muttered. "I honestly think you could kick someone's ass all by yourself if they tried to mess with you."

"Money can only buy so much," Eden said in amusement. "But no, I'm not just a pretty face, not that I ever thought you thought so. My brothers and father have always taught me to defend myself and I'm actually an excellent shot with both pistols and rifles. And as I told you previously, though you showed me up quite nicely, David and Micah had been working with me on self-defense moves and a variety of martial arts techniques."

"I'm more than happy to take over that aspect of your training," Swanny said, a grin pulling at the corner of his mouth.

"Enough flirting, you two. I'm starving," Skylar said. "And I'm excited to see the city at night from the river. I think this is going to be so cool."

Swanny glanced up at Edge. "We all set?"

Edge nodded. "Car is around back waiting."

Swanny reached for Eden's arm, pulling her into his side, wrapping his arm around her waist as they stepped from the entry to the hotel room. The door swung closed and Swanny ensured it was shut tight and not ajar and then tightened his hold on Eden.

"Then let's get on with your night, honey. I want you to enjoy yourself."

"Oh I will," she said in a low voice as the others went ahead of them. "How could I not when I'm with you?"

The surge of satisfaction that filled his chest lasted the entire car ride to the riverside dock.

CHAPTER 25

SWANNY relied on his gut for just about everything. It had saved his ass—and others'—more times than he could count. His teammates joked and said he had a sixth sense for sniffing out danger, but they didn't argue that when he spoke, they listened. They accepted without reservation when he hesitated and they acted accordingly.

Six months ago on a seemingly simple extraction, it had all gone to hell and they could have all died if it weren't for Swanny and his legendary "gut." They'd been sent to go in and out, cover and protect an ambassador's wife and daughter and take them from a precarious, escalating situation in an unstable country.

Swanny had known something was off the minute they retrieved the wife and daughter. Joe had started to lead the way to the back of the house where a helicopter was landing to complete the extrication, and Swanny had frozen, calling out to Joe as he stepped from the house.

Thirty seconds later, they would have been in the chopper when it exploded into fiery pieces, courtesy of a grenade launcher.

So now as he stood with Eden, Skylar and Edge, preparing to board the dinner boat, he marveled that his gut was quiet. No screaming at him that there was imminent danger or that he was an idiot for giving in to Eden's request for dinner on a fucking boat.

Eden looked as excited as a child at Christmas, and even Skylar had a wide smile on her face. Eden's enthusiasm was infectious because he swore he actually saw Edge give her an indulgent smile.

Swanny shook his head. He wondered if anyone was safe from Eden's charm.

They were seated near the head of the boat, and true to Eden's word the tables around them were empty with only a few occupied toward the middle, close to the cabin. The back of the boat was filled to capacity, but there was very much a feeling that they were the only four on board.

Quiet descended as the boat disembarked and a waiter appeared to pour them their choice of wine. Swanny, Edge and Skylar declined, opting for water instead while Eden chose a red, sipping it, seemingly savoring every taste.

"I can't thank you enough for this," she said, a broad smile lighting her face, her eyes twinkling in the lights of the city. "The city is so beautiful at night. There's a magic to it."

And yet she'd never opted to take the trip before. What was it she'd said? That there'd never been someone else she would have considered going on such a trip with.

Swanny's heart swelled, as did other parts of his body, to his eternal disgust. The least he could do was get through the evening without a perpetual hard-on. He was already looking forward to taking her back to the hotel and making love to her the entire night.

He knew he had to be gentle and patient. She would be tender from the night before, but he was imagining a dozen ways he could accomplish just that without causing her a moment's pain.

He sat, watching Skylar and Edge actually relaxed and laughing, Eden joining in, their enjoyment of the city and the lights and landmarks, and he marveled at how normal it all felt.

Was this what normal couples in normal relationships did? Normal wasn't something he was very accustomed to. Sure, he'd seen members of KGI fall and fall hard for the women they loved, but in no way could one ever call their courtship or resulting relationship *normal*.

He hadn't ever realized he'd even craved normal. Or craved a relationship at all. He'd always assumed anything more than a one-night-stand or at best a brief arrangement was out of his reach. And in his line of work, what woman would be lining up to sign up for something like that even if he wasn't damaged goods?

The Kelly women seemed to have no issues with what their husbands did, but then it was "normal" to them. It was how they'd met their husbands, not some surprise sprung on them after months of dating and then the guy casually says, *Oh, by the way, I kill people for a living.*

Not that killing was their official goal. In fact, they always made the effort to make their missions as clean and effort-less as possible, but there was always the possibility of it all going to hell and at that point it was either kill or be killed. No one had to ask their preference on that matter.

They floated gently down the Seine, soft music playing as accompaniment to the shimmering water and the twinkling lights of the city.

His enjoyment, however, wasn't the scenery or how beau-tiful the city might be at night. He was riveted to Eden, his attention focused solely on her, absorbing every smile, every expression of delight. And he found himself more lost under her spell than ever.

She was so beautiful to look at that it hurt sometimes. Like looking directly into the sun. And she was his. Later he'd take her back to their hotel room and he'd make love to her as tenderly as he'd ever made love to a woman. Eden deserved the best. Special treatment. Because she was a spe-cial woman, indeed. A breed apart from any other woman Swanny had ever met.

Their dinner entrées were delivered and Swanny was happy to see that Eden had actually ordered real food. He doubted she'd eat all of it, but at least she'd enjoy some of the succulent feast before her.

His own steak looked cooked to perfection. Seared on the outside, providing a delicious crust, and when he cut into it, the meat was just the right shade of pink. Not quite raw, but not too well done either.

Edge had ordered a steak as well, while Skylar chose the seafood platter with a variety of succulent selections.

They ate in companionable silence, occasionally commenting on a sight that passed. But Swanny's attention was solidly fixed on Eden and savoring her enjoyment of the evening out. His chest puffed out a bit, first at the knowledge that he'd been the only man she'd ever chosen to take this trip with, despite her many visits to the city, and second that he was the one to give her this experience she wanted so much.

She'd asked him. No one else. She'd waited for *him*.

At one point, Eden shivered delicately, the breeze picking up and blowing off the water. Not even giving it a thought, Swanny scooted closer to her, pushing their chairs until they were bumping. Then he leaned over and pulled Eden into his arms to provide her warmth.

She let out a contented sigh and snuggled into Swanny's arms, melting bonelessly into his embrace.

"This has been the most perfect evening ever, Swanny. Thank you for doing this for me," Eden said sweetly.

Didn't the woman know he'd get her the damn moon if that was what she wanted?

For the rest of the dinner cruise, they sat, Eden swallowed up by Swanny's arms, conversing between the four of them as if indeed they were simply two couples enjoying a romantic evening.

Swanny owed Edge and Skylar a huge thank-you later. This was certainly out of the line of duty for them, and the last thing he wanted was to cause discomfort between the two since they roomed together.

When they reached the end and docked, Swanny waited, wanting the other passengers to disembark before he, Skylar and Edge flanked Eden to take her to the waiting car.

As before, Skylar rode on Eden's other side, with Eden in the middle, while Edge rode up front. Eden curled into Swanny's side, seemingly uncaring of what anyone thought of their relationship.

He knew his teammates likely thought he'd lost his mind. He was always the most reserved, the quiet, observant one. It wasn't like him to take a personal stake in any mission, or at least that was the appearance he gave. In fact, every mission they went on, Swanny felt deeply. Like Donovan, he had a special place in his heart for children. Donovan's new family had quickly wormed their way into Swanny's heart, especially the youngest, Cammie.

He would have done anything in the world to protect that little girl.

Eden nestled her head against Swanny's shoulder, seemingly content to just sit in silence as they headed back to the hotel and what Swanny knew—anticipated—was waiting. He just hoped Eden was still on the same wavelength as him, as she'd hinted earlier.

When they got to the hotel, Swanny quickly did a sweep of Eden's suite while Edge and Sky waited with her in the hallway. Once he cleared the interior he sent Edge and Sky on to their room and told Eden to go ahead and get ready for bed. He made a quick call to check in with Nathan and Joe to let them know all had gone well tonight, as well as to go over the plans for the following day and to discuss the upcoming soiree and the best way to handle security for Eden.

Once his conversation was completed, he headed to Eden's bedroom, anticipation beating a strong pulse in his throat. He found her nude, lying in bed as though she'd been waiting for him.

"You've got some catching up to do," she teased. "I'm already three steps ahead of you. I've showered and undressed and am in bed waiting for my man to come satisfy me."

Swanny let out a low growl, tempering the urge to strip down where he was and immediately get into bed with her and spread those silken thighs. But he made himself go into the bathroom and take the world's quickest shower. He came out moments later, still toweling the moisture from his hair, but he, like Eden, was wearing absolutely nothing and his dick was straining upward, hard, the head nearly purple with the blood rushing to his groin.

"Mmm, I'm guessing you won't need any seductive wiles tonight," she said, soft laughter in her voice.

"Just looking at you is seduction all in itself," he rasped out. "But honey, I need to make certain you're ready for this. We made love last night and I don't want you to be so tender that I hurt you tonight."

She smiled and pushed the covers down farther so more of her body was bared.

"The only ache I have will only be assuaged if you make love to me," she whispered. "You won't hurt me, Swanny. I trust you. You were wonderful last night. Taking it so slow and being so tender. I'll never forget my first time, thanks to you. It couldn't have been more perfect."

Remembering that he'd planned to have a "relationship" talk with Eden tonight, he pondered briefly when would be the most appropriate time. Right now he wanted to make love to her so badly he hurt. And what he had to say might well dampen the whole mood, particularly if Eden wasn't on the same wavelength he was.

After they made love. During the postcoital glow and snuggle time, then he'd talk to her about what he wanted to discuss. Right now? The sexiest woman in the universe was lying naked in her bed, inviting him to make love to her. How the hell was he supposed to resist *that*?

She glanced shyly at him as he approached the bed, and he could see that she had something on her mind but was hesitant to reveal whatever was causing her shyness.

He stopped at the edge, wondering if perhaps she was harboring second thoughts.

"I have something to ask you," she finally said, her voice breathy, as though she'd been holding her breath until she spoke.

"I think we've already covered that you can tell or ask me

anything, Eden," he said seriously. "You never have to worry about angering me or upsetting me."

Her cheeks went pink and then, as if gathering her courage, she blurted it out in a quiet voice.

"Can I make love to you tonight? I mean, I want to touch you and explore you like you did me last night. Last night was what I wanted, I mean, I wanted it to be perfect and you did exactly that. But tonight I'd like to take more . . . control, I guess you could call it, and make love to you. At least until the end," she added with a blush. "I don't want to be on top or anything. I'm not even sure I'd do it right."

He cut her off before she could ramble any further because he could tell with each passing word that she was growing more and more self-conscious.

He leaned over, pulling one knee onto the bed, and pressed a kiss to her luscious mouth.

"Honey, there isn't a man alive who wouldn't respond with a resounding 'Hell, yeah!' to a proposition like that. I'll lie here and let you do whatever your little heart desires and if any time you feel out of your element just tell me. We'll work through it together and when you're ready for me to take over, just say the word."

She smiled, relief lighting her eyes, and then her gaze flickered over his nude body as he stretched out on the bed, nothing hidden from her view.

She knelt up over him, her hair cascading, a curtain of silk, teasing his skin with those light brushes.

She pressed a kiss to his chest, directly over one of the scars, and then kissed a line up to his neck and the hollow of his throat. She nibbled delicately at his jaw before moving to his ear, where she sucked the lobe between her teeth.

Swanny was one hot mess of seething, extremely aroused alpha male. Her every touch drove him to the brink of insanity. And then his heart swelled with emotion—love—as she oh so tenderly laved her tongue over the scar on his cheek and followed up with little tiny kisses, covering every inch of the mangled flesh.

"Do you know how beautiful you are to me?" she whispered.

He couldn't speak for the knot in his throat. He could only nod, though it was a lie, because no, he couldn't imagine her finding him beautiful. Or even handsome. There were so many other men out there without the baggage he came with. Without the hideous scarring and imperfections he wore inside and out.

But she was fast slipping past the exterior, the visible scars, and fast easing into his heart and soul where the most painful scars resided. She soothed him in a way he'd never found peace before.

How could he ever let her go? He'd never find another woman like this. One who could so easily see beyond his imperfections to the heart of him and recognize that he was a good man with a good heart. No one would even try. Had never tried. Not until Eden.

She slid her mouth downward again, repositioning her body until she knelt right at his hip and hovered over the apex of his legs.

Tentatively she wrapped long, gentle fingers around his straining erection. He gasped, already feeling moisture beading the head and leaking onto her hand. With measured strokes, she moved her hand up and down, bringing him to a new frenzy with every upward and downward pull.

With her free hand, she cupped his balls, gently squeezing and rolling them in her palm, exploring every inch of his most sensitive region.

She glanced up at him, her hands still working their magic on his dick and balls. There was a gleam in her eyes, almost laughter.

"Um, are most men this size?" she asked. "You obviously know I have little experience and it's not like I Google naked pictures of men so I don't have much to go by, but you seem a little . . . big."

Swanny chuckled. "Can't say I've whipped out my dick and measured it against other men, but the average penis size is between five and a half and six inches fully erect. I, um, have more than that. So I'm not the biggest guy for sure, but I do fall above the average."

"Now why doesn't it surprise me that you'd be above average," she teased. "You certainly are in every aspect of your body. I have to admit I was worried last night. I didn't know how the heck you were going to get that thing inside me."

He stroked her cheek, pushing her hair behind her ear. "You were made for me, Eden. Just as I was made for you. We fit. We just fit."

She smiled and then resumed her careful exploration of his dick. Then she leaned her head down, her hair spilling downward to obscure his view. Oh hell no. He wasn't missing a second of this.

He reached down to snag her hair and held it up and out of the way just as her tongue flicked out and delicately licked the tip of his cock.

His entire body leapt like he'd been delivered an electric shock. He arched his hips upward, automatically. Wanting—needing—more.

"You like that," she murmured.

"Hell yes, I like it," he said in a guttural tone he didn't even recognize.

She grew bolder then, swirling her tongue around the head and then finally, *finally*, she sucked him between her lips, into that hot satiny heat of her mouth. And his eyes rolled back into his head at the explosion of pleasure that burst through his body.

If he died right now, he'd die a happy man and wouldn't have a single regret. Being with Eden was like being bathed in indescribable warmth. Sunshine and honey all mixed together.

But he also knew he couldn't let her continue much longer or he'd come and then she'd be left behind and like hell he was going to be that selfish.

"Eden, honey," he gasped. "You have to stop or I'm going to come all over your mouth and down your throat and I want you with me. I want you to feel as much pleasure as you're giving me."

She slowly released suction and lifted her head, her eyes half-lidded and heavy with desire.

"I think I could come just by pleasuring you and making you come," she admitted. "I'm so on edge right now that it's not going to take much."

"That makes two of us," Swanny growled. "Get over here and get on your back. This is going to be way quicker than I intended, but you've driven me beyond my breaking point."

She smiled but quickly complied with his guttural command. She laid out her body like a cat stretching in lazy contentment. Fire burned in her ocean eyes, making them more vivid, the sparks of green glowing even more brightly against the darker blue that at times dominated.

He rolled over and onto her, spreading her thighs to position himself at her opening. But before he pushed in, he slid a finger in, testing her readiness. He didn't want to hurt her and even if it killed him to wait, he was going to make damn sure she was wet and ready for him.

She moaned softly, partly in dismay that it was his finger and not his dick entering her. Her pussy clutched at his fingers as if demanding more. The walls were liquid velvet, so satiny and plush. He stroked the inside, pushing farther until he hit her G-spot, and she nearly came off the bed and his hand was suddenly bathed in wetness.

Satisfied that she was more than ready for him, he withdrew his fingers and then grasped the base of his dick and began to push inward, feeling her stretch around him to accommodate his size.

This time her moan was one of deep satisfaction. She gripped his shoulders, her nails digging into his flesh, and she tilted her hips upward, meeting his thrusts, drawing him deeper inside her.

"Wrap your legs around me and hold on. This is going to be fast and hard. If I hurt you in the slightest, you tell me to stop and I will, no matter how far gone I am."

"Stop worrying about hurting me," she said softly. "I want you. I want this. I want everything you have to give me.

Show me how much you want me, Swanny. Take us both over the edge."

Her words had the effect of a whip, galvanizing him to action. He slid his hands down her breasts, cupping them gently before caressing a line down her sides to her hips. Then he slipped his palms beneath her ass and lifted her to meet his more forceful thrusts.

At the very first plunge, he was lost. A haze fell over him, sucking him into a violent vortex of pleasure and desire such as he'd never experienced. He powered into her, retreating the barest of inches before planting himself as deeply as he could go. Until they were one person, joined intimately, him taking up where she left off.

There was no Swanny. No Eden. There was only Swanny and Eden. Together. One person. Two pieces of a whole. Finally complete.

She clung to him tightly but gave no indication that she was in any pain. Her soft moans and cries of ecstasy reassured him that she was with him.

He removed one hand from her bottom and worked his thumb between where they were joined to stroke her clit. Her entire body shook and then tightened and he knew she was as close as he was.

"Hang on, honey. We're almost there. Stay with me. I'll get us there. I swear."

"Hurry," she whispered. "I'm burning up, Swanny. I can't take this any longer. I feel like I'm going to break apart."

He began thrusting hard and fast, as much as his strength would allow. His vision blurred as his orgasm rose and flashed and he began spilling into her silken depths. She arched upward with a violent cry. A frenzied noise of utter satisfaction and completion.

He continued to stroke in and out of her, slowing his movements, even after he'd finished pouring the last of himself inside her. He couldn't bring himself to leave her yet. He felt cold without her. Only with her did the parts inside him that had remained untouched by warmth for so very long begin to thaw.

He needed her. In a way he'd never needed another person in his entire life.

And that scared the holy hell out of him.

He settled into sleep, his last fleeting thought that he'd never brought up the topic of their "relationship" as he'd planned to do.

CHAPTER 26

THE night of the soiree, Swanny dressed while Eden donned her evening finery, and instead of leaving her gorgeous hair down, she arranged it in an elegant updo with tendrils floating delicately down the slender column of her neck.

She'd done her eyes in a dark smoky look with a hint of glitter on her eyelids and affixed dangly diamond earrings to her ears, and she wore a matching choker around her neck.

She looked every bit the supermodel she was. The heels she wore made her nearly as tall as he was, and he was a tall man, but he liked the idea that she fit him just right. He could tuck her underneath his shoulder and he didn't have to lean down to kiss her.

She checked her watch. "Can you see if the others are ready? Fashionably late is one thing, but late-late is altogether different. I don't want to piss off the Aria representatives by showing up when the party is nearly over."

Swanny gave her a small salute and then went next door to check on his teammates. Nathan and Joe were inside Edge and Skylar's room and Skylar was laughingly helping her male teammates with their suits and straightening their attire.

"You guys ready?" Swanny asked from the door. "Eden's ready to go. Everything in place?"

Joe nodded. "Yeah, we'll take the lead. You follow behind with Skylar and Edge."

Swanny shook his head, unease creeping up his neck. "No, Skylar rides with you. Edge is with me. Put Skylar between you. Too much exposure up front."

Joe and Nathan gave him a concerned glance but didn't argue. "Okay, man, we'll play this your way," Nathan finally said.

Swanny nodded and then walked back toward Eden's suite with the others in tow. He slipped his key card in and then cracked the door partway.

"Everyone's ready if you are."

"Perfect! Let me just get my clutch."

Eden collected the beaded, sequined small purse off the bar and then went to meet them.

They immediately fell into step around her and escorted her down the stairs to the back entrance where the cars waited.

The drivers on hire were big burly men, well versed in personal protection. Swanny had no doubt they were packing as well, and it gave him a measure of relief that they had two extra men on Eden's protection detail.

While his gut wasn't screaming, it wasn't exactly quiet tonight and he couldn't pinpoint why. This was precisely why it didn't pay to become personally involved with a client. It could be that he didn't want her on display for dozens of wealthy men to salivate over. It could be that there was a real danger to her.

Things had been too quiet ever since Eden's brush with death when a sniper had taken a shot at her, and if Big Eddie Sinclair was to be believed—and the man was not prone to overexaggeration or bouts of hysteria—a very real threat lurked in the shadows, waiting and watching for an opportunity to enact his revenge against Eddie.

They weaved through busy Paris traffic the short distance to the upscale bar and restaurant that offered a private room.

Swanny had already been over with his team to see exactly what they were dealing with.

They'd marked areas in the room Eden was to never be in. Where she'd present an easy target from a sniper shooting through a window. They also arranged for one of them to tail Eden the entire night, and she wasn't to go to the ladies' room without Skylar and Swanny to escort her, with Skylar going in while Swanny manned the door, temporarily shutting off access until Eden had exited.

They'd prepared well for the event. So why was his gut eating a hole in his insides?

Eden reached over and slid her long slender fingers through his much larger ones, his hand engulfing hers. As if sensing his sudden turmoil, she smiled sweetly and leaned over to kiss him, uncaring that Edge sat on her other side.

"Relax," she murmured. "What could possibly go wrong when I have Superman protecting me? I trust you, Swanny. You won't let anyone hurt me."

Her words settled over him, warm and comforting, but they did nothing to dissipate his sudden agitation.

The closer they got to the restaurant where the soiree was being hosted, the more twisted up he got inside. He knew he could very well jeopardize Eden's career or her account with Aria if he fucked this up for her, but he could ignore it no longer. Her life was worth far more than some million-dollar cosmetics campaign. At least to him it was. Damn anyone else.

"Turn around," he barked into the small mouthpiece affixed strategically to his collar. "Abort. Abort, goddamn it."

To the driver's credit, he didn't hesitate. He executed a perfect J-turn in the middle of traffic and Swanny caught sight of the car carrying Nathan, Skylar and Joe doing the same, falling in behind them.

"What's up, Swanny?" Joe asked tersely. "What's going on?"

"My gut is screaming like a motherfucker, that's what," Swanny said sharply.

Radio went silent. They were all preparing for the worst. No one on his team doubted his gut, as ridiculous as it might

sound. It was just another reason he fit in so well with his
teammates.

"What you feeling, man?" Edge murmured from his
place on Eden's other side. True to Edge's nature, he never
hesitated. He was always prepared for anything. He already
had a gun pulled and was reaching for the other from the
opposite shoulder harness.

"It's wrong," Swanny muttered. "It's all goddamn wrong."

"Swanny?" Eden whispered.

He turned to Eden, expecting anger or even outrage that
he'd pulled the plug on what was a very important night for
her, but all he saw were eyes wide with fear. Whether she was
conscious of it or not, she was gripping both his and Edge's
hands, her knuckles as white as the color in her face.

"What's wrong? What should I do? Tell me so I don't get
in the way."

He admired her calm when she had to be scared to death.
Swanny knew he wasn't exactly a pillar of reassurance at the
moment, his features locked in stone and examining every
single car, person, business as they barreled by.

He carefully squeezed her hand and then reluctantly let it
go. He needed both hands, not just one.

"You stay behind me at all times," Swanny said as calmly
as he was able when his insides were screaming that Eden was
in danger. "If for whatever reason you can't get to me, you
stick to Edge. He'll protect you. Do not, and I repeat, do not
present an open target. If you can't take cover behind me or
Edge, then you hit the ground behind the vehicle.

"This car has bulletproof glass and a reinforced steel
frame. It will withstand an impact that would demolish most
other cars. You have your seat belt on?"

She nodded, her eyes still wide.

"Good girl. Now try to keep calm so I can get you back to
safety."

No sooner had the words escaped his mouth when the
world simply exploded around them. The front end of the car
lifted, nearly flipping it over backward before slamming back
to the road, fire and smoke billowing from the front.

The driver's head was lolled to the side and Swanny reached up to check for a pulse, all the while gathering Eden to his side in preparation for escape.

"What the fuck?" Edge yelled hoarsely. "That was a fucking RPG!"

"Driver's dead," Swanny said grimly. "Everyone out on my side! The shot came from the right. Eden, as soon as I pull you out, you hit the street and *don't* move until you're told. Nathan and Joe will cover you."

"Swanny, you're bleeding," Eden said, a hitch in her voice. "And where are you going?"

"I'm going after the motherfucker who attacked us."

"I've got your six," Edge said.

"One, two, three, go go go!" Swanny urged, kicking open the damaged back door and pulling Eden to the street, shoving her down roughly so she didn't present a target.

Nathan, Joe and Skylar ran up, guns drawn, cursing a blue streak.

"Cover Eden," Swanny barked. "Edge and I are going after this fucker. Do *not* let anything happen to her."

"We won't, man," Nathan said softly. "I've been in your shoes. I know how it feels. We'll take care of your girl."

Swanny shot him a look of gratitude and then ran down the street, his tux disheveled and blood-smeared. With the way people ducked and ran he must have looked like an angel of wrath, bent on the destruction of everything in his line of sight.

Mentally he went over those first moments when the world had gone all to hell. The driver had suffered a direct hit but the shot had come from the right side, not the left. And why the driver? The assassin could have just as easily targeted the backseat and they might or might not have survived. The car was reinforced, and for the sole purpose of protection, but not many vehicles outside the military could withstand a direct hit from a rocket-propelled grenade.

Edge pounded the pavement behind him, guns drawn. Already in the distance sirens could be heard, and Swanny knew they had one giant clusterfuck on their hands.

"Son of a bitch!" Swanny swore as he skidded to a stop.

Edge came to an abrupt halt beside him and the two stared down at the discarded AT-4. An older model, not the recoilless version found in more recent editions. Swanny glanced quickly around, taking in the disturbance in the soil, then snapped his attention back to Edge.

"Fuck. The French police are going to be all over this. You got anything on you to do a check for prints?" Swanny asked.

Edge grimly nodded. "They don't call me Mr. Prepared for the Worst for nothing."

He reached into one of the breast pockets of his suit and pulled out a box containing gloves, tape and dusting powder.

"You got about one minute before we're made, so put it in high gear," Swanny muttered, listening as the sounds of the sirens grew louder.

Edge quickly went to work on his examination, carefully bagging evidence and dusting for prints. His gaze drifted to the same area of disturbance Swanny had already observed, and he lifted one eyebrow.

"Seems our asshole can't afford more up-to-date equipment."

Swanny's gaze swept the area again, this time noting small patches of blood likely caused by the recoil. He wished the fucker had blown himself up, but it was obvious he'd escaped. This time. If Swanny had his way, he wouldn't get another chance to get to Eden. It was time to crack down and crack down hard, which meant calling in Sam and putting every bit of KGI's might behind tracking down this son of a bitch.

"Let's get out of here," Swanny said. "I want to get back to Eden. She has to be scared out of her mind."

Swanny and Edge hurried back toward the scene. Swanny cursed vividly when he saw a swarm of reporters and news crews all homed in on Eden's pale face. Nathan, Joe and Skylar were doing an admirable job of keeping the vultures back, but police were questioning all four, which made crowd control next to impossible. After all, it wasn't every day a vehicle got RPG'd right in the middle of Paris.

There were murmurs and shouts all between tossing question after question the policemen's way.

"They want to know if this was a terrorist attack," Edge translated.

Swanny lifted an eyebrow at his friend. "Since when are you fluent in French?"

Edge grinned. "My mother is French. I actually have dual citizenship and was born in America. My dad was military, so I followed in his footsteps for a while but found fighting was more of a challenge. I thrived on the adrenaline."

As they strode rapidly to the scene, Swanny glanced over at his friend. "So why'd you give up MMA?"

Edge shrugged. "I was getting older. The competition was getting younger. I wanted to go out on top so when I won the belt in the heavyweight division I announced my retirement a few months later. But I was still restless and wanted the adrenaline. I wanted to make a difference. I guess it's what bothered me most when I quit the army to pursue a career in MMA, because at least in the army I was making a difference. It wasn't all about me and my ability to pound a guy in the ring. When I heard about KGI, it seemed the perfect compromise. I knew I was qualified. I was a ranger. My skills weren't rusty because even after I left the army I still kept to my military regimen. Kept my shooting skills up. I guess even back then I missed it and realized I'd made a bad decision."

As soon as Eden looked up through the crowd and saw Swanny coming toward her, she broke away from the police and reporters and shoved her way through the resisting crowds. She threw herself into his arms and held him tightly. She shook violently against him. There wasn't a single part of her that wasn't quivering. Her teeth chattered and her skin was icy cold.

Swanny swore as he gathered her in his arms, covering as much of her as he could. She was in shock and it was obvious no one had made any effort to get her medical attention.

He buried his face in her sweet-smelling hair, such a contrast to the smell of fire, smoke and melting rubber. Even the scent of blood hung obscenely in the air.

"I was so scared for you," she whispered brokenly. "Oh God, Swanny, never do that to me again. I died a thousand times waiting for you to come back, so afraid you wouldn't."

Tears slipped openly down her cheeks as she swallowed back a raw sob. He tenderly kissed each drop of moisture away and then clung to her, anchoring her through the storm.

With Edge translating, Swanny got his point across in a blunt, take-it-or-leave-it fashion. Swanny wasn't leaving Eden exposed a minute longer. He was taking her back to her hotel and if the police wanted to question her, it damn sure wouldn't be at a precinct.

The officers on the scene put up a token protest until Skylar very sweetly informed them exactly who Eden Sinclair was and that she was considered one of the most beautiful women in the world and it wouldn't look good for the police to hold a shaken, in-shock, scared-out-of-her-mind woman against her will.

The commanding officer on the scene couldn't backpedal quickly enough. He immediately arranged a police caravan to ferry Eden and her entourage back to the hotel, though Swanny made a mental note to check out and find another hotel. As soon as the news got out—and it would—the journalists, both legitimate and paparazzi, would be circling like vultures, which would put Eden in an even more vulnerable position.

Swanny quickly led Eden to their suite, holding on to her because she was far from steady on her feet. As soon as they were inside, she collapsed on the couch, leaned forward so her elbows rested on her knees and buried her face in her hands.

Silent sobs shook her shoulders, hell, her entire body. She lifted her tear-drenched eyes to his, and it cut out his heart to see her in such distress.

"Why, Swanny? Why? I don't understand," she said, her voice cracking under the weight of emotion. "Why would someone want to blow up my car? Who could possibly hate me so much that they'd go to such horrible lengths to kill me? I don't u-u-understand."

Her voice broke off and she dropped her face into her hands once more, her shoulders heaving with the force of her sobs.

He went to her. He couldn't do anything else. A man who didn't comfort his woman when she needed it the most wasn't much of a man. She turned blindly to him, clinging to him like a burr, burying her face in his neck, wetting the collar of his shirt with her tears,

"I don't understand," she whispered brokenly. "I just don't understand."

Swanny sighed because, goddamn it, her father should have been straight with her from the start, and now it was left to Swanny to piece together the entire puzzle so at least Eden could gain some understanding of what was going on around her. Something she should have been aware of from the start. And right now he didn't give two shits if it pissed her father off and he fired KGI.

Because whether or not KGI was still assigned as her security detail, there was no way in hell he was leaving Eden's side until the assassin was taken out. Permanently.

CHAPTER 27

SWANNY gathered Eden close in his arms, her face buried in his neck. He rubbed his hands up and down her back, offering her comfort and bracing himself for what he was about to tell her.

He'd do anything at all to spare her this pain, but if it saved her life, if it made her more wary and alert, then he'd lay it out to her as delicately as possible.

He stroked her hair and then gently pulled her away so he could look her in the eyes.

"Listen to me, honey. There's something—a lot—I need to explain to you. Something that you should have been told from the very beginning, and I'm risking a lot by going against your father's wishes, but you need to be told . . . the truth."

Her eyes widened in shock, a glazed look falling over her delicate features.

"My father? The truth? Swanny, I don't understand. What do you mean my father should have told me the truth? Are you saying he *lied* to me?"

Distress was a beacon in her eyes radiating to the rest of her body. She looked utterly bewildered, betrayed and devastated. Her lips quivered and tears crowded the corners of her lids, glistening on her eyelashes. God, but he hated what he had to do. Normally it wasn't something he would do. KGI answered to the party footing the bill, even when they disagreed.

But this was a different situation entirely and he couldn't—wouldn't—allow Eden to exist in ignorance a moment longer. Her father be damned. KGI be damned. If it lost him his job, he didn't give a fuck. All he cared about at this moment was the woman staring at him, sorrow and confusion shining in wounded eyes.

And so he started at the very beginning, telling her everything her father had related to him and his team. She visibly flinched and her hand flew to her mouth as tears gathered and ran down her cheeks when he told her that her mother's death was an act of vengeance and not an accident.

By the time he finished the entire sordid tale, she was openly sobbing, her shoulders heaving as she tried to gulp back her sounds of anguish.

He felt like the worst sort of bastard for destroying her illusions. For turning her world upside down and for exposing long-held secrets and the endless cycle of revenge.

He stared at her in sorrow, unsure of whether to hold her, try to comfort her, but he didn't know if she was angry with *him*. He didn't know if he should touch her or maintain their current distance, because the moment the ugly story had been spilled, she'd withdrawn, putting space between them, and now she sat, hands fisted in her lap, staring straight ahead sightlessly as tears streamed down her beautiful face.

"Eden," he said softly, no longer able to bear her agony. He felt it as keenly as if someone had driven a knife right through his heart.

And then his dilemma was solved because she whirled, her face ravaged by grief, and threw herself into his arms, fisting his torn shirt with both hands. She pressed her body as close as she could without him putting her into his lap, so he promptly rectified the matter, dragging her into his arms and wrapping them tightly around her.

Though her sobs had quieted, her body still shook and he could feel the dampness on her cheeks where her tears had left silvery trails down her face.

"I'm so sorry, honey," Swanny said, regret a physical ache in his chest. "I wouldn't hurt you for the world. Please forgive me this, but I thought you deserved to know. I've thought it from the very beginning before I even met you, but your father was adamant. He was trying to protect you."

"*How* could he keep something like this from me?" she asked tearfully. "God, it's been a lie. All these years. A complete lie. And *more* lies. What else has he kept from me? How long has he been controlling my life—and, my God, I've allowed it. I allowed him to hire Micah and David because I didn't want him to worry. He hired you and then lied about why. I couldn't figure out at the time why no one except me seemed relieved that the shooter had been arrested, and now I know it's because everyone knew I wasn't safe except the most important person in this equation. *Me*."

He couldn't argue a single point with her because she was exactly right, and his guilt intensified, because she should have been told the truth from the start even though it wasn't his place to make that kind of decision.

But all of that changed for him the moment he and Eden connected, when she came to mean so much more than just a job to him. Her father might argue that Swanny had no rights when it came to his daughter, but that was bullshit. His commitment to Eden went far beyond the normal client relationship for a regular mission. This was deeply personal to him and he was willing to risk everything for her. Censure, the loss of his job, his very identity.

He recognized that Eden was a total game changer for him. His priorities had shifted, and he was a man who always placed his loyalty and commitment to his job above all else. But Eden had reordered his priorities. Her protection, her happiness, her life came first. Nothing else mattered as much to him. He'd go to the wall for her and damn the consequences.

"I know this was hard to hear, Eden," Swanny murmured against her hair. "And I'm so damn sorry. You have to know

I'd do anything not to hurt you. But with this attack, you need to know what you're up against so you can take the proper precautions. Don't get me wrong. I'm going to protect you with my life. My team is going to protect you. But you needed to be aware of what exactly is at stake here."

"Thank you," she whispered, stunning him. Why was she thanking him for tilting her world on its axis? Shouldn't he be the bad guy here?

She lifted her head, a watery sheen still evident in her ocean eyes, but the tears had stopped streaking down her face. What he saw in her eyes blew him away. There was no anger. No condemnation. There was sincere gratitude, and he could tell she was valiantly pulling herself together and trying to regain her composure.

"Baby, what are you thanking me for?" he asked hoarsely.

"For trusting me with the truth," she said in a low voice. "For wanting me to know from the start. For telling me now what my father should have told me a long time ago. I don't want you to apologize to me, Swanny. Not for telling me the truth. It means a lot to me that you would risk so much for me. Your life. Your job. I'm humbled by the lengths you've gone to, to protect me physically and emotionally."

She leaned forward, pressing her lips to his so sweetly it made his gut ache. There was a wealth of emotion in the light brush, like a butterfly's wing against his mouth. Soft and delicate, just like her.

She pulled away, breathless, her cheeks pink and no longer pale with shock. And then her eyes became troubled again, shadows dimming them.

"I know I should call my father, not to confront him, but to assure him I'm all right, but I just can't face him right now. I need a little time to digest this—what he kept from me," she said in a faltering tone. "Does that make me a terrible, selfish person?"

His reaction was instantaneous, nearly explosive. "Hell no it doesn't. You deserve as much time as you need to process your shock. God only knows how hard this must have been for you. I certainly can't claim to even understand what it's done to you because I've never been in your situation. You'll get no judgment from me. You'll never get anything from me but complete support and understanding."

Emotion swamped her expression, her eyes warming, the shadows from just moments prior dissipating.

"I—"

Whatever she was about to say was cut off when a sharp knock sounded at the door. Swanny cursed, even though he knew their time together would be very short lived because not only would the police be involved, but his team would also be gathering to put together the pieces and plan their next move.

"Stay put, honey," Swanny said, brushing his mouth across her forehead. "Just sit here and try to relax. I'm afraid the next hours are going to be long and stressful for you."

"But you'll be here, right?" she asked, her brow furrowed anxiously.

"I'm not leaving you," he vowed. "We're in this together. You're mine to protect, Eden. You go nowhere without me."

Relief shone brightly in her eyes as she sagged against the back of the couch. Another impatient knock sounded and Swanny turned, checking the peephole to see two policemen and Swanny's entire team.

He opened the door and gestured for them to come in. But he stepped in front of the policemen and then turned to Edge. "Translate this for me. Tell them they are not to over-tax Eden. They aren't to press her too hard. She's upset and in shock and I won't have them upsetting her further."

"I'm perfectly able to understand English," one of the policeman said in a dry voice. "I understand your concerns and we will most certainly be mindful of Miss Sinclair when we question her."

Swanny nodded and then extended his hand. "Daryl Swanson, but everyone calls me Swanny." He shook both the inspectors' hands as they introduced themselves to him in return as being part of the Police Nationale's anti-terrorism unit for this jurisdiction.

They quickly explained that they were investigating this

as an act of terrorism, and if there was no evidence to support terrorism, the case would be turned over to the criminal investigation section of the Police Nationale.

Damn it, but Swanny needed time to discuss with his team exactly how they were going to approach this. Pretend ignorance and play up the angle that Eden was the victim of yet another random brush with death? It was hardly plausible, but the last thing he wanted was for his team to get kicked off the case, so to speak, and have people who weren't as diligent as he and his team protecting Eden.

Over his dead body was that happening. His line was drawn in the sand and he wasn't budging.

He exchanged quick glances with Nathan and Joe, and Joe held up a finger to his lips behind the investigators' backs, signaling that for now, they were playing it cool and not showing their hand.

As a courtesy or perhaps because Swanny's expression had immediately become fierce when he'd issued his dictate as to how Eden was to be handled, the investigators let Swanny take the lead as they walked farther into the suite, where Eden was huddled on the sofa.

She'd dragged one of the throws from the arm of the couch and pulled it around her, almost as though when he left her he took her warmth away. The color that had briefly returned when she kissed him had washed away, leaving her pale and haunted-looking again. She surveyed the approaching investigators with clear apprehension.

Swanny leaned over, lifting the blanket as if securing it more firmly around her and whispered close to her ear, "Just play it cool, honey. Follow our lead. We don't want to tip our hand and involve them."

She gave an imperceptible nod, as if moving so Swanny could arrange the blanket just so, and then Swanny took a seat next to her on the couch, sitting close enough that their bodies touched. He gestured for the two detectives to take seats in the two armchairs across from the couch separated by a coffee table.

Skylar took a seat on the other side of Eden, and Nathan, Joe and Edge stood, forming a perimeter around the seated members. Edge leaned against the arm of the sofa where Skylar sat, and Nathan and Joe stood on either side of the investigators, their arms crossed, expressions indecipherable.

The investigators were clearly uncomfortable with the obvious disadvantage their seating gave them, surrounded by the KGI team.

Inspector Mercier cleared his throat and then leveled his gaze on Eden. Inspector Dubois remained silent, allowing his partner to take the lead.

"First let me express my regret for your traumatic experience, Miss Sinclair. I want to assure you that our department has made this case an absolute priority and we fully intend to apprehend and bring to justice the person or persons responsible."

"Thank you," Eden murmured.

Underneath the blanket, Eden's hand slid over Swanny's leg as if seeking reassurance from his touch. Uncaring of how it appeared to the others, Swanny slipped his hand over hers, laying it atop hers so that it was trapped between his leg and his palm.

She immediately relaxed, and some of the anxiety eased from her forehead and the tight lines around her lips disappeared.

They questioned not only Eden but the entire team for the better part of four hours. Swanny could tell it was taking its toll on Eden, but he wanted it done with. The investigators questioned why she had such an extensive security team and if there had been serious threats made against her.

They frowned upon learning Eden had received a close call so recently, but Joe explained that the shooter had been arrested and charged and that the tighter security was simply a guard against possible copycat occurrences given the media coverage of the shooting in Boston.

The investigators seemed to become increasingly frustrated because while every question was answered, the responses were purposely vague, not volunteering anything more than what the investigators asked. On the surface they appeared completely cooperative and forthcoming, but it was clear the investigators were getting nowhere in their minds.

As the end of the fourth hour approached, just when Swanny was about to call an end to the entire thing, the investigators finally stood and gave their thanks for their cooperation and promised to follow up if any leads turned up.

Eden's shoulders sagged in obvious relief. Swanny wasn't sure how she'd made it this far without collapsing. She had to be exhausted and was still reeling from all Swanny had told her. He wanted to get her to bed and then meet with his team to determine their next course of action.

Sam would need to be called in with the latest developments so he could relay the information to the team tracking the source of the threat. And though he'd certainly made it clear to Eden that she was in no way obligated to call her father, Eddie Sinclair *would* have to be notified. Once he learned of the event—and he most assuredly would hear of it—he'd want to barge over, and that would only draw more attention to Eden and compromise her safety. It may even be the killer's motive. To draw out Eddie and set up a scenario where Eddie had to witness his daughter's death.

Eden would sleep tonight, but Swanny and the others wouldn't. There was too much to sort through and decisions to be made in regard to Eden's protection.

CHAPTER 28

THE next morning, Swanny's team had gathered in Eden's suite to discuss the day's events and schedule. They'd spent the entire night tirelessly setting into motion plans for Eden's protection. Joe had contacted the director and the executives at Aria and had arranged to reconvene to an undisclosed location for the shooting to resume. In turn, the filming crew had spent the night relocating and setting up. The security was tightened and more added, but only KGI would have direct access to Eden and be in charge of her transportation and handling.

Swanny was reluctant to expose Eden in any manner, but she'd been firm when she said "the show must go on" and that she wouldn't allow some asshole with a grudge to dictate her life or ruin her career. He had to admire her determination even as it scared the shit out of him.

There were two more days of filming before the launch party, and the very last thing Swanny wanted was a repeat of the last time Eden had ventured out for an event. But Eden was adamant that filming wouldn't be delayed and the launch party would be held as scheduled. Too much time and planning had been put into this campaign, and Eden refused to be the one responsible for its delay.

Joe had reported in to Sam, who had relayed the intel to Rio's team, which was taking the lead on tracing the source of the threat. Not that KGI had ever taken the threat to Eden lightly, but Sam was even more determined to track down the bastard and take him out. He called in Steele and his team and put them on the job along with Rio's team so they could cover more ground and dig deeper, flushing the ass-hole out from underneath his rock.

And oddly, when Swanny himself had called Eden's father, Eddie's response hadn't been one Swanny had expected. He hadn't lost his shit. Hadn't freaked the fuck out and boomed out that he and his sons would be on the next flight to Paris. He'd even agreed with Swanny that for now he and his sons should stay put and not risk giving the attacker what he may likely want. The Sinclairs together. Eddie had agreed that it would be putting Eden in more danger and had signed off on KGI's handling of the situation. That phone call still twisted Swanny's gut, and his senses were screaming at him that something was decidedly off. But he put that away, because his focus wasn't on Eddie or whatever the hell he was think-ing. Swanny's sole priority was Eden.

Eden had just come from the bathroom after dressing for the day of filming when a pounding on the door put everyone on alert.

Swanny immediately drew his gun and headed for the door, his team on his six. He checked the peephole, stunned to see *Hancock* standing outside, a murderous expression on his face.

What the fuck? What was Hancock doing here? And why? Any time Hancock made an appearance trouble was usually in his wake, and Swanny's hackles immediately rose.

"Hancock," he mouthed to the others.

The what-the-fuck looks abounded, matching his own reaction. Hancock pounded on the door again and it was clear he wasn't going anywhere.

Swanny held up his hand and motioned for Edge and

Skylar to take the other side of the door while Nathan and Joe stood just behind Swanny, and Swanny reached to unlock the door.

The minute Swanny opened the door, Hancock was in his face, hands gripping Swanny's shirt in tight fists, so fast and furious that Swanny had no time to react. His team immediately raised their guns and trained them on Hancock, and Joe barked an order for Hancock to stand down or he'd shoot.

"Where is she?" Hancock demanded, ignoring Joe's threat.

Hancock was one pissed-off ball of bristling male, anger pouring off him in waves. Before the rest of Swanny's team could follow through with Joe's threat or Swanny could get his own gun up and between them, Eden's voice echoed through the room.

"Guy? What on earth are you doing here?"

And then to Swanny's utter shock, she pushed by Swanny, inserting herself between the two men, and threw her arms around Hancock, hugging him tightly. More baffling was the fact that he returned her hug just as fiercely, his fury seemingly diminished now that Eden was there in front of him.

The looks on Swanny's team members' faces were a mixture of what-the-fuck and utter bewilderment. Had the entire world gone insane? How the hell did Eden and Hancock even know each other, much less be on such intimate terms?

Hancock was visibly relieved as he held Eden tightly against his body, and Swanny realized that Hancock's anger had in fact been worry. What the hell was Hancock's connection to Eden? Hancock was a rebel, following his own set of rules and morals. Swanny wouldn't have believed him capable of feeling emotion for another person.

"You scared the hell out of me, cupcake," Hancock said gruffly.

Everyone's mouths fell open, even Swanny's. Cupcake? What the ever-loving fuck? And she'd called him Guy. Hell, Swanny didn't even know Hancock's first name or if Hancock was his first name. He knew very little about Hancock at all other than the little that had been gleaned from his run-ins with KGI on two missions.

But there was a softness in his expression that was never present. Swanny had never seen the man appear anything except cold and reserved, but he was anything but that with Eden. There was honest-to-God relief and tenderness in his eyes as he hugged Eden again.

Skylar's lips parted, and she stared at Hancock as if an alien had suddenly descended. *Cupcake?* she silently mouthed. *For real?*

Swanny was every bit as bewildered as the rest of his team. This wasn't a contingency they'd planned for at all. How could they have? Sure, Hancock had shown up and had crossed paths with KGI in the past, but he'd never had a personal stake in any of them. And it appeared he most certainly had a close relationship with Eden.

A tight fist wrapped itself around Swanny's neck as jealousy and a sense of territory violation assailed him. He considered Eden his, and he didn't like the fact that another man, especially Hancock, was evidently on intimate terms with her.

When Eden pulled away, Hancock looked her up and down, his eyes narrowing as if studying her for injuries.

"Are you okay?" Hancock asked in a soft voice.

The KGI team was utterly bewildered, and it was reflected in all their expressions. Swanny's teammates lowered their guns but didn't holster them, and Swanny kept his up, on constant guard because he didn't trust Hancock in the least.

"I'm fine, Guy," Eden said. "They've taken very good care of me. Why are you here? How did you know? I don't understand. Have you spoken to Dad or Ryker or Raid?"

"Because I saw your name splashed across the news as having been car-bombed by a fucking RPG," Hancock growled. "If they were taking such good care of you, then why the hell were you ever in that position to begin with?"

"Not to interrupt an apparent reunion here," Joe said dryly, "but can someone tell me what the fuck is going on here? How the hell do you know Hancock, Eden?"

She turned startled eyes on Joe. "The question is how do you know Guy? And why are you all treating him like the enemy?"

Hancock slid an arm around her shoulders, pulling her into his side, and brushed a kiss over her brow. Swanny had to swallow back the growl forming in his chest. He didn't like what was going on here and he definitely didn't want Hancock touching Eden.

And yet suddenly so much made sense. With a startling moment of insight, Swanny recalled her asking if Hancock had talked to her father or brothers, as though it was an absolutely normal event to have occurred. It would certainly make Eddie's reaction make sense, and explain why he hadn't gone off the rails and caught the first flight to Paris.

Because Eddie knew Hancock was on *his* way.

"It's all right, cupcake. Let's just say that me and KGI go way back and have a somewhat tumultuous relationship."

"That's an understatement," Nathan muttered under his breath.

"Come and sit. All of you," Eden said in a firm voice. "I've had enough information withheld from me and it's not going to continue. I want to know what's going on here."

"You aren't the only one," Swanny said pointedly.

Hancock followed Eden into the sitting area, Swanny and his team close behind.

As soon as Hancock was seated next to Eden, his hand engulfing hers in a reassuring manner, he pinned Swanny and his team with his steely gaze.

"What the hell is going on, and I want it all. I don't give a shit what your orders are or if this is some classified crap. I want to know exactly what the situation is here."

"I only just learned of it myself," Eden murmured. "Swanny told me, thank God. My father and brothers kept me in the dark. They didn't want me to know."

Tears welled in her eyes, and it was all Swanny could do not to forcibly remove Hancock from Eden's side and pull her into his arms to give her comfort. But at the moment, there was the very real issue of there being a connection between Hancock and Eden that Swanny didn't understand. It was obvious that Hancock had feelings for her. The question was in what capacity?

They obviously hadn't ever had a sexual relationship because she'd been a virgin when Swanny made love to her. But she'd mentioned an obvious connection to her father and brothers as well. There were a dozen questions buzzing in his head because nothing made sense right now.

"You found out about your mother," Hancock said in a low voice.

Eden's eyes widened, going even glossier with a sheen of tears. "You knew? Am I the only person who *didn't* know?"

Hancock squeezed her hand. "I would have been here much sooner, but I was in deep cover and didn't get your father's calls until I saw the news and then checked my messages and spoke to Eddie. I'm sorry, cupcake. I should have been here to protect you. You have to know I'd never allow anyone to hurt you."

She sniffled back the tears that threatened and gave him a watery smile. "I know, Guy. And please, don't feel badly. As I said, Swanny and his team have been taking very good care of me. I have two more days of shooting and they've made provisions for my safety. It all ends with a launch party after the wrap-up of production, and then I'll be done with this job and can go back home and be safe."

Swanny flinched at how casually Eden spoke of going home and being safe. He damn sure wasn't ready to let her go, but neither did he want her in danger for a second longer than necessary. Hell of a note when the only way he got to be with her was if she was in danger. He wanted to *mean* something to her. Something more than a protector, a temporary bodyguard, whom she would forget when it was all over with.

Hancock looked at Swanny, obviously picking up on the fact that though Nathan and Joe were the team leaders, Swanny was lead on this mission.

"Give me the rundown," Hancock said, his expression now hard and focused.

Swanny glanced at his teammates, wondering just how much he should relate to a man who was nebulous at best, though he had come through twice and had saved Maren, Steele's wife, by taking a bullet for her, not to mention getting her out of a messy situation and back into KGI's hands and protection.

"Tell him," Eden said softly. "I trust him with my life. He deserves to know."

"Just what is your relationship?" Swanny asked carefully, stalling before he got into the details with Hancock.

"Her family pretty much adopted me," Hancock said, uncharacteristically breaking his habit of not revealing anything remotely personal. "I owe her father and mother a lot. Eden has always been like a sister to me. It's because of them that I survived."

This time Eden squeezed Hancock's hand and smiled at him. Then she turned to Swanny. "He's family."

Swanny sighed and then related the story from start to end, including everything Eden's father had told him. Eden steeled herself, her features locked in stone as she heard for the second time about the events that had unfolded over all these years and how it was affecting the present.

Hancock's expression grew colder and colder, fury tightening his features.

"So you have the other teams tracking this son of a bitch?" Hancock demanded.

Swanny nodded. "Rio and Steele are both on the job. We hope to find and eliminate the source of the threat as quickly as possible."

"Not soon enough, apparently," Hancock said in an icy voice.

"Eden is our top priority," Swanny said just as coldly.

Hancock suddenly rose, pulling Eden to stand beside him and engulfing her in another huge hug. "I'm going to run, cupcake. There's apparently a lot I need to do. I'll check back in with you in a few days."

Shit. This was not a good sign. Hancock could well blow KGI's mission all to hell. Swanny would have to warn Sam ASAP of the new development and of Hancock's involvement in yet another of KGI's missions. Sam was going to be pissed.

She hugged Hancock back, and he kissed her cheek and

then strode out of the suite, not saying a word to Swanny or his team.

"Well," Skylar said, breaking the awkward silence that had descended. "That was, um, interesting."

Eden sat back down but checked her watch. "We need to leave soon. I don't want to be late and cause more disruption to the filming. But I'd like to know exactly how you all know Guy. I'm completely confused."

"We've bumped into him on a few missions," Joe said. "Let's just say our relationship is tenuous at best. We haven't ever figured out exactly what his motives are, but he has helped us in the past as well as hindered us. We don't know a whole hell of a lot about him. Our exposure to him has been brief at best. We kind of have a tacit agreement to stay out of each other's way."

Eden frowned. "So he does what y'all do?"

Swanny glanced quickly at Joe to silence him. If Eden considered him family but wasn't aware of who and what Hancock was, he didn't want to further disillusion her any more than she already had been.

"Hancock is a law unto himself," Swanny said. "We aren't sure ourselves exactly what he does, but I think it's safe to say that it's mostly classified and military."

"Oh," Eden said. "That makes sense. He did join the military. Followed in my father's footsteps. It's just that we rarely see him, so I figured whatever he did was top secret. He's often gone for months at a time and I haven't seen him in two years."

Swanny wasn't about to tell her why or give details as to Hancock's activities or go into any further details about his role in the two KGI missions. There was simply no need, and she'd already been dealt enough shock. He wanted her as stress free as was possible given the circumstances, and more than that, he wanted her to have faith in him and his vow to protect her and keep her safe.

"We should go," Joe announced. "The car is here. The new hotel has been secured and security measures implemented. You'll be checked in under an alias and officially checked out of this hotel. With the new filming location, it's our hope that we've laid the groundwork for it to appear as though you've left the country."

Eden looked perplexed by Joe's explanation.

"We had a double visibly leave the hotel and head to the airport, complete with paparazzi coverage. She's currently on a plane to the U.S. under your name. The car that will be taking you to the studio is tinted so no one will be able to see inside, and we're all cramming into one so it won't look suspicious for a caravan to suddenly depart the premises."

Eden's eyes rounded. "You've thought of everything."

"I hope to fuck so," Swanny said. "We're not taking any chances with your life, Eden. I won't lie. I wish you *were* on a plane back home, but I also understand how important this is to you and your career."

She touched his arm, her eyes warm, as she met his gaze. "Thank you, Swanny."

"Okay, let's roll," Joe said, a hint of impatience in his voice. "Take your places and let's get the hell out of here."

CHAPTER 29

THE tension in the studio on the outskirts of Paris was thick, a tangible air that permeated every single person working. Except Eden. Swanny didn't know how she did it, but she pulled it off with perfection. Smiling as if she didn't have a care in the world. Playing to the camera. Saying her lines in a smoky, husky, sexy-as-hell voice that kept him hard for the better part of the day.

There was posted security around the entire perimeter, and Skylar and Nathan had taken position on the roof with their sniper rifles, doing constant recon and reporting to Joe every half hour.

Every single member of the filming crew, including the director, much to his displeasure, was thoroughly searched before being allowed in, and Swanny's team had done a sweep of the entire studio much earlier that morning before returning to the hotel to bring Eden in.

Swanny, Joe and Edge were on the inside with Eden, standing just off the set and out of the camera range but close enough to cover her quickly if things went south. Swanny was the closest to her, purposely positioning himself in front of Edge and Joe so he could keep close watch over Eden.

Even the director was uncharacteristically silent. He was on edge, nervous and jumpy, and his mood quickly spread to his crew, who were every bit as agitated as he was.

It was clear they were scared shitless, but there was also admiration in the director's eyes each time Eden pulled off a flawless performance and he called it a wrap.

Eventually her calm spread to the rest of the crew, and by the afternoon, the tension had dissipated and the mood was much more relaxed. No one jumped at the slightest noise any longer. It was as if she held them all in her thrall, and, well, he supposed she did just that. He knew he certainly wasn't immune to her. She just had a way of putting those around her at ease, and yet Swanny knew just how scared and upset she was behind the calm facade.

It only made him admire her all the more for being able to maintain her composure and act as a reassuring presence when it was he and his team who were supposed to have that job.

Every once in a while, between shoots, Swanny could see the calm slip just a bit, and he saw the fatigue and fear in her eyes. The sorrow as she was still processing all she'd learned in the last twenty-four hours. And hell, the woman could have died. Again.

Two brushes with death in a short period of time and yet she was stalwart and a consummate professional. He'd never met a woman like her. Never met her equal and he knew he never would. There would never be another woman for him. Not after her. How could any other woman ever measure up? Who else would accept him and his faults? His scars, both external and internal.

She looked up as if sensing his gaze, and her eyes immediately warmed and she smiled, the tiredness and fear drifting away as if she drew comfort and strength from his presence. Ironic, since everyone else was drawing comfort and peace from her.

"If we can get in another hour, we'll be ahead of schedule and can wrap up by noon tomorrow," the director announced. "Great job, everyone. And Eden, you're fabulous as always."

A cheer went up from the crew, and Eden smiled with her

usual grace. "I'm sure under a different director we would indeed be behind schedule. You did a wonderful job, Lonnie. As always. I can't imagine working on this project with any other director."

The director flushed at Eden's praise and dragged his finger around his collar as if uncomfortable. The cantankerous, brusque director was as enthralled with Eden as everyone else, though he tried to hide it with his bark. Right now, though, Swanny was imagining a satisfied cat cuddled against Eden while having its head stroked as the director preened and actually smiled—a genuine smile—at Eden.

And the hell of it was that Eden had been utterly sincere. She really was just too damn nice. Swanny would have told the director to go fuck himself on several occasions, but Eden had taken it all in stride and performed to expectation. Beyond expectation, in Swanny's opinion. Considering all she'd been through, it was a damn miracle that she could even perform at all.

Swanny's team immediately kicked it into high gear, preparing for Eden's departure to the new hotel, where she'd be checked in under a false name. Joe had used one of the many aliases KGI possessed for just such occasions as this.

Before departing, Eden donned a black wig and wore heavily tinted, large sunglasses that covered nearly the entire upper portion of her face and a scarf wrapped around her neck and pulled up over her mouth. She also wore a coat with extra padding so it appeared she was several pounds heavier than she was, and she wore flats to make her appear shorter. She'd been instructed to hunch slightly to solidify the illusion of her being shorter and heavier.

Swanny's team had dressed casually, looking like normal people instead of the operatives they were. Though it made him extremely uneasy, they didn't completely surround Eden, because they didn't want to draw any attention to the fact that they were protecting her.

The crew was instructed to remain until thirty minutes after Eden's departure.

Joe and Nathan went out first to get into the waiting SUV

and then Swanny came out with Eden at his side, Skylar and Edge following casually behind.

Swanny was on heightened alert, scanning their surroundings while appearing to be casual as he headed toward the car. One hand was inside his light blazer, resting against the butt of his pistol in case he needed to act fast. He knew Skylar and Edge were similarly prepared and that Nathan and Joe, already in the vehicle, would both have their weapons drawn, ready to leap out at the first sign of danger.

When Swanny got Eden into the middle seat, Skylar went to the opposite door while Edge took the front seat next to the hired security specialist driving the SUV.

Swanny didn't like Edge being in such a vulnerable position. After what had happened when their vehicle had been hit with an RPG and the driver had been killed, if a similar attack happened, Edge was an open target. The very last thing Swanny wanted was to lose a teammate. A brother.

Eden was more at ease as they drove to the hotel. She was relaxed, leaning into Swanny's side, snuggling as if seeking his strength and warmth. Uncaring of how it appeared to his teammates, he wrapped his arm around her, pulling her closer to his body. She laid her head on his shoulder and let out a sigh.

"One more day of shooting and then the launch party and we'll be done with this," she said, relief evident in her voice. "I won't lie. I'm ready for this to be over with. It scares me that you and your team are in the line of fire. I'd never forgive myself if one of them—or you—were hurt or killed because of me."

Swanny frowned because she sounded like she was ready to be done with it all. Including him.

He was suddenly struck with a raging case of nerves. He could feel his palms growing clammy. What if she didn't feel the same way about him as he did about her? What if when this was over, she moved on, leaving him behind, only the memory of him being her first lingering in her mind?

He tried to block out his doubts and focus on the positive and hope for the best. It scared him to death to put his heart on the line. To open up to her completely and to be so direct in his planned conversation with her.

His head told him he was an idiot for even considering that a woman like her would have any interest in seeing him beyond the time they spent protecting her, but his heart clung to the tenuous hope that he was more to her than her bodyguard.

What if he got shot down?

He wished he could be more confident. But his demons wouldn't go away. His dreams were still tormented by his time in captivity, though he had noticed that when Eden slept with him, she chased away those demons, calming his inner beast and soothing away the pain of the past.

But he had visible reminders of his captivity. Could a woman like Eden look beyond those? In her career, where beauty and elegance was a part of her daily life? He couldn't imagine her ever wanting to show up to an event on his arm.

Beauty and the Beast. Literally. Only real life wasn't a fairy tale and no happily-ever-afters were ever guaranteed. He'd seen love work with the Kelly brothers. Other members of the KGI team. But he'd never considered it for himself. Never thought he would even entertain the thought.

And yet he knew in the deepest recesses of his heart that he loved Eden beyond measure. He felt the worst kind of fool for setting himself up for such a huge fall. He wasn't even sure *when* he'd fallen for her. She'd certainly had his attention from the moment he met her, but looking back he couldn't pinpoint an exact moment when love had happened.

It seemed he'd always felt it toward her, growing even more the first time they made love and he discovered he was her first. That had humbled him in a way he'd never been humbled in his life. It still had the power to bring him to his knees. It was a gift he'd treasure forever, no matter what happened between him and Eden.

But he knew one thing. No matter where life took him, he'd never love another woman as he did Eden. Nor would he ever meet another woman of her caliber.

CHAPTER 30

EDEN issued an audible sigh of relief once Swanny and part of his team had entered her suite and swept the interior while Edge and Skylar had remained in the hallway with her, flanking her protectively and watching for any sign of anyone in the hallway.

They'd rented out the entire floor of rooms so they'd be the only occupants, and the hotel had put a block on anyone stopping on their floor on the elevator. But the stairway presented an issue because they couldn't lock it in case they needed to get out fast, and they damn sure needed more than one option for escape.

Now everyone was gone except Swanny, and she sank onto the couch, only wanting Swanny next to her, his arms around her.

"Want to get undressed and into more comfortable clothing?" Swanny asked before he sat next to her. He stood just in front of her, as if waiting to see what she wanted before he decided on his position.

"Only if you'll come to bed with me and hold me," she said, watching for his reaction.

It bothered her that she was still so unsure of herself, or rather of him. She wasn't used to being anything but confident in her life and career. But this was something she'd never encountered before.

She'd completely lost her heart to Swanny and she had no idea if he reciprocated her feelings. She knew he cared about her. No question there. But when this was all over with, would he simply move on to the next mission and she'd go back to her life and career as if they hadn't ever held such a close bond?

His expression immediately softened and a heated glow entered his eyes as he stared warmly down at her. He held out his hand to help her to her feet and then pulled her into his arms.

"I'll hold you all night, honey. But first there's something I want to give you and then . . ." He hesitated briefly, uncertainty flashing in his eyes giving him an almost vulnerable look. He let out his breath as he pulled her a little farther away from his embrace. "Then, I'd like us to go to bed because there's something I want to discuss with you."

He blurted out the last, as though it had taken him a moment to gather his courage and say it before he changed his mind.

She looked curiously up at him, a sudden attack of nerves making her stomach flutter. Was he going to tell her they were over? That he'd made a mistake by making love to her? How did the saying go? Something like women got way more emotional when it came to sex and how they read far more into the act than a guy did? Had she set herself up for a monumental fall?

Some of her panic must have shown on her face, because Swanny immediately looked contrite and pulled her back into his arms. "I'm sorry, Eden. That probably came out badly. I'm not so good with words, and I'll man up and admit, I'm nervous as hell. But it's nothing bad. God, I hope not anyway."

Something in his voice immediately soothed the tension that had knotted her insides. She could hear the nervousness in his voice, see the same tension she had felt in his features. It made her want to comfort him instead of seeking comfort for her own bout of nerves.

"What do you want to talk about?" she asked, deciding to take the plunge. Like a bandage. Rip it off quickly and cleanly.

Instead of answering her, he took her hand and pulled her toward the bedroom. When they were standing by the bed, he reached into his pocket and pulled out a silvery strand. At first she wasn't at all certain what it was until he held it up.

It was a delicate necklace with a heart charm that twinkled and caught the low light from the lamps. Her pulse ratcheted up. She was delighted with the gift, but she saw the uncertainty in Swanny's expression and her heart immediately softened.

"I'd like for you to wear this," he said gruffly. "I know you can't wear it all the time, like for your shoots or the launch party. But in between and especially if you aren't with me, I'd like for you to wear it."

There was an odd note to his voice. She cocked her head to the side, studying him for a moment. Then she brushed away the oddity and decided he was simply nervous over whether she'd like something so simple. He likely thought nothing but the most expensive jewels ever adorned her body.

Even if she didn't like his gift—and that certainly was not the case here—she'd never in a million years crush him by rejecting something so precious.

Reverently she took it in her hands, sliding it carefully from Swanny's fingers.

"I love it," she said, a knot forming in her throat.

"Really?"

She swore she could see sweat on his brow.

She extended it toward him and then turned when he took it from her.

"Clasp it for me?" she asked.

He fumbled behind her neck, and she smiled when he muttered a curse. Finally he secured it and she turned around, walking into his arms, hugging him tightly.

"Thank you," she said. "I really do love it."

He returned her hug and then tilted her head back with a nudge to her chin and his mouth covered hers. Heat scorched a path up her spine and yet she shivered as if chilled in reaction to the pleasure radiating in waves over her skin like the softest of whispers.

She broke away, panting slightly, desire a strong, steady presence. It weighed down on her, filling her with need, desperate need.

"If we're going to discuss anything, then I suggest we get to discussing before we get sidetracked with other matters entirely," she said breathlessly.

Again she saw vulnerability creep into his eyes, giving her an unfettered glimpse of raw emotion shimmering back at her. It made her want to hug him to her and tell him it would be all right. But how could she when she had no idea what it was he had on his mind?

After the last bomb he'd dropped on her, she'd be a fool to think whatever it was would be insignificant.

"Get undressed for bed and comfortable. Give me a minute to wash up and change myself. Then we'll get into bed and talk."

She swore he was delaying it, almost as if he were still gathering courage to broach whatever topic he had on his mind. It only made her more nervous, and she wanted to blurt out that he should just tell her now, because the wait was killing her.

But she also recognized that whatever it was, he needed a moment to collect his thoughts. For him, she could wait, because she never wanted him to feel uncomfortable with her. Not when she was so at ease with him. There wasn't anything she felt as though she couldn't tell him, and she wanted him to feel the same way about her.

"Okay," she said softly. "It won't take me but a moment, but take as long as you need. I'll be in bed waiting."

Relief registered in his eyes and he turned abruptly, heading to the bathroom. A moment later she heard the shower turn on. She stripped out of her clothing and chose a comfortable pair of silk pajamas. She certainly had sexier options

to wear, but she didn't want to distract Swanny from whatever he wanted to discuss. The desire between them had
been a tangible force in the room, but she'd also registered
the importance of whatever it was he wanted to talk to her
about, so she pushed thoughts of lovemaking from her mind
and mentally prepared herself for what lay ahead.

Hoping for the best, she took a steadying breath and
climbed into bed, pulling the covers up to modestly cover
herself, and waited for Swanny to return.

She didn't have long to wait. It wasn't even five minutes
before Swanny returned, wearing a pair of boxers and a
form-fitting T-shirt that had her drooling over his muscled
physique. He paused at the edge of the bed, uncertainty once
again filling his eyes.

Taking the initiative, she pulled the covers back and patted the space beside her.

"You can talk to me about anything, Swanny," she said
softly. "I never want you to feel as though you have to hold
anything back. Not from me. Never from me. I feel closer to
you than I've ever felt to anyone else in my life outside of my
father and brothers."

His features relaxed and he climbed into bed beside her
and turned on his side facing her, propping his head up with
his palm, elbow down on the pillow. He fiddled with the
sheets a moment, his gaze lowered, but then finally he seemed
to gather his courage and he lifted his gaze to meet hers.

She waited patiently in silence, not wanting to press. She
sensed this was something huge. At least to him. But still,
she couldn't stanch the tiny tendrils of dread that wrapped
themselves around her heart.

"I know I'm not good enough for you," he said gruffly.

She opened her mouth to voice an immediate denial, but
he put a finger gently to her lips.

"Let me finish," he said quietly. "There's a lot I want to
say and I need to get it all out before I completely wimp out."

She promptly closed her mouth, her heart aching at the
vulnerability in his voice.

"I—I guess I want to know where this is headed," he said

in a faltering voice. "You and me, I mean. You have to know I have feelings for you, Eden."

He stopped and shook his head.

"That's not accurate. I'm in love with you. Completely and utterly in love with you. There's no doubt in my mind about how I feel about you. And I need to know if you have any feelings for me. When this is over, I need to know where that leaves us. You aren't just a job to me. You never will be. And I don't want, when this is all over with, for us to go our separate ways and pretend that we didn't share such a deep connection, and I guess what I'm asking is if you feel that same connection or if it's one-sided on my part."

He grew quiet, the anxiety in his gaze heightening. Her heart was racing, near to exploding. He'd laid himself bare before her. The courage that must have taken with his insecurities over not being good enough for her, not fitting into her world, his scars both internal and external. God, she couldn't fathom such courage when she hadn't even had the courage herself to tell him how she felt about him. She was suddenly shamed that he'd had to be the one to bring the topic up. That she hadn't had his courage and had forced him into such a vulnerable position. If only she had as much bravery as he had. If she had only been willing to face her own fears, he would never be in this position, placing his very heart and soul in her hands when he had no idea if he'd face rejection.

Tears burned her eyes and she made no effort to wipe them away. They slid soundlessly down her cheeks and for a moment she simply couldn't breathe. Couldn't possibly say a word. Her throat was clogged with emotion, her chest heavy. Close on the heels of raw emotion came overwhelming relief. He wasn't blowing her off. God, he'd just said he loved her. The very thing she'd wished the most for. The thing she'd lacked the courage to offer him first.

She still couldn't find the words that were filling her heart, her mind, her very soul, so she did the only thing she did find herself capable of. She threw her arms around him, knocking him onto his back. And then she kissed him. Raw, heated, pouring every ounce of what she couldn't summon to say into her kiss.

Her tears spilled onto his skin. She could taste them, salty and warm on their tongues as he returned her kiss in equal measure. She framed his face in her hands, gently caressing the scarred side, and then she kissed the corner of his mouth, the one where the scar just reached and affected that side's ability to tilt upward as much as the other, and then she followed the path of the scar all the way up his cheek to where it ended near the corner of his eye.

"I love you too," she said brokenly, finally able to speak around the huge knot in her throat. "I love you so much, Swanny. I'm so sorry I haven't said it before. I guess we were both afraid. I'm so sorry I forced you into this position when I should have been the one to be honest with you the moment I knew I was in love with you."

"Oh God," he whispered. "Thank God. I was so scared, Eden. You have no idea. I've never put myself on the line like this. Never thought I would. It scared the shit out of me. It's taken me days to work up the courage to tell you everything in my heart. I know I'm not good enough for you, but God, I want you. I love you so much. I don't want to be without you. Ever."

She growled in response, her eyes narrowing as the tears stopped and she glared down at him as ferociously as she could, given the emotional magnitude of the moment.

"I swear to God, Swanny, if I hear the words 'I'm not good enough for you' one more time, I'm going to strangle you. That's the most ridiculous, absurd thing I've ever heard in my entire life. Not good enough for me? What the hell is that supposed to mean?"

She was huffing with indignation, and he smiled. Then he laughed, the sound light and carefree, as if it had been years in the making. He relaxed beneath her, joy spreading over his features, warming his eyes. He'd never been more beautiful to her than in this moment. Lying beneath her so happy and at ease. As if she'd single-handedly slain every one of his demons. She realized then the power she had over him, and it didn't make her feel good at all. She wanted them to be equals. She didn't want the power to hurt him, ever. But she also realized now that they both had the power to hurt each other because they were too intertwined, too connected. Soul deep.

Soul mates.

It might sound corny as hell. Something from a book or a movie. But it fit. Because she knew to her bones that Swanny was the only man for her. There'd never be another after him. How could there be?

"Promise me you'll never say it again," she said, taking a more serious, quieter tone. "Only I get to decide who's good enough for me, and I say you're perfect for me. Excuse my potty mouth, but I don't give a flying fuck what anyone thinks. And if you think I'm going to hide my association with you or refuse to be seen in public with you, then I'll kick your ass from one end of this room to the other."

He burst into laughter again and then gathered her tightly in his arms, hugging her to his hard body. He pressed a kiss into her hair and then inhaled, squeezing her even tighter until she could barely breathe. And yet she didn't mind. She was locked against him, where she belonged. She'd never felt safer and more secure than she did right here in this moment with him wrapped solidly around her, a barrier to the outside world where danger lurked and someone stalked her, waiting and watching for an opportunity to harm her.

"I guess this means we're an item, then," he said, an obvious grin in his voice.

"Damn straight we are. I know we have some things to work out. Namely our careers. But for now I vote we put that conversation on the back burner and focus on here and now and the fact that what I want most is for you to make love to me."

"Never let it be said I denied my lady anything," he said cheekily, tugging playfully at her hair.

"I like your attitude," she said in a sassy voice, matching his own playfulness.

God, but she loved this. That she could be herself. The real Eden Sinclair. No cameras. No acting. No glamour or makeup. No fancy clothes. Not the supermodel the rest of

the world saw. With Swanny she was just Eden. A woman
with needs just like every other woman in the world. Normal. And she'd found perfection. *Utter perfection.* What
more could she possibly ever ask for?

He rolled suddenly, reversing their positions so she was
beneath him. He stared down at her, his eyes glittering with
molten desire.

"Then you'll like this a whole lot better," he said, just as
he lowered his mouth to hers.

Oh yeah. She did like it a whole lot better now that he was
kissing her. Sealing their love with more than just the words.
He was fulfilling the promise of so much that the word
entailed with his body. His tongue. His gentle hands as he
caressed the length of her body.

He seemed impatient with her pajamas. Sliding his hands
underneath her top as if desperate for the feel of her skin.
She arched like a cat into each touch, purring her delight as
he inched her top higher until finally he ordered her to put
her arms up so he could hastily yank the material free of her
body for good.

Willingly, she complied, and then he went to work on her
bottoms, pulling them down in mere seconds, tugging them
from her ankles before sending them sailing in the opposite
direction her top had landed.

Then he chuckled softly as he stared down at her completely naked body from his position on his knees at her feet.

"You cheated," he accused. "You set me up, planned for
this. No underwear? How daring, sweet, innocent Eden. You
may have the face and the heart of an angel, but you have the
soul of a wicked temptress. Swear to God, you'll be the
death of me yet."

She merely grinned, then arched her body invitingly. "You
just going to sit there and list all my faults or are you actually
going to do something with me now that you have me naked
and in bed?" She stared pointedly at his still-dressed body.
"Seems to me you have a lot of catching up to do."

"I can sure as hell fix that," he muttered, already reaching
to strip his T-shirt off, his muscles rippling with the effort.

She held her breath when his hands immediately dropped to his boxers. His cock was bulging the material outward and if he moved an inch in either direction, his erection would spring free through the opening in the crotch.

He shoved downward and she sighed at the beauty of his male physique as he leaned back on the bed so he could work the underwear free and toss it aside. She hadn't lied or plied him with insincere compliments. He was absolutely beautiful to her.

Yes, scars crisscrossed his body. No area had been left undamaged by his captors when he'd existed in hell. But to her they were a testament of his honor, of his will to live despite impossible odds. That they hadn't been able to break him. How many men could say the same? How many men would even survive, much less survive with their sanity intact? And yet he continued on, still holding a job that put his life on the line on every single mission his team went on.

A movie title floated through her mind—it was silly, but she was so absorbed in her study of him and her thoughts, her admiration, that she couldn't help but think of the words *Uncommon Valor*. It suited him, and all his teammates, to a T. But especially Swanny. Her man. The man she loved and God, he loved her too!

It was as though it were only just sinking in that he returned her feelings. Her love. A giddy rush invaded her veins, making her bold and yanking her from her perusal of his beautiful body. She leaned up, reaching for him, pushing herself up to her knees so that he was turned to the side, his feet on the floor where he'd only moments before stepped from his boxers. She framed his face, pulling him in to meet her kiss.

Hot, lush, she kissed him with wild abandon she would never have believed herself capable of. She poured every ounce of emotion, the depth of her love, into her kiss.

He wrapped his arms around her and fell with her, her back landing with a thud on the soft mattress, his mouth still fused to hers. She let out a soft moan when he slid his mouth down the line of her jaw to her ear, where he licked and toyed with the lobe before sucking it firmly between his teeth.

The rhythmic suckling motion only heightened her anticipation for when he'd do the same to her breasts. And to her
clitoris. An all-over body shiver quaked through her in
remembrance of his mouth on her most sensitive flesh, how
expertly he'd brought her mind-blowing ecstasy.

Whoa, she was getting way ahead of herself here. *Stay in
the moment, Eden. Savor every second. Don't let it be over
too quickly.* This was a night she'd never forget as long as
she lived. The night Swanny told her he loved her and then
showed her his love in the most tangible way a man could
show his woman his feelings.

"You with me?" Swanny asked gruffly, his head just above
hers as he stared down into her eyes.

She cursed herself for getting so carried away with her
internal reflection, because now Swanny held a look of hesitation, as though he worried he wasn't pleasing her. That
she'd drifted away from the here and now.

She reached up to touch his scarred cheek and gently
caressed it. "I was just savoring the moment and thinking
how I'd never forget this night as long as I lived because it's
the night you told me you loved me and now we're making
beautiful love. So yeah, I'm with you. I'm so with you. Never
without you. Even when you aren't right there by my side . . .
At the shoots when we have to be apart, even though I know
you're just a short distance away, I'm still thinking about
you. Wishing you were touching me. Just holding my hand
or wrapping your arm around me. All those sultry sexy
looks I had to give the camera? They were all for you. I
imagined you making love to me, me inviting you to make
love to me, and poured every single emotion I felt for you
into what the camera captured."

"Jesus, Eden," he muttered, just before his mouth crashed
down on hers again.

When he came up for air and they were both sucking
huge breaths into their starving lungs, he stared down at her,
his eyes boring intently into hers.

"You can't know what that means to me. You can't possibly know because there is no way in hell I can ever put into

words what it means. There aren't enough words in any language to describe what you mean to me."

"Just show me," she said simply. "Our bodies communicate much better without words."

Without responding, he lowered his head to her breasts and flicked his tongue out, teasing one nipple into rigidity. He circled the puckered ridge, leaving a warm, damp trail before nipping ever so gently at it.

She bowed upward, her gasp of pleasure whistling past her lips. Her body undulated, greedy, wanting more, but he didn't respond to her silent demands. Patiently he teased and pleasured one breast before finally moving to the other to give it equal treatment. Eden was a writhing mess, nearly out of her head with desire for him to take her. To possess her. Own her. Cement the declaration of their love with the joining of their bodies.

He pressed a gentle kiss between her breasts and then kissed a line to her navel, where he circled it teasingly with his tongue before going lower and lower still.

Eden was always careful to keep her bikini area waxed. She often modeled swimwear or lingerie. She'd always considered it part and parcel of the job and had never been concerned about upkeep when it came to a man. But now she was glad she was neatly trimmed as Swanny nuzzled through the soft tuft of curls that formed a small triangle at her groin.

With gentle fingers, he parted her folds and then swiped his tongue from her entrance all the way up to her clitoris. She nearly came on the spot.

"Swanny!" she panted. "You have to stop. I'm going to come and I want you with me. Especially tonight. It has to be together tonight."

He lifted his head, his eyes filled with so much warmth and understanding. "We'll go together, honey. I guarantee it. I just want to make sure you're with *me* and prepared fully for me."

"I'm so ready."

The words were nearly a groan. Her body was strung tight, seemingly pulled in opposite directions as the tension increased, her orgasm building and swelling until she felt completely out of control.

As if sensing she was hanging just off the edge, Swanny rose up over her, his big body covering hers, his heat scorching against her skin. He nudged her thighs wider apart and then he slid his hands down, burrowing between her body and the mattress so he could cup her behind, lifting her as he pushed inside her.

The angle he held her at made it possible for him to slide all the way into her. They both let out strangled sounds and she realized he was just as precariously close to release as she was.

She slid her hands up his muscled arms to his broad shoulders and then stroked and caressed his back as he lay there above her, his face creased with strain as he held himself still inside her.

"It's okay, Swanny," she whispered. "I'm there. Don't hold back. Don't worry that this isn't perfect. Perfection isn't marked by time or length of a special moment. It's marked by the effort made. Take us both over. I'm ready."

He let out a loud groan and then lowered his head so their foreheads touched, their mouths a mere inch apart, their breaths mingling. There was something decidedly intimate about them simply being. The gesture was warm and affectionate and spoke far more words than could ever be said.

"You ready?" he whispered, adopting the same tone she had.

"Yeah," she whispered back, her eyelashes fluttering as their gazes molded together from being such a short distance apart.

He shifted, withdrew and then thrust forward. Deep. Hard. Like iron coated in velvet. Her breath hitched and her fingers dug into his shoulders, anchoring herself for the impending storm. She closed her eyes and surrendered to the magnetic pull of ultimate release.

Each time he thrust forward, he hit just the right spot in the inside and out. Her clitoris was straining and every brush of his groin over the hypersensitive flesh was like experiencing an electrical surge.

"Please," she begged.

"Never have to beg," Swanny vowed. "I'd give you the world at your feet if you wanted it. Anything that is in my power to give you will always be yours."

He kissed her, sealing his vow, his body moving hotly over hers. Limbs tangled, hearts entwined, they both climbed and fell at the same time, spiraling into the vortex of dizzying ecstasy. Eden was only aware of Swanny. Swanny who loved her. Swanny who would protect her with his life.

He settled over her like the warmest of blankets, his chest heaving, an exact match to her own. She wrapped her arms and legs around him, effectively putting her stamp, her claim, to this gorgeous—inside and out—specimen of a delicious alpha male.

No one could possibly be more satisfied or happier than she was right now. There was no feeling in the world to match this sense of completion. The future looked so incredibly bright. Nothing was impossible. She and Swanny would find a way to stay together. It was a vow she made to herself, one she fully intended to see through.

CHAPTER 31

SAM Kelly immediately answered the secure phone, anxious to get a report from Steele or Rio. After what had happened in Paris, Sam was more determined than ever to use any and all resources he had at his disposal to rid Eden of the threat to her.

"Sam," he said shortly.

"This is Steele," Steele said curtly. "Someone got to Sanchez before we did and Jesus, it's a bloody massacre. Everyone is dead. Sanchez, his men. The place is trashed. It's a complete clusterfuck."

"Goddamn Hancock!" Sam swore. "I should have seen this coming after he reared his head in Paris and promptly disappeared and fell off the radar. I'm one hundred percent *sure* he's behind this. He has close ties to Eden and her family, and it's just like him to take matters into his hands and take out any threat to what he considers his family."

"Well, he fucked us on getting intel," Steele said, obviously as pissed as Sam was. "I'm having my team go through the pieces to see what, if anything, we can learn, but I have a feeling Hancock took anything pertinent to our investigation. What do you want us to do now, boss man?"

"Complete your sweep," Sam replied tersely. "I'll call Rio up and tell him to stand down. I'll report in with Nathan and Joe. Tell them the developments. If Sanchez hired an assassin, he'll quickly discover that he's not going to get paid, so I think they can breathe a little easier. I'll tell them to continue their security until the shoot is over but that they can relax a little. It should take a lot of pressure off Eden as she winds this down."

"Will do," Steele said. "We'll let you know if we discover anything, and then we're pulling out and heading home unless you need us for something else."

"Things are quiet right now," Sam replied. "All we have going on right now is Eden's protection, but I'll let you know if things change. I know you're anxious to get back to Maren and Olivia."

There was a pause before Steele gruffly responded, "Yeah, I am. But we'll get the job done and report in with anything we find."

Sam disconnected and then sucked in a deep breath. Fucking Hancock. At times it seemed they couldn't move for tripping over him. He always popped in from nowhere and they never knew what side he lined up on, despite the fact that he'd saved Maren, Steele's wife, at much risk to himself.

He shook his head. Who knew Hancock had actual human ties to anyone? He was more machine than man. The news that he considered Eden and her father and brothers "family" had been a shocker because Hancock was most certainly a lone wolf. Always going his own way and answering to no one. He was definitely a wild card. Someone Sam was always wary of, no matter the circumstances.

He didn't trust Hancock as far as he could throw him, no matter that he'd actually been helpful to KGI's cause in the past. And Sam wasn't deluded enough to think that Hancock helped out of the goodness of his heart. The man always had his reasons for every move he made.

With a shake of his head, he called Joe and relayed the news to him. After listening to Joe mutter the same curses Sam had uttered himself upon receiving the news, they hung up, with Sam issuing the warning that although they could relax, they were not to stand completely down and to treat the situation as if there were still an existing threat to Eden.

They had only a short time left before Eden wrapped up and would be returning home. At that point, KGI could sign off, collect their paycheck and put another successful mission down in the books.

CHAPTER 32

EDEN hummed as she dressed for the launch party. With the relieving news that the threat to her had been eliminated, she felt lighter and carefree. She was in *love*. Even better, Swanny loved her. Nothing seemed insurmountable in light of those events.

She hadn't asked for details. Didn't want them. And to Swanny's credit he didn't give her anything more than, "The threat to you has been taken care of."

She trusted Swanny, and she trusted his team and organization, for that matter. She knew that while Swanny's team had been front and center, KGI had been working behind the scenes to get to the bottom of the whole mess. So if they said everything was good, then she believed them.

Swanny, much to his consternation, had been shooed from her room so she could dress for the launch party. He and his team waited for her in the lobby. She wanted to surprise Swanny by wearing the necklace he'd given her. She couldn't wait to see the look on his face and love warming his eyes when he realized she was wearing his gift.

No, it didn't exactly meet the standards of the designer dress she was wearing, but she didn't give one damn. She loved the necklace and she was wearing it, choosing it over the many jewels designers would kill for her to wear for the event.

She had just finished securing the clasp when she heard her hotel door open. Frowning, she stuck her head out the bedroom door, her hand covering her chest where the necklace pendent rested, prepared to reprimand Swanny and tell him to get his ass back down to the lobby, but it was maid service pushing her cart inside.

Smiling, Eden walked farther into the living area. "There's nothing I need. In fact, I'm just about to leave if you want to give me five minutes and then come back."

Even as she said it, a prickle slithered down her spine because she remembered that Joe had arranged for them *not* to have maid service during their stay. Swanny always picked up linens, towels and other necessities straight from the front desk. For that matter, *no one* was allowed on her floor.

But perhaps now that a threat no longer existed they had relaxed their restrictions. She'd have to ask Swanny about it when she met him downstairs.

"It is no problem, miss," the maid said in a heavily accented voice. "I just leave you new towels and give you turn-down service so when you return everything is perfect, yes?"

As the maid spoke, she closed the distance between herself and Eden, a warm smile on her face. She had darker skin, but Eden couldn't place the accent. It sounded more Central American than Mexican. It definitely wasn't French, but then many immigrants to France came from all over the world and took jobs in hotels and restaurants.

"That's fine," Eden said faintly.

She started to step around the maid to collect her clutch and head to the elevator when suddenly the woman moved with speed that astonished Eden. Then Eden felt a prick in her arm and she stared aghast at the woman just before the room sort of fizzled around her and grew fuzzy.

She opened her mouth to scream for help but found herself incapable of saying anything at all, much less screaming.

The maid grabbed her arm and jammed the barrel of a pistol into her side, her expression menacing as it yawned and blurred in and out of Eden's vision. God, she had to get herself together. Make herself overcome the effects of the drug. This time she had only herself to rely on to get out of trouble. And there was no way in hell she was going to let Swanny down.

"Now you listen to me," the maid said, all traces of her accent gone. "You're coming with me and we're going out the side maintenance entrance and if you make one wrong move, make a single *sound*, I'll kill you where you stand. Nod if you understand."

It took considerable effort for Eden to nod. The drugs had her impaired enough, but terror paralyzed the rest of her.

She stumbled as the maid started forward, her grip painfully tight on Eden's arm and the gun digging into her side, most assuredly bruising the skin.

The maid all but dragged her toward the elevator and then pressed the button for the subfloor, one level beneath the lobby, that was restricted to employees only. The maid inserted a card that identified her as a hotel employee and the elevator descended to the basement level.

To Eden's utter horror, when the maid yanked her from the elevator, she nearly tripped over the body of another maid. There was an obvious gunshot wound to her forehead, right between the eyes, and the woman's head lolled to the side, eyes open and glassy with death.

Eden's stomach lurched and the world went even dizzier around her, the drugs rendering her incapable of doing anything but being meekly led to the exit. The maid threw open the door, did a quick survey of the alleyway and then shoved Eden into the backseat of a small Peugeot. She leaned in over Eden and quickly taped her mouth shut and then roughly turned her on her side, jerking her arms behind her and cuffing them together.

It all took but a few seconds, but time had yawned for Eden and everything was moving in slow motion, terror and helplessness filling her as she realized she was being kidnapped.

The woman, whoever she was, had already killed at least one person to gain access to the hotel. It was obvious killing meant nothing to her and now she held Eden's life in her hands.

Tears gathered in the corners of her eyes as the car eased out of the alleyway and into Paris traffic. She was certain this woman meant her to die. But where was she taking her? And *why*?

Swanny, her father and her brothers flashed through her hazy consciousness. She'd never see them again. Worse, they'd likely never know what happened to her. Tears slipped from her eyes, hot against her chilled skin. She wept for all she'd lost and for the pain her disappearance would cause Swanny and her family.

And then she prayed that Swanny and his team would somehow, some way, miraculously find a way to rescue her before it was too late. Swanny hadn't given up when faced with the unthinkable. He'd survived months of torture and degradation and come out the victor, never giving the animals who tried their best to break him the satisfaction of doing so.

She drew on his strength now, the memory of all he'd endured. He deserved someone of the same caliber, the same never-quit attitude and the determination to come out the victor.

She gathered those things to her, holding them tightly, letting them—and Swanny—burn brightly in her mind. Because something in the deepest part of her soul realized that she was going to need to tap reserves she wasn't sure she possessed. But damn if she was going down without a fight.

CHAPTER 33

SWANNY was waiting impatiently in the lobby with his teammates, checking his watch and muttering under his breath. He didn't like leaving Eden, no matter that the threat to her had been eliminated. His gut wasn't quiet. It was going off like a mofo.

Deciding to fuck it and risk her disappointment since she wanted to surprise him, he turned to stride toward the elevator just to ease his screaming gut when Hancock stormed through the entrance to the hotel, his features creased with rage and . . . *worry.*

It was the worry that stopped Swanny in his tracks, because nothing worried Hancock. The guy was an automaton and he only had one expression. Well, that wasn't exactly true. When he'd come to Eden's room, it was as if an alien had temporarily taken over his body because the man had actually shown emotion and tenderness with Eden. There was obvious affection between the two, and Swanny still couldn't get over the fact that Hancock considered Eden and her family his own family. And he called her *cupcake.* For the love of God . . .

"Where the fuck is Eden?" Hancock demanded.

Typical no greeting, no pleasantries. That wasn't Hancock's way and, well, it wasn't Swanny's either. They both got straight to business without meaningless chitchat getting in the way.

"She's in her room finishing dressing for tonight's launch party," Swanny supplied. "She should be down any minute."

"Son of a bitch!" Hancock swore. "You left her unguarded even for a few minutes? What the hell kind of operation are you running here? I have intel you need immediately."

At that, Swanny's entire team came to attention and crowded around, all business, as they waited for Hancock to continue.

"Well, since you obviously eliminated the threat to her, it doesn't make a hell of a lot of sense that you're freaking the fuck out," Joe drawled, staring pointedly at Hancock to let him know that KGI was well aware of who got to Sanchez.

Hancock swore again. "He wasn't the threat. He never *was*."

"What the fuck are you saying?" Swanny demanded. The dread in his gut intensified. Goddamn it, he knew something wasn't right, and he damn well should have put his foot down and never agreed to give Eden ten minutes to finish dressing alone.

"Short version," Hancock clipped out. "Eddie had it all wrong. He thought the mother and daughter were killed when their mission went FUBAR. He assumed it was the son seeking revenge after I took out the father after he killed Eden's mother. But it never made sense to me. If he was seeking revenge, a wife for a wife, then why wouldn't he have killed Eden then? Wife for wife, daughter for daughter."

Swanny's panic level was reaching epic proportions. He didn't like where this was going a damn bit.

"Let's get to her room," Hancock barked. "I'll give you the rest on the way up. I want to make damn sure she's safe because the threat to her has *not* been eliminated."

At that, Swanny and his entire team broke into a run, Swanny pounding on the elevator call button.

As they piled into the elevator, Hancock continued.

"The daughter survived. It was only *thought* she was killed in cross fire. It's not the goddamn son after Eden. It's the daughter. It explains how inept the attempts on her life have been. This isn't some hired assassin after Eden. The daughter is coming after Eden herself."

"Son of a bitch," Swanny swore. "Goddamn it, Hancock. Haven't you ever heard of a fucking phone? Why the hell didn't you let us know immediately instead of waiting until you got here to spill? You talk about us not doing our job, but if Eden means so goddamn much to you then, why the fuck didn't you immediately get on the horn and warn us?"

"Because I thought you'd keep doing your goddamn job," Hancock snapped. "I came straight here after taking out the son and his security. It was there I found correspondence from his sister and him begging her not to go after Eden. To stop the cycle of revenge and retribution. In all of this, it appears the son is the only halfway intelligent one. I didn't discover this until after I'd taken him out. I fucked up. I admit that. I should have made him talk because he didn't deserve to die. He tried to talk his sister down, but she's batshit crazy and is obsessed with making Eden and Eddie suffer and taking Eden out. She wants Eddie to know, to see his daughter suffering, and that may be the only goddamn thing that gives us time to find her before she kills Eden."

The blood in Swanny's veins froze. Dread clutched him by the throat and wouldn't let go. *Oh God, please let Eden be in the hotel room where she's supposed to be.* No matter what, he wasn't leaving her side until the crazed lunatic trying to kill her was taken out for good. He cursed himself for relaxing his guard even for a moment. No matter how prettily Eden had asked for a few minutes to dress and meet them in the lobby, he should have insisted on remaining with her the entire time. He hoped to hell his fuckup didn't cost Eden her life. He could never live with himself. He could never live without *her.*

They rushed off the elevator, guns drawn, and when they got to her suite, Swanny went cold with dread.

The door wasn't completely closed, a maid's cart partially obstructing the entrance. He shoved it inside, gun up, his team flanking him as he burst into the room.

"Eden!" Swanny bellowed. "Eden, are you here?"

They rushed in, spreading out quickly. Swanny ran into her bedroom only to find it empty. A quick check of the bathroom turned up nothing, and he began to sweat as panic gripped him by the balls.

"She's not here," Hancock yelled. "Fan out. We have to search the hotel from top to bottom. Go, go, go!"

Somehow Hancock got paired with Swanny and they hit the stairway, running full tilt down each floor. Nathan, Joe and the others would do a floor-by-floor sweep, but Swanny knew if Eden had been abducted, her kidnapper wouldn't have stuck around.

They ran to the basement floor and used the access key provided by hotel security to open the door leading to the stairwell. As they rounded the corner where the elevator stood, Hancock let out a vicious curse.

Swanny saw the maid lying on the floor, eyes glassy with death, a bullet hole low on her forehead, directly between the eyes. Blood had already congealed and she was cold, and rigor was starting to set in.

Son of a bitch. The crazy-ass daughter had gotten into Eden's room by posing as a maid and used the key card from the cleaning lady she'd shot and killed.

Swanny bolted up and ran toward the exit, throwing open the door, ducking out, hoping against hope that he wasn't too late and could get a bead on the crazy bitch who'd taken Eden from her hotel room.

What bothered him the most and filled him with over-whelming panic was how she got Eden out with no issue. Eden was trained in self-defense. She could handle herself in a bad situation. So the only way someone would get her out of a hotel with no one knowing and without one hell of a fight was if Eden had been drugged.

Thinking back on the hotel room, there was no sign of a struggle. Nothing had been out of place. Just the maid's cart, and the door had been left ajar. She *had* to have been drugged. It was the only explanation.

With a maid coming in, Eden being Eden would have

been nice and welcoming, never suspecting a maid could be a danger to her. Especially since Swanny had assured her the threat to her had been taken care of.

Stupid fucking idiot.

This was his goddamn fault. He'd never get over his complete idiocy. Never would be able to make it up to her even if he got the chance, and he prayed he'd have that chance. That he'd find her before it was too late. He couldn't entertain any other option or he'd lose his mind.

"Quit beating yourself up," Hancock said gruffly. "This is as much my fault as it is yours. There's nothing to be accomplished by either of us going over the woulda, coulda, shouldas at this point. We have to get it together and find her."

"We need the video surveillance stat," Swanny said grimly as he and Hancock completed their sweep of the alley and parking lot.

"Leave that to me," Hancock said. "I may not be the geek your Donovan is, but I know my way around computers and electronics. You can be the heavy and I'll pull up what we need."

. They both hurried inside and went straight to the security desk. Confronted by two very large, very pissed-off men, the head of security didn't even protest. He brought them into the surveillance room and let Hancock take over.

"There was a blip earlier," the security guy said in impeccable English, his expression grim as he related the information. "It blinked and went out for a few minutes, which is likely when Miss Sinclair was taken. But we have a camera in the alleyway, so if they went out that way, and it's likely given the location of the murdered maid that they did, you may pick up footage of the vehicle and get a plate at least."

Hancock typed furiously, skimming through footage before the blackout and then homing in on the alleyway when the cameras had gone back online.

"Son of a bitch," Hancock breathed.

Swanny leaned forward to see a woman shoving Eden into the back of a maroon Peugeot and then leaning over her for several seconds. When she backed away they could see

Eden lying in the back, the shiny glint of handcuffs on her wrists.

The kidnapper's face was averted from the camera. Longer dark hair hung down her back and her skin was darker toned. She was shorter than Eden but way stockier. Her arms were muscled as if she had a strict exercise regimen. Her shoulders were broad and square and there was no hint of the curve of breasts through the maid uniform she'd appropriated from the employee she'd killed.

Then the Peugeot drove away and Hancock zoomed in on the plate. Hancock barked the number to the security guard and instructed him to contact the police to put out an APB for the vehicle with the plate number.

Swanny radioed his team, told them to stand down from their room-to-room search of the hotel and reported what he and Hancock had discovered.

"We need to widen our perimeter and make damn sure we cover the borders, airports, train stations, any public transit and get the word out on the car and plates. We need as many eyes and ears on this as possible," Swanny said in a grim voice.

"I'll call Sam. Get the teams this way so we have all our manpower focused on finding her," Joe responded.

"It'll be too fucking late for that," Hancock snapped. "She won't survive long enough for fucking Rio and Steele to ride into town. We have to find her and find her now."

"No shit, asshole," Swanny growled. "If you think I'm waiting on anyone to find her, you can go fuck yourself."

Hancock went silent and stared long and hard at Swanny. "You're in love with her," he said softly.

"My relationship with Eden is none of your goddamn business," Swanny said icily.

Hancock shoved into Swanny's face, going nose to nose with him.

"That's where you're wrong," Hancock growled. "Eden's my sister in every way that counts except blood. Her family is the closest thing I have to family, and I will do *whatever* it takes to protect her."

"Then quit fucking around and let's get moving," Swanny bit out. "Because we're not doing her any good bickering like fucking children. She's my *life* and I refuse to rest until I have her back."

"Fair enough," Hancock said quietly. "Let's get going."

CHAPTER 34

TWO hours into the extensive search for Eden, Swanny was in absolute despair. With every passing second, he felt Eden slipping further and further away. He prayed as he hadn't prayed since he and Nathan and their mates were imprisoned in an Afghani hellhole.

Shea and her sister Grace were angels sent from God. Swanny knew that in his heart. But now he needed another miracle. Like the one he and Nathan had been given when they'd made their escape.

It was also times like these that Swanny wished Shea's gift of telepathy weren't random. That she could somehow reach out to Eden and help them find her. Grace would be of more help, but by the time Rio would be able to get her here, it would be too late for Eden.

His stomach was in a permanent knot and even though he refused to even consider the worst-case scenario, that Eden was already dead, he couldn't help the surge of grief that threatened to buckle his knees.

He couldn't lose her. His life had been fine before. He wouldn't consider himself happy, but neither could he have said he was unhappy. His life was well ordered. His absolute focus had been KGI and his team, their missions and the bond he had with the Kelly family.

Marlene Kelly, the matriarch of the Kelly clan, had pulled him into the fold, instantly adopting him as her own, and she mothered him just like she mothered her actual sons. That love and loyalty extended to her daughters-in-law and everyone else who'd been adopted into the Kelly family.

But now? He couldn't bear the thought of going back to his sterile existence. He couldn't imagine his life without Eden. She was his own personal ray of sunshine, her warmth enveloping him just by being in the same room.

Mentally he reprimanded himself. Such dire thoughts did no good whatsoever, and he wasn't giving Eden the credit she deserved. She was a fighter. She would find a way to survive until Swanny reached her.

And he would find her. If he had to turn the whole god-damn world over in his search, he'd find her or die trying.

His secure cell rang and he yanked it up, knowing it was one of his teammates. Hancock paused, slowing the vehicle he and Swanny occupied, and tuned in to the conversation.

"Swanny, it's Joe. Where are you right now?"

Swanny leaned over to check the street name just a few feet away from where Hancock had pulled over. He related the intersection to Joe and heard Joe's sigh of relief.

"We're five minutes out. Stay put. Eddie has heard from Eden's kidnapper and you need to see this, man. But you're going to have to keep your cool and keep your head straight. Eden needs you—all of us—and you can't let emotion cloud your judgment because we're going to have to go in and hope to hell we aren't too late."

"What the fuck?" Swanny roared. "What do you know? What the hell did Eddie say her kidnapper said?"

"It's not what he said. It's what he sent me. Just stay put. We'll be there in three minutes now."

Swanny swore a vicious blue streak when Joe disconnected with no further explanation. Then he pounded the dash in frustration, his blood pumping wildly through his veins.

"What the fuck did he say?" Hancock demanded. "Joe heard from Eddie? Why the hell wouldn't he contact me? I'm the one who fucking told him, Raid and Ryker to stand down when they lost their shit after the RPG attack. I told them I'd take care of the matter and they'd just get in my way. They damn well should have sent whatever intel they received to *me*."

"I have no fucking clue," Swanny ground out. "I couldn't give a shit about the whys and wherefores about who called who and why. Joe said Eddie sent him something and then told me not to lose my shit and remain focused. Now you tell me. Does that sound good to you?"

The heavy sarcasm—and a healthy dose of terror—was registered by Hancock. He lost some of his belligerence and he actually paled.

"Jesus," he whispered. "What the fuck could it be? God, don't let it be a picture of her dead body."

"Shut the fuck up," Swanny raged, uncaring that he was precariously close to losing all control and simply imploding. "Joe said we had to go in and get her out before it was too late. That means she's not dead. Yet."

Hancock fell silent and kept glancing at his watch. A few moments later, Swanny's team roared up in two vehicles, having split up to cover more ground. Swanny was out and running in Joe's direction before Joe could even get out.

Hancock was right on Swanny's heels, ignoring the incessant honking by pissed-off drivers whom Hancock had blocked by parking at the corner of the intersection.

"Show me," Swanny said bluntly.

Joe hesitated, which made Swanny's insides twist into one huge ball. He could barely breathe for the dread gripping him.

"Just show us, goddamn it," Hancock demanded. "We're wasting fucking time by standing here. Is she alive? Whatever it is, get on with it."

Joe dragged a hand through his hair and then pulled out his sat phone.

"Eddie called a while ago freaking the fuck out. Eden's kidnapper sent him a video because she wanted Eddie to see what she was doing to Eden. She taunted him by saying she was drawing out Eden's death. Told him her revenge would be complete because she was going to kill Eden and she wanted him to watch her die. Which leads us to believe she's going to send another video."

"Show it," Swanny said, his nostrils flaring.

Joe sighed. "This isn't easy to see, man. But you need to keep it together. Donovan is working on a trace to see if he can track her location. Hopefully he'll strike gold and be able to give us a specific location, or hell, if he can just get us in the general vicinity, we'll find her."

Before Swanny or Hancock could tell him to quit delaying and show the damn video, Joe turned his phone around and hit the play button for the video.

Hancock's sudden intake of breath was heard over the noise of traffic and the incessant honking.

Swanny felt sucker-punched as he stared at the events unfolding in front of him. He was numb, utterly numb. He'd never felt horror to this degree. Not even when he and Nathan had been tortured and starved for two months in hell.

Eden was bound to a chair and blood covered her face as her kidnapper made yet another cut to Eden's face, carving a meticulous line from her cheekbone to underneath her chin.

Eden's shriek of pain brought hot tears to Swanny's eyes. He closed them, unable to bear it any longer. He didn't even bother to wipe the tears away. He was devastated by what he saw Eden having to endure. The woman was systematically torturing her and taunting her with her impending death.

"Focus, goddamn it," Hancock shouted. "We need to study the video, see if we can see anything that helps us pinpoint her location. Put it away, Swanny. Eden needs us. You can't help her if you lose your shit now."

Swanny visibly shook off his grief and rage and refocused his attention on the tear-blurred screen in front of him.

"Start it over," Swanny choked out. "Hancock's right. We need to look beyond Eden to see if we can locate anything that helps us. She doesn't have long. When this crazy bitch grows tired of torturing Eden and taunting both her and

Eddie, she'll kill Eden and the next video we receive will be of her dead body."

It took everything he had to push aside his emotions and look at this with the detachment he always had on other missions. He couldn't look at this when his mind was clouded and consumed with fear for Eden. He had to put it away and do the job. At any cost.

Bracing himself and forcing himself to study the video with objectivity, he zeroed in on the surroundings. This time Joe muted it because the only sound was Eden's scream and Swanny couldn't bear to hear it again. Knowing she was in agony was hard enough. Listening again would send Swanny right over the edge. And he was precariously close to losing his shit. One push and he'd be gone.

Something caught his eye and his pulse ratcheted up, so much so that he could feel it beating at his temples and in his neck.

"Back that up," Swanny ordered.

He leaned in, taking the phone from Joe, and then hit play again, bringing the phone closer to his vision.

There. There it was!

Oh God. She had his necklace on!

He thrust the phone at Joe, his movements frantic as he dug out the GPS locator from his pocket. Goddamn it. Why hadn't he thought of it before? He was so rattled in the hotel room, he hadn't even thought about looking for the necklace. He'd assumed she'd wear something far more glamorous to the launch party.

"What the hell?" Hancock demanded. "What's going on? What did you see?"

"The necklace," Swanny rasped as he yanked out the locator. "I gave her a necklace with a tracking device. I told her to wear it when she wasn't filming or at an event. I never expected she'd wear it tonight. That must have been the surprise she'd planned for me and why she didn't want me to see her dressing. Yes, I gave it to her as a gift, something special, but my primary focus was on having a way to make sure she was safe if I wasn't with her for whatever reason. But she didn't know it had a chip. I didn't want her to misinterpret the gesture."

Everyone pushed forward as Swanny fumbled with the locator, his hands shaking so badly he could barely punch in the commands to get a bead on Eden's location.

"Come on, come on," Swanny chanted in frustration. "She can't have gone too far in this length of time."

Bingo! Relief crushed him with its weight. There was a blinking dot on the map of Paris. Eden was still in the city!

"Got her!" Swanny shouted. "Let's roll."

CHAPTER 35

THEY scrambled into two vehicles, shoving in clips, lifting assault rifles into place and positioning knives and flashbang grenades.

Swanny had given the GPS locator to Joe, who was driving him and Hancock while Nathan, Edge and Skylar brought up the rear.

By using satellite imagery, they were able to pull up a picture of the exact location that gave Eden's position. It was a house on the outskirts of Paris, just to the south, in a suburb with houses spaced short distances between them.

They had to make damn sure their entry was clean and not have an innocent caught in the cross fire. Swanny prayed the entire way. He prayed that Eden was alive. He prayed her kidnapper hadn't figured out the necklace was a tracking device and left it in its current position as a decoy. Because if that was the case, they were well and truly fucked. They'd be starting from zero again, and every precious minute counted.

"Drive faster, goddamn it," Swanny seethed.

"I've got it to the floor, man," Joe replied, his expression grim. "Get yourself together. We can't afford to let emotion cloud your judgment. We don't know for certain she's where the tracking device is, and we don't want to burst into a civilian's home and blow them all to hell."

Swanny ground his teeth together. Bullshit. Let his judgment be clouded by emotion? How the hell could he not be up to his eyeballs in emotion and adrenaline? Not to mention bloody fucking terror. The woman he loved was suffering horribly. He knew only too well what she was enduring, and he'd been trained to withstand torture in the military. Violence hadn't touched Eden until recently. She wasn't meant for pain and disfigurement.

Tears gathered and burned in his eyes, but he blinked them away, knowing he needed perfect vision and his senses sharp. They might get only one shot at this. If threatened, the crazy-ass woman would probably take Eden down even knowing she was about to die herself.

Hancock, who'd been studying the close-up map of the neighborhood, lifted his head.

"Looks like there are two entrances. Judging by the background in the video, my bet is the basement level. It was dark with concrete walls and the floor had appeared dusty and damp."

"So we go in quietly, undetected, and then we take her by surprise with a flashbang. Eden will be disoriented but she's likely already so from the drugs," Swanny said in a grim tone.

"Nathan and I will take the front," Joe said from the driver's seat. "You and Hancock go in the back. Sky and Edge will cover front and back just in case she gets by you."

"Like hell she's getting by me," Swanny vowed.

Hancock nodded his agreement, almost looking insulted by the idea that *anyone* would get by him.

Ten of the longest minutes of his life later they pulled to a stop three houses down from the one that signaled Eden's presence.

They piled out, quickly spreading out, guns up. Joe motioned for Nathan and then gave a hand signal for Edge and Skylar to each take an exit while Swanny and Hancock broke into a run, quickly clearing one of the iron fences between a neighboring house and the back of the house where Eden was being held captive.

The door was locked, but Swanny quickly jimmied the lock and pushed the door quietly inward, stepping lightly and soundlessly across the floor. Hancock followed closely behind, a pistol in one hand and an assault rifle cradled in his other arm, the strap wrapped around his arm to anchor it in a shooting position.

They froze just at the stairway to the basement when they heard a chilling scream shatter the silence.

Relief and rage vied for top reaction to Eden's shriek of pain. Relief that she was alive, and rage that the crazy bitch was cutting her up piece by piece.

Swanny and Hancock crept down the stairs, only pausing when they heard a slight noise above them. Swanny swiveled, gun up, but then relaxed when he saw Nathan and Joe following them down.

Satisfied that they had backup, Swanny resumed his quiet descent. He stopped when the wall cut away, giving a way to see inside the basement. He didn't want the woman to have a clue anyone was here. He needed to get a bead on Eden and her captor so they could attack strategically.

Moving inch by careful inch, each one seemingly taking hours, Swanny peeked around the edge of the wall and into the dimly lit basement area.

He caught his breath when he saw Eden tied to the chair she'd been bound to in the video. Her head was drooping, blood sliding down her face from multiple cuts. Her tormentor had her back to Swanny and his team, and her laughter filled the room.

"One more video, I think," she said in a smug tone. "Something to give your father to remember you by. Then I'll slice you open and let you bleed out and film the entire thing. Your father will pay for all he's done. For taking my mother's life. My father's life. For taking *my* life from me for so many years."

Eden lifted her head sluggishly, her unfocused gaze on the

woman. Her lips curled and she gave the woman a look of pure hatred and distaste. It was obvious to Swanny she was in shock and likely still sluggish from the drugs. But it was what she did next that surprised the hell out of Swanny and filled him with pride even amid his rage and fear for her.

"Go fuck yourself," Eden croaked.

Swanny made the go signal before the woman could retaliate. In her anger she might well kill Eden on the spot.

Swanny lobbed a flashbang so it landed right beside Eden's chair and ducked briefly behind the wall so he and his teammates wouldn't suffer the effects.

The room exploded with sound and two different sets of cries went up as Swanny rushed in, Hancock and the others hot on his heels. The woman was on her knees holding her head but she still reached blindly for her gun, lifting it in Eden's direction.

Swanny didn't hesitate. He put a bullet into the back of her head, crumpling her the rest of the way to the floor. Then he rushed over to where Eden was tied to the chair, tears that had nothing to do with the explosion burning a trail down his cheeks.

He ripped off his shirt and placed it to her face to stop the flow of blood covering her cheeks and forehead. Hancock dropped behind her and quickly sliced through the rope securing Eden to the chair.

She immediately sagged forward and Swanny caught her in his arms, swinging her upward, cradling her securely.

"Eden! Eden, honey, talk to me, please. Can you say anything? Are you hurt anywhere else?"

She blinked, confusion furrowing her brow. For a moment her gaze locked with his and relief swamped her eyes before going glossy with tears. It ripped his heart right out of his chest to see her so fragile and vulnerable. He pressed his lips to her forehead, uncaring of the blood that smeared his own face.

"Swanny," she whispered, her voice hoarse from her screaming.

"Yes, baby. It's me. I've got you now. You're safe. No one can hurt you now."

"L-love y-you."

He lost the battle and broken sobs welled in his throat. "I love you too, honey. God, I thought I'd lost you. I thought I'd lost you. I couldn't bear it."

She closed her eyes, pain contorting her features.

"Stay with me, Eden," Swanny said as he turned to take her up the stairs. "Stay with me, baby. I'll get you to the hospital. Everything will be all right. I swear it on my life."

"S-stay with m-me."

Her voice was so faint he had to strain to hear her. He kissed her hair, just wanting to touch her, reassure himself that she was alive and in his arms as he made quick work of the stairs.

"I'll never leave you," he vowed.

CHAPTER 36

SWANNY charged into the hospital in central Paris, cradling Eden in his arms. She hadn't regained consciousness since she'd told him she loved him, and that worried the hell out of him. Who knew what else she'd been subjected to? And he hadn't been able to bring himself to let her go from his arms long enough to assess the rest of her body to see if there were additional injuries.

His heart was bleeding for Eden. He was so overcome with grief and guilt that he could barely maintain his composure. But he had to be strong for Eden. Had to make sure she got the care she so desperately needed. No matter what it took. He'd hit his retirement and investments to pay the cost if that was what he had to do.

He was met by a startled nurse and, thank God, Edge was with him since the nurse didn't speak a word of English.

"I want the best possible care for her," Swanny said, an edge of steel lacing his voice. "And I want the very best plastic surgeon called in to repair the damage to her face. I won't accept anything less."

There was an instant flurry of conversation between Edge

and the nurse and then the nurse's eyes widened, and she immediately got on the phone and spoke rapidly into the receiver.

"What the hell did you tell her?" Swanny demanded.

And why the hell hadn't they taken her back yet? She needed immediate medical attention. She needed X-rays and a complete head-to-toe examination to ensure that all injuries were accounted for. He prayed with everything he had that her only serious injuries were to her face, but he had no way of knowing exactly all she'd been subjected to, and that gutted him. He wanted a report. Wanted to ease his mind, even though his worry over those cuts was overriding all else. But as long as she lived—as long as there were no serious, life-threatening injuries—he could deal. Because no matter how she looked, he loved her. Her. Not her stunning beauty or the professional face known to so many. He loved who and what she was. The heart of her. He didn't give one fuck about scars, but he refused to allow her to endure that kind of pain, a constant reminder of her nightmare for the rest of her life. He knew all too well how that felt, and if it was within his power, he'd make damn sure Eden never had to suffer that.

"I simply explained who Eden was and that it wouldn't do for her not to have the absolute best plastic surgeon in the region. She's on the phone now calling in the top doctor in the plastic surgery field to see if he can come in immediately."

After a few more moments, the nurse hung up and rushed around to where Swanny stood with Eden. Then she spoke rapidly to Edge, glancing at Swanny as she talked.

"What?" Swanny demanded. He hated this language barrier. He wanted to know exactly what was going on with Eden.

"She wants to know your relationship to Eden and whether you have authorization to grant permission for surgical procedures."

"You tell her I'm her goddamn husband and I'll be the only person authorized to grant permission for medical procedures and I want to know exactly what's going on every step of the way."

Edge relayed Swanny's response, and the nurse looked

appeased by the explanation. Then she gestured for Swanny to follow her back. Knowing he'd need Edge, despite his desire to have Eden to himself, he motioned for Edge to come as well.

The nurse hurriedly ushered her into a private cubicle and then explained to Edge that while they waited for the plastic surgeon they would do a complete medical examination including X-rays and that they would prep and clean her wounds on her face so that when the surgeon arrived they could take her straight back to surgery.

"Just let her know I'm not budging," Swanny said stubbornly. "Tell her not to even bother trying to throw me out because I'll tear this damn hospital down to get to where she is."

A smile hovered on Edge's lips as he translated Swanny's threat. The nurse's eyes widened and she took a hasty step back as if Swanny's tone and expression had thoroughly intimidated her. But she nodded her agreement and instructed him to lay Eden on the stretcher.

Swanny was reluctant to leave her even for a moment, but he grudgingly arranged her on the bed and took a step back so the medical staff could do their job. But he made sure he remained close and kept Edge in the room to translate because he didn't want to miss a single word.

He stood, arms crossed, his gaze never leaving Eden as the medical personnel scurried back and forth, performing their examination. Swanny's rage only increased as they removed her clothing and he saw extensive bruising to her rib cage and kidney area.

He curled his fingers into tight fists, tension bristling in tangible waves. His edgy mood bled over to the medical staff and they made certain to keep Edge in the loop over every discovery and the fact that they'd be bringing in a portable X-ray so they didn't have to move her from her current position.

Swanny nodded his approval, but his expression stayed grim. He kept checking his watch, waiting for the damn surgeon to arrive. He didn't want Eden waking up and seeing her face this way, even though she'd see the bandaging. She'd know they—the cuts—were there. But he'd be damned before he ever let her suffer as he had, nor did he want her to carry permanent memories of such a horrific experience. He didn't give a flying fuck that legally he had no right to be making medical decisions on her behalf, but he'd fight any-one who opposed his decisions.

At one point she seemed to stir and Swanny immediately snapped to attention. He barked an order for Edge to relay to the nursing staff. He wanted her sedated until she went to sur-gery. No way in hell did he want her to wake up to the horror of what had happened to her. Not until Swanny could be cer-tain she had received the absolute best care and that the cuts to her face were fixed and would heal flawlessly.

An hour later, a physician bustled in wearing street clothes. He went immediately to Eden's bedside and removed the loose dressings on her face. He studied extensively, muttering to himself as he completed his examination.

Swanny was fidgeting with impatience, waiting for the surgeon to tell him anything. More importantly, if the dam-age could be undone.

Finally he turned to face Edge and Swanny. To Swanny's relief he spoke flawless English.

"We are fortunate in that the cuts to Miss Sinclair's face aren't deep. I don't believe there will be any tissue damage. The cuts are very precise, not jagged. It's my opinion a scal-pel was used to inflict the cuts, which certainly makes my job easier."

"Thank God," Swanny whispered.

"They'll prep her for surgery and I'll go get scrubbed down and change and be waiting in surgery for her to arrive. Expect them to move her within the hour, and of course we'll keep her comfortable throughout the entire process."

Swanny extended a shaking hand to the doctor. "I appre-ciate this. Thank you for coming so soon. This means the world to me."

"It's no problem. I'm well aware of who Miss Sinclair is and she's graced the covers of so many magazines. I will make it my utmost priority—and pleasure—to ensure that no permanent scarring remains. I'm very good at what I do," the doctor said in a serious tone. "I have no reason to believe that the surgery won't be one hundred percent successful. She'll need time to recover, of course. She won't be back to work immediately, and she'll likely need additional procedures. It won't happen overnight, but in my professional opinion the damage can be corrected."

"She won't be lifting a finger," Swanny said gruffly. "And she won't be facing those additional procedures alone. I'll ensure she has everything she could possibly need or want at her disposal."

The surgeon hurried out and in a matter of moments the nursing staff came back in and began the task of prepping her for surgery. After a few minutes, one of the nurses turned regretfully to Edge, though she included Swanny in her gaze.

"We'll take her to the OR to finish prepping her. We have to make sure we're in a sterile environment. I know it's hard not to be able to see her or be with her, but I promise she's in the best of hands. If you'll wait in the surgery waiting room on the second floor, we'll update you periodically, and then when she's brought to recovery you'll be able to see her."

Swanny let out a strangled breath, fear and relief swamping him. What if the surgery wasn't a success? Eden wasn't a vain woman in the least. But there was no way in hell he wanted her to suffer as he had done with his facial scarring. Her face and body were her career, and he had no desire for her to be forced to retire early. He wanted her to have choices, even if those choices forced her in a different direction than him.

"Come on, man," Edge said quietly, putting a hand on his shoulder. "Let's go find the others and hit the waiting room. If I had to guess, Eddie and her brothers are already in the air flying over. They're going to want to know everything."

Swanny nodded and reluctantly allowed himself to be led from Eden's room. They went into the emergency department waiting room where the others were sitting. Hancock surged to his feet, worry etched into every groove on his face.

Before anyone could ask, Swanny quickly relayed the situation to them all. Hancock swore and pounded his fist on one of the chairs in front of him.

"This is my fault," he said furiously. "I took out the wrong person."

"None of us were looking for the sister," Joe said quietly. "We'd been told both mother and daughter had perished in the mission Eddie headed that went all to hell. It only made sense to focus on the brother after the threat Eddie received. We all carry part of the blame for not finding this out until it was too late. We accepted Eddie's word since it had happened years ago, and we should have thoroughly researched the entire situation and broadened our scope beyond the son."

But no matter who was taking the blame, Swanny knew in his heart that he and *only* he was responsible for Eden's kidnapping and subsequent torture. He never should have left her. He should have insisted on being with her the entire time. The kidnapper posing as the maid would have never made it through the door of Eden's suite if Swanny had been there.

It was a regret he'd live with for the rest of his life.

CHAPTER 37

THE hours stretched, seemingly days. Each minute ticked by with agonizing slowness. Swanny was unable to sit. He paced the small confines of the surgery waiting room while Hancock and the rest of his team sat on the sofas and chairs, their expressions somber.

They didn't even try to force Swanny to keep his cool or sit down and try to relax. They all knew how he felt about her. They also knew, despite the fact that he hadn't verbalized it, that he held himself responsible for Eden's kidnapping and torture.

At one point, as if no longer able to contain herself, Skylar rose and went over to Swanny. To his surprise, she hugged him fiercely, and he had to lean his head down toward her much shorter frame to hear what she whispered.

"Try not to worry so much, Swanny. I know you love her, but Eden is strong. She'll recover from this. You've seen the worst in so many situations, but you've also seen the close calls with the other wives. KGI hasn't failed in a mission yet, and we damn sure don't intend to fail now. We've eliminated the threat for real this time. All Eden has to focus on is recovering and getting well, and I know you'll see that that happens."

Swanny managed a half smile and then hugged her back. "Thanks, Sky. I won't lie. I'm one beat away from completely losing my shit like I did earlier, but it does Eden no good. I could have fucked up and not seen the necklace if I hadn't calmed down and viewed the video objectively. And then she'd still be in that bitch's grasp, likely dead by now. I can't get that image out of my head no matter what I do. Bursting in and seeing Eden so bloody and defeated. I'm not sure I'll ever get over that. Especially knowing it was my fault."

An angry glint entered Skylar's eyes. "The fuck it was your fault. Swanny, this was no one's fault. We got bad intel and we acted on it. And because of you we were able to locate Eden before it was too late. Remember that and forget the rest."

"Appreciate it," he said in a choked voice.

He couldn't say any more because he hadn't lied to Skylar. He was precariously close to losing control. The longer they sat—or rather stood—waiting, the more fear and worry knotted his insides.

His thoughts were interrupted when Eddie, Raid and Ryker burst into the waiting room, Eddie's eyes wild. He looked about ten years older. Exhaustion ringed his eyes and his hands were shaking.

"How is she? Where is she?" Eddie demanded. "I want to see her immediately."

Hancock stood, placing himself between Eddie and his sons and Swanny and the rest of the team.

"This was my fault," Hancock said in a low voice. "I took out the wrong man. The daughter you thought had died in cross fire survived. She's the one who has been stalking Eden and trying to take her out."

"That's who was on the video?" Eddie asked hoarsely. "She didn't say anything, though she sent a message afterward taunting me. Telling me that justice would finally be served, but I had no idea. I mean I thought maybe it was some crazy stalker who'd become obsessed with Eden. Goddamn it. I never even thought to focus on anyone except the son. Nothing else made sense!"

"Don't beat yourself up over it," Hancock said. "We all

share responsibility in not protecting Eden as well as we should have."

"Where is she?" Raid asked bluntly.

At that Swanny stepped forward, no longer willing for Hancock to take the lead with Eden's family.

"She's in surgery," Swanny explained. "A plastic surgeon—the best—was called in to repair the cuts to her face so there'll be no permanent scarring. She had other injuries but nothing serious. They took X-rays and did a thorough exam. She took a beating but nothing is broken. The only issue is the cuts on her face, and the surgeon assured me that he could start the process of returning her face to its normal appearance."

"And who the hell authorized all this?" Ryker demanded.

"I did," Swanny said calmly, bracing himself for the fall-out that would likely ensue.

Eddie and Raid gave him puzzled looks before Eddie finally found his voice again.

"Why was I not consulted? I'm her family. I should have at least been kept in the loop, and I damn sure should have been the person to grant permission for any treatment or surgery. What the hell do you even know about this surgeon? Did you research him?"

Swanny held up a hand, his harsh expression stopping the tirade in its tracks.

"I love your daughter, Mr. Sinclair."

He included Eden's brothers in his gaze as it swept over Eden's family.

"And she loves me."

At that, shock registered in her family's eyes. Eddie's lips parted as though he were about to say something, but Swanny ruthlessly continued on. He wanted to draw the line in the sand right here and now just in case Eddie got any ideas of taking over and leaving Swanny out. Like hell that was going to happen.

"I made the decisions. I told the staff I was her husband. I may not be right now, but I certainly plan to be if Eden will have me."

He fingered his scar, purposely drawing attention to it, something he would have never done in the past.

"You see this? Is this what you really want for your daughter? Your sister? There is no way in hell I'll ever put her through having her face permanently carved up and scarred. Her career is important to her, and I'd never do anything to take her choices away. It'll be up to her what she wants to do afterward but by God, she'll have choices."

There was grudging acceptance in Eddie's and his sons' eyes.

"How long has she been in, and do you know when she'll be out?" Ryker interjected.

Swanny sighed, frustrated because it had already been hours. And there was still yet another issue he had to address.

"They came out half an hour ago and said she was still in surgery but doing well. The surgeon is taking his time and being extremely careful to ensure there will be no permanent scarring. After she's taken to recovery, someone can go back to see her. And just so you know, that person's going to be me."

He stared down Eden's family unflinchingly, as if he dared them to argue.

"When she's moved to a room you'll all be able to see her," he said.

Eddie looked like he wanted to argue. There was obvious conflict in his eyes as he weighed the matter and decided whether he wanted to protest.

Then he looked up at Swanny. "You love my daughter? And she loves you?"

"Yes, sir," Swanny said without hesitation.

Eddie's shoulders sagged a bit as if all the air escaped him at once.

"All right. I won't object to you going into recovery. But I'll want to see her as soon as possible."

"There's another thing you should know," Swanny said as Eddie took a seat in one of the chairs. "Eden knows everything. I told her the night her vehicle was attacked. I needed her to understand the magnitude of the danger to her, and she deserved to know what the hell was going on when her car was blown up, killing the driver."

Eddie buried his face in his hands, emotion overcoming him. His voice was thick with tears.

"God, this is my fault. All of it. I swore nothing would ever touch my children. And now Eden is paying for my past sins. I don't know how she'll be able to ever look at me now."

Swanny softened at the older man's obvious grief.

"Sir, there is one thing I've learned about your daughter in a very short time. She has the biggest, most tender, forgiving heart in the world. Yes, she was upset and shocked at the time. But I have no doubt she will not be angry with you, nor will she refuse to see you. She loves you, her entire family, too much. And that's not who Eden is. She isn't one to hate. To harbor resentment."

"You do indeed know my daughter well," Eddie said quietly.

Swanny jerked around, forgetting all about Eden's family and the other occupants of the room when his name was called by a nurse who'd just entered the waiting room. He rushed toward her, hoping for news about Eden.

He was greeted by a broad smile.

"Miss Sinclair is out of surgery and in recovery. She's awake but still a bit groggy and confused. You can come back to see her now. She'll remain in recovery for forty-five more minutes before we transfer her to the floor. We just want to make sure her pain is under control and she suffers no nausea from the anesthesia."

"But she's okay?" Swanny asked, holding his breath until he was light-headed.

The nurse smiled again. "Yes, she's just fine. Come now. I'll take you back to see her."

Without a backward glance at the others, Swanny hurried after the nurse, eager to see Eden for himself. To reassure himself she was okay and awake. Because then he had to address the subject of whether she could ever forgive him for allowing this to happen to her.

The nurse showed him into recovery and motioned toward Eden, who was being monitored by a nurse at her bedside.

Swanny slowly approached the bed, his stomach clenched as he took in all the bandages covering her face.

"Is she awake?" Swanny whispered to the nurse at her bedside.

The nurse smiled and nodded and then gestured for him to take the seat on the other side of her bed.

"Eden? Eden, honey, can you hear me?" Swanny asked in a low voice.

Slowly, Eden turned in his direction, her eyes instantly going warm as she registered his presence.

"I knew you'd come," she whispered hoarsely. "It was the only thing that kept me sane. I knew you'd come. I was so scared I'd never see you again."

Tears clogged Swanny's eyes, and the nurse attending Eden's vitals discreetly stepped away.

"How can you even look at me, knowing that I failed you," he choked out. "It's my fault you were taken. I never should have left you alone. I don't know that I can ever live with myself."

Weakly she lifted a hand to his cheek and gently caressed his face with cold fingertips.

"Not your fault. I was too trusting. I should have known but it was too late by the time it dawned on me she shouldn't be there. You taught me better and I didn't listen."

Swanny reached up for her hand, pressing her palm to his lips as tears slid soundlessly down his cheeks.

"I brought you here and insisted on the best plastic surgeon Paris had to offer. I couldn't allow you to live with constant reminders of what happened to you. I know how important your career is to you. So I made the decision to have the cuts to your face repaired. The surgeon said that in a few months, and with additional procedures, you'll look good as new again."

She smiled up at him, so much love in her eyes that it took his breath away. God, *she still loved him*. Had told him as her last conscious thought when he'd taken her away from the horror she'd endured.

"I don't care about my face or career, Swanny. I only care about you," she said, sincerity ringing clear in her voice. "As long as I have you, as long as you love me, nothing else matters."

He had to take a long moment to compose himself. To try to rid himself of the tears and the emotion knotting his throat so tightly he couldn't speak—or breathe—around it.

"I love you," he said brokenly. "I love you so much, Eden. You're a miracle. My miracle. A gift I never dreamed of receiving. I'm so damn grateful for it. You'll never know how much you mean to me, but I can tell you every day for the rest of our lives just how much I love you."

Her eyes widened and her hand slid from his grasp as she stared up at him.

Clearing his throat and understanding why she was staring at him in shock, he made an attempt to repair his completely botched effort of proposing.

"Marry me, Eden," he said in a husky, tear-laced voice. "Be with me. Stay with me forever. I know we have a lot to work out with our respective careers and I want you to know that I'll always support your decisions. I'll never stand in the way of your career. I just want you."

This time it was Eden who teared up, her eyes going glossy and bright. But there was such a joyous smile on her face that seemed incongruous with their surroundings. She was in recovery just coming out of surgery. She had to be in pain and groggy and yet she lit up the room like sunshine in July over Kentucky Lake.

"I'll marry you, Swanny. I love you so much. And you're right. We'll work it out in time. But for now, all I want is to go home with you. Spend a few months recovering and regrouping. Then we can tackle our careers and make compromises. That's what love is all about."

He leaned over and gently kissed her lips, one of the few places she didn't have a bandage covering her face.

"I don't have a ring—yet. But you can be damn sure when you leave this hospital you'll be wearing my ring. And then I'm taking you home to Tennessee. I'll buy you the perfect house on the lake and you can sit out on the deck and enjoy the water and do nothing more than rest and recover while I wait on you hand and foot."

Her smile broadened and she slipped her hand into his, squeezing.

"My dad will want to give me away and my brothers will want to be there. But otherwise I don't want a big fuss. No paparazzi, no public announcement of our engagement or marriage and certainly no damn pictures of the event plastered all over magazines. It will be our day and I want to keep it that way. Intimate and private."

"Speaking of your family, they're all here. They arrived just a short while ago and they're worried sick about you. When you get moved to your room I'll let them know it's okay to see you. But for now? I don't mind being selfish and keeping you all to myself until they move you."

Her eyes sparkled despite the grogginess from the anesthesia and the pain he knew she had to be feeling.

"I'm on board with your selfishness, because trust me when I say I'm going to be very possessive of you and spending time with you, just the two of us. I can't think of a better way to recover than to spend it with you, in our home, with someone I love more than I ever imagined loving another person."

Swanny's heart filled to bursting. He didn't even mind the tears that once again crowded his eyes. This woman lying in a hospital recovery room was so strong and yet infinitely gentle and so very loving and giving.

He whispered a thanks to God for seeing her safely back to him. Where she belonged.

And he was already envisioning the perfect house on the lake. With a perfect deck and a dock overlooking the water, not far from the KGI compound, but he had no desire to sequester himself and Eden behind the walls of the compound. He wanted a special place of their own. Their sanctuary where they could focus on each other and a future that was brighter than the sun.

EPILOGUE

EDEN stretched lazily on the lounge chair situated on the sprawling wood deck that was just yards from the water's edge. Sunshine warmed her, spreading comfortable lethargy through her body.

She felt like a satisfied cat sunning herself.

It was a lazy day. The best. Contentment settled over her and she eyed her laptop sitting on the little table next to her chair.

Eh. It could wait.

She focused her gaze on the water, a shimmering sheet of glass catching the sun's rays, sparkling like diamonds scattered liberally across the surface. She sat there several more minutes and then reluctantly checked her watch.

With a sigh she reached over to retrieve her laptop. Swanny would be home soon and she needed to be apprised of the details so they could discuss the situation when he arrived.

He was at the compound for a meeting to give the rundown of his team's latest mission to the older Kelly brothers.

A surge of pride washed over her as she thought of Swanny and his job. Though he expressed reluctance to leave her for the first time since that awful time in Paris, she'd encouraged him to go. It was a righteous mission, a word she'd quickly picked up by being around the members of KGI. Swanny's family. Now her own extended family as well.

She was closer to her father and brothers than ever. They had come for every surgery she'd endured since the first in Paris. They'd been there at Swanny's side, supporting her— and him—through every procedure as her face slowly resumed its normal appearance.

Now? There was no sign of the slight scars that had been present after the first surgery. The first surgeon had done an impeccable job of meticulously keeping the scarring minimal. And the ensuing surgeries had been performed by the top plastic surgeon in the US.

Each time, Eden had been flown out on a KGI jet to California, where she'd quietly been checked into the hospital to undergo the process of making her appearance flawless once more.

She hadn't minded the scars, but Swanny had been adamant that she never be permanently disfigured, as he was. Ruefully smiling, as she always did when she considered his adamancy on the subject, she'd allowed him his way because he'd been so determined.

He loved her. And she knew that because he loved her, he wanted the absolute best for her. He wanted her to have choices. He supported her in returning to her career, just as she supported him in keeping his own.

Yes, it was dangerous. Yes, she lived with the fear that he may not return from a mission, but it was a fear that every single wife of the KGI members shared. It was a bond between them, one that had drawn Eden close into the ranks of the Kelly wives, and the wives of the other team leaders as well.

Maren, the wife of one of the other team leaders, was a top-notch physician who practiced locally, and she checked in on Eden often, always ensuring that Eden was recovering well from each of her surgeries.

All the wives had accepted her without hesitation. They embraced her, and it was obvious that Swanny was held in high esteem and that Eden was loved if for no other reason than the fact that she accepted Swanny as he was and saw him for the wonderful man he was beneath the surface.

Eden opened her laptop and then went to her email to look for the message from her agent regarding Eden's return to modeling. Ironically enough, for Aria.

They wanted to do a second campaign. This time for yet another new product. The last campaign had been a huge success—although Eden was certain all the press coverage over the attempts on her life certainly hadn't hurt. But they wanted her for their next launch. And, well, she was ready.

Before? No, she hadn't been. She'd thoroughly enjoyed her solitude with Swanny. The two had been married on Kentucky Lake, behind the walls of the KGI compound where they could be assured absolute privacy.

Her father and brothers had attended, and as Eden had wanted, the ceremony was small and intimate. No photographers, paparazzi, long guest list, etc. Just the other members of KGI, their wives and children, her family and, of course, Swanny.

She still smiled when she remembered her wedding day. She'd insisted on someone taking a photo of her and Swanny, despite the fact that her face hadn't completely healed at that time and the faint lines were evident in the photo.

But she and Swanny had both been smiling so hard that they glowed. She wouldn't trade that picture, that moment, for anything in the world.

"Hey, beautiful."

A shadow fell over her, right before warm lips covered hers and even warmer hands slid up her bare legs to the hem of the shorts she was wearing. She smiled. Her husband was home.

"Hi there yourself, handsome."

Eden got a kick out of the lengths Swanny went to in order to reassure her she was still beautiful. As beautiful to him as he was to her. What a pair they made.

"How are you feeling?" he asked as he plopped into the chair next to her.

She drank in the sight of him. He was dressed in fatigues and a white muscle top. It made her want to climb on him and have her wicked way with him right out here on the deck, and damn the outside world.

"I'm fine," she assured him. "Was just looking over the email Nigel sent me about the Aria account."

"Ah," Swanny said. "And? You going to do it?"

No displeasure. No judgment. Just encouragement in his voice. Nothing to register what he thought she should do. It was one of the things she loved most about him. He wasn't remotely threatened by her career and he'd gone to great lengths to ensure she would still have a career.

He was leaving the choice solely up to her, but she didn't fool herself for a moment by thinking her choice wouldn't affect him. He'd made it abundantly clear that he supported her unconditionally and that she was free to pick and choose her assignments. However, he insisted on going with her to every one. He would act as her personal security, along with Micah and David.

She wasn't sure he'd ever truly move past that awful day in Paris when she'd been abducted and subjected to the torture she'd endured. Though he might not hinder her in any way in continuing her career, he'd arrange to take a leave of absence for all of her shoots no matter how short or long they might be. He still lived in terror that she would be taken from him, and he made certain that he would be with her every step of the way when she did choose to go back to her career.

She studied him lovingly a moment and then, because she could and because she could never say it enough, she blurted, "I love you."

His eyes warmed, catching the sun and the reflection of the water in his green eyes. "I love you too, honey."

"And yeah. I'm going to do it," she said decisively.

"Good. I'm proud of you. I know it took a lot of courage to make that decision."

Her heart swelled. How well he understood her. In the short time they'd been married, they'd spent virtually every minute together, learning, growing. Already so far ahead of most couples with only a few months behind them.

He well understood her hesitancy. Her self-consciousness when it came to wondering if the scars were evident. He understood that only too well, having lived it for the last few years. He was her rock. Her support. And her biggest cheerleader. Always telling her how beautiful she was.

"When do we leave?" Swanny asked.

Just like that. So simply laid out. No questions. No reservations. Just a solid reminder that he was with her every step of the way. God, she loved this man.

"Next week," she murmured. "Is that enough time to give your team notice that you'll be out of action for a bit?"

He nodded. "Yep. Already have all that down. When I'm with you, they either don't draw a mission or, if they absolutely have to, then one of the Kelly brothers fills in for me. Nathan and Joe are considering taking on another teammate anyway. We're smaller than the other teams and we could use a sixth for times just like this. And, well, when I am in action, an extra teammate at your side never hurts."

Eden pondered Swanny's words and then glanced over at him.

"What's on your mind, honey? I know that look. You're thinking something."

"Have y'all ever considered talking to Ryker about joining your team? You served together and he's still sort of in action with what he does."

Swanny grinned. "Is my girl psychic? Or maybe you've been listening in on our conversations."

She lifted one eyebrow. "No. But now you've got me curious."

"We have considered it actually. Depends on how rusty he is and how much he's kept up his skills, but yeah, we've talked about it. It all boils down to how much training time we'd have to devote to him."

Eden sighed. "I feel like a dumbass for even suggesting it, regardless of whether you all have already talked about it. I must be a masochist for even thinking about adding another person to worry about when your team does draw a mission."

Swanny gave her a tender smile and then reached across to take her hand, squeezing it before lacing their fingers together.

"I'll always come home to you, beautiful. You give me a reason to come home. Every damn time."

"Just like I'll always come back home to you," Eden returned, her smile as tender as his. "No matter that you go with me. We'll both always come home to Kentucky Lake."

He leaned over her just as she herself was leaning in, but that didn't surprise her. They were both so in tune with each other. Their mouths met in the sweetest of kisses. Bathed in the sunshine dancing off the lake, they sat there, hands twined. Knowing that no matter where life or their careers took them, that they'd always have "home" to come back to.